SHATTERED DREAM

ALSO BY THE AUTHOR

Fiction by Rebecca Carey Lyles

PRISONERS OF HOPE SERIES

Shattered Dream (Book One)

Tangled Truth (Book Two)

Hidden Path (Book Three)

KATE NEILSON SERIES

Winds of Hope (Prequel)

Winds of Wyoming (Book One)

Winds of Freedom (Book Two)

Winds of Change (Book Three)

Short Stories by Rebecca Carey Lyles & Friends

Passageways: A Short Story Collection

Nonfiction by Becky Lyles & Friends

It's a God Thing! Inspiring Stories of Life-Changing Friendships

On a Wing and a Prayer: Stories from Freedom Fellowship, a Prison Ministry

PRISONERS OF HOPE SERIES
BOOK ONE

SHATTERED DREAM

REBECCA CAREY LYLES

PERPEDIT ✓ PUBLISHING, INK

COPYRIGHT © 2019

DEDICATION TO SURVIVORS OF RELIGIOUS CULTS

Before writing the *Prisoners of Hope Series*, I was privileged to talk with former members of a variety of religious cults. No matter the ages of the individuals, how long they stayed in such groups, whether the cults originated in America or elsewhere, the stories I heard shared many similarities. *Shattered Dream* is dedicated to those brave people who dared to break free from abusive, exploitive, tyrannical institutions. Their courage was evident as they recounted painful aspects of their controlled cult lives for me, oftentimes in tears.

Whether they were born into or drawn into a religious cult, escape was never easy and the long-term effects of trauma impossible to avoid. For their protection, I will not name the individuals, but I will say you are heroes and heroines who inspire others to walk the difficult healing journey that grows a person from victim to victor. May God richly bless you as you banish the ghosts of your pasts, spread your wings and fly into freedom. Thank you for gifting me with your stories and allowing your experiences to encourage others to flee bondage and regain their true selves.

PRISONERS & PROPHETS

"Return to your fortress, you prisoners of hope…"
Zechariah 9:12a (NIV)

"Those prophets lie by claiming they speak for me, but I have not even chosen them to be my prophets. And they still think their words will come true." Ezekiel 13: 6 (CEV)

CHAPTER ONE

Eight orange-clad women—nine, including myself—are waiting to use one of two phones. I'm the last inmate in the slow-moving line. Like the others, I've been standing on the linoleum-covered cement floor for almost an hour.

I shift my weight to the other foot. My feet ache. My back spasms. The jail-issue boots don't help. I'd love to sit, but the only chairs in the room are the stools attached to the phone kiosks. We're not allowed to plop on the floor.

The women grumble and gossip or fidget with their hair and stare at the wall. Two of them argue in hushed tones about who got there first. We're all anxious to connect with the outside world. And we're all frustrated with the newcomer who's exceeded the ten-minute call limit by two minutes and shows no sign of hanging up.

The inmate ahead of me, a gaunt gray-haired woman, turns. Her dull eyes, pinpointed by tangled wrinkles, are unreadable. Contempt curls her creased lips. She aims a thumb at the newcomer, and through broken yellowed teeth, rasps, "She'll learn."

Her smoker's breath assaults my sinuses. We've just come from the yard, where twice a day she chain-smokes and I walk the track. Stifling a cough, I glance at the guard standing inside the doorway, but he doesn't care how long we talk or what we say. He's only there to keep the peace.

The residents of Gallatin County Detention Center are the ones who enforce a ten-minute maximum and "discourage" those who monopolize the phones from repeating the infraction. They'll deliver a crystal-clear message to the new woman tonight, a message she'll remember for a long time. If nothing else, she'll learn not all rules are written.

For the umpteenth time, I check the big black-rimmed clock that hangs above the phones. An hour and five minutes of afternoon phone time left. The new girl has now talked thirteen minutes. Snuggled into the booth, the phone pressed against her cheek, she's probably whispering sweet nothings to her boyfriend.

The other caller, a big muscular woman who works out every day in the weight room, sits ramrod straight on the stool. Elbow out, she grips the phone like a weapon and nods her head in short bursts, as if answering questions. She's either taking care of business or speaking with a lawyer. I'd bet my last chocolate bar her call will be short.

The small room is warm, as always. I close my eyes and fan my face with my hand. But at the sound of footsteps behind me, I pivot, having learned long ago to watch my back. Several clones of myself—women wearing orange t-shirts tucked into elastic-waist pants of the same lovely hue—drift into the room on their sturdy brown boots. My cellmate, Serena, is one of them.

She lifts her chin in greeting and resumes talking to Nelda, her latest best friend. I don't care who Serena has for friends. However, she and Nelda are both heroin addicts who talk nonstop about how much they itch for another fix, an obsession that's not aiding their recovery.

One inmate has a bounce to her step. She stops two feet from me, grinning like I'm *her* latest best friend.

I backstep to regain my personal space.

"Hi, my name is Roxie," she says. "I'm from right here in good ol' Bozeman, Montana." She giggles like she told a joke. "Born and raised here."

I give her the onceover. *Must be new. She's entirely too happy.* Newbie inmates either keep to themselves, cry all the time, or try too hard to fit in.

Roxie, whom I immediately dub Rookie Roxie, is perky and cute, despite the sores on her face and the shadows beneath her red eyes. She doesn't look old enough to be incarcerated with adults. But then, I've seen plenty of eighteen- and nineteen-year-olds in the women's facility. At twenty-eight, I'm not that much older, yet some days I feel I belong in the nursing home with my grandma. Alcohol can do that to a person.

Roxie extends her hand, expecting a handshake, I assume.

I ignore it. Touching is against the rules at GCDC.

"I'm new here," she says.

Yep, and still high or in shock from your arrest. I catch a whiff of stale perfume, another clue she recently came from the outside.

She grabs the ID card hanging from my neck. "Cassie Anita True. That's a nice name."

Roxie is lucky I'm not the volatile type. Some inmates would knock her hand away, breaking a finger or two in the process. "Remember the rules," I say. "Hands to yourself."

"Sorry." She drops the ID. "I forgot."

"Happens to all of us." I peek at the guard to see if he noticed— he didn't—and tell her, "You can call me Cat."

She glances from my ID to my face. "That's, uh, different."

"My initials."

"Oh." She giggles again. "I get it." Without pause, she adds, "You're so exotic. What's your nationality?"

"You jump in with both feet, don't you?"

She gives me a funny look.

I don't bother to explain. The girl apparently has no filters. "My mother is Jamaican," I tell her, "and my father is French-Canadian." Before she can ask if I grew up in Jamaica, France or Canada, I add, "They live in Oregon."

4 | Rebecca Carey Lyles

One of the bickering women shouts the "B" word. I twist in time to see her shove the other woman, who swears and pushes her against the wall. The rest of us step away. Jailhouse squabbles can escalate to the hair-pulling, eye-clawing stage in a nanosecond.

Fists clenched, the enraged duo stand nose to nose, screaming expletives at each other. The room reverberates with their screeches. I cover my ears.

The guard does an about-face, his jaw hard as stone, and strides toward the red-faced pair. I silently plead for him not to kick us all out.

"She started it," yells one of the women, waving her arms.

"No, I didn't," shrieks the other. "She did."

He raises a palm, and they hush, arms stiff, fists tight.

I clasp my hands. The room is so quiet I can hear my heartbeat.

The guard calls in their names and booking numbers on his radio, tells them they can't use the phones for a week, and orders them to return to their cells. Another guard is waiting for them at the door.

I rub my sweaty hands on my pants. Maybe I'll get to talk with my parents after all. This could be my last chance. The line shuffles forward. If the smell that now permeates the room is any clue, I'm not the only one traumatized by the outburst.

The weightlifter slams the phone and stomps away. Another inmate quickly takes her place. We have to act fast. Sometimes people jump ahead and grab a phone the instant it touches the cradle.

The inmate who was monopolizing the telephone stumbles past. Tears drip from her cheeks, forming dark splotches on her orange t-shirt. Along with heartbreak, she's sure to suffer physical consequences for that long call. I'm tempted to pat her shoulder, but I don't.

Now, only three residents stand in front of me.

Behind me, Roxie is chatting with another inmate. I'm glad she found somebody else to talk to. I'm about to leave GCDC, and I don't need anyone bent on self-destruction in my life. Like others I've met in this jail, she's too much like the old me.

To be honest, I can't say the classes and therapy sessions here have transformed me, but they help. I try to believe I'm in transition—eager to move on and anxious to meet the new Cat. Despite my best intentions, however, the "transitioning me" struggles with random alcohol cravings. This is one of those occasions.

I've learned to search for the source of my need, or my *alleged* need, as the jail counselor regularly reminds me. My guess is the current trigger is either boredom or anxiety, probably anxiety. That's partially due to the fight but mostly because I'm excited to tell my parents my good news. For too long, I've been their "bad news" daughter.

I'm now close enough to the phones to catch snatches of one-sided conversations.

"I'm, uh, wondering if I still have my job. I get out on…oh…" The girl's stringy brown hair hides her face.

The other caller tucks a strand of her chin-length blond hair behind her ear. "Mama loves you, darling. I'll be home soon, and we'll bake peanut butter cookies together."

I hate it when people lie to their kids. That woman is not going home. She's going to prison. She told me she's waiting for the judge to decided which one.

The next person punches in a number, waits, and then replaces the handset. Her disappointment is evident in her lowered head and drooping shoulders. I feel her letdown, remembering the times I couldn't talk because no one was home to accept my call. But my empathy is short-lived.

In fact, I'm inwardly cheering. Thanks to her departure, I'm one person closer to calling home. Two people now stand between me and a telephone.

I can't wait to tell Mom and Dad I'm done with denial and ready for rehab. Really ready, this time. I want to put the past behind me, to stop clinging to my addiction like a life raft. For years, I convinced myself alcohol was my salvation, when in truth, it sucked me to the depths and nearly drowned me.

The airless room is suffocating. I gather my hair in a ponytail and fan my neck. Thinking about my dependency makes me think of Eric and where it all started. And thinking about Eric makes me sad. Painfully sad. I drop my hair and step nearer the phones.

For me, *heartache* is not a metaphor. My entire being aches for my deceased husband, but I've gotten to where I no longer cry myself to sleep. Instead, I stuff the hurt and dwell on the magical night we met at the downtown Bozeman coffee shop where I sang and played my guitar on weekends.

Unlike Rookie Roxie, I moved here ten years ago to attend Montana State University on a music scholarship. Music was everything to me, until my sophomore year. That's when a friend introduced me to Eric True. Then my life became music *and* Eric. He was an amazingly talented art major, also a sophomore. I still remember how our artistic souls connected that night, like two ends of a seatbelt clicking firmly into place.

We were married as soon as we finished finals the following spring. At least, that's how my dad tells the story. I was twenty and Eric was twenty-one. Both of us were beyond-the-stars thrilled to say *I do* and take off on our honeymoon.

Remembering our first few months together makes me smile. Our marriage was far from perfect—no surprise when two passionate, sensitive, immature individuals come together. Yet, we were happy. And making up after a fight was always so much fun.

I eye the clock. I should have enough time for a quick call home.

I taught Eric music basics and how to play the ukulele. He taught me how to shape clay into plates, bowls and cups. The dishes weren't fancy. Still, we loved them, and they worked fine for us.

We spent a lot of time outside our cozy little apartment, biking around town, hiking the mountains, kayaking the river, or gliding over our favorite lake in Eric's old canoe. Always competitive, we raced the three flights of stairs to our place almost daily, plus we played frisbee golf and had watermelon-seed spitting contests.

In the winter, we threw snowballs at each other. In the spring, we splashed through rain puddles. And in the summer, we skipped rocks across the lake to see whose rock bounced the farthest.

One of our favorite pastimes was to sing our way through the grocery store, using words from the signs and the package labels. I'd point to a sign, Eric would pluck a string on his ukulele, and I'd start singing. He'd strum along, sometimes singing with me on the repeat or adding a verse of his own.

Prime rib...ooh, baby... You are my prime rib, my prime rib. Buh-bum-pah... Ooh, baby... At twenty-five dollars a pound, I'm leavin' you for a cel-er-y rib, a cel-er-y rib. Buh-bum-pah... Prime rib...ooh, baby...

We prided ourselves in accomplishing two goals at once—weekly grocery shopping and entertainment that fit our college-student budget. We laughed and laughed at our crazy lyrics, but to our great disappointment, people rarely stopped to stare or clap. In fact, they tended to avoid us. We were never asked to leave the store. But then, this *is* a college town.

Our fun and games ended when Eric began having night sweats. His back, arms and legs ached constantly, and he tired easily. He no longer challenged me to stair races or shopped with me. When he continued to lose weight, no matter how many protein shakes I made him drink, I convinced him to see a doctor.

Staring at the phone room ceiling, I blink away tears, which is what I do every time I recall that dreadful day. The doctor sat on one side of a big desk, hands folded. The two of us sat on the other side, clutching each other's hands. My mouth was dry, and I had a big lump in my throat that wouldn't go away, no matter how many times I swallowed.

I can still hear the doctor clear his throat, twice, before calmly telling us Eric had stage-four bone cancer and months, not years, to live. My first instinct was to cover my ears and scream, "That's a lie!" But I didn't want to make the horrible, life-altering moment any worse for my husband. I jumped out of the chair and pulled Eric to his feet. "We're going home."

We didn't ask the doctor any more questions. We didn't say goodbye. We didn't stop at the front desk.

I drove us straight to our apartment complex, where we climbed the three flights of stairs one at a time, arms around each other's waists, grasping the railings with our free hands. Eric's pale face and labored breathing broke my heart. Once we were inside our apartment, we closed the door, locked it and didn't come out for three days. Day three was our ten-month anniversary. We "celebrated" by making an appointment for his first chemo treatment.

My mind fast-forwards through Eric's treatments, which consumed the last eight months of our marriage. In retrospect, I regret we decided to try the chemo, hoping it would trigger a miracle. Instead, it made him horribly, miserably sick. I'm grateful for every minute I had with my husband, but I wish with all my heart he hadn't suffered so much pain and nausea.

Watching the pallbearers lower Eric's casket into the ground was worse than watching him die. Only my parents' unyielding grip on my arms and my brother's strong hands on my shoulders kept me from throwing myself onto the plain pine box that held my love. I would have gladly been buried with him.

I swipe at my damp cheeks. Good thing I don't have access to alcohol in jail, or I'd be tempted to drown my sorrow, again. I remind myself I have happy news to share with my parents. Talking with them should keep me from diving any deeper into the pain.

Only the smoker precedes me in line. And soon enough, she's sliding onto a kiosk stool. We have thirty-five minutes until supper. I should have plenty of time to explain my plans to my parents.

Weeks or maybe months following the funeral—I have no idea how much later—my neighbor Anna rang my doorbell. I rarely answered the door after Eric died, but for some reason, I did that day. She had a pan of brownies in one hand and two big narrow-necked bottles in the other. I asked how she managed to ring the doorbell. She said she thought of using her nose, but her elbow did the trick.

Over the course of a long melancholy afternoon, we ate all the brownies, and Anna introduced me to huckleberry vodka lemonade. Things went south from there. Yet, truth be told, I still harbor a certain degree of gratitude for her misguided kindness. Booze may have stolen my life, but it helped me forget the agony, for a while.

Behind me, Roxie says, "Good, the line's moving fast. I need to talk to my boyfriend."

I turn.

She scratches at a sore on her neck and then rubs her hands together, all the while blinking and bouncing on her toes. Withdrawal jitters. She's coming down and will land in the detox tank before the night is over. I don't envy her.

Edging toward the phones, I say, "Does he know where you are?"

"Yeah, but I need to warn him…" She jerks her chin toward the guard. "You know…stuff."

"Does he shoot up, too?"

Her forehead crumples. "How did—?"

I shift my gaze from her face to her arms.

"Oh." She stares at the ugly red scars that trail from the orange t-shirt's short sleeves down her forearms. "Normally, I wear—"

"Yeah, and you are so strung out you believe that's all it takes to fool people." One of the phones becomes available, and I drop onto the stool. "Lay off, Roxie, before your teeth look like hers." I nod at the smoker, who's facing our direction.

The woman obligingly opens her mouth.

Roxie retreats, bumping into the inmate behind her, who curses and tells her to stomp on her own feet.

I dial my parents' home number. One ring, two rings, three… Voicemail will activate on the fifth ring. If Mom doesn't answer the house phone, I'll call her cell number, but she should be home from volunteering at the food pantry by now. On the fourth ring, she answers. "Hello."

Thank you, Jesus. I wait through the detention facility message. My mother accepts the call, like I knew she would. She always does.

"Hi, it's me." I smile.

"Cassie, sweetheart. I'm so glad you called." I love that my mother still has a hint of her rich Jamaican accent.

"Glad I caught you home, Mom."

"Perfect timing," she says. "I just walked in. Made a quick grocery stop. How are you?"

"I'm great. How about you and Dad?"

"We're both fine, though a bit concerned about your brother. He's mountain climbing in New Zealand this week, says he's 'doing the Southern Alps.'" She laughs, and I picture her wide smile and the crinkles around her eyes.

"He and his friends can't climb one or two mountains and call it a day," she says. "No, they have to climb them *all.*"

Kip's exploits distract our parents from the heartbreak I cause them, and that's okay with me. He told me a while ago the Southern Alps have seventeen peaks, so I'm fairly certain they're not climbing all of them in a week. But, maybe they are. They're a crazy bunch. I wrap the phone cord around my finger. I'd give anything to be with my brother, breathing fresh mountain air and feeling a sun-warmed breeze on my face.

"Of course," Mom adds, "we fret about you, too. Can't be easy—"

A loud buzzer sounds, and a woman's voice blares from the loudspeaker above the doorway. "Lockdown. Deputies, do a headcount and report."

The guard bellows, "Off the phones. Everyone, queue up."

I groan. "Gotta go, Mom. I'll try again after supper."

CHAPTER TWO

The moment we're allowed out of the mess hall, I make a beeline for the phone room, burping spicy spaghetti sauce as I go. Two women ahead of me swing their arms and walk so fast they're almost trotting. The female guard who's about to unlock the door barks, "Slow down." They comply.

Three others catch up with me, including Rookie Roxie. We trail the speed-walkers into the phone room. They rush to the phones and slide onto the stools. Both of them know to keep their calls short.

Out of habit, I check the clock. The phone room is only open for two hours after dinner, but that gives me plenty of time to speak with my parents. I hope they don't have meetings or are visiting Grandma Hunt. I really, *really* need to talk with them tonight.

A phone becomes available. I settle onto the stool and make my call, smelling the last caller's breath on the mouthpiece. She must have eaten more than her allotted one slice of garlic bread with her spaghetti and meatballs. Some women have no qualms about asking their tablemates for food they don't want.

Dad answers on the second ring. "Hello."

His deep resonant voice tugs me home. I see him in his recliner, the phone at his ear, a big grin on his face. Together, we wait through the detention center message, and he accepts my call. "Hey, how's my girl?"

No matter how low I've sunk or how often I've disappointed my dad, I've always been "his girl." And I know I always will be. Jail has made me more grateful for his love than ever before. Many of the girls here have no idea who their fathers are. And those who do know don't usually have healthy relationships with them.

"Hi, Dad." I grin. "I'm doing great. How about you?"

"I'm good, except I wish I wasn't on my way out the door. The library board meets in a half hour. I came into the office to gather my notes and only answered the phone because your mom said you might call."

My heart sinks. "Bummer." He's the board chairman. I know how important those meetings are to him. "I have good news, and I wanted to tell you and Mom together."

"Tell me quick, or I'll squirm all through the meeting."

"No way, Dad. You're too professional for that." I laugh at the thought of him wiggling in his chair. "The short version is that I'm getting out of jail early."

"Good for you, Cassie! That's great news, unexpected news." He chuckles. "Your mom is here, hanging on my shoulder. I'd better give her the phone before she rips it from my hand."

Dad tells me he's proud of me, we say our goodbyes, and Mom comes on the line. "I'm so glad you were able to get through, Cassie. Your first call was way too short."

"I have good news, Mom."

"I got that idea from your father giving me a thumbs-up, grabbing his notes and kissing me goodbye, all at the same time."

We share a long laugh. I can picture her adjusting Dad's collar, which was probably half in, half out of his sports jacket, and smoothing his gray hair that tends to spring several directions at once.

"So, what's your good new?" she asks.

"I'm going to be released in two days." I nearly bounce on the stool. "I'm super excited."

"Two days?" She gasps. "That's amazing. I thought you had a year to go."

"I connected with this rehab place called Transformation Way, and the judge—"

"What's the name?"

The lack of enthusiasm in her voice slows me down. "Transformation Way. Don't you love how it's descriptive yet poetic?"

"Huh." She pauses. "Never heard of it." I'm not surprised her interest downgraded to caution at the mention of rehab. I don't have a stellar track record with rehabilitation programs.

"Me, neither," I tell her, "but it's church-based." That should impress her. "And they help people with all kinds of addictions—drugs, alcohol, even overeating and pornography."

"Sounds wonderful, dear. How did you learn about this organization?" I have to give her credit for at least trying to sound excited for me.

"Women from the church come to the jail chapel twice a month, and—"

"You attend chapel services?"

"Yes, Mom. Sundays, Tuesdays and Thursdays." I pause to let the revelation sink in. Chapel attendance has been a part of my routine for months. I haven't told her because I didn't want her to ask me about it every time we talked. My reemerging faith is a personal matter between me and God.

Eric's sickness and death created a huge chasm that separated me from my Creator—or at least I thought it did. Not only did God end my brief marriage, he took the love of my life, a sweet man he'd gifted with incredible talent. A man who loved his Savior dearly and who wanted to use his art to make the world a better place. What was the point of his death?

The cellmate I had before Selena begged me to attend chapel with her. She said the music and the speakers' talks helped lift her depression. Maybe chapel would encourage me, too.

Finally, I conceded. "I'll go with you once," I told her, "but if I don't feel better, that's it. No more."

I'd been raised in church and didn't see how a religious service could magically make me happy again. But when the guitar-playing pastor from a local church had us sing my grandpa's favorite hymn, "Amazing Grace," I lost it at "how sweet the sound."

Grandpa Hunt died the week after I became incarcerated this last time. I was unable to attend his funeral service. To not be there to support Grandma and Dad and the rest of the family felt as if I'd descended to the level of pond scum. I truly was a "wretch," like the song says.

Yet, as the song also says, the amazing grace that saved my soul when I was a young child could also save the wretch I'd become. I'd lost my way, but God hadn't lost me. At that instant, I knew I'd found my way back into his arms, thanks to his tenacious love. Grief and anger had blinded me to the truth of his presence, but now I could see. *Amazing grace, how sweet the sound.*

I was in an Alcoholic Anonymous group at the time, working through the twelve-step program. The second step states "we came to believe a power greater than ourselves could restore us to sanity." That day was the beginning of my restoration to sanity and my return to faith, the third step in the program. "We made a decision to turn our lives and our wills over to the care of God."

Later, I switched to Celebrate Recovery, a Christ-based version of AA, and based my recovery on the Scripture provided for the second step, Philippians 2:13. "For it is God who works in you to will and to act according to his good purpose." Every day, I need him to give me the desire and power to do what pleases him, to turn my back on the mind-numbing pleasure of addiction.

"What's the name of the church?" Mom asks. "I might recognize it."

My parents live two states away, but I tell her anyway. "Faithful Followers of the Way."

"Haven't heard of it." She pauses. "Odd name for a church."

"Churches aren't called First Presbyterian and Second Baptist anymore. They have names like River, Rock, Journey, Life—more down-to-earth names than the traditional ones. At least, that's how I see it."

"If you say so…"

Before she can ask more questions, I continue. "The women sing some songs and then one of them tells how Transformation Way changed her life. They have a lot of success stories. And they dress really nice. Not quite your style, Mom, but you'd probably approve."

Being a fashion writer for a Jamaican magazine puts Mom in a colorful class all her own. She loves primary colors and vibrant stripes and plaids layered in wild combinations.

"Business suits?" she asks. "Rather than office casual?"

I can tell she's trying to form a mental picture.

"Not exactly. I'd say a step above business suits—and expensive. Some are black with fancy trim, but most are in primary or pastel colors, and the fabric has a sheen to it. Satin, I suppose. The tops and jackets are usually accented with sequins and beads that catch the light. Kind of like modest formals with jackets. You'd enjoy the bright colors."

I'm not all that interested in clothes. However, thanks to Mom, I have a fairly good sense of style and can make a t-shirt and a pair of jeans look classy, with appropriate accessories. The church women's ankle-length straight skirts and dresses are, in my opinion, a bit odd and confining. Definitely not my taste. I prefer loose natural-fiber skirts. But that's me, not them. A different lid for every pot, as my father would say.

The women all wear red lipstick, have perfectly straight white teeth, and grin the whole time they're on stage, whether they're speaking or singing. I doubt I see that many smiles in a month at GCDC. I'd love to have teeth like theirs. Mine are stained by alcohol and tobacco, and a couple of my front teeth were chipped when I tripped over a curb in a drunken stupor.

"Interesting," Mom says. "The visitor information the jail gave us instructed us to dress down, wear very little makeup and leave jewelry and watches at home."

I chew at my lip, not sure what to make of her comment. The Faithful Followers wear blinged-out jewelry and big flashy watches. Maybe volunteers have different rules than regular visitors.

"Who knows what's up with that." I rest my head on the side of the kiosk. "What I like about these people, Mom, is that they can actually sing, unlike some groups that come here."

"You and your perfect pitch." She laughs. "You used to get so annoyed when Opal Moody sang at church. You once told the pastor not to let the lady with the funny voice sing any more. You were three at the time."

The mental picture of a little girl setting her pastor straight makes me laugh. "I remember a woman with a voice that hurt my ears," I tell her, "but I don't remember talking with the pastor." I've always been quick to speak my mind, a trait authorities don't seem to appreciate.

"If I understood you," Mom says, "you're leaving jail in two days and going straight to the rehab center. Right?"

Leave it to my mother to cut to the chase. I have a feeling she doesn't want me on the streets for even an hour.

"Here's the amazing part, Mom. The Transformation Way women were in chapel a couple weeks ago, and one of them talked with me afterward." I'd been watching them pack their things and thinking, *These people have their stuff together. I want what they have.*

"She said she'd noticed how much I enjoyed the music. And when she learned I was only halfway through my two-year sentence, she offered to have the Transformation Way director speak with the judge and suggest I finish my time at their facility."

"She made that offer based on your love for music?"

"Well, actually, she also said I appeared to be someone seeking to better myself and the fact I attended chapel services indicated I understood where to go for guidance."

"I see. So, she talked with the director, and the director talked with the judge, and..."

"To my amazement, Judge Snow signed off on the idea. I'll finish my sentence in the one-year Transformation Way program, and then I'll be free to get on with my life. Noreen—that's the woman's name, Noreen Nystrom. She promised to pick me up the morning of my release to drive me there."

"Amazing. The wait time at some of the other places we checked was months, sometimes years."

"I remember."

When I told Noreen early release wasn't possible for me, she'd winked and whispered, "Let's just say we have friends in high places." I didn't know what she meant, and I didn't want to know. Early release was all I cared about. I'm anxious to overcome alcoholism. I'm also anxious to reestablish my reputation as a viable musician in the region.

After I dropped out of college, I tried to support myself by performing at restaurants and clubs, concert halls, weddings and parties. Anywhere I could find a paying gig. Thanks to my less-than-professional behavior at times, I've been banned from most venues in Montana, Wyoming and Idaho, including the sleaziest of joints. They want nothing to do with me, possibly due to the fact I pilfered cash when I was sober enough to search for it.

I'm hoping the Faithful Followers will help me get on my feet musically, as well as spiritually and financially. Noreen mentioned the possibility of finishing my degree. One way or another, I'll learn what I need to learn and move on. I can't see myself having a long-term relationship with the group, nice as they are.

"Wish I could be there when they release you," Mom says. "I'd take you to lunch and on a shopping spree, maybe even to a spa for shared pampering. Been too long since we had a girls' day out."

I smile. "I'd love it so much, Mom. Let's plan on a year from now."

"Is this place in Bozeman?"

I smell perfume, feel a hand on my shoulder and turn my head. Roxie is hovering beside the kiosk. She taps the top of her wrist with a trembling finger. "I really need—"

All the girl *really* needs is another hit. I wave her away and resume the conversation with my mother. "According to Noreen, the Faithful Followers' campus, as they call it, is several miles outside Bozeman. In addition to a sanctuary, they have a school, a gymnasium, the treatment center, dormitories, a dining hall and other buildings."

"You've tried treatment before..." She's stating the obvious, yet my mother lets the fact hang like a bridge for me to cross.

"Twice, Mom. I haven't forgotten those programs didn't work for me." I take a steadying breath. "But this place is different. It's affiliated with a large church. They'll not only help me spiritually, they'll help me find a part-time job and get a car. They'll also provide housing and food. Noreen said they'll even give me a cell phone. I'll be able to stay in touch with you and Dad."

"It all sounds wonderful..." She pauses. "But treatment is expensive. How are you going to pay for it?" Ah, a subtle reminder she and Dad don't plan to cover the cost, which they did for the other two programs. I don't blame them. They've seen a lot of money disappear down the wayward-daughter drain.

"That's the beauty of Transformation Way," I say. "It's funded by the church. All they ask is for me to commit to the program for one year." Actually, the judge committed me, so to speak. I don't have a choice.

"I'm ready, Mom, ready to go forward with my life, which means not only overcoming alcoholism, but..." I twist side to side on the stool. "Returning to my music."

"Cassie..." Her voice rings with delight. "That's fantastic. You're such a gifted musician and songwriter."

"I've been writing." Hearing myself say *I've been writing* sends a zing along my spine. "I have sixteen new songs stored in my head. Most them are worship songs, but I don't know if they're any good. I can't wait to pick out the chords on my guitar."

I stopped singing and playing my guitar after Eric died. He loved, loved, *loved* my music. When he left my life, the joy of music seeped from my soul, and I got the crazy idea singing would somehow dishonor his memory. I guess you could say alcohol replaced the music.

"I'm sure your songs are as beautiful as ever," Mom says. "You have a marvelous ability to integrate poignant words with stirring melodies."

"Thanks, Mom."

"Do you have an address for the rehab center? I'll ship your guitar to you right away."

"No, I don't have an address, but I'll let you know as soon as I learn what it is."

"This is so exciting, Cassie. You're about to be released *and* you're making music again."

I look behind me. The line is growing. I could chat longer, if I wanted. After all, I'm leaving soon, and I've befriended those who rule the roost—every community has its pecking order. But I've said what I needed to say, and I'll soon be able to talk as long as I want.

"I'd better get off the phone, Mom, before someone has a panic attack. You know how it is around here. I'll be in touch as soon as I have a cell phone in my hands." Sharing a phone is only one of a thousand things about GCDC I won't miss.

CHAPTER THREE

The day of my release, Noreen meets me at the detention center's front desk shortly before noon. She's beautifully groomed and impeccably dressed, as always. I'm wearing the same stained t-shirt, torn jeans and grubby hiking boots I had on the day I was arrested. To the officer at the desk, we must be quite a contrast, a filthy street urchin in the perfumed shadow of a princess. I showered this morning, but my clothes reek like the inside of a laundry basket.

Apparently, Noreen anticipated my need for clean clothing. She hands me a Macy's bag and sends me to the lobby restroom to change. Inside a stall, I pull out black polyester pants, a ruffled rose-colored top with cap sleeves, a flowered jacket and a pair of black flats.

I examine the clothing that's so new the tags are still attached. Not my style, for sure. But… I snap the tag off the jacket. Beggars can't be choosers.

I dress as quickly as I can, anxious to walk out GCDC's front door. When that happy moment finally arrives, I step from under the curved blue portico that shades the entrance and onto the asphalt parking lot. My bag of old clothes in one hand and my boots in the other, I stretch my arms wide and raise my face to the sun. Sucking in the crisp spring air, I savor the miraculous confluence of early release and springtime in Montana. Only Eric could make this morning better.

Noreen doesn't let me bask in my freedom for long. She grabs my arm and whisks me to a shiny pearl-white Lexus parked at a distance from the other cars. It practically glows in the sunshine, so clean you'd think she drove it off the showroom floor this morning.

She holds her hand over the Lexus symbol on the trunk lid. It slowly rises. I carefully lay my meager possessions in the spotless interior. After closing the lid, she walks to the driver's side. I go around to the passenger side and open the door.

A new-car aroma greets me. I touch the seatback. It's upholstered in soft, unblemished, ivory leather. The floormat looks like it's never been touched by a shoe.

"Hop in." Noreen is already in the driver's seat. "And be sure to buckle up, buttercup."

I lean inside, smiling at her silly rhyme. "I know I'm wearing the new clothes you brought me. Still, I'm afraid I'll dirty your immaculate car."

"Nonsense, Miss True." She pushes a button near the steering wheel, and the engine purrs to life. "The Lord gave me this car for his service."

I sink into a seat as comfortable as an easy chair. The phrase *cradled in opulence* comes to mind, and a song begins to form in my head. "You can call me Cat." I fasten my seatbelt. "That's what my friends call me."

"We'll see about your name later. But for now—"

"What's wrong with my name?"

Ignoring my interruption, she continues. "We've got a big day ahead, beginning with…" She glances at the clock on the woodgrain console. "Lunch at Restaurant des Delices in ten minutes. We have just enough time to get there."

I've never heard of the place, but it sounds expensive. "I can't pay—"

"No worries. It's all part of the program." She flutters her hand, and her perfume mingles with the new-car scent. "You'll love the food there. The chef and most of his staff are fow members."

"*What* members?" I thought she might have said "fowl" or "foul," but neither word makes sense.

"F-F-O-W is an acronym for Faithful Followers of the Way. Instead of saying the full name or the initials each time we mention the church, we say 'fow.' You can do the same."

"Okay..." My breath catches in my throat, and I realize I'm having a hard time breathing. Maybe it's the airless car with all its odors. I put my finger on the window button. "Do you mind if I open the window?"

Noreen's headshake is nearly imperceptible. For the first time, I notice the Bluetooth headset protruding from beneath her perfectly coiffed blond hair. She touches the console, and air whooshes from the vents. It's cold air, but I can breathe easier.

I get the hint and drop my hand. She wouldn't understand how I've longed to inhale outside air. In fact, she might question my sanity. Bozeman's atmosphere includes the jail's atmosphere. I understand that reality. Yet, knowing I'm no longer on the inside makes the air fresher, cleaner, more invigorating. To me, it has the wonderful smell of freedom.

On the other hand, the tight seatbelt and the new clothes bind my body. After months of baggy inmate apparel, I feel like I'm wrapped in elastic. Fighting the urge to release the seatbelt, I focus my gaze beyond the car windows at a view of Bozeman and the Gallatin Valley I haven't seen in months.

Bozeman is surrounded by beautiful mountains, some close and some distant. Several of the peaks are still capped with snow, yet their rocky slopes calm my spirit and help me reorient to the real world. I'd love to keep driving, maybe all the way to the top of one of those mountains.

What I'd really like is to climb aboard Eric's motorcycle. It was repossessed long ago, but if I had it, I'd ride and ride, up and over our favorite mountain passes. I want to feel the wind in my hair, my cheek against my husband's shoulder, my arms around his waist. I want to hear the engine's purr and the tires' hum.

I swallow my rising sorrow. Riding Eric's motorcycle without him would reduce me to a blubbering lump blinded by tears. I'd have to pull over at the first turnoff, wait until I could see, and return to my lonely, aching, solo existence.

All too soon we arrive at the restaurant. My stomach has been in knots since I first learned I'd been granted early release. I'm not hungry, but who am I to refuse a free lunch? I'm penniless as well as homeless.

Crossing the Restaurant des Delices threshold is surreal, like I stepped from Bozeman into Paris. I had no idea such a fancy restaurant existed in the Montana cow town I've called home all these years. Due to our tight budget, Eric and I rarely ate out. When we did, our options were limited—Taco Tuesday at the Mexican place near campus or Twofer Thursday at the burger joint on the corner.

I'm glad Noreen had me change out of my stained t-shirt and dirty jeans. The female diners in the room are dressed to the nines. And the men mostly wear button-down shirts and dress pants, not exactly normal attire in a western college town that majors in outdoor activities.

The short dark-haired maître d´ leads us to a table near the rear of the restaurant, giving me an opportunity to survey the premises. The place looks as delicious as it smells. After months of plain beige walls, my culture-starved psyche struggles to take it all in.

Black chandeliers hang from wooden beams, and heavy sea-green drapes border the multi-paned arched windows. Huge flower baskets grace the alcoves, while wheat bundles stand at attention in the corners. All around the room, hand-stenciled vines ramble over textured walls.

And the paintings...oh, the paintings, including two prints by Eric's favorite French artist, Camille Pissarro.

Once more, grief nearly overwhelms me. Eric and I promised each other we'd celebrate our MSU graduation with a trip to Paris. He planned to immerse himself in the Louvre Museum, and I hoped to check out the music scene, including the street performers.

The maître d´ seats us, hands us menus, and with a twitch of his black handlebar mustache, describes the lunch special. I try to act interested in pecan-crusted trout with the chef's award-winning orange-rosemary butter sauce drizzled over it. But I'm thinking Eric would have loved the artwork in this restaurant.

The gorgeous landscape behind the maître d´ features a frozen lake surrounded by a dark forest. Moon shadows and Milky Way glimmers intermingle on the ice. On the far side of the lake sits a small cabin. Smoke rises from its chimney and light shines through its solitary window.

I pull myself from imagining the cabin's cozy interior and focus on the flickering candle in the center of the table. The squat pale-green orb sits on an off-white pottery base. Wonderful aromas waft around us—fresh-baked bread, seafood, coffee, and other tantalizing smells I can't quite identify. Soft classical music emanates from speakers high above. Restaurant des Délices would have been a wonderful place to celebrate anniversaries with my husband, something we never had a chance to do.

On our one and only anniversary, he wanted to buy me a card and flowers. But he was too sick from the chemo to leave the apartment, which made him sad. I told him to get well, so we could celebrate our two-year anniversary and many more.

A lot of good that did.

I sigh and turn my attention to the maître d´, who gives me a questioning glance before saying, "Your waiter will be with you shortly." He twists one side of his mustache into a tighter curl, pivots on his heels and marches away.

I open the leather-bound menu.

"You okay?" Noreen asks. Her perfect eyebrows pucker, no longer following her brow line.

"I'm not very hungry." I offer an apologetic shrug. "Do they have something small, other than salad?"

"Oh." She seems shocked. Maybe she expected me to be ravenous after a year in jail. "How about a crepe?" She smiles. "Giles—he's the head chef—makes very good crepes. I think that's what I'll have."

Our waiter, a dark-haired man with an olive complexion a little lighter than mine, arrives with a water carafe. He greets Noreen and tells me his name is Robert. His accent sounds more Hispanic than French.

"This is Miss True," Noreen says. "She's interested in becoming a church member, like you."

I smile and nod. "Nice to meet you, Robert."

"The pleasure is mine." He fills our water goblets without spilling a drop on the linen tablecloth, all the while asking what we'd like to eat. I order a spinach crepe with Mornay sauce, and Noreen orders a chicken-and-mushroom crepe. I watch him go. He seems rather serious.

Despite the ceiling fans that circle lazily above us, I feel extra warm, probably due to layers of synthetic fabrics I'm not accustomed to. Slipping the jacket from my shoulders, I'm about to take it off when Noreen says, "Leave it on."

"What?"

"Leave it on."

I lift my chin. "I'm hot."

"Our members, whether male or female, never bare their arms. And we never show flesh above the ankle, if we can help it, and certainly never above the knee."

"Why is that?" I don't try to hide my skepticism.

Her gaze hardens. "Put on the jacket."

Although I'm not a member of her church, or any other church, I shrug the jacket onto my shoulders. "I don't understand what's so bad about arms and legs."

"You will." She smiles mysteriously. "In time."

Why she can't tell me now is the mystery, but I say no more.

Our lunch arrives on white earthenware plates. Fresh mesclun salads accompany the crepes. I chew slowly and carefully, relishing each tasty bite. Jail "cuisine" can't begin to compare.

I dab the corners of my mouth as I eat and manage not to dribble sauce on the new jacket. Noreen hasn't said it's mine to keep. Not that I want it. My mom might appreciate the bright flowers, but my taste is subtler.

Between bites, Noreen asks about my family, my education and my marriage. The fact she knows I was once married tells me she's done her homework. I'm not sure how I feel about that.

Before she can ask how I landed in jail, something she's probably already researched, I inquire about her family. She's wearing a wedding set on her left hand. The large diamond in the center is surrounded by several smaller ones.

She laughs. "The head count is ever-changing. Bruce and I have three children of our own, but others come and go."

"Are you foster parents?"

"Not exactly. We take in church children from time to time, depending on the need. At their parents' request, of course."

I tilt my head. "Seems to me acquiring parental permission would be a given."

"Why, yes…certainly." She lays her fork at the top of her plate. "I only wanted to make that aspect of our ministry to families clear." Daintily patting her lips with her napkin, she glances at her watch.

I savor one last bite of the spinach crepe and make a mental note to treat my parents to dinner here when they visit. According to the menu, a string quartet performs each evening from seven until ten. Mom and Dad would enjoy everything about this place— the food, the ambience, the music. I place my fork on the top edge of the dish.

Noreen reaches for the brown portfolio she carried into the restaurant along with her white leather purse. "Before we get on with our afternoon, we should go over some paperwork."

So that's what she has in the portfolio. I should have guessed and primed myself for this moment of spilling my guts. The rehab place will want to know all the details of my tawdry past.

"We have a busy afternoon ahead." She opens the case and pulls out a folder and a pen. "This is a good time to get your signature on the documents."

I set my plate aside, wondering what she means by *busy afternoon*.

She lays two legal-size forms on the table and slides one over to me. "This one is for Transformation Way."

I stifle a groan. Here we go again. I hate listing my arrests, my incarcerations, my hospitalizations, the treatment programs I've failed. "The judge's order isn't enough?"

Robert appears beside me. He gathers our plates and silverware. I notice a gold band on his left ring finger. Maybe I'll run into him and his wife at the church.

I hand him my napkin, whispering my thanks.

He nods and leaves.

"We want your *commitment* to the program," she says. "We want to know you're joining us because of your desire to become a better person, not solely because a judge sent you to Transformation Way."

She pushes the second sheet across the tablecloth until it's even with the first. "This one is for Faithful Followers of the Way. If you'll recall, you're required to join the church as well as participate in the program."

I've signed for student loans, college admission and treatment centers, but why does a church have something for me to sign? Maybe it's an application for membership. Then I see that both documents are titled *Liability Release*. I scan the Transformation Way form and then the one for the church. They're each one page in length and, for the most part, identical.

"This doesn't ask for background information." I raise my eyebrows. "Other programs require—"

"The sheriff already provided us with that information." She smirks. "We probably know more about you than you know about yourself."

I ignore her patronizing smile and read the rehab-program form line by line.

> *Transformation Way directors, counselors and therapists provide mental and emotional counseling and therapy. The Transformation Way staff and students, along with Faithful Followers of the Way pastors, leaders, employees, members, associates and students pray for deliverance and healing, cast out devils, speak in tongues, and receive and extend words of wisdom and exhortation. No guarantee is made by either entity that mental or emotional illness will be relieved, addiction of any nature cured, or personal relationships and issues healed.*

> *No guarantee is made by either entity that injuries, congenital maladies, illnesses or diseases will be healed, that devils will be exorcised, that souls will be saved, or that words of wisdom and biblical exhortation will equate to professional advice.*

> *Faithful Followers of the Way pastors, leaders, employees, members, associates and students do not claim any education or experience in family counseling, marital counseling, mental health counseling, emotional counseling, financial counseling, psychiatry or psychology, nor are they experts in any medical field. Counseling, healing, casting out devils and deliverance are done through teaching and applying God's Word, laying on hands, subjecting the spirits, and prayer.*

I skim the other document, see that its language is similar, and glance at Noreen, who seems to be observing my every movement and facial expression.

She asks, "More questions?"

"I can understand why the release forms might be somewhat alike, but these are almost identical. What's the deal?"

"It's simple. The state requires both entities to disclose ministry practices and provide agreement forms for adherents to sign. We have a similar one for the school."

"But these suggest no experts are on either staff. The church might not have professionals in psychiatric or medical fields." I tap the questionable section. "But, surely, the treatment center has qualified individuals." I assume private and group counseling are part of the program, and I'd prefer to have *trained* therapists and facilitators, not wannabes.

"Let me see that form."

I hand it to her, showing her the paragraph in question.

"I see what you mean." A crease forms between her perfect eyebrows. "I'll mention a possible wording change to the director."

Something about her tone makes me doubt her sincerity, but I resume my reading.

> *My desire is that Faithful Followers of the Way pastors, leaders, employees, members, associates and students assist me and direct me to receive God's blessings as led by the Holy Spirit through teaching the Word, providing words of wisdom and exhortation, prayer and laying on hands, be it for healing, subjecting and exorcising devils, deliverance, or any other physical, emotional, mental, spiritual or financial need.*

> *I release the pastors, leaders, employees, members, associates and students of Faithful Followers of the Way from any and all liability regarding any complications that may result, whether directly or indirectly, alleged or confirmed, from ministry endeavors.*

I grew up attending church with my family and can't imagine how harm could come through prayer. The document goes on to say the signer waives the right to sue for damages resulting from "physical, emotional, mental, spiritual or financial injury."

I lift my gaze to meet Noreen's. "What kind of injury comes through prayer? I don't get it."

Pressing her lips together, she slowly shakes her head. "We've had two, let's say, *unstable* individuals threaten us with lawsuits. The first was a man who didn't receive the healing he desired. Obviously, God had a different plan for his life. The other, a woman, accused one of our pastors of emotional abuse when confronted with evidence of sin that hindered her relationship with God and others.

"As expected..." The smirk returns. "Their threats didn't go far. However, the notion that ungrateful or unstable individuals could sue our church disturbed us and altered our focus, which made serving God difficult. After the second accusation, our pastor decided we had to close the barn door before, not *after* the horses get out, if you know what I mean."

I reread the section that bothers me the most. Space is provided for the signer to name his or her children and list their birthdates. And then the signer agrees to waive the right to sue the church regarding ministries they "perceive" to negatively affect those children.

If Eric and I had had a child, would I feel comfortable with that clause? It seems to give carte blanche permission to do whatever they want with kids. I look to Noreen for an explanation.

"You're at the part about children, right?"

"Yes."

"Everyone stumbles over that. We've had issues in the school as well as the church. Out of hundreds of satisfied parents, three disgruntled parents of children who'd been disciplined at our school banded together to seek damages.

"The judge eventually tossed the case for a lack of evidence of mental, physical or emotional harm. In addition, those parents had each signed a consent for corporal punishment when they enrolled their children at Triumphant Way School." She jiggles the pen she's holding in her fingers. "Discipline at Triumphant Way is firm, yes, but it's also loving. As with the previously mentioned situations, we couldn't let three people set a precedent for other parents. Lawsuits distract the administration and teachers from the work God is doing in young lives."

She offers the pen to me. "Ready to sign?"

I've signed plenty of documents that protected other parties from liability and litigation, yet I hesitate. For some reason, these release forms make me uneasy. Are other churches this concerned about lawsuits? Is this a result of our litigious times? I chew at my bottom lip. Maybe I'm being overly cautious, still watching my back.

Or maybe it's the last line on both documents that reads: *This contract remains in force as long as the member lives or until nullified by Faithful Followers of the Way leadership.*

Noreen is drumming the pen on the tablecloth, but I ignore her and take the time to reread the strange sentence. What kind of church expects lifetime membership? Weird. Better wording would be—*until the member leaves the group.* Which is exactly what I plan to do the moment I'm ready to reestablish my music career.

I sit back. "These are strong words. I need more time to consider the forms before I sign them, *if* I sign."

CHAPTER FOUR

Arms folded, I wait for Noreen to give me a a week or two to decide if I'm going to sign the forms. But when I see her kindly benefactor facade twist into a scowl very much like that of a peeved jail matron, I know it's not what she's thinking.

Forearms on the white tablecloth, she juts her chin at me. "Have you forgotten you've been *sentenced*—" She hisses the word. "*Sentenced* to Transformation Way? And *sentenced* to attend our church services?"

"No, I haven't forgotten. However, the judge's decree is one thing. This paperwork is something else."

"Without your signature on both forms, we cannot allow you into the program."

"Really?" I lift an eyebrow.

"Really." She lowers her voice. "Either you sign, or I call the cops. They'll arrest you right here, right now, with all these people watching." With a wave of her hand, she indicates the diners seated around us. "The officers will cuff you, lock you in their cruiser, and drive you straight to jail. Remember how that feels?"

She drops the pen.

We stare at each other.

Neither of us blinks.

Finally, I pick up the pen. The church leaders have reason to include language that protects the ministry. Still... I blow out a breath, sign and date both papers and hand them to her, along with the pen. I hope I haven't done something stupid. But what choice did I have?

Noreen completes the witness sections and drops the forms into her portfolio. When she lifts her head, she has a wide smile across her face, as if all is wonderful in her world, as if she didn't just threaten me.

I, on the other hand, am sickened by what I did.

For twelve months, I followed orders, went where I was told to go, signed where I was asked to sign, and said "yes, ma'am" and "no, sir" to judges and officers. But I'm no longer in that environment. To launch my relationship with this group in such a kowtowing manner is not what I expected to happen today.

"Congratulations," Noreen says, a new gleam in her eyes. "Now, you're one of us. But we must do something about that hair. Next stop, the beauty parlor."

"I can't afford—"

"Your dental work will commence early next week."

I put my hand over my mouth. "Dentist?" I mumble. "I can't pay—"

"No worries." She flutters her hand. "It's all part of the program. You'll see."

With its gilded mirrors, ornate tables and massive flower bouquets, Salon Bellissima Tu is almost as stunning as the French restaurant. The salon name is stenciled in a fancy font on the wall behind the reception desk, where red bricks peek through aged plaster. The place smells better than the average beauty shop, like spices, not perm solution and nail polish.

Why haven't I heard about this beauty shop before? Bozeman isn't all that big. Could be my oversight was due to the fact it's also a spa tucked into a secluded corner of one of the city's nicer neighborhoods.

All three women at the desk seem to know Noreen, and they welcome me with broad smiles. You'd think I was a long-lost cousin. The happy atmosphere is a Hallmark commercial for the way life should be.

Noreen walks me to my hairdresser's station.

"Let me guess," I whisper. "They all attend Faithful Followers of the Way."

I'm not yet ready to say "fow." It still sounds to me like a word for filth or for chickens. If I let my mind imagine the women here as chickens, I'll giggle until I snort, and I won't be able to explain what's so funny. Eric would get the humor, but these people might not.

"*Most* of them are members." Noreen checks her hair in a mirror and slips a stray lock into place. "We're working on the others."

Two-and-a-half hours later, I leave the salon with the cutest haircut I've ever had. My long, dry, straggly light-brown hair is now shoulder-length, shaggy yet stylish, and shining with rose-gold highlights. My nails, which I've kept short since I started playing the guitar, are polished in a gold-swirled creamy pearl, a nice contrast to my brown skin. And my face is coated with so much makeup it feels heavy.

I've always applied eye makeup, foundation and blush with a light touch, even for performances. And I never wear lipstick. But according to the mirror, it's all there, including copper eye shadow.

This process required several phone calls to a mystery person and repetition of the mantra, "We must match the gift of God within you." I don't know what that means, but they all seemed determined to make me look my best.

After months of not wearing makeup, my first thought when the esthetician finished was, *I could pass for a streetwalker.* I didn't say anything because everyone else was blabbering on and on about how the new hairdo and makeup brought out my natural beauty. I haven't made any attempt to enhance my personal appearance since Eric died, so I have to admit the change is an improvement.

On the way to the mall, where a "shopping adventure" awaits me, I ask about Faithful Followers of the Way. After all, I just joined a church I've never seen, let alone attended—not that I had a choice.

"Oh, my…" Noreen grins. "FFOW is hard to describe."

The legal forms still trouble me. I don't appreciate the fact I was coerced into signing them. Yet, I'm willing to do whatever I need to do to conquer alcoholism, grow spiritually and return to the concert circuit. Those documents and the judge's order guarantee my admission into the rehab program.

"You have to experience FFOW to believe it," she says. "And even then, you'll occasionally need to pinch yourself to confirm it's real." Her eyes sparkle. "You'll be amazed at how your life changes. I know I was. In fact, I'm still amazed. I came to FFOW years ago, and I've never been the same. The old ways are behind me."

Old ways? I give her a curious glance.

She waves a dismissive hand. "I'll tell you about it someday, Lord willing."

"I met a lot of people from the church today." I stroke my newly polished thumbnail. "It must be really big."

"By Montana standards, it is. We have over two thousand regularly attending members, not including children. Some churches have that many members, but they don't attend every Sunday, like ours do."

"I've lived in Bozeman for several years, yet I hadn't heard of the church until your group came to a chapel service."

"You probably didn't hear about us because we're located outside of town," she says. "FFOW's early days go back almost fifty years. It started out small and had a different name and location. After our current pastor came on board, three regional churches with a vision to focus on healing and deliverance ministries banded together. They purchased acreage and started building. God led people from all over the West to join together to do the impossible. And that's exactly what we did."

She pulls into the mall lot and parks at a distance from the other cars.

We're close enough to Macy's that I assume it's our destination.

"Hundreds of total strangers," she says, "have become one big happy family."

"Everyone I met today seemed super happy."

"We're all full of joy. We don't have time for grumpiness because we're too busy serving the Lord."

I open the car door. No wonder the women at the jail whine constantly. Sitting around doing nothing day in and day out makes a person grumpy. I'm ready for joy and happiness, for positive people. I'm ready to serve the Lord.

Noreen loads my arms with carefully selected items—ankle-length dresses and skirts, long-sleeved blouses, dress pants and flannel nightgowns plus a robe. Every clothing choice, including the nightwear, is based on Noreen's phone conversations with the mystery person and the magic mantra, "We must match the gift of God within you."

I stop at the Levi's rack, but she pushes ahead, carrying slips and underpants. Lace-free bras dangle from her fingers. Frilly bras, she says, are "of the devil."

I don't argue. She can believe whatever she wants to believe.

Inside the dressing room, she helps me hang the items on hooks. I'm relieved when she steps out. I was afraid she might remain in the tiny mirrored room to give her opinion on what works and what doesn't—based on the gift of God within me, of course.

Alone for the first time all day, other than quick restroom visits, I slip on an expensive ankle-length outfit, turn to the tall mirror and gasp. With my highlighted hairdo and over-the-top makeup, I could be one of the FFOW women who visited the jail. I grimace. If I felt like a clone in jailhouse orange, how is this any different? Have I exchanged one uniform for another?

This morning, while watching me gather my things, Serena said, "I envy you, Cat. I have five more months in this hellhole and, as you know, orange just isn't my color." We'd both laughed, but the truth is, very few people look good in orange. Eric, with his fiery red hair, was one of them.

I twist to see the back of the outfit in the mirror. Because it's long, it might be considered old-fashioned. However, the light-blue fabric is satin, not cotton, and the skirt is straight, not gathered. Does some manufacturer design special clothes for this store to sell solely to FFOW women?

The style is definitely not something I'd choose. But I can wear whatever they tell me to wear. For a year. Then I'll dig out my blue jeans and tank tops.

I have to admit I look better, more like the girl who walked the aisle to take Eric's hand and say, "I do." I unbutton the top, reminding myself this is a *new* day, a *new* way. The Transformation Way. Time to leave the past and the memories that drove me to addiction behind. Maybe this place is the key to unlock—

"Does everything fit?" Noreen calls from the other side of the door. "Need a second opinion on anything?"

Startled out of my thoughts, I rip off the top and grab another one.

"I don't mean to rush you," she says, "but we have two more stops to go before dinnertime." Despite her words, she sounds anxious.

I hold a blouse to my shoulders. "Almost done." Tossing it aside, I grab a dress. "Just a couple more outfits to try."

On the way to the shoe department, Noreen stops at the jewelry counter.

I switch the clothing bag to the other hand. "I'm not much for jewelry, so you don't have to—"

"Nonsense." She holds a beaded necklace to the light. "You'll want the *altogether look* at FFOW, and this does that exactly. It's a perfect match for your blue outfit."

The *altogether* look has never been *my* look. Eric called me a modern-day hippie. With my long straight hair, tie-dyed tops, faded jeans and ever-present guitar, he said I would've fit in with the sixties crowd. But he didn't want me to change. Like my parents and my brother, he loved me just the way I was.

I pass a tall glass case and catch sight of my reflection. At first glance, my family might not even recognize the new me. I hardly recognize myself. One more reason to finish the program and move on.

Noreen is an experienced shopper. In no time flat, she's selected and purchased earrings, necklaces and bracelets to match the clothes plus a pricey watch with a decorative metal band. The total cost so far for the Macy's shopping spree is well over a thousand dollars. I've never purchased so much stuff all at once.

Thank God, everything is a gift. A generous gift. I should be grateful.

As we trot through the store, exhaustion grips my shoulders. I'm sure I'll be more appreciative when I'm not feeling so tired and overwhelmed. I haven't been this active since college days. The more I lag behind, the faster Noreen marches forward. I'm tempted to drag the heavy bag on the smooth tile floor, but I'm fairly certain she would *not* approve.

We stop, this time at the fragrant cosmetic counter. Noreen speed-dials the mystery number and talks at length with the person on the other end as well as with the salesclerk. Without consulting me, they discuss what shades of foundation, blush and lipstick enhance my *nutmeg* skin tones and also match the gift of God within me.

Whatever that is. I'll ask later. I don't want to delay our departure from this endless store.

The two women hold bottles and tubes to my face and debate the options. I try to tell them I'll buy something cheap at the drugstore, which is what I've always done, but they shush me. I shift my weight from one sore foot to the other. The new shoes are killing my feet. Noreen shoots me a scowl that brings me to a standstill.

Somehow, I survive the cosmetics department and make it to the shoe department, where I stumble into a chair, relieved to finally be able to sit. My feet feel too swollen to try on shoes, but I accept the nylon footies the salesman hands me. He looks near my age and has dark hair and blue eyes like my brother.

Noreen calls him by name. "Corban, we'll need three pairs of pumps in off-white, black—"

"Thank you, Noreen," I interject, "but I can't wear pumps."

The way Noreen and Corban stare at me, you'd think I spurned the Hope Diamond. "I have a foot malformation," I tell them. "My podiatrist says I should never wear heels higher than half an inch." I point to some cute leather sandals. "I can wear those."

Noreen frowns, and the salesman looks to her for direction, like I don't exist.

Her sigh holds a hint of exasperation. "We'll have to pray for deliverance."

Deliverance? For my feet?

"Bring out flats, in white, beige and navy blue." She turns to me. "Size seven-and-a-half B, correct?"

"Uh, yes." Is there anything she doesn't know about me? "But the ones I'm wearing are—"

"And a pair of tennis shoes," she adds as he starts to go. "For outside work."

Outside work? At a recovery center? "I hate for you to spend the money when I have hiking boots. They're great for outdoor stuff."

Corban hesitates.

Noreen wrinkles her nose. "Hiking boots? Uh, no." She motions to him. "Remember, no Nikes."

"No, ma'am. Never." He disappears into the backroom.

I give her a questioning look. "No Nikes?"

"As they say, the devil is in the details. With Nikes, it's literally true." She sits beside me. "Not many people know Nike was the Greek goddess of victory. We at FFOW choose to honor the God of heaven, our real source of victory, not some fabricated Greek goddess."

"I had no idea." I tug off the shoes, praying the others fit better.

"That's how it is at FFOW. God blesses our leader with words of wisdom no one else receives."

"Oh." *No one else?* Does God have favorites?

Corban hurries to us with a stack of shoeboxes in his arms.

Noreen jumps to her feet. "I need to visit the ladies' room. I won't be long."

The salesman plops onto the stool in front of me and deposits the boxes on the floor. But he's looking toward the opposite side of the aisle. I follow his gaze and between racks see Noreen entering a restroom.

He grabs my sweaty feet and places them on the stool's angled surface, too close to his nose for my comfort, and turns them this way and that.

"Uh, sorry." I cringe with embarrassment. "I forgot the nylons." Pulling my feet away, I slip on the footies.

Corban grabs one of my stinky shoes. "Aha, exactly what I thought. Size seven." He balances it in his hand. "These shoes are new. Where did you purchase them?"

"I didn't buy them." I don't want to tell him I just got out of jail. "Noreen, uh…"

"That's all I need to know. The shoes came from here." Opening the top box, he pulls out an identical pair of black flats. With any luck, the leather smell will negate my foot odor. After another quick peek at the restroom door, he says, "Quick, put these on and tell me what you think."

I do as he says then walk to a mirror. "Even with swollen feet, they feel better than the others." I sit again.

"The way you were walking, I could tell the shoes didn't fit right." He places the original pair in the box and slides it under a chair. "I'll change the label later." Taking the lid off another shoebox, he says, "In theory, these navy shoes are identical to those, but you should try them on to be sure they're okay."

His eyes shifts to the side. I can tell he's watching the restroom. "You heard my name," he murmurs. "What's yours?"

"Cat."

He arches an eyebrow. "Is that an approved name?"

"It's my nickname, if that's what you mean, the name my friends call me."

Corban helps me out of the navy shoes and into the white ones. "No, I mean—" He jerks his earlobe.

I stare. Does his ear itch or what?

Without moving his lips, he whispers, "Look at your feet."

His behavior puzzles me, but I follow his lead.

"Walk around." He clears his throat, and in a louder voice, says, "See if these feel as good as the others."

Before I can get to my feet, Noreen bustles into the shoe department in a wave of fresh perfume. "Let me see what you brought out."

He flips the lids off the boxes, one at a time. She approves of all but the tennis shoes. Without explanation, she deems them "inappropriate."

Corban is heading for the backroom, when she eyes her watch. "Forget it, Corban. We're running out of time. These will do." She scurries to the purses. "Tally everything while I gather a few more items."

He winks, catching me off-guard. I blush, and he chuckles. His wide grin is so contagious, I can't help but smile. I help him repack the shoes and carry them to the counter, where he scans the UPC codes and places the shoeboxes one by one into a big bag.

I nearly groan out loud. Another huge bag to haul around the store.

Noreen flits amongst the racks like a whirling dervish. Without a single mystery-person phone call, she grabs nylons, socks, slippers, belts and scarves, and drops them beside the cash register. And then she goes for more—of what, I can't begin to imagine.

I try to make small talk with Corban.

He nods and continues working.

Fatigue threatens to overwhelm me. I lean against the counter. This sudden shift in environments is a lot to process. I've gone from a year behind bars to racing around the mall, from wearing the same orange clothes every day to a bag full of fancy outfits. For the first time in years, my straggly hair is pretty again, and I ate lunch at a French restaurant instead of the jail dining hall.

I ought to be happy. After all, I've never been treated to so much nice stuff all at once. I'm about to enter my final treatment center, the one that'll do the trick, as Dad would say. From there, I can move forward with my life and my career. I should be happy *and* excited, but I miss my mom. Shopping with her would have been leisurely and fun, and lunch would not have included a threat to send me back to GCDC.

Frowning, I think of the red flags from today, words like *approved name, liability release, never bare flesh, consent for corporal punishment, words of wisdom no one else receives, Nike...* And then there's Corban's odd behavior. He seems nice enough, but...

On top of it all, I'm beginning to feel like a project, which if I'm honest with myself, is what I am. I wanted a do-over, I'm getting one—a full makeover, inside and out. The outside today and the inside over the upcoming year. I'm determined to endure to the end. But already, I'm exhausted.

An urge to rush home to my parents who've never tried to force me into a mold washes through me. They want me to stay sober and out of jail, of course, but they've always encouraged me to be myself. If I had cash and a car, I'd drive straight to Salem, Oregon, stopping only for gas, just to feel their arms around me and to let them know I'm okay. Even a hug from my ornery brother would be good.

"Hang on." Corban whispers. "It'll get easier."

I give him a grateful smile, but his attention is on Noreen, who comes running with a shiny pink purse about the size of two cell phones placed side-by-side. *Pink purse?* I hope it's for her, not me.

She throws it on the counter. "Isn't this the cutest little thing?"

"It's, uh…dainty." *And more fitting for a child than an adult.*

Noreen hands Corban a credit card. After everything is tallied, she asks him, "When do you get off work tonight?"

"Seven o'clock."

"Be sure to be on time for the service."

Something clicks in his eyes, like he switched off the lights. He nods without comment.

She must have noticed my weariness because she says, "I'll go get the car and meet you at the east entrance. But first, I'll purchase your bath linens." Leaving me with the clothing and shoebox sacks, she takes the smaller ones and dashes off, nearly tripping over a child.

I thank Corban and reach for my bags. "I'll probably run into you at church."

He dips his head, but he doesn't smile or wink, and his eyes are blank, as if the door to his soul slammed shut.

CHAPTER FIVE

Happy to be relieved of the heavy bags, I push the button to close the Lexus trunk lid and climb in beside Noreen. "Thank you for all the nice things you bought for me today." I reach for the seatbelt. "I don't know when I can pay you back, but—"

She shakes her head and drives toward an exit. "No worries."

I fasten the seatbelt. "Where are we going now?" With any luck, a bed with a softer mattress than the one I had in jail is in my near future.

At the exit, she looks both ways and then pulls onto a highway leading out of town. "Wednesday night is mandatory potluck night at FFOW."

My heart sinks. A potluck means I'll have to remain upright and sociable for at least another hour, probably two. Beginning a new life is a thrill, but I'm ready for a long nap.

"Mandatory?" I study her profile. "For church members or Transformation Way students?"

"Both." She checks the clock on the console. "You're not expected to contribute a dish tonight. But next week, be sure to read the rotation calendar on your household's refrigerator to learn what your assigned food item is."

"Okay…" I'm still trying to comprehend I heard the word *mandatory* used regarding a church activity. Another word to add to my list of confusing FFOW terms. And what does she mean by *household*?

"Your five-dollar admission fee is also waived for tonight."

I don't try to hide my surprise. "The church charges the people who contribute the food for the potluck?"

"Yes, and we love it. Such a privilege, praise God." She waves a hand in the air. "It's a brilliant way to collect money for our overseas work. We funnel thousands of dollars each month into the orphanages and schools we've established in underprivileged countries."

She tilts the rearview mirror her direction. "The concept came from another word of wisdom given to our leader. We call them FFOW-wows."

"Fow-wows?" *As in bow-wow?*

"Yes." She brushes hair from her forehead.

I try not to snicker. "What's your leader's name?"

"*Our* head pastor—yours and mine—is a wonderful woman named Ruby Jade Paradise." Readjusting the mirror, she adds, "You'll have an opportunity to meet her soon."

"Ruby. Jade. Paradise." I search for something nice to say about the strange name. "A unique name, for sure."

We stop before a wide gate with a FAITHFUL FOLLOWERS OF THE WAY sign on it. At the bottom, in smaller print, are the words "No Trespassing." A church with a gate and a "No Trespassing" sign? Most churches beg people to visit their services. They open their doors to the community by providing food and clothing and sometimes housing to those in need. I know because I've been the recipient of their generosity more than once.

Noreen rolls her window down and punches buttons on a metal box beside the road. The iron gate slowly swings opens.

I open my mouth to ask about the gate and the sign, but Noreen speaks first. "God gave Ruby Jade a new name many years ago. It's perfect for her."

"So that's not her real name."

"It's not her birth name, but it's her legal name." She hits the gas and surges ahead, past a street sign that reads "Paradise Path." Touching her earphone, she speaks in a low voice, something she's done several times today. "Yes, through the gate." Has she been reporting our every move?

The winding road is lined on each side by meticulously groomed trees and bushes. We whiz past so fast they're almost a blur. The grassy expanse stretching into the distance reminds me of a golf course. How big is this place?

"We're going to arrive on the dot." Noreen's knuckles are white on the steering wheel. "I don't want to miss announcement time. As soon as I stop the car, hop out and follow me."

We pass Triumphant Way School and then zip alongside a tall structure I assume is the sanctuary. A covered walkway with arches runs the length of it. Huge pansy-filled planters are centered within each arch.

Next is a long single-story building that also has an arched walkway and more pansies. Noreen screeches the car around the corner and into a parking space marked "Noreen" directly in front of the building. She stops with a jolt that would have sent us both through the windshield if we hadn't been wearing seatbelts.

Turning off the engine, she unbuckles and jumps from the car. I'm two steps behind. We dash toward carved double doors that stand at least twelve-feet high. Noreen grasps one of the cross-shaped metal handles and yanks the door open.

Inside is a wide foyer and a second set of ornate wooden doors with cross-shaped handles. "This is the rear of the dining hall," Noreen whispers. "Follow me to the front."

She opens a door and hurries up a wide aisle toward a stage much like those found in school auditoriums, high heels clicking with each step.

I pause inside the doorway, taking in the scene before me. Beautiful women and handsome men, all nicely dressed, are seated at long tables on both sides of the aisle. The children with them appear to be wearing their Sunday best.

Conversations and food smells I can't quite identify waft around me, but no one is eating. Are they waiting for us? I rush to catch up with Noreen, feeling the stares as we pass table after table. By the time we reach the stage with its maroon velvet curtains and microphones and lights hanging from the ceiling, the huge room is eerily quiet.

She leads me onto the platform and over to a mic on a stand. Smiling, I clasp my hands behind my back. Thank God, I've spent plenty of time in front of people. Otherwise, I'd be a nervous wreck. This is a large crowd. I wonder if I'm seeing all two-thousand FFOW adherents and their children or only a portion of the congregation. Some members, like Corban, may still be working.

I've had plenty of practice calculating potential income from concerts based on ticket prices and approximate numbers of attendees. Rather than count the tables and the people at each table, I figure two-thousand diners times five dollars each. Am I really looking at ten-thousand dollars, not counting the food and the fancy clothes or the rows of late-model cars parked outside? These people must be well-off. And ten-thousand times fifty-two weeks in a year would equal a pile of money for the church's outreach work.

Noreen has her hand over her ear, listening—I assume—to the mystery person again. Strange timing. An entire congregation is waiting while they talk.

The huge room is plain, not ornate like the building's exterior, but the women, who all wear red lipstick, are colorful. Their hair is flawless and their outfits expensive. Dresses and skirts seem to be the norm for the potluck. I don't see any females in pants. The men wear dress pants and long-sleeved dress shirts, either white or light blue, buttoned to the second button from the top. No ties. They're all smiling, including the kids, who sit at attention, somehow reminding me of well-trained circus dogs.

"Hello, Faithful Followers." Noreen adjusts the microphone. "We have a special guest with us tonight. Please welcome Miss True, our newest FFOW member."

Everyone jumps to their feet, clapping and cheering. I've had good responses at concerts but nothing like this. I start to bow, as I would at a performance, then catch myself and dip my head.

Noreen motions for the people to take their seats, which they do without hesitation. She turns to me. "Would you care to say a word, Miss True?"

I narrow my eyes at her. A warning would have been nice. We had plenty of time today for me to gather my thoughts and plan what to say.

She smirks, which is apparently a regular habit of hers.

I step to the mic. "First of all, thank you for such a warm welcome. I'm overwhelmed."

They smile and nod.

"Because I'm new, I need to clarify that I'm actually *Mrs.* True. I was married to Eric True for a year and a half before bone cancer took him from me."

Soft moans emanate from the group, but their expressions are mixed. Some seem sympathetic. Others glance about, as if they're searching for someone.

Noreen nudges me aside. I hear a voice coming from her earphone, the same one I've caught snatches of throughout the day. "Ask if she remarried."

Noreen parrots the question. "Have you remarried?" An arrogant lift of her brow follows.

I shake my head. She knows the answer.

She listens again and then says, "Technically, you're single and a *miss*." She laughs a humorless burst. "To clarify, that's 'miss' not *amiss*."

Nervous titters run through those seated at the tables.

I open my mouth to defend my stance. My marital status can properly be designated either *missus* or *miz*, but I'll never be a *miss* again. When the flint in Noreen's eyes suggests I keep my thoughts to myself, I close my mouth. A public disagreement in front of my fellow congregants would be in poor taste, to say the least.

The voice on the phone is sharp though soft enough the sound system doesn't pick it up, as far as I can tell. "Noreen, apologize for Miss True's deceptive appearance."

I touch the jacket lapel. The real me wouldn't dress this way, but... I raise my gaze. Noreen is gawking at me, a shadow of the in-charge person who whisked me away from the jail. I get the impression she hasn't had much practice apologizing.

I tilt closer to the mic, remembering the jail chaplain's favorite phrase. *Transparency is the key to transformation.* Might as well take the first step now. What better time and place?

"One more thing," I tell the onlookers. "These are not the clothes I put on when I dressed this morning. Instead, I donned a jailhouse-orange t-shirt and matching cotton pants, something I've done every morning for the last year as a GCDC resident."

Chins lift, eyes widen, but if the listeners are shocked, they don't show it.

I continue. "Noreen not only gave me a ride when I was released, she graciously provided a nice outfit to change into before I left the facility. My own clothes were dirty and torn." My transparency does not include my final thought. *And far more comfortable than what I'm wearing right now.*

Noreen blows out a long breath, and a swirl of color and rosewater floats between us on a tinkling undercurrent. I gasp and step away, my mind reeling. Did an angel or a fairy descend on us? But then I see the whirlwind is a short heavyset woman swathed in silk of every imaginable hue. Dark curls streaked with silver tumble down her back.

Where did SHE come from? I glance behind me. The velvet curtains are moving back and forth as if touched by a breeze. I twist to catch the audience's reaction to the newcomer. Apprehension and adoration vie for dominance on most faces, especially the children's. Others reveal no emotion.

The woman yanks the microphone down to her level and shouts, "Pea-jee-eye-ech!"

I jump backward at least a foot.

Without blinking an eye, Noreen and the hundreds of other members yell, "Pea-jee-eye-ech!" The stage vibrates with the roar, sending tremors through my feet and into my ribs.

Wide silk sleeves rise before me like multicolored wings. Throwing her head back, the newcomer reaches for the ceiling with jewel-laden fingers. Diamonds sparkle and her long purple fingernails glisten. The metal bracelets encircling her thick wrists jingle.

A sea of undulating hands wave before us like marine plants on a coral reef.

She repeats, "Pea-jee-eye-ech!"

I steel myself for the response, which is louder than the first blast. Even the window coverings quiver. *What language is this?*

Noreen motions, and the people sit in unison. Not one person misses the cue. I've never seen a more attentive audience. She readjusts the microphone. "Good evening, Ruby Jade. Thank you for blessing us with your presence."

Oh, so she's—

Ruby Jade spreads her short arms wide. "Pea-jee-eye-ech!"

Still seated, the people respond, "Pea-jee-eye-ech!"

By now, I'm not quite so startled by the exchange. However, the intensity is unsettling. You'd think they were at a hometown football game.

Her voice at a normal volume, Ruby Jade says, "Prepare the microphone for me, Noreen."

Noreen releases the mic from the stand and holds it in front of Ruby Jade, who takes my hand but faces the audience. "Children, please stand and tell our newest member what 'pea-jee-eye-ech' means."

Several hundred children rise to their feet, hands raised.

Ruby Jade extends her arm like a choir director. "All together, now." The silky sleeve swings.

They recite in unison, "Praise-God-in-heaven."

"Thank you." She lowers her arm, palm down.

The children sit.

Oh... Finally, I get it. They were saying P-G-I-H, not speaking in tongues or a foreign dialect. Weird. But at least I won't have to learn another language to be a part of this group.

Ruby Jade grasps both of my hands, and Noreen maneuvers to keep the mic before the leader's mouth.

"Miss True." Ruby Jade smiles, revealing perfectly aligned whiter-than-white teeth. Her face is surprisingly slender. She has flawless porcelain skin and high cheekbones. Heavy black eyeliner and glittering gold eyeshadow emphasize her most remarkable feature, gold-flecked violet eyes.

"I am pleased to meet you," she says, "and delighted almighty God in heaven led you to join us. Here among the Followers is where you'll find righteousness, happiness, success and the path to heaven." Her thick red lipstick has a hint of purple in it. "I sense beauty waiting to be unveiled in your spirit."

Beauty waiting to be unveiled... A song lyric, perhaps?

"My name is Ruby Jade Paradise," she continues. "I am the pastor, prophetess and psalmist for the Faithful Followers of the Way. My utmost privilege is to receive and deliver God's words for his children to his children." She flourishes a hand over the congregation, her wide sleeve shifting with the movement. "You, Miss True, are now included among God's children, hallelujah."

I'm about to say I was already God's child, when the audience bursts into another round of handclapping punctuated by loud shouts. "Hallelujah, hallelujah!"

Following my coffee-shop performances, Eric would tell me my music was amazing and "the applause was thunderous," which made us both giggle. But in this place, it's true. The way these people clap could literally raise the roof. I eye the ceiling. No cracks yet, though the hanging mics shudder, sending vibrations up the wires that hold them.

When the noise lessens, I respond. "I'm pleased to meet you…" I hesitate. "Do I address you as Mrs. Paradise or as Pastor or—?"

"You may call me Ruby Jade." Her purple eyes probe, as if she's searching my soul, but her smile is gracious. "That's what all my dearest friends…" Once more, she waves her silk-draped arm toward the crowd. "That's what these dear people call me."

She releases my hand and grabs the microphone from Noreen. Hand up, palm facing the ceiling, she faces the group. "Faithful, let us pray." Her sleeve slides down her arm, revealing a nasty-looking rash I didn't notice earlier.

Everyone stands, heads bowed, arms raised. I close my eyes.

"Great God in heaven," she loudly proclaims, "we thank you for the meatloaf, green beans, Jell-O salad, yeast rolls and apple crisp you have provided from your bounty. Amen."

I open my eyes and look around. That's the oddest meal prayer I've ever heard, other than my brother's prayers. Kip used to list the food just to make everyone laugh. Ruby Jade, on the other hand, appears entirely serious.

The sound of chair legs scraping the floor fills the room. I'm happy the Faithful can finally eat. If Noreen hadn't taken the time to introduce me, they'd be finished with their meal by now.

Ruby Jade leaves through the curtain, and Noreen takes me by the arm. She leads me onto the steps and across a stamped-and-stained concrete floor similar to my parents' patio. We stop at a table in the middle of the huge room.

My "household members," as Noreen terms them, are waiting for me, hands in their laps and smiles on their faces. Although I'm touched by their thoughtfulness, I hate being the cause of further dinner delay, especially for hungry children.

One by one, I'm introduced to the eighteen individuals seated at the large table. The "household guardians" are Olivia Pritchard, a big-boned, dark-haired woman, and her husband, Owen Pritchard, a mousy but kindly sort with thinning light-brown hair.

They have four brown-haired children—two polite teenage boys, two smiling elementary-age girls—plus a sad-faced little boy with curly red hair named Zachary Russell.

"Zachary resides with us, but he's not one of us," Olivia says.

Her comment strikes me as an odd way to state the relationship, but because he has a different last name than the others, I assume he's a foster child.

Olivia's mother and aunt also live with them. Her mom is a thin, severe woman with dyed black hair. The distaste on her face suggests she's not exactly thrilled I'm joining the household, probably something to do with my ex-con status.

In contrast, the aunt's smile is welcoming. Her soft roundness and short silver curls remind me of my grandma, but her eyes are alert and probing, unlike Grandma Hunt. Dementia has stolen the light from my nanna's eyes.

A man named Scott introduces his wife, Candice. They're both blondes, and she's patting the tiny baby boy snuggled on her shoulder. Another brown-haired couple, Michael and Deanna, have two girls and a boy who are also brunettes, and who all look to be elementary age.

I have a feeling jail was quiet compared to this household when everyone's home. I also have a feeling hair color is probably not the best way to distinguish the residents. I should have used one of those memory techniques, like picturing a bowl of candy on Candice's head, or whatever. All the women, except Olivia's mom and aunt, have highlights in their hair.

Last of all, I meet my roommate, Marcela, a pretty girl with shoulder-length strawberry-blond hair, green eyes and a sweet smile. My guess is she's several years younger than I am, but she seems nice, and I'm sure we'll get along fine. For the most part, the group is kind and welcoming. I should enjoy living with them. At their grumpiest, they have to be more pleasant than crabby inmates who whine about every little thing.

Many of their voices, including those of the children, are raspy. They sound as though they're coming down with or getting over laryngitis. Communal living has its problems. Colds and flu bugs swarmed the jail like bloodthirsty mosquitos, but I was only sick once at GCDC. I trust my immunity is still strong enough to withstand the germs.

Noreen directs me to the empty seat beside Olivia and moves on. Some sort of tension seems to dissipate—I feel it more than see it, and we begin passing the food back and forth across the long table. Olivia, who seems to be the no-nonsense type, asks me questions about myself.

I answer as best I can in my befuddled state. I feel the same way I did the first time I was incarcerated. Numb. I know I'll eventually adjust. But at this moment, I can't decide which I want more, a drink or sleep.

By now, I'm beyond hunger. To be polite, I put a little of everything on my plate when the food is passed my way. Sure enough, we're eating meatloaf, green beans and Jell-O salad, which I thought only elderly people like my grandma ate, plus yeast rolls and apple crisp. It's all served in foil pans, including the Jell-O.

I sneak a peek at a nearby table. From what I can see, those people are eating similar food from foil containers. This is more like a school cafeteria or the jail mess hall than a cafeteria. The local dollar store must love to see these people walk in the door. Or, maybe the church has a wholesaler for the hundreds of pans needed each week. Good thing I'm too tired to attempt to unearth the reasoning behind such uniformity.

Beyond that "household," a wide-shouldered, dark-haired, thirtyish man makes eye contact with me, drops his gaze to my chest, and raises his fist in a brazen thumbs-up.

I avert my eyes from his lecherous grin. What was that about? Did it really happen in church? Or did I imagine it? I'm so tired, anything is possible.

CHAPTER SIX

I pick at my food, listening to my housemates' congenial banter. They somehow manage to talk and bolt their food at the same time, eyes on the huge clock above the double doors. Zachary, the sad-eyed redheaded boy, doesn't eat. Instead, he twists this way and that, scanning the room.

Olivia pushes away from the table and marches to the other side. Bending over his shoulder, she whispers so loud I can't miss her words, despite a roomful of conversations. "That's enough, Zachary. Turn around and eat, or you'll get a paddling."

"But—"

"No buts." She grabs his shoulders, a bit too forcefully, and faces him forward. He starts to cry.

She kneels beside him, dark eyes flashing. "Stop it. Now."

He closes his mouth and stares straight ahead.

"That's better."

I seem to be the only one concerned about the interchange. The others are chatting as if nothing unusual is happening. Olivia takes her seat beside me, breathing hard. Could be Zachary is a challenge to control, especially in public.

I've eaten a bite of everything but the apple crisp, when a loud buzzer jolts me to attention, followed by the painfully loud grating of chair legs on the cement floor. Except for the teenage boy who shovels in another mouthful of food, those around me gather their plates and silverware and stand.

Without comment, they walk to rubber basins stationed on a motionless conveyor belt at intervals along the walls. I follow. The only sound is that of our shuffling feet—until those ahead of us begin scraping food scraps into basins. Silverware clanks into separate basins, and plates and cups are deposited into others.

My group returns to our table. The women collect the serving utensils and walk them to yet another rubber tub. The men gather the foil pans, stack them and shove them into one of the oversized trash receptacles teenage boys are wheeling about the room.

A youth from our table collects the paper napkins and throws them in the bin. The other teen helps Marcela wipe and dry the heavy plastic tablecloth, fold it, and place it in a cupboard beneath the conveyor belt. I'm impressed by the efficiency of it all. Within fifteen minutes, all the tables are cleared, and we're heading toward double doors opposite the ones Noreen and I entered.

Marcela comes alongside me. "Next…" She clears her froggy throat. "We go to the sanctuary for the Wednesday praise-and-petition service."

I peek at my new watch. Seven-twenty.

The sanctuary, which we access by way of a covered walkway, reminds me of a Jehovah's Witness Kingdom Hall. Similar to those meeting places, this one has no windows. However, it's several times the size of a typical Kingdom Hall. The interior walls are painted pure white, including the trim and wainscoting. Huge crystal chandeliers hanging from the high white ceiling sparkle with brilliant elegance.

The blue-carpeted floor angles downward from the doors to a curved stage. Row after row of royal-blue chairs arranged in three sections follow the platform's arc. Three stair-stepped levels lead up to the wide platform, and three giant pastel wreaths hang on the stage wall. They're the largest wreaths I've ever seen. The flowers must be silk rather than fresh.

Less than a minute inside the sanctuary, and I'm convinced the decorating committee included mostly women. No guy would design a church to resemble a fancy restroom—a women's restroom, that is, especially one reeking of rosewater.

A musical ensemble is seated at one side of the platform, instruments ready. The shoe salesman, Corban, is one of them. He has a trombone in his hands and is moving the slide in and out.

Marcela leads me down to a row of chairs where women of all ages are already seated. She whispers, "This is the unmarried women's section. I have permission to sit with you tonight."

"Permission?" I quirk an eyebrow.

She murmurs, "I'll explain later," and puts her finger to her lips.

Permission? Designated seating?

I relive the very public conversation I just had with Noreen regarding whether or not I'm a "miss," and anger churns in my chest. I stifle it, knowing I must accept the fact I'm no longer married. But I'd like to know why we're segregated by marital status—and why Marcela needs permission to sit with me, or anyone else, for that matter.

She sandwiches me between herself and a girl who looks barely out of high school, which leads me to another question. I open my mouth to ask Marcela about segregation and ages. But before I can speak, she motions with her chin toward the front.

A group of men dressed in identical dark suits with baby-blue handkerchiefs in the breast pockets, white shirts and blue ties are filing onto the platform from a side door. They arrange themselves on the steps. Robert, the waiter I met at the restaurant, is one of them.

The instant the last person is in place, trumpets blare. I jerk, as startled by this new noise as I was by the buzzer in the dining hall. Words flash onto the wall above the musicians, and the men begin to sing, apparently at the top of their lung capacity. Their volume is amazing.

Those around me leap to their feet and join the loud singing. I stand, but I don't know the song, so I don't sing along. I'm disappointed the musicians and the singers play and sing in unison. No one, as far as I can tell, adds harmony. At least they're on pitch, for which I'm grateful. As tired as I am, one discordant note could dissolve me to tears.

The music goes on and on. Like the group that visited chapel services, the men all sing with wide smiles, including Robert. I love music, but this set of songs is loud and long, and my sore feet and tired body are desperate to sit.

No one else is seated, not even the elderly ladies in front of me. If they can keep standing, I can too. I don't sing, but I clap when the congregation claps, and I raise my hands when they raise their hands. Marcela is smiling and clapping in time with the others.

Closing my eyes, I concentrate on the words to get into a worshipful state of mind—that is, until Marcela elbows me.

I blink.

"We worship with our eyes open," she whispers, "so the demon of piety can't steal our spirits."

"What?"

She puts her finger to her lips.

Finally, the singers leave the platform, but the instrumentalists remain, including Corban. Everyone plops into their seats, and Noreen strides from the side door to the transparent acrylic podium. She adjusts the microphone. "Good evening, Faithful."

The unison reply comes. "Good evening, Noreen."

I'm struck by the fact she and Ruby Jade are addressed by their first names. Why, then, do they refer to me as *Miss True*? I blow out a long breath. Just one more of many questions to ask someone. I'm not sure who it would be, but maybe I'll start with Marcela.

"Before Ruby Jade comes to bring God's latest word to us," Noreen says, "we'll spend time petitioning him." She extends her hands. "For those of you new to Faithful Followers of the Way, we worship God with music at this praise-and-petition service and then present our needs to him. He provides when we ask."

A picture of flags appears on the front wall—a red, white and blue American flag and a blue Montana flag with its scenic portrayal of the state's resources in the middle. "Ruby Jade is tireless in her attempts to connect with our governor and our president," Noreen says, "yet only their underlings respond. God has told her to speak his word directly to our top officials and not allow a third party to distort the purity of the message."

She leans closer to the microphone. "Our mayor and police chief listen to her advice, our sheriff, district attorney and judges receive her calls. Our senators and representatives at both the state and national levels are attuned to her tutoring.

"It's time…" She points at the flags. "It's time for the governor of the State of Montana and the president of the United States of America to hear from God!"

As one, the church members jump to their feet, cheering and shouting, "Amen! Amen! Hallelujah!" Amazed by behavior usually reserved for sports events, I slowly stand. This is even more overwhelming than my welcome. I catch sight of Corban, who from the stage is trying to make eye contact with me. His brow is tight. He taps the fingers of one hand on the palm of the other. I get the impression he's telling me to join the applause.

Because his expression is one of worry, not disapproval, I start clapping. He gives me a slow wink, or maybe it's something in his eye, and then stares straight ahead with what looks like a forced smile. His cadenced clapping is robotic.

Noreen lowers her hand, and the cheers stop, just like that. In a whoosh of displaced air and rustling clothing, the congregation sits. All attention is focused on Noreen. No one fidgets or whispers to their neighbor. Everyone's hands are in their laps, including the children's hands.

My parents' pastor would have asked for other prayer requests, but Noreen instructs us to "go before the throne." All around me, arms spread upward and outward. I'm reminded of branches on trees planted too close together. Whispered words buzz, growing louder and louder. If I didn't know better, I'd think a swarm of bees had invaded the room.

Marcela elbows me. "Pray."

I whisper, "I am praying."

"Out loud."

I'm not sure whether to pray in English or to fake-pray in tongues, which I assume is what I'm hearing, at least from some of the nearby women, including Marcela. The girl on the other side of me speaks so softly I can't tell what's coming out of her mouth.

Aiming my palms heavenward, I hold them near my face because I don't want to tangle with the arms in front of me. "God," I whisper, "I'm not sure what to say. This is so different—"

A loud "amen" reverberates from wall to wall. I open my eyes in time to see the lights dim. Music swells and colors spin onto the white walls—purple, silver, gold. Circled by a spotlight, Ruby Jade sashays across the stage in an undulating silky haze, arms dancing, sleeves swaying. Every now and then, I catch sight of the red rash on her arms, but it's mostly hidden.

Her lips and kohl-lined eyes are more lavender than I remember, and her face is white beneath the bright light. The crowd rises, cheering like she's a rock star.

I slowly unfold to join the adoring mob and sneak a glance at my watch. Eight-thirty, and the main attraction is just now arriving.

Laughing, Ruby Jade embraces us in a wide figurative hug. "PGIH!"

This time, I join the others in repeating, "PGIH!"

She motions for us to be seated, rings twinkling. "Wasn't that fun?"

A young male voice calls, "Do it again." Laughter ripples through the room.

"I thought I'd add a bit of color to our midweek service." She clasps her hands and rests them on the lectern. "And, yes, we might have a do-over one of these days."

The sanctuary lights come on, but not all the way, and the spotlight remains on her pale face. I can't decide if she resembles an exotic dancer or an evil clown. I blot the thought from my mind. She's a pastor who enjoys a bit of spectacle.

I could swear the podium is lower now than when Noreen stood behind it. How did they do that?

Rotating her thumbs, one round the other, Ruby Jade quotes a scripture verse I recognize from the Old Testament, probably Genesis. "And God saw that the wickedness of man was great in the earth, and that every imagination of the thoughts of his heart was only evil continually."

She steps to the side, one hand resting on the podium's acrylic ledge. "*Every imagination* was evil continually. Sound familiar?"

"Amens" pepper the congregation.

"Outside of these walls," she continues, her voice growing louder, "evil abounds. It abounds in the form of thieves, liars, cheaters…" She stabs the air with each word. "Adulterers, idolaters, murderers, coveters, profaners and…" She drops her voice. "More, much more."

What follows, "for the children's sake," she says, is a description of each sin she's listed, along with related scripture verses, all from memory, unless she has a teleprompter I can't see. I pinch my earlobes to stay awake. Unlike me, the others hang onto her every word. When I've had some rest, I'll be able to concentrate better.

Hands on her ample waist, Ruby Jade tips toward her attentive audience. "I'd like to tell you those of us inside the fold are protected from evil," she whispers. "I'd like to tell you evil can't touch this church." Her volume rises. "I'd like to tell you everyone in this room is pure and free from deceit. But that would be a lie straight from the devious devil—*and you know it.*"

She thrusts both arms straight out in front of her. Index fingers extended, she sweeps her aim from one side of the auditorium to the other. I can't help but think of a soldier panning enemy territory with his rifle. She stops, her purple nails pointed at the single women's section, my section.

Her eyes flash. "You know who you are…s-s-sinners-s-s." The word hisses from her lips.

I hug my ribs hard and swallow. I'm a sinner. I know I am. But I've asked God for forgiveness. The Bible says he removes our sins as far as the east is from the west. So, why is my heart hammering my ribs? And why do I feel like she's targeting me, and no one else?

Lowering her arms, Ruby Jade stands silent and motionless, except for her eyes. Her glittering gaze shifts from side to side. "You know who you are," she whispers. "You know who you are."

I gulp.

But then she smiles, and her features soften. She becomes a different person, almost motherly. "More on this subject later. Stay tuned for God's Word explained in full."

I release the breath I didn't know I was holding. Others around me do the same.

"Dear ones," Ruby Jade says, "Don't look so relieved." She flips her hair behind her shoulders. "Only fools claim to be without sin and ignore the truth of their depravity. First John one-eight tells us God will forgive and cleanse, but you must first confess. That's first John one-nine.

"You *must* confess and be cleansed. As I've told you over and over, confession and cleansing are good for the soul and necessary for salvation. I *will* continue to provide you opportunities for deliverance from the devious devil, every time the Spirit leads."

Without further fanfare, she walks out the platform's side door. The lights come on, and Noreen approaches the podium, which is tall again. Naming two men, she says, "Meet me here at the front after the service to discuss building repairs."

She then asks for volunteers to scrub the nursery furniture and paint the walls on Friday morning. When no one raises a hand, she says, "By not responding, you are rejecting an opportunity to serve the Lord *and* to serve our children. Do you not care for the health and well-being of our precious little ones?"

Several women raise their hands, and she tells them to meet her in the nursery at eight a.m. Friday morning. She checks her notes one more time then extends her hand. "Faithful, you are dismissed."

I raise my watch. Nine forty-five.

Trailing Marcela out of the building, I ask if I can catch a ride to the house with her.

"Where's your luggage?"

My sacks aren't exactly luggage, but I tell her, "In Noreen's car."

"Then you'll have to ride with her."

My vision of slipping between sheets for a long sleep evaporates like fog at noon. I step to the side of the murmuring throng exiting the sanctuary behind us and wait until only two or three people straggle through the open doors. When I return to the sanctuary, Noreen is talking with two men and apparently not happy about something. "She asked for cherrywood."

"The lumberyard didn't have cherrywood," one of the men responds. "We stained a piece of hardwood to match what's in her office and inserted it where she wanted. That short section, by the way, is behind a door. It's a mere two-and-a-quarter inches long." He indicates the length with his finger and thumb. "And it perfectly matches the rest of the molding."

"You should have ordered it."

"She wanted it done that day."

For a moment, Noreen appears at a loss for words. "Well, then, order authentic cherrywood and replace the defective wood when it arrives."

"We'll do that."

The men pivot and march toward the door, jaws set, fire in their eyes. "I should have paid for it myself and not submitted the receipt," one of them mutters. "That's the *only* way she could have known what we did."

Noreen is still behind the lectern, reading something. Not wanting to disturb her, I take a seat on the front row. But after a couple minutes, I realize she doesn't know I'm waiting for her. I clear my throat.

She lifts her head.

A man enters a side door and begins to straighten chairs.

"I'm over here, Noreen." I wave a hand. "Please finish what you're doing. I can wait." Logic says she'll want to go home to her family soon. She's been gone all day.

"Miss True..." She seems surprised to see me. "I'll deliver you to your household in a minute." She gathers her papers and motions to the man. "I'm leaving now, Boyd. You can lock up."

CHAPTER SEVEN

The upstairs bedroom I'm to share with Marcela isn't large, but it beats a jail cell. Similar to a jail cell, it lacks decoration. No pictures on the walls, no headboards for the two single beds, no knickknacks on the narrow dressers and nightstands—only alarm clocks and lamps. The furniture is painted brown with gray drawer fronts. Those colors might work in an Army barracks, but...

I stifle the critical thoughts, thank Noreen and drop my load on my appointed bed.

While I fill my dresser drawers with underwear, socks and nightgowns, Marcela hangs the skirts, blouses, dresses and pants for me. She also arranges shoes on my side of the closet, which now smells like a clothing store. The lineup includes the "inappropriate" sneakers as well as my old hiking boots.

I'm glad Noreen left after she dropped me off and didn't catch the look Marcela and I share when she holds the shiny pink purse under the closet light. Evidently, I'm stuck with the silly thing.

I compare my new watch's time against that of the small alarm clock on the nightstand. The words "time to serve Jesus" are taped across the top. It's midnight already. "I'm so sorry for keeping you up, Marcela. I had no idea the service would go so late and I'd have to wait for Noreen."

She shrugs. "You'll get used to it."

"You mean, services are always long?"

Her green eyes glaze over. "Let's brush our teeth and get ready for bed. Tomorrow will be here before you know it."

Mystified by the sudden change of subject, I follow her into the attached bathroom. The small room's only color is the pink towel hanging from the towel rack.

She starts the sink water and leans close, meeting my wide-eyed stare in the mirror. "The bedroom has a video camera." Her voice is barely a whisper. "With a microphone."

I rear back. "Are you kid—?"

She puts her finger to her lips. "I don't know how much it can pick up," she murmurs, "but we must be very careful what we say and do."

"Who…?" I close the door. "Can see us?"

She opens the door. "A branch of Security called the Sentinels."

"Why did you do that?" I squint at her reflection.

"If we're in here together with the door closed, they'll get suspicious."

"Suspicious of what?"

"You know…kinky stuff."

What?

She dampens a toothbrush, spreads toothpaste on it and turns off the water.

I search through the toiletries I brought from jail and find my well-used yellow toothbrush plus a small toothpaste tube. Barely aware I'm brushing my teeth, I focus on the ceiling.

Why are the Sentinels watching our bedroom? Do they watch all the members' bedrooms, or only ours because we're single? Or because I'm a criminal. Is Marcela a criminal too?

We finish our teeth and rinse our toothbrushes.

Marcela wets a washcloth.

I bend toward the mirror. "Are they monitoring our room in case someone breaks in?"

"If only." Her eyebrows pinch. "Actually, they hope to prevent the kinkiness I mentioned."

I shake my head, disgusted by the notion. "This *special service* is for singles, not married couples, I assume."

"*Especially* for married couples."

Again, I'm speechless.

She runs the cloth over her face. "Ruby Jade determines when we can have, uh, you-know, and when we can have children." Shutting off the water, she says, "Someone will hear water running in the pipes. We'll get in trouble for wasting it."

Eric and I had wonderful intimacy. I can't imagine another person invading, *monitoring* something so private. I whisper, "Surely not married couples…"

Marcela sighs and holds her left hand in front of her face. She's wearing an engagement ring *and* a wedding band. I don't know why I didn't notice her rings before. The set is simple, but the diamond is huge. She wets another cloth and hands it to me. "Welcome to my world."

"I don't understand." I stare at her in the mirror. "Why are you here, not with—?"

"Long story. I'll tell you one of these days. Right now, I need to sleep."

"Me, too." I press the warm, damp cloth over my tired eyelids. It feels so good I moan. Maybe in the morning I'll wake up to the realization this was a nightmare to top all nightmares.

"One more thing," Marcela murmurs in my ear. "Noreen told me to remind you to keep your hands outside the bed covers."

I lower the cloth. "Why?"

"Shh…" She shakes her head. "Same reason we can't wash our private parts with a cloth."

"How are we s'posed to—"

"You'll figure it out."

I've just closed my eyes, when a loud noise awakens me. I peer through the darkness and see Marcela fumbling with something on her nightstand. *Good. That's her alarm, not mine.* Pulling the covers over my head, I will my body to once more drift into oblivion.

But then a click resounds, and Marcela is calling, "Miss True, Miss True. Wake up. You and I are helping with breakfast this morning."

Miss True? Why does everyone call me that?

I push away the covers and sit, blinking to adjust to the light. The sound must have been Marcela switching on her lamp. A reflection of lamplight on the camera lens catches my eye. I grab the robe I left on the nightstand and slide my arms into the sleeves. Our jail cells were more private than this.

Marcela is already making her bed.

"You can call me Cat," I tell her. "The name my friends call me."

"No, I can't do that." She frowns. "It's not your approved name."

What's with names around here? "Approved name?"

"Yes. My approved name is Marcela Renee Perez."

"What's your real name?"

"Well, that is my real married name. My family and friends used to call me Marcy, but not since we came to FFOW. Ruby Jade doesn't approve of nicknames."

"I like Marcy."

"She says it's frivolous." Marcela folds the chenille spread over her pillow. "You should get out of bed. If we don't hurry, we'll make people late for work, including me."

I'm about to ask her where her husband is and where she works, but she hurries into the bathroom and closes the door. Thanks to our midnight conversation, I know to wait—not that I would have barged in on her.

Ten minutes later, we exit the bedroom together. A whiff of fresh-brewed coffee greets us at the top of the stairs. "Smells good," I tell Marcela. "After our late night, I'm going to need it."

"If you're anything like the rest of us," she says, "you'll be drinking buckets of coffee."

I add "buckets of coffee" to my red-flag list. Over the years, I've known plenty of heavy coffee drinkers, including my grandpa. But what does it mean when *everyone* drinks buckets of coffee?

I follow her down to the kitchen to help prepare a traditional American breakfast of sausage, eggs, pancakes and orange juice. Marcela squeezes oranges and I make scrambled eggs according to Olivia's very specific instructions. Is every FFOW household eating the same thing this morning?

Dining for the second time with my housemates is a pleasant though quiet affair and not as rushed as last night. We eat at a long rectangular table in an even longer dining room. The walls are bare except for a black-rimmed clock that reminds me of school and jail clocks, and a big picture of the leader. She is truly a beautiful woman, but it feels weird to have her image stare at us while we eat.

Seeing the home in daylight, I get an idea of how large it is, which it needs to be to house so many people. Does everyone in the church live communally?

Last night, I noticed the church's property is located away from other buildings and houses. This neighborhood—Fellowship Neighborhood, according to the engraved rock at the entrance—is also some distance from town. It seems to be an isolated group of homes, not a subdivision.

The others at the table look as tired as I feel, especially the kids. No one asks how we slept, probably because the night was so short. But they do ask about each other's plans for the day. They all have several activities scheduled. That is, everyone except me.

I'm planning my return to bed, when the male household guardian, Owen, opens the Bible beside his plate and says, "Miss True…"

"Yes?" *Am I about to be treated to another sermon, one prepared specially for me?*

"You may not know the Faithful follow a reading schedule of three-to-five verses per day. Ruby Jade calls it her ten-year guide. Because we're all so busy serving the Lord, she's directed the household guardians to provide the reading each morning from the King James Version. Olivia and I alternate. This morning, our passage from the KJV Old Testament is Lamentations three, verses nine through eleven."

He clears his throat, yet his voice remains hoarse. "He has enclosed my ways with hewn stone. He has made my paths crooked. He is to me like a bear, lying in wait, and like a lion hiding in secret places. He has turned me off my ways and pulled me in pieces. He has made me desolate."

He closes the Bible and glances around the table, nodding like a bobblehead doll. I expect the others to discuss these strange verses and enlighten me regarding their context. Instead, they push back their chairs and carry their dishes into the kitchen. Zachary and I stay at the table to finish our pancakes.

Similar to Eric, the little boy has green eyes, flame-red hair and a smattering of freckles across his pale cheeks and button nose. He's a cute kid yet somehow sad and listless. His nose drips, and he wipes it with his sleeve. Maybe he has a cold.

Olivia charges into the dining room. "That's enough, Zachary." She gathers salt and pepper shakers from each end of the long table. "Take your plate to the kitchen and go get ready for school."

His lower lip puckers.

She scowls at him. "Stop acting like a baby and obey me."

Head bowed, he picks up his silverware and his plate with the half-eaten pancake and shuffles toward the kitchen.

"Move it, Zachary. Upstairs, now. Blow your nose before you brush your teeth."

She seems impatient with him, but maybe he dawdles every morning. "Miss True," she says, "your breakfast duties today include helping Marcela rinse dishes and load the dishwasher. That won't require much time. I'll be glad to drive you to work when I deliver the children to school in half an hour."

What? "Uh, thanks, but I don't have a job to go to. I'm in the—"

"Oh, but you do." Judging by her haughty expression, I'd say she's enjoying an *I know something you don't know* moment.

Owen walks in carrying a briefcase and holding a corduroy sports jacket over his shoulder. He chuckles. "We don't let grass grow under our feet around here." After a quick peck on Olivia's cheek, he says, "I'll see you both this evening," and hurries through the kitchen toward the garage.

I stand and gather my tableware. "Where will I be working?"

"You're now a teacher's aide at Triumphant Way." Olivia's smile is proud. "That's the name of our church's school. You'll be in the third-grade classroom with Zachary."

"Morning or afternoon?"

She gives me a funny look, as if she's forgotten I'm here for the rehab program or doesn't know. "All day," she says, "regular school hours."

I thought the state had laws against schools employing criminals. I also thought I'd start the rehab program and *then* find a part-time job. Evidently, I thought wrong. "I've never worked in a classroom, and I didn't apply for the position."

"Ruby Jade is a very good judge of character. If she believes you'll be a good teacher's aide, then the teacher will be happy to have your assistance."

Ruby Jade doesn't know me and neither does the teacher.

Zachary calls from the kitchen, "Our other aide ran away with her boyfriend."

Deanna and Michael's oldest daughter, Heidi, who's collecting the syrup and butter, says, "They're both damned to hell."

"Hush, you two," Olivia orders, "and get ready for school."

After I help Marcela load the dishwasher, I pour myself another cup of coffee. I have a feeling it's going to be a long day.

Because I don't have time for a shower, I rinse my hair in the bathroom sink. Marcela comes in to do her makeup while I blow-dry my hair. I step close, meeting her gaze in the mirror. "I just learned I'm going to work at the school, starting this morning."

Her eyebrows crumple. "I submitted an application to be a classroom aide months ago."

"Where do you work?"

"Receptionist in a plastics factory. Ruby Jade assigned me to that job two years ago. All my efforts to transfer somewhere else have been useless." She sighs. "I should be grateful for work. Some people in our congregation are unemployed. But the factory is cold in winter and hot in summer." Lowering her voice, she adds, "Plus, it stinks and the work is boring."

With upward strokes, she coats her eyelashes with mascara. "The worst thing is my office doesn't have any windows. I stare at gray walls all day, every day, and I never get to go outside."

And then you come home to this dreary place.

She pulls a hairbrush from a drawer. "I'd rather be with children. They're sweet and fun, and they smell better than plastic. Plus, they have recess breaks." She grins. "I know it's silly, but I miss recess. I loved going out to play and run with my friends."

"I totally understand about recess," I tell her. "But I don't have the foggiest idea how to be a teacher's aide. Maybe they'll fire me and give you the job."

She huffs a bitter laugh and runs the brush through her hair. "Fat chance."

Finished with my hair, I switch off the blow dryer and put my brush away. "I'm confused, Marcela." I drop my voice to a whisper. "Are you saying the plastics factory is somehow connected to the church?"

She slips her brush into a drawer. "FFOW owns that factory plus a pasta manufacturing plant, a flower shop, an auto-parts business and twenty-seven other businesses around town."

"I've heard of churches owning businesses, but I didn't know they could tell members where to work."

"Around here, it's about matching the gift of God within us. Only Ruby Jade can discern whose gifting is best for what business. I just wish…" She lowers her head.

"What do you wish, Marcela?"

"I wish God would change his mind and let me go to school to be a teacher."

I walk into the third-grade classroom with Zachary. He's excited to introduce me to his teacher, Mrs. Watkins. "This is Miss True," he says, a wide smile on his freckled face, the first real smile I've seen on him. "She's new in the house where I live."

Mrs. Watkins thanks Zachary for the introduction and shakes my hand. "Welcome to Triumphant Way Elementary School." She's a pleasant fifty-ish woman on the fluffy side, as my father would say. Similar to so many others, she has blond highlights. And her voice is hoarse. I'm beginning to see a pattern.

"Thank you." I dip my head. "I hope I can be helpful here, but you should know I've never worked in a school before."

"That's not…" She studies me for a moment. "That's not what I was told."

I raise my right hand. "God's truth."

"Well…" She shakes away the controversy. "If you can add and subtract, read and spell, you can work with third graders."

"I can do all that." I nod. "Plus, I remember the songs I learned in third grade in Oregon." Truth is, I remember every song I learned in elementary, middle and high school music classes and choirs, but I have no reason to bore her with my personal trivia.

"Great. These children love to sing. Type the words onto separate sheets of paper, and we'll submit them to Ruby Jade for approval. I'll give you the password for the computer in the corner."

"Okay…"

She shows me around the classroom. All the while, I'm trying to make sense of what she said. Why do song words need to be approved, and why does Ruby Jade do the approving, not the teacher or the principal? Seems I have more protocol questions here than I did at GCDC.

The classroom is orderly—not a scrap of paper or a pencil on the floor. And it has a school scent about it. But something is missing. Why I think that, I don't know. I haven't been inside a third-grade classroom since I was in the third grade. I look around, and then realization smacks me between the eyes.

The room is nearly colorless. No bright posters or student art on the walls, no reading charts in primary colors, no bulletin boards, no multicolored maps of the United States, no construction-paper chains hanging from the ceiling. The only hints that young students utilize this classroom are the low chairs, desks and tables. The chairs are black plastic, and the desk and tables have woodgrain tops.

Throughout the morning, the kids move from station to station. Some read aloud to me with their halting little voices, while others glue pre-painted macaroni to construction paper in a cross shape. As they work, the teacher tells them about Jesus dying on the cross. I assume she'll have follow-up burial and resurrection projects for them later. Easter is only a couple Sundays away.

Thank God I was released in time to celebrate Palm Sunday and Easter. The jail chaplain does his best to make holidays special for the inmates, yet it's never quite the same as a real church service. I know Jesus said wherever two or three are gathered in his name, he's in their midst. That's great. However, no one can deny "Up from the Grave He Arose" sounds a whole lot better with more than a handful of voices.

And next year… Next year, I'll celebrate Easter with my family.

A college student named Taylor mans the math station. He told me he attends afternoon classes at MSU with several other FFOW members. The third graders seem to really like him.

With the everchanging activities, including recess and bathroom breaks, the morning passes so quickly I'm surprised when a prerecorded female voice over a loudspeaker announces lunch in the gymnasium. I glance at my watch. Eleven-thirty.

The children stand, push their chairs in, and form a line at the door. Taylor goes to the head of the queue.

Mrs. Watkins motions to him. "Take the children to the lunchroom. Be sure to say 'grace' before they eat."

I turn to her. "Am I supposed to go with them?"

Chapter Eight

Talk about on-the-job training. So far, I haven't known what I'm expected to do until it happens. The administration should have given me a schedule and explained about lunch.

Mrs. Watkins opens a desk drawer to retrieve her purse. "You eat here, Cassandra, unless you have an approved reason to leave the campus. I'm excused to go home for lunch because I need to let our dog out of the garage."

She pulls her keys from the purse. "If you don't have cash today, they'll put it on a tab."

"How long do we have for lunch?"

"Forty-five minutes. Believe me, it goes fast." She edges toward the door.

"Can I eat with the kids and then go to the teachers' lounge? I want to write my parents a note." I'll have to borrow a pen and paper from her and ask Marcela to loan me a stamp.

Her demeanor changes from congenial to stern, as if I'm a student to reprimand. "Followers do *not* lounge—that's what lazy people do, and we *never* enter a lounge where alcohol is sold. Never say *lounge* and never, *never* say *kid* or *kids*."

"Kid?"

"Ruby Jade says the word refers to baby goats. She has a good point. Our precious little ones are not goats. They're children. Be careful not to use that word, or you'll be the recipient of—" She eyes a camera I hadn't noticed before and lowers her voice. "Public rebuke and correction."

I learn something new every hour at FFOW, including the fact video cameras are ubiquitous.

I wander around the school until I find the gymnasium. Several women are clustered at one table, three men plus Taylor at another. Children of all ages are seated at a couple dozen more tables, girls on one side of the room and boys on the other.

Their quiet chatter sounds happy. No arguing, shoving, food-throwing or loud talk. They were as well-behaved on the playground earlier. No wonder they were so good during the service last night.

I spot a serving window at the far end of the gym and walk over, expecting to find the typical school cafeteria setup. Instead, three McDonald's bags line the ledge, and no one occupies the kitchen. A sheet of paper has "LUNCH" printed at the top and the date and lines for signatures below.

Back when I was walking the streets, someone gave me a McDonald's coupon, which I promptly used. I was grateful for it, but my stomach roiled for two days after eating there. The experience might have been a fluke, but I make it a practice to avoid The Golden Arches, no matter how hungry I am.

One of the women seated at a nearby table says, "Welcome aboard, Miss True."

"Thank you." I walk over to the group.

The women introduce themselves with trademark raspy voices, and the men at the other table raise their hands one by one and call out their names. I ask the staff if they always eat with the kids and then quickly add, "Children, that is." Some say it depends on whether they have permission to run an errand or to grade papers at their desks, and a couple of them say they usually do. Taylor says he always does.

"Is it McDonald's every time?" I ask.

"No," says one of the women, "thank God." She dips a French fry in ketchup and pops it into her mouth.

"Is fast food the norm?"

"Except when it's prepared by the Home Economics class. Are you going to join us?"

I smile. "Maybe another time."

From there, I head out into the sunshine. Such a beautiful day. You'd hardly know it inside the windowless gym or the classroom with the blinds half-closed. I inhale a long breath of fresh air and start around the building. It's separate from the church and the dining hall but within walking distance of both. A sea of emerald-green grass surrounds the buildings.

Arms out, I lift my face and smile into the brilliant blue sky. My freedom to enjoy a gorgeous day on the "outside" is almost too much to take in. *Thank you, Jesus.*

Yellow daffodils and bright tulips color the corners where sidewalks meet. Dark evergreens and newly leafed deciduous trees dot the lawn. In the distance, across a valley greened by prairie grass and fledgling crops, white clouds touch snowcapped mountaintops. The springtime beauty I can see from here is astounding.

Some distance beyond the dining hall, a single-story building is bookended by two taller structures that resemble college dormitories. Are those for the rehab residents? If so, why am I living with the Pritchards? I shake my head. Trying to make sense of this place may drive me nuts.

The FFOW compound is at the base of a mountain blanketed with evergreens. Strolling along the edge of the property, I come across a trailhead leading into the woods. Off to the side is a graveled parking lot and a wooden sign, which I can't read because it faces the parking lot.

Though I haven't hiked since Eric died, something stirs inside me. The trail would be a wonderful way to get fresh air and exercise during the lunch break. Already, the scent of pine trees has invigorated me. I'll bring a sack lunch and eat as I walk. With forty-five minutes each day to work on the tunes and lyrics floating in my head—

"Ma'am," someone yells. "Excuse me… Ma'am."

I pivot. A man is hurrying across the grass. I've been focused on walking the trail, if he called to me earlier, I didn't hear him.

"Who are you?" He stops a half-dozen feet from me, breathing hard. I have a feeling he doesn't do much running. "And where are you going?"

I squint at the man. A wide-brimmed black hat with "FFOW Security" on the front shadows his face, but I glimpse a salt-and-pepper mustache and sideburns. He's wearing a navy-blue sports jacket with "FFOW Security" sewn on the pocket and khaki pants tucked into black lace-up boots. One hand holds a two-way radio. The other rests on the butt of a holstered pistol.

Keeping the gun in my peripheral vision, I survey our surroundings, preparing to run into the trees if he threatens me.

The two-way crackles, and a male voice says, "Come again, Hank?"

"Pete," Hank yells into the radio, "I have detained a solitary female at the property line near the trailhead." He lifts his chin and peers at me, one eye focused on my face while the other wanders to the side. "Dark skin. Indian, probably. Streaked hair. Eyes…"

I narrow my eyelids.

"Age approximately twenty-five, height five-and-a-half feet or thereabouts, weight around one-hundred-and-fifteen pounds."

Who is this bozo? He's wrong on most all counts, but I must admit I'm slightly flattered he underestimated my age and weight.

I fold my arms and give him my most ferocious glare. "Who are *you?*"

"Faithful Followers of the Way Security." With a proud lift of his chest, he taps the words on his jacket pocket. "What are you doing on private property?"

"I work here."

His head jerks, his jaw drops, and his elbows jut, like I've given him the shock of his life. "No—you—don't."

"Third-grade aide," I tell him. "Mrs. Watkins' classroom."

"Security is always informed regarding newcomers."

"I came to FFOW last evening—you may have seen Noreen introduce me at the potluck dinner—and started work at the school this morning. Maybe whoever informs you hasn't had a chance to contact you today."

He pushes a button on the radio. "Pete, call the office and ask about the new aide in Mrs. Watkins' class." To me, he says, "What's your name?"

"Cat."

He arches an eyebrow. "Cat?"

I nod. "Cat True."

"What's that?" Pete's voice over the two-way suggests he and Hank are near the same age. They both sound gruff, not hoarse like the others.

"True." Hank holds the radio close. "Last name, True."

"Gotcha. Over and out."

"While he's investigating my legitimacy…" I give Hank my sweetest smile. "I'll go check out the trail for future use."

"No." His brow lowers, and his eyes align. "You can't do that."

"Why not? The sign says it's a Forest Service trail, and Forest Service trails are open to the public. They even provided a parking lot."

"This is private property. You can't access Mount Killjoy from here."

"I'm a member of the church that owns this property, *and* I work at the church's elementary school. What more do you want?"

"Being a member doesn't mean you're free to roam. You must—"

"Wait a minute." I interrupt him. "Did you say Mount *Killjoy*?"

"Yes. Members—"

"How did it get such a negative name?"

He appears miffed by my interruptions, yet he answers me. "Can't say for sure, but rumor has it some old codger was ticked because the trail is deceptive. At first, it's smooth and easy, but then it becomes a series of switchbacks that go straight to the top. The view from there is supposedly impressive, but the climb is a killer, or so they say."

I study the trailhead. *How did Eric and I miss climbing Mount Killjoy?*

"Ruby Jade had us sign a petition to change the name, but so far, the Forest Service is ignoring the will of the people."

"What name does she want them to use?"

"Faithful Mountain, to reflect the proximity of our church campus."

"Oh." Mount Killjoy is definitely a more intriguing name. And from what I've seen of the church so far, possibly a more appropriate name.

"Members…" he says, apparently determined to finish his thought. "Members go to their appointed meetings and obligations and stay off the grass."

"That's crazy." I spread my arms. "All this beauty and no one gets to enjoy it?"

He shakes his head.

"Then I'll be the first."

"No–you–won't–young lady." Hank glowers at me.

"Why not?"

"Ruby Jade doesn't want anyone wandering the property or going into the woods. She says evil things happen in forests. Devils live there."

Devils? Really? She's read too many fairytales. I check my watch. I have just enough time to return to the classroom. "I'd better get to class, but I promise you, I *will* walk this property on my lunch breaks and hike that trail one of these days, all the way to the top." *With or without devils.* I step back, trying to see the summit, but I'm too close.

"You can't do that. I'd have to—" He stops.

"Do what? Shoot me?"

"No, I'd never—"

I take off at a trot across the grass, calling over my shoulder. "Nice to meet you, Hank."

The afternoon speeds by like a fast-forward video, other than the long moment when Hank and a white-haired man step inside the open doorway. I'm seated at a short table, helping a student with a science worksheet about weather. Hank and I make eye contact. He nods and moves on. I have no reason for concern, yet I'm glad they didn't make a scene.

After school lets out, the household children and I climb into the big van Olivia drives. She asks them about homework and then instructs us regarding the afternoon chores. We will all help mow, trim and rake the five acres of lawn, trim the trees and bushes, and clean the flowerbeds. Then the children will tackle their homework, while two of the girls and I assist with supper preparations.

As she pulls into the long driveway, Olivia eyes the rearview mirror. "Hannah and Heidi, whispering is of the devil. If you can't say it aloud, it doesn't need to be said."

Their muted replies are barely discernible. "Yes, ma'am."

"What do you say?"

Louder, they repeat in unison, "Yes, ma'am."

"That's better. Now, what were you two talking about?"

Neither girl answers.

Olivia stops the vehicle.

One of the girls says, "I told Heidi I need to go to the bathroom, bad.'"

"Hannah doesn't want to, you know, have an accident," Heidi says. "That would be of the devious devil."

I struggle to keep a straight face. She mimicked Ruby Jade perfectly.

Without comment, Olivia hits the gas and drives straight into the garage, almost before the door has raised all the way. The van jerks to a halt, the side door slides open, and the girls hop out.

So much for today's whispering lesson.

I've changed into the jeans and t-shirt I brought with me from jail and am tugging my hair into a ponytail when Marcela walks into the bathroom.

She gasps. "What are you doing? You can't dress that way."

"Olivia said I'm supposed to do yardwork. I don't want to ruin the pants and blouse I wore to school today. They're brand new."

"You have to. Followers *never* wears jeans, except some of the men who do construction. Ruby Jade says they're worldly trappings—"

"Of the devious devil."

She opens her mouth but doesn't say anything more.

I slip off the jeans and pull on the polyester pants. "I s'pose I have to wear the new tennis shoes, even though they'll get grass-stained and dirty."

"We're each responsible to wash and iron our clothing and clean and polish our shoes. How we represent God to the community is very important."

"The *community*," I say, making quotation marks with my fingers, "is not going to see us. This is a huge chunk of property, with trees around the perimeter. The nearest neighbors are a block away. Besides, they're all church members, so what does it matter?"

"You're being rebellious, Miss True." She waggles her finger at me. "Please stop, or I'll have to report you."

"Report me?"

"Yes, now leave, so I can have some privacy." She waves me out of the bathroom and shuts the door.

Marcela and I are on our hands and knees in the backyard, trimming the grass around a flowerbed filled with wonderful-smelling orange and yellow tulips. The Bozeman area is experiencing an early spring and greening fast. To be outside without a jacket this time of year is a rare treat.

"Marcela, can I ask you a question?" I snip grass along the bricks bordering a flower bed.

"Sure."

"What's your husband's name?"

"Rodrigo, but his approved name is Robert."

"Is he Hispanic?"

"He's from Argentina."

"I met a waiter named Robert at a French restaurant yesterday. He had dark hair and an accent." Was that only yesterday? So much has happened, I feel as though I've spent a lifetime with these people. "Could he be the same guy?"

"Were you at Restaurant des Delìces?"

"Uh-huh." I pluck a weed that's popped up between tulips, toss it aside and continue clipping grass.

"He works there, but don't call him a *guy*. He's a young man. And we are not *gals*. We are young women."

I can only assume I'm hearing another Ruby Jade directive. "He was a nice *young man*, and I have to say, when God was passing out good looks, he gave Robert a double dose."

Marcela blushes but doesn't respond.

"How did you meet and marry someone from another country?"

"Like I said, it's a long story." She glances both ways before continuing. "The short version is he came here to work and go to school, and Ruby Jade got a word from God he was supposed to stay in America. The easiest way to stay is to marry a U.S. citizen. Ruby Jade picked me. She said we'd make beautiful children together."

"Beautiful children? Are you kidding? She didn't say you'd be happy together or you'd learn to love each other or be a good match to serve God together?"

"Well, no…" She seems surprised I would suggest options.

"Or maybe you should date a while to see if you fall in love and actually *want* to marry each other?"

"She hears from God." Marcela begins to trim grass again. "Which is all that matters. The key purpose of approved couples is to keep the FFOW nursery filled with cute children."

"No homely babies allowed?"

"Miss True…" She checks the area. "Followers don't say such things."

"How can you make beautiful children, if you don't even *live* together?"

"One of these days, we'll be together again."

"Do you love him? I've heard love sometimes happens in arranged marriages."

"Yes." She smiles. "We had several college classes together, so we knew each other, a little. He's really nice. I was happy when Ruby Jade told us God wanted us to be a couple."

I wonder if she and Rodrigo had any say in the matter, but it's a question for another day. "You haven't said why you separated." I snip some more grass. "Was it a culture clash?"

The riding mower steered by one of the teenage boys heads our direction from across the wide lawn, the sound growing louder by the second.

"No, we, uh…" Her cheeks flame. "We discovered we enjoyed, well…you know, bed stuff when we went to Louisiana for my grandfather's funeral. We stayed a couple weeks to help my parents sort through his belongings and prepare his house to put it on the market. When we came home, we forgot about the camera and…" Her voice trails off.

"You mean someone actually watched you?"

"I…well…I guess so." She winces. "Anyway, we didn't have permission to…you know, so Ruby Jade separated us for six months."

I open my mouth but can barely choke out the words. *"Six months?"*

"That's why I moved here." Her shoulders droop. "He's in the men's dormitory."

"Do you two talk on the phone or email or text?"

She shakes her head.

"Do you sit together in church?"

"I'm assigned to the sanctuary with the married women. He's in the discipline room at the side of the sanctuary and watches on a screen. Men and women are separated in there, too."

"Eric and I would have gone nuts to be so close but not be able to be together. How soon will you be reunited?"

"Three more months."

"Marcela…" I groan. "This is the craziest thing I ever heard. How can you be so calm about it?"

"Inside, I'm not calm. I cry a lot." She slaps her hands to her mouth. "I shouldn't have said, I mean—" Her words are muffled. "I let go."

Confused, I look around. "Let go of what?"

Eyes wide, she blurts, "I shouldn't have said anything. Please, Miss True, please, *please* don't tell anyone I let go of Jesus."

The mower noise is growing louder. I smell the fresh-cut grass, which for a city girl like me, is the essence of springtime. Yet, a storm is brewing in Marcela's soul.

The moan that escapes her open mouth becomes a howl. "Oh-h-h…" She crosses her arms, her fists clenched on her chest, and rocks back and forth.

I long to hold her and tell her everything will be okay, that I'll help her however I can. But like before, the light has disappeared from her eyes, leaving a dull green stare behind.

"Don't let me lead you into sin, Miss True. If Jesus tells you to—"

Before the mower can drown our words, I say, "Trust me. I'll never, ever—"

"Not how it works." She jumps to her feet. "I let go of Jesus, and I have to pay the consequences."

Watching her dart behind a shed, I long to run after her to tell her she can't let go of Jesus. His name "Immanuel" means *God with us*. He told his disciples he'd always be with them, that he would never reject or drive away anyone who comes to him. He said he does his Father's will, and the Father's will is that he not lose those who believe in him.

I forgot Jesus' tenacious love for too many years—or chose to ignore it. But all the time, he never let go of me. The Bible says *nothing* can separate me from God's love. His Word is all about his promise to be with us, the very reason he came to earth.

Jesus, our never-let-go God and Savior, holds onto Marcela. She doesn't have to hold onto him. I hope someday I'll be able to share that truth with her.

CHAPTER NINE

Thursday nights are household nights for FFOW members. Everyone gathers in the living room, where I'm told we have a choice of things to do together. We can make popcorn, although we may not add salt or butter—Olivia's rule to protect the furniture—and watch videos of Ruby Jade's sermons or past FFOW events. We can also do an approved work project, at the church or elsewhere.

Or, we can do a prayer walk around the church property, if we call ahead for permission in time for Security to be notified. No one mentions the trail. I'd like to know if any of them have hiked it, but I decide to save my questions for private conversations.

When Owen stops listing the options, I want to say, "Don't you people ever do anything fun?" Judging by the bored expressions on the kids' faces, they feel the way I do about the limited list of odd possibilities.

Olivia suggests we watch the winter concert to give me an idea of what to expect at the spring concert in a couple weeks. One of the girls jumps to her feet. "Rosaline and I can make the popcorn...if that's okay with you, Mother." Olivia nods, and the girls hurry into the kitchen.

Between the three couches, two recliners and several dining-room chairs, we all have a place to sit. I'm on a couch beside Candice and her baby boy. His wide toothy grin and sweet coos make me smile.

Other than a huge gold-framed picture of pink peonies above one of the couches and a big vase of artificial flowers in the corner, the room is devoid of decoration. The oval window at the top of the door is pretty. It has flowers etched in the opaque glass.

While Owen searches for the DVD, I work on learning names. Deanna and Michael Alquist's three children are Hannah, Heidi and Bradford. Such a big name for a little guy who looks all of five or six.

Olivia and Owen's daughters, Rosaline and Rhonda, are the girls in the kitchen making the popcorn. Their teenage sons are Judson and Jeffrey. The "not one of us" red-haired boy is Zachary Russell, a name I remember from last night. Olivia's mom is Alice Jenkins, and her aunt is Marjorie Boyer. Alice gazes straight ahead when she states her name. I get the feeling she'd rather I didn't know it.

Candice and Scott Johnson's baby is named Tristen. I'm tempted to ask if that's his "approved" name. Did Ruby Jade okay the name before his birth certificate was signed?

I get up to find pen and paper to write the names, but Olivia tells me to sit down. "You need to learn to use the memory God gave you," she says. "It's an amazing gift from our Creator."

"I'll try." I don't mention the sad fact alcoholism messed with my memory. Thank God, my recall is getting better every day. I've always been able to remember phone numbers and songs, and they mostly stick, but names can be elusive.

"You'll be quizzed at breakfast."

No pressure…

A popcorn aroma fills the air. My mind flashes to the last movie I watched with Eric from his hospital bed. I snuck in popcorn and we picked a cartoon we hadn't seen because we needed to forget his illness and have a good laugh—and it worked. We laughed so hard the nurses came in to find out what was so funny.

Before I can sink too deeply into my memories, the girls return with a big plastic bowl and smaller paper bowls and napkins, which they pass around the room. I scoop out popcorn for Candice and myself and hand everything to the next person.

Other than FFOW DVDs, Olivia informs me, televisions are only used to display the weather channel. "Followers do not read the pagan world's books, magazines or newspapers. And we do not listen to the radio or watch movies or television, other than the weather channel, which is a necessity for daily living."

I'd wondered why the TV was always on, always muted and always tuned to the local weather station. Now I know. The station is currently predicting the unseasonably warm weather will continue through Easter. That should make the Faithful happy.

I'm amazed the TV is so big. My guess is it has a sixty-inch screen. Why they need such a huge screen to watch the weather, I don't know. But when the video starts, I get it.

The recording opens to an orchestra playing a beautiful song I don't recognize. The sound is high-quality, and the cameramen obviously knew what they were doing. They briefly pan the audience. The sanctuary is full.

When Ruby Jade saunters into the spotlight, singing an African-American spiritual in a rich contralto, I nearly choke on my dry tasteless popcorn. She's wearing a full-length shimmering gold gown with long sleeves and a black-and-silver sash. Her streaked hair is piled high on her head and circled by a tiara.

"I know what you're thinking," Candice whispers. "She's not only beautiful, she has a gorgeous singing voice."

Actually, I'm thinking the gown does nothing to hide her girth. If anything, it emphasizes it. But who am I to talk? After Eric died, I lived on donut holes, cheese pizza, ice cream—and alcohol.

I gained enough weight that on rare trips to the grocery store, I could walk by college friends without them recognizing me. My stringy hair and baggy clothes probably added to my unintentional disguise. Sometimes, they'd hesitate, but no one ever stopped to talk, which was okay with me. Their stories of fabulous careers, happy marriages and amazing children might have sent me running out of the store.

Ruby Jade's style is lush and smooth. I easily picture her beside a grand piano in a lounge—God forbid—entertaining an intimate, appreciative audience.

Slender women in silver gowns and thin men in black suits with gray shirts, black-and-silver ties and silver handkerchiefs in their breast pockets croon a luscious four-part backup, swaying in unison. You'd swear it was a Hollywood production. Yet, when Ruby Jade leaves the spotlight, the others stiffen and stare straight ahead, presumably at the rear wall, and morph into the singing style I heard last night.

They sing an unfamiliar melody at top volume, in unison. What happened to the harmonies they sang earlier? Following them, group after group of children, then teens and then adults file onto the stage. I'm told they're organized by Sunday school classes, which include all boys or all girls, all men or all women.

Each class performs another loud, unfamiliar, harmony-deficient tune. Three of the groups hop while they sing. I'm impressed they can maintain their loud volume and do aerobic exercise at the same time.

Also noteworthy, at least to me, is the fact not one Christmas song is included in the FFOW winter concert. Those seated in the living room don't have much to say other than to tell me which group they're in, so I can watch for them.

Even the toddlers, who appear late in the video, are divided by gender. The older singers were dressed alike, but these are arrayed in expensive kid clothes. The little ones are adorable. Did their cuteness come naturally, or was their genetic makeup predetermined by Ruby Jade?

After the toddlers, Ruby Jade comes back onstage, but she doesn't sing. Instead, she thanks the visitors for attending the FFOW winter concert. "If you'd like to visit a regular service, please call our office, and we'll block off chairs for you. Our sanctuary fills fast."

Huh. I've never heard of a church reserving seats. Maybe it has something to do with the gate and the no-trespassing sign.

The "credits" at the end include the date, December twenty-third of last year. So close to Christmas, yet no hint of the season was apparent in the sanctuary. And I don't remember any of the singers wearing red or green.

This place may be more like the Jehovah's Witnesses than I first suspected. Did the attendees know they wouldn't hear Christmas carols, or did they leave disappointed? I, for one, would have felt let down, maybe even betrayed.

The video ends, and the music is replaced by crying. Zachary is huddled in the corner, his forearms on his knees and his face buried in his arms. "Owen," Olivia snaps, "he saw her, and now we've got this to deal with. Take him to his bedroom and give him a good paddling."

"I don't believe it's—"

"Owen…" Her threatening tone sends chills down my spine. I can't imagine talking to Eric with such malice in my voice.

Owen sighs and walks over to the sobbing little boy. He bends down, puts his hand on his little shoulder and says, "Come with me, Zachary." Owen's voice is gentle, a distinct contrast to Olivia's harshness. "Let's go."

"Make him wipe his nose," Olivia orders.

"We'll stop by the bathroom." Owen leads Zachary toward the stairs.

No one else seems as concerned as I am about Zachary. Maybe they're accustomed to his tears. Olivia sends the younger children to bed. I get up to follow them, but she says, "The fun is only beginning, Miss True. Please have a seat."

I'd love to suggest they have fun without me. I'm too tired for a game. But, oh, no—we're not so lucky as to have a game. Instead, we discuss the four-month-old video. The others rave about Ruby Jade's solo, the quality of the recording, the beautiful music and the adorable children. I'm shocked they can find so much good to say.

In time, I realize they're repeating what others said. I fight to keep my eyes open and act interested. When Owen joins us again, he asks me for my comments. I mumble, "Amazing uniformity." No one seems to know how to respond to that, and he sends us all to bed, encouraging us to not give over to unworthy dreams.

Whatever.

Marcela and I say very little to each other while we ready ourselves for bed. I have plenty of questions. However, I'm too exhausted to remember what they are, except, who is the female Olivia referred to, the one Zachary saw? Why was he crying? And what in the world are *unworthy dreams*?

My clock blinks one-fifteen in digital red as I fall into bed. I don't care whether the mattress is soft or firm or lumpy. To lie prone for even a few hours is a blessed relief—my hands outside the covers, of course.

Four hours later, our clocks buzz in unison. This morning, I'm charged with baking blueberry muffins from scratch. One sniff of the vanilla extract, and I'm tempted to drink the entire bottle. The thirty-five to forty percent alcohol content, a percentage I remember from my drinking days, could help me forget this insane place, at least for a while.

"Where did you find such a huge bottle of vanilla extract?" I ask Olivia. "I've never seen one so large."

"If you'll look closely at the label, you'll notice it's written in Spanish. I bought it in Mexico during our last south-of-the-border outreach. Vanilla is inexpensive there. I purchased several bottles."

Hmm. Maybe Mexican vanilla has an even higher alcohol content than the American version. "Sounds like a good deal," I say, "especially for a household this size." I manage to add a mere teaspoon to the mix and return the tall container to the cupboard. As far as I can tell, it's the only vanilla extract on the shelf. Good thing I don't know where the other bottles are stored.

Marcela stirs oatmeal made from oat groats that soaked overnight and fries two pounds of bacon. Deanna juices orange after orange. The combination of pungent aromas makes my mouth water. I pour the muffin batter into the paper-lined tins and slip them into the oven.

Sure enough, Olivia asks me to identify each household member by name while they eat. To her obvious surprise, I pass the test with flying colors. Maybe I didn't destroy all my brain cells after all. Zachary seems pleased I remembered his name, first *and* last. Then she reads Lamentations three, twelve through fourteen, another depressing selection of strange verses. No one seems to put much thought into what we heard.

On the way to school, Olivia tells me she'll drop me off at the church for a meeting in Ruby Jade's office.

"What about my class?"

"I'm sure they'll tell Mrs. Watkins. If not…" She glances in the mirror. "Zachary, if Mrs. Watkins asks where Miss True is, tell her she's in a meeting with Ruby Jade."

I twist to smile at him, wondering if he cried himself to sleep last night. Probably not. Olivia would have nixed his tears.

"Yes, ma'am." He nods obediently.

Turning to Olivia, I ask, "Any idea what the meeting is about?"

"Ruby Jade…" She stops for a light. "Gives every newcomer a brief orientation."

"Great."

Olivia's side stare seems to say, *Are you sure?*

"Maybe she'll tell me when the Transformation Way program begins."

"I forgot you're doing T.W."

"It's why I'm here. Court order."

The quiet chatter behind us dissolves to silence. Had the kids forgotten my jailbird status?

"I'm excited," I say, "ready for transformation."

"Good for you. Ruby Jade should finalize staff positions soon."

I tilt my head. "Staff positions?"

"The director and his wife, who served as the program's mental health therapist, resigned several weeks ago and left the church, a foolish move on their part. I'm sure they already regret their reckless decision." The light changes, and she takes off. "Needless to say, the program is a bit shorthanded at the moment."

"But the center is still operating, right?"

"Uh, right…" She hesitates. "As best they can."

I'm five minutes early, yet the church secretary, Evelyn, ushers me directly into Ruby Jade's oversized office. FFOW's pastor, prophetess and psalmist is across the room, talking with Noreen and another woman. While Evelyn and I wait for her to acknowledge our presence, I survey the elegant office with its cherrywood floor and matching bookshelves, which display far more art than books. The marble-topped cherrywood desk in the middle of the room is bare except for a red folder and a red pen.

A huge fireplace consumes most of one end of the large room. It's framed by white marble and red roses. Judging by the fragrance floating in the air, the roses are real. A white leather couch and two overstuffed chairs straddle the fireplace. Between the sofa and chairs is a coffee table of the same design pattern as the desk. Classical guitar music plays softly in the background. My mom would love the decor.

The three women are standing near closed French doors that face the forest I attempted to visit. All are dressed in the group's signature satin suits, the skirts of which land at their ankles. Their high heels match their outfits.

I feel underdressed in my navy polyester pants, blue-and-white striped blouse and navy flats. Surely, Ruby Jade will understand I'm dressed for work. I discovered yesterday helping third graders with their lessons requires constant bending.

Noreen's presence makes me feel a bit more comfortable. I was nervous about meeting alone with Ruby Jade. The third woman looks me up and down, her eyebrows pinched with what I interpret as disdain. I saw similar facial expressions often when I was homeless.

As if just now seeing us, Ruby Jade says, "What is it, Evelyn? I told you not to disturb us. And who is this with you?"

Her words and tone make me feel like an intruder. Evelyn, who shrinks into herself, must feel the same way.

I smile at her before turning to the three women. "My name is Cassie True. I have an appointment with Ruby Jade."

Evelyn whispers, "She's new to FFOW."

Ruby Jade looks from me to Evelyn and back, a puzzled expression in her purple eyes.

Noreen says, "You need to give her a name."

What?

"Oh, yes, of course." Comprehension clicks, and Ruby Jade says, "You may go now, Evelyn." The condescension in her voice grates against my ears.

Evelyn smiles a fake FFOW smile—I'm learning to recognize them now—and slips out, silently closing the door behind her.

Ruby Jade motions me toward the couch. "Please have a seat, Miss True." All business now, she's back to form. Maybe she didn't get much sleep last night.

Before we sit, she says, "Miss True, I don't believe you've met Inez Curtis. She and Noreen act as my right and left hands." Noreen and Inez eye each other over Ruby Jade's head, silently sparring over who's the left and who's the right. That's my impression, anyway.

Inez and I shake hands. "Pleased to meet you," she says. But her noodle grip and impassive gaze through cool gray eyes suggest I'm a bug she'd prefer to squash.

I nod. "Nice to meet you, Inez."

Ruby Jade and Inez sit on the chairs and place their hands in their laps, leaving Noreen, who now holds the red folder and pen, to settle on the couch beside me. She doesn't act pleased. Maybe notetaking is beneath her paygrade.

I decide to pretend I called this meeting. "Thank you for taking the time to meet with me. I have lots of questions for you." I rest my palms on my polyester-clad thighs.

Ruby Jade leans forward, a portly picture of grandmotherly concern. Her makeup is not nearly as dramatic as it was the other night. "This is all new to you, dear," she says. "I'm sure you've had a few surprises."

"I'm mostly concerned—"

Her eyes, more violet than lavender today, shutter like a camera lens. "Miss True, this meeting is *not* about your concerns."

Something in her voice tells me the meeting is also *not* going to be fun and games.

"Let's begin with your name and get it out of the way."

"Good. I'm tired of everyone calling me *Miss True*."

Her horrified expression is mirrored by Inez. You'd think I threatened to bomb the church.

"Makes me feel like a schoolmarm. I—"

Noreen clears her throat.

I stop babbling.

Ruby Jade straightens. "State your name."

I sit taller. "Cat True."

"Your parents named you *cat*?" Her twisted lips suggest disbelief *and* disgust. She crooks her fingers into claws and aims the long purple nails at me. "S-s-s-s. Cat is a wicked name. Those nasty creatures s-s-scorn s-s-submissive obedience." She draws out the last syllable.

As quickly as she went into cat mode, she sits back, drops her hands and lifts her chin. "I'm a dog person, myself. I haven't been a cat person since—" She shakes her head and seems to return to reality. "What were your parents thinking?" Clasping her hands, she begins circling her thumbs, one around the other.

I blink, not yet recovered from the cat act. Surely, this isn't a serious question.

"I asked you..." She scowls. "What–were–your–parents–thinking?"

"My mother and father, who are both wonderful, God-fearing people..." I pause to let my description of my parents sink in. "They named me Cassie Anita Hunt. When I married Eric True, I became Cassie Anita True. It didn't take my husband long to figure out my initials spelled a word. He started calling me Cat, and the nickname caught on with our friends."

"Cassie. Anita. True." Her eyebrows twitch. "Is this your full, *real* name?"

"Yes." My gaze is trapped by Ruby Jade's unwavering focus on my face, yet in my peripheral vision, I see her thumbs twirl the opposite direction. Her pupils are mere pinpoints. Odd. The room's lighting is muted.

"Your last name is ill-chosen."

What? "I didn't choose the name. I chose the man with the name."

She flips her dark hair behind her shoulder, diamonds sparkling on her fingers. Stabbing a long fingernail at me, she declares, "You, young woman, have not honored your name."

I wait, unsure of where this is leading.

"You live a lie. You are not truly *true*."

"I try to be honest."

"You were in jail for a reason."

"Yes, but now—"

"So, you assume living in our hallowed midst for less than forty-eight hours makes you an honest person."

"That's not it at all. I—"

"I don't want to hear your excuses." She turns to Noreen. "Make a note her last name is *Turner* until she *turns* her life around and becomes a woman worthy of the name *True*."

CHAPTER TEN

"Please," I beg, "my husband's name is all I have left of him. Please don't take—"

Ruby Jade's eyes flash. "Quiet."

I close my mouth.

Noreen opens the folder.

"Now, to your first name." Ruby Jade closes her eyes and sways from side to side, all the while twirling her thumbs. "We must match the gift of God within you." She repeats the phrase twice more before her voice fades away.

The others wait patiently. Apparently, this behavior is common.

I maintain my rigid posture. Before I can delve into why I'm allowing a stranger to change my name, Ruby Jade opens her violet eyes. "Cassie Anita is childish," she declares. "Why didn't your parents name you Cassandra?"

Assuming she wants an answer, I start to tell her they'd often said *Cassie* was a perfect fit for me. But she stops me with a raised palm. "Because they were ignorant. Cassandra has two meanings, one pagan and one Christian. The pagan meaning is 'she who entangles men,' and the Christian is 'helper of mankind.' In Greek mythology, Cassandra was an unheeded prophetess." She blinks. "But we don't give credence to such nonsense."

She must have researched the name earlier. Those definitions didn't come out of thin air.

"Up to now, you've been an entangler of men. With our assistance, you will become a helper of mankind, a *true* person, the *true* woman Jehovah God designed you to be. From this moment forward, you are Cassandra Turner and will remain so until I determine you've become a *true* woman of God."

I shake my head. The only person I've ever entangled is myself, with the aid of alcohol.

Her thumbs stop, her pale cheeks color and her eyes harden. "Are you disagreeing with my decree?"

Decree? "I've never entangled anyone. I love and respect my parents and I loved my husband with all my heart. Still do."

"Well, there you go. Misguided allegiance."

What?

Her face softens. "You'll learn here how to give your love to God alone." She hoists her hands above her head. "PGIH!"

"PGIH," repeat Inez and Noreen, their voices robotic.

"I love God," I say.

"You don't love him enough." Ruby Jade checks her watch. "I have a full schedule of appointments today and need to move on to more important matters."

I'm digesting Inez's snicker and the suggestion I'm wasting their precious time, when Ruby Jade bends toward me, smiling benevolently. "I see beauty waiting to be unveiled in your spirit. What are your dreams, Cassandra Turner? What do you believe is the gift of God within you?"

I hesitate, partly because she's used the "beauty waiting to be unveiled" line before and partly because I'm unwilling to answer to the name she's given me. "As you might guess," I say, "I dream of the day I graduate from Transformation Way and begin a new life on the outside, as they call it in jail."

"But what will you do in your new life?" she asks. "Have you thought ahead? What's your training, your background, your passion, your favorite thing to do…?" She touches my hand. "Your secret dream?"

"No doubt you already know I'm a performance musician." I glance at the folder in Noreen's lap.

The only indication of prior knowledge is Noreen's nod.

I plow ahead. "I love music and I love to entertain, to see how the melodies, harmonies and words of my songs touch hearts and make people happy. Eric, my husband, loved my music. I want to honor his memory with music. My dream is to teach songwriting classes and to perform gigs with my guitar."

"Gigs?" Ruby Jade's lips curl.

She knows what a gig is. I can see it in her eyes, but I tell her anyway. "Concerts."

"Do you write the songs you sing?" Inez asks.

I'm surprised she spoke without Ruby Jade's permission. "Yes, I perform my own material."

Inez looks at Ruby Jade, whose shoulder lift must give her the okay to continue. "Ruby Jade is FFOW's psalmist," Inez says, "or songwriter, if you will." Her gray eyes have turned to steel. "Our *sole* songwriter. God gives *her* the songs he wants our congregation to sing. Please don't ever presume to—"

"Wouldn't dream of it." I'll keep my songs to myself until I can present them to appreciative audiences. In fact, when I leave this room, I believe I'll go talk with Judge Snow, even if it means I have to walk all the way to town. I bet he can find another program for me, one where they won't insult my name, my parents, my *misguided* love for them and my husband, my—

"We'd like…" Ruby Jade seems thoughtful. "We'd like to have someone with your experience, training and background join one of our singing groups, possibly lead a group. I've been told you're quite talented."

Her last few words seem to come out in a slur, but maybe I imagined it. She scratches her arms, and I glimpse the rash beneath her long sleeves. It looks painful.

Inez blinks several times. Noreen crosses and uncrosses her legs. Their boss must have caught them both off-guard. I wonder if she saw the disconnect in my eyes and decided to change tactics. I'm also curious to know who in her circles would have a clue whether I'm talented or not.

"Interested?"

I open my mouth to refuse her offer and walk out the door. Yet, I know if I leave now and the judge has nowhere else for me to go, I'll be sent to jail, again. And break my parents' hearts, again. If I stay, music involvement might make the church's craziness tolerable. It's only a year. I can do this.

I repeat my new mantra to myself. *Only a year. Only a year.*

Dipping my head, I swallow and say, "Yes," wishing I was downing something stronger than my own spit.

"Good." Ruby Jade beams like a Cheshire cat with a mouse under its paw. "We'll talk later." She pushes out of her chair and walks to her desk, speaking over her shoulder. "Noreen, please accompany Cassandra to Mrs. Watkins' classroom."

I take the hint and stand.

Ruby Jade whips around, stabbing a finger at me. "Never forget, Cassandra Turner, your name may be Cassandra, but I…" She taps her collarbone. "I, Ruby Jade Paradise, am the FFOW prophetess." Her eyes spark. "Any prophetic utterances on your part will go unheeded. I advise you not to waste your breath."

I open my mouth but then close it, not sure what to say. The thought hadn't entered my mind.

To Inez, she says, "You and I need to go over the income report. I'll have Evelyn bring us a cup of tea." She walks to a shelf and takes another red folder from a stack.

I stand, feeling like I've come through a thick fog. "Thank you."

Both Ruby Jade and Inez frown at me, obviously annoyed I'm still there.

"Yes, later." Ruby Jade flicks her wrist.

I swivel and walk to the door.

Outside Ruby Jade's office, I whisper to Noreen, "About a cell phone…"

"Oh, yes. I'll get it for you. Follow me."

I wave to Evelyn as we pass her desk. "Bye." Her smile, which is similar to my mom's smile, reminds me how anxious I am to talk with my mother. She must be worried sick. I'm surprised she hasn't called FFOW. Or maybe she has, and they haven't told me.

The muscular, thirty-something, breast-ogling guy I saw at the Wednesday-night dinner enters Evelyn's office. He's wearing a form-fitting t-shirt and tight jeans. *Jeans?* I thought—

"Hello, Vance." Noreen's voice has an edge to it.

"Ahhh…" He lifts an eyebrow. "I finally get to meet our newest member."

His lascivious undertone twists my stomach, and his over-the-top aftershave twists it a second round.

"You know who she is." Noreen blows out a breath. "And you know what your mother said. No more conquests." She presses her red lips into a tight line.

He snickers. "I don't know what you're talking about." Holding out his hand, he says, I'm Vance Longpre, the pastor's son. Have you received your *approved* name?"

I should have known. He has Ruby Jade's dark hair and pale skin, but his eyes are a deep blue. With straight white teeth, dark eyebrows and black curls falling onto his forehead, he'd be handsome, if his lips weren't contorted in a sneer.

I take his soft uncalloused hand. He grasps mine with a possessive firmness.

"You may call her Cassandra," Noreen says. "Cassandra Turner."

"Cas-*san*-dra." He draws out the syllables. "That's a *fa*-bu-lous name, one I'm sure I'll use often."

I yank my hand away. Weird…

He snickers and pats the knife sheath attached to his belt before heading to his mother's office.

Noreen glares at his back but says to me, "Don't mind him."

Over her shoulder, I catch sight of Evelyn. We make eye contact and she shakes her head, ever so slightly. Is she trying to warn me about Vance? I appreciate her concern, but she doesn't have to worry. He's not someone I'd *ever* be interested in.

Three doors down the hall, Noreen stops before a windowless door and pushes buttons on a keypad. It flashes green, and she opens the door.

I start in behind her.

She says, "Please wait in the hall."

I backstep, but not before I see a wall of electronic equipment with screens and blinking lights and hear men's voices.

She shuts the door.

While I wait, I wander the hallway. None of the other doors have keypads, but some of them have windows. I peek inside. They're empty and appear to be classrooms. Maybe they're Sunday school rooms. The walls are bare, so it's hard to tell.

One large room has a grand piano and several rows of chairs arranged in a semicircle. I'm peering through the window when Noreen exits the mystery room.

"There you are." She comes over and hands me a box with "True" written across the top in black marker. "It's charged and ready for use. Be sure to read the instructions."

"Thank you." I tap the window. "Can you tell me about this room?"

"This is where our music groups practice and warm up before services and appearances." She smiles. "In fact, from what Ruby Jade said earlier, I assume you'll be spending a lot of time here."

"Can we go inside?"

"I don't have my keys with me, but here comes Corban."

SHATTERED DREAM | 109

The shoe salesman is walking toward us, carrying a trombone case. His face seems to come alive when we make eye contact. But maybe I'm reading too much into his smile.

When he's closer, Noreen says, "I assume you borrowed a key to the music room from Security."

"Yes." His eyes go blank.

"Miss True..." She clears her throat. "Cassandra Turner, that is, is going to be working with one of our music groups. She'd like to see the music room."

He glances my direction. "I'll open it for you and then run the key to Hank."

My buddy Hank. I wonder if he's been told about my name change yet.

Corban sets the case on the floor and unlocks the door. "I'll be right back."

Noreen swings the door wide. I grab the case, and we go inside. Ah, the look, feel and airy smell of a music room. I'm not sure if it's the big windows, the wide-open area, the rows of chairs, or the baby grand piano front and center that thrills my soul. I love it all.

I smile at Noreen. "This is perfect, a musician's dream."

"The acoustics in this room make our practice sessions a pleasure."

I walk over to the piano and rub my fingers across its satiny finish before I lift the fallboard that covers the keys. Playing a series of chords, I finish with arpeggios into the upper octaves and turn to Noreen, who has a bemused expression on her face. I smile. "This piano has a beautiful tone."

"Ruby Jade purchased it in Denver and had it delivered not too long ago. Their piano tuner flew over to tune it for us."

Corban comes bounding into the room. "Do you know where—? Oh, there it is." He glances from Noreen to me. "Thank you for bringing my trombone in for me."

"You're welcome." I dip my head. "Are you here to prepare for something?"

"Sunday's music." He sets the case on a chair and opens it.

Noreen's phone chimes. She studies the screen. "I need to go deal with one of my charges." High heels clicking, she marches out the door.

Corban stares from her retreating figure to me and then follows her, mouthpiece in one hand and the trombone slide in the other.

I stand there, mouth open, wondering if I'm expected to leave too.

He pivots in the doorway. "Single people who aren't the same…you know…require a chaperone," he says. "Without Noreen here, we could—"

His face reddens. "I mean, if someone…" He tugs at his earlobe, and his gaze flits from ceiling corner to ceiling corner. "You know, *saw* us together." Slipping a finger around the mouthpiece he's holding at his side, he crooks it, twice.

I step closer, but not too close.

"It's very possible," he murmurs, "this could be a test."

"A test?"

"To see what we'll do without a chaperone."

"Weird."

He sighs. "Yes." Most people I know would say "yeah." But he seems careful with his words. Is that another Follower thing?

"Whatever." I shrug. "I should get to my classroom."

"Are you a teacher?"

"Teacher's aide. Third grade."

"Mrs. Watkins is nice."

"Yes. She's good with the kids…I mean, the children."

"She was my third-grade teacher."

"You went to school here?"

"All twelve grades."

Ah, his education could be the source of his formal language.

He looks as though he has more to say on the subject. Instead, he murmurs, "How are your feet?"

"Much better, thanks to you."

"Good." He checks his watch. "I'd better put in some practice time before I leave for work."

"And I'd better go before Mrs. Watkins sends out a search party."

He moves into the hall and steps to the side.

"I just got a phone." I brandish the cell phone box on the way out the door. "We should exchange numbers."

He shakes his head. "Singles aren't allowed to share telephone numbers."

"Really?" I catch a whiff of his spicy aftershave. I like it.

He sighs. "Really."

"Which is the fastest route to the school?"

"Walk to the end of the hall, make a left and then a right." He points down the hallway. "You'll see double doors at the end. Go through there, and the school will be in front of you."

"Thanks."

"See you around, uh…Cassandra, is it now?"

"You can call me Cat or Cassie, but as of a few minutes ago, my *official name*—I make finger quotes—is Cassandra Turner."

"Cassandra Turner." He studies me for a moment. "I'll remember that." Lowering his voice, he adds, "and your real names, too."

"Thank you, Corban. What's your last name?"

"Dahlstrom." He grins. "That's my real name."

"Thank you, Corban Dahlstrom. I'm glad to know someone around here cares enough to connect with the real me."

"Same here." He winks and steps into the music room.

When I return to the classroom, Mrs. Watkins is alone, working at her desk. I check the clock. The kids—children, that is—must be at recess. I tap on the doorframe. "Good morning."

"Good morning to you." She stands. "We missed you earlier, but I hear congratulations are in order."

I raise my eyebrows. *What now?*

"I heard you received your approved name." She smiles. "*Cassandra Turner.* Such a beautiful name. What a blessing."

"Uh, thank you." *I think...* Her reminder of the maddening name-change episode skyrockets my blood pressure. Sucking in a quick breath, I blow it out through my nose. I can feel my nostrils flare.

Mrs. Watkins frowns. "Something wrong?"

"No, not at all. What would you like me to do?"

What's left of the school morning zips by, and once again, I'm without a lunch. Rather than eat the fast-food offering of the day, I head outside to do what I've been itching to do all morning—call my mom. I now know better than to walk the property, but surely, sitting in the sunshine won't rile Security.

I step out the front door and look around. The air is fresh, and the sky is cloudless. In the distance lies a cemetery I hadn't noticed earlier. It's beautiful, with tall trees and well-manicured grass. I have a feeling I'm not supposed to walk in there or use a headstone for a seat, not that I would want anyone to desecrate Eric's headstone that way.

Yet, for all the parklike beauty, not a picnic table, bench or rock is in sight. I opt for the school's shaded front steps. I'll be able to see the phone screen better here than in the sunshine.

I open the box and find a folded paper with "Read This First" printed in bold letters on the outside. I unfold the sheet. At the top is a large-print heading: PROPER USAGE OF A FOLLOWER PHONE.

Oh, so that's the deal. This isn't *my* phone. I'm only borrowing it. One more reason to regain my own life the instant I finish the program. I sigh and read through the phone dos-and-don'ts.

Do not call friends or family members who are former members. Do respond to leadership texts and emails immediately, but do *not* call them unless you have a true emergency. Don't talk with family members for more than fifteen minutes at a time or more than once a month. Do not call acquaintances outside of FFOW. Don't talk with other Followers for more than ten minutes at a time and no more than twice a month, unless the call is related to a church activity, event or ministry. Don't attempt to activate the camera feature or internet service. Don't…

The list goes on, but I can't continue reading. I need to talk with my mother before I return to the classroom. If we talk longer than fifteen minutes, so be it. The instant that thought flits through my brain, I catch sight of italicized words printed in red at the bottom of the page. *Disregarding the above directives will result in forfeiture of this cell phone.*

Okay, okay. I'll keep an eye on my watch and not talk a second longer than the allotted time. Some staff person must go through the bills with a magnifying glass to ensure no one uses too many minutes. Or maybe the computers in the mystery room do it automatically.

I refold the paper and lift the phone from the box. It's a flip phone, which surprises me. I didn't know flip phones were still being manufactured. After it powers on, I tap "contacts" to start my contact list, beginning with my family's numbers. Luckily, I have those memorized.

Several numbers are already inputted, those belonging to Ruby Jade, Noreen, Inez, Mrs. Watkins and Security. That makes me laugh. Not only am I on a first-name basis with Hank and Pete, I have their number.

The phone dings and buzzes in my hand. I jerk, nearly dropping it. Who would send me a text before I have a phone?

I open the texts. Twelve. All from Ruby Jade. I tap the first one, half afraid of what I might read. It's a reminder to be on time for this morning's meeting. Because her time is precious. Good thing I was early to the meeting she forgot.

I read the other messages. All eleven are group messages exhorting the members to smile for Jesus, be faithful in the small things—whatever that means, be on time for the Sunday services and on and on. I delete them all.

CHAPTER ELEVEN

After I add my parents' home number, their cell phone numbers, and my brother's number, I dial my mother's cell. She answers after three rings with a tentative, "Hello…"

"Hi, Mom."

"Cassie, sweetheart. I thought that Montana prefix might be you. Is this the cell phone you talked about?"

"Yes, this is my new number. Seems like forever since we talked, even though it was less than a week ago."

"Same with us. We knew you were transitioning, but we didn't know the details."

"I just got this phone, and I'd love to have a good chat. However, I'm on my lunch break, which will be over soon."

"You have a job already?"

"I'm working as an aide in a third-grade classroom. The kids, or children, I should say, are really sweet."

"Wonderful!"

Before she can ask how someone with my background can work in a school, I ask how she and Dad are doing.

"We're fine. Busy planting masses of pansies—you know how I love my pansies—and prepping the garden area, trimming bushes, raking winter debris. The usual spring routine. Are you doing the program *and* working too?"

"I haven't started the program, but I had a brief orientation this morning." In a weird sense, it was an orientation of sorts to my strange new world. Thinking about the name change makes me angry, but I'm not about to tell Mom. "Monday morning will probably be the official start. To be honest, I don't know how the job and the program will work out. Maybe I'll do half-days at both. Or maybe I'll go fulltime with the program next week."

To distract her from more questions about Transformation Way, I change the subject. "Did Kip come out of the mountains yet?"

"Not as far as we know. He said he'd call us on Monday, if not before. You two keep your dad and me close to our phones."

"Sorry, Mom."

"Don't be sorry. We love hearing from you. And now that you're free, I hope we can all get together this summer. If not here or there, maybe at your brother's place in Spokane."

"He'd have to clean his apartment."

"You're a smart girl." Mom laughs. "You figured out my ulterior motive."

"When you and Dad come to Bozeman, I want to treat you to an amazing restaurant I discovered. I know you'll both love it."

"Sounds intriguing. I'll definitely be anticipating it. Before I forget, I should get your address. Give me a minute. I'm driving and need to pull over to grab a pen and paper from my purse."

I glance at my watch. I have a minute, maybe two left of my lunch break. My stomach growls. I'll have to stop by the water fountain on my way to class and fill up on water.

She comes back. "Okay, ready."

I tell her I live with a family and give her the Pritchards' address, but I don't suggest she send the package to "Cassandra Turner." I also don't tell her the name she gave me is *childish* or that my married name is *ill-chosen*. My guitar should reach me via my real name, but I'll worry until it does.

"I'll send your guitar tomorrow," she says, "with lots of padding. I'll also insure it."

"Thanks, Mom. I can't wait to play it."

"What's the last name of the family you live with?"

I tell her Olivia and Owen's last name, but I don't mention the others. She'd ask all kinds of questions.

"I can't wait to meet them."

"I'm sure you'll like them. They're very, uh…" I struggle to think of something nice to say about Olivia and Owen. "They're committed to helping people."

A bell blares above my head, and I jump.

"Sounds as though it's time for you to return to work," Mom says.

"Good guess. The bell scared me half to death."

"It was plenty loud on this end."

"I love you, Mom. I'll call again later."

"I love you, my sweet Cassie."

Thank you, Mom. She has no idea how much her use of the name she and Dad gave me comforts me and reminds me who I really am.

My after-work chores, according to the chart on the refrigerator, include helping the younger children with homework before dinner and the older ones later in the evening. When Zachary whimpers and says he wants his mama, I console him and hand him a tissue, so Olivia won't notice his tears.

In between tutoring sessions, I assist with dinner preparations. By the time the last of the dishes are done and the final math problem conquered, the grandfather clock in the downstairs hallway is chiming one a.m.

Marcela is in the bathroom with the door open when I walk into the bedroom. I join her and pull my toothbrush from the drawer. "I can't believe we're still awake. I feel like I've been on a weeklong bender."

"You'll adjust."

Someone else said something similar. Who was it? Oh, yeah. The shoe guy, Corban. He told me things would get better. I sure hope so.

I smile, remembering his winks and ear tugs. I wish I could have hung around the music room to listen to him play his trombone. He seems like a nice guy, although a little skittish. But then, that's how people are around here. Skittish.

Saturday morning, breakfast is served at six-thirty, as usual. No sleeping in for this bunch. Marcela says I'll adapt, but I'm so tired I could lay my head on the table and instantly fall asleep. Instead, I drink two cups of coffee. Before our household climbs into the van to go distribute flyers at a flea market, I drink another cup. My stomach burns, but I'm now wide awake and anxious to get out of the house.

We'll be promoting the spring concert. FFOW, I'm told, only opens its doors to the public when it has concerts or special seminars. Maybe they focus on Armageddon the way Jehovah's Witnesses do. I remember JW couples, usually women, knocking on my parents' door every couple of years with invitations to attend end-times conferences. It's one of the methods they use to suck unsuspecting individuals into their twisted belief system.

Everyone is participating except the two older women, Alice and Marjorie, who'll be watching the young children. The list of dos-and-don'ts the children are given before we leave rivals the phone-usage list. How can they be so happy when their fun is so limited? Maybe it has something to do with the admonition to "smile for Jesus" every time they act the least bit grumpy.

What disturbs me is the flash of fear in their eyes before big fake smiles break across their little faces. The teens, I've observed, are more adept at hiding their emotions. But I've been around enough hurting people to know they're not happy campers.

While Owen drives, Olivia informs us of our own behavior list. No wandering about the grounds—we're going to the flea market to work, not to squander the morning. Two FFOW members of the same gender must remain together *at all times*. Short bathroom breaks are allowed as long as we remain in pairs.

Someone snickers, and she tells us to stop giving over to devil thoughts. I'm hoping that mandate doesn't mean we're expected to step into the stalls together. No thanks.

Finally, she reaches the end of her flea-market rules and faces frontward again. I sense a silent unified sigh of relief. The rest of the way, conversation in the van is muted. The others only seem to tune in when they congratulate me on my approved name, repeating it each time. Do they think I don't know what it is? *Weird bunch.*

The flea market shimmers with energy. Walking among the colorful awnings, I encounter a series of tantalizing aromas—roasted chili peppers, barbequed beef, deep-fried turkey, cotton candy, kettle corn... By the time we reach the Followers gathered in the middle of the market, I'm salivating like Pavlov's dogs.

Like those from my household, the women are wearing long-sleeved blouses and dark polyester pants. The men are dressed in long-sleeved Oxford shirts, either white or light-blue, and black dress pants. I don't know about the others, but I feel overdressed for a flea market.

A man and a woman I haven't seen before introduce themselves and tell us they're the outreach overseers. He hands stacks of flyers to each of us, while she designates who should go where. Marcela and I are paired with Corban and a guy named Logan, whom Corban introduces to me as his younger brother. They're about the same height and look a lot alike, but Corban has blue eyes and Logan has brown eyes. Logan's shirt is white. Corban's is blue. Guess they didn't want to look like twins.

"I'm only twenty-nine," Logan says when we're introduced. "My brother here is over-the-hill. He just turned thirty-one."

Corban slugs his brother's arm.

They know how to joke around, a refreshing change from the other members I've met. Maybe we can relax a little and enjoy ourselves. But then I notice they always stand at least four feet from me and Marcela. Though they smile wide FFOW smiles, their tight shoulders, wary eyes and constant head movements betray them.

They remind me of a pair of watchdogs. If those two can't drop their guard, I can't drop mine. Too bad. This had the potential to be a fun day.

"For Cassandra's information," Marcela says, "You didn't have a birthday party."

"Uh, right." Corban's expression is serious. "Followers don't do birthdays."

I'm about to ask why they don't do birthdays, when Vance comes running. "I'm with *her* group," he calls, pointing our direction. I assume he means Marcela until I realize he's looking at me. What an idiot. Just because he's the leader's son, he—

"We're short over here." The male leader beckons to him. "You can join us."

"I don't think so." Vance stops beside me, and I catch a whiff of… Weed?

"I'm with Cas-*san*-dra." He raises his eyebrows and glances around the group with an expression that clearly states, *I'm the leader's son. Don't you dare question my choice.*

Corban, Marcela and Logan eye him, that switched-off stare on each of their faces. I can't tell what's going through their minds, but I feel their tension. Despite being their beloved leader's son, Vance does not appear to be a FFOW favorite. Without comment, Logan leaves us to join the others.

Walking single file through the noisy, milling crowds, we find our assigned intersection, one where we can each take a corner. Corban continues to keep his distance, but Vance sticks to me like gum to a shoe. I wonder if he colors his dark hair, which shines almost navy blue in the sunshine. He's a head taller than Corban and broad-shouldered. I'd swear he puffs his chest whenever a twenty-something female walks by.

The knife sheath is hanging from his belt again. What does he need a knife for? A lot of Bozeman outdoor guys carry knives for skinning their kills, cleaning fish or working around a campsite, but he doesn't strike me as the hunter-camper-fisherman type.

Marcela reminds Vance he's supposed to cover the corner across from me. He ignores her. Every time I distance myself from him, he sidles close again, bringing his sweaty marijuana smell with him. I'd like to tell His Royal Muscularness to flake off. However, I suspect that wouldn't be wise.

He's apparently more interested in talking to me than in distributing the invitations. I pretend not to hear him. People are talking all around us, and I'm trying hard to convince anyone who'll stop that they should attend the concert.

I get the feeling Vance is spoiled and used to having his way. After all, his mother is the most important, most powerful figure in the church, as far as I can tell. Is his father in the picture? I haven't seen Ruby Jade with a man, but that doesn't mean much. I've been with the group less than three days. Does Vance have siblings? Are they as obnoxious as he is?

I frown. Why am I pondering this jerk's family when I could be asking Marcela and Corban about theirs? Mimicking my Follower friends, I put on a fake smile and offer a flyer to a guy with a wide-brim leather hat and black dreadlocks.

He grins, takes the paper, folds it and sticks it in his back pocket. Touching his hat brim, he nods and continues on.

Across the way, I see Robert from the restaurant stop beside a pottery display. People are milling all around him. Marcela hasn't noticed, and I don't draw her attention to him, though he's gazing at her—his wife—with such longing it breaks my heart. What an insane situation. He disappears in the crowd.

"Did you see that?" Vance snickers. "The dude is a glutton for punishment."

I ignore the comment, like I've ignored all his other snide remarks about the passersby.

We're breaking for coffee at a small kiosk in the middle of the huge market, making small talk as we wait in line, when Vance's phone dings. He pulls it from his pocket and shows it to me. His mother's face is on the screen. It's a photo, not a video, but he certainly has a fancier phone than the one I was given.

He steps away but returns moments later to hand his flyers to Corban. "Mom..." He angles his chin toward me. "That's Ruby Jade to you. She's taking me to Restaurant des Delices for Saturday brunch. Sadly..." He shimmies his broad shoulders. "I'm forced to leave you peons without supervision."

I don't respond, and neither do the others.

With an arrogant lift of his dark eyebrows, he looks me up and down. "Try to manage without me, Cas-*san*-dra." I refrain from slapping him because I'm so glad he's leaving.

After Vance disappears in the crowd, Corban offers to buy me coffee and a pastry, but Marcela elbows him. "Corban..."

He sighs and says, "You're right."

I'm about to tell them I don't need anything, when Marcela says she'll get mine. I don't know what those two were alluding to, and I don't ask.

The coffee kiosk has three small metal tables with chairs, all occupied. About the time our order is ready, a couple at one of the tables leaves, and we fall into the chairs. I'm grateful for a chance to get off my feet.

Marcela voices my thoughts. "I'm so happy to sit, I don't mind this hard chair."

I bite into the apricot pastry and follow it with a sip of coffee. "Mmm, that's good."

Corban nods. "Not bad."

Sitting back in our chairs, we people-watch while we drink our coffee and eat our pastries. Snatches of conversation from the ever-moving throng intermingle with the rich aroma of roasting coffee beans.

Aware this may be a unique opportunity to learn more about my new friends, I lay my snack on the napkin. "Tell me about your families. I know Marcela is married to Robert, and that you have a brother, Corban. Do you two have other relatives at FFOW?"

Funny how, already, I so easily utter "fow" along with everyone else.

"Just Logan and my parents," Corban says. "We're all members."

"I have a younger brother and a sister still at home." Marcela clutches her cup with both hands. "My parents, who used to be members, left shortly after Robert and I were married. They tried to get us to go with them, but Ruby Jade convinced us to stay." Her voice has lost its hoarseness.

"Why did your parents leave?" I ask. Before she can respond, other questions come tumbling out, one on top of the other. "And what did Ruby Jade say to convince you to stay? If I understood the instructions that came with my cell phone, you can't have contact with your parents. Is it true? I'd be a wreck if I couldn't talk with my parents. They're my lifeline."

She opens her mouth and closes it.

"Sorry." I rub my temples. "I have so many questions bouncing around my brain. Every day, I discover more about FFOW I don't understand."

Marcela gives Corban a hard stare.

He lifts a palm. "Mum's the word."

Another look I can't decipher passes between them.

"I miss my family." She sighs and gazes above the crowd ambling through the flea market. Like a kaleidoscope, the colors and patterns are ever-changing. "But I try not to because Ruby Jade says it's clinging to family, not Jesus."

"Is that why you don't have pictures of them in our room?"

"No one displays family pictures," Corban says.

Now that he mentions it, I realize I haven't seen any family photos around the house. One more "don't" to add to my ever-growing list of things to remember not to do.

Marcela stares into her coffee, her lips trembling. "If Robert and I ever have children, they won't have grandparents in their lives. His parents are too poor to fly over here to visit, and Ruby Jade probably won't let us go there. It's…it's hard." She lifts her head and wipes tears from her cheeks. "I shouldn't focus on what will never be. Really, I shouldn't."

"I'm so sorry." I put my hand on her arm. Touching wasn't allowed in jail, but I assume it's okay in this setting. "Why did your parents leave, when they knew they might never see you again—or their potential grandchildren?"

"Ruby Jade wanted my dad to sign his building supply business over to the church the same as other business owners have done. But he said he couldn't give the management of the lumberyard his grandfather built from the ground up to someone who knows nothing about lumber or the building trades. It flourished under both his grandfather's and his father's guidance, and he's doing his best to honor them by following in their footsteps."

She twists her cup round and round. "My father makes a good living, and he gave a lot of money to the church. Plus, he hired FFOW members and was training Robert to work alongside him. At the time, Robert and I lived with my parents and my siblings, so we were able to have private family discussions about what to do."

"Wouldn't happen at the Pritchards' house." I make a face. "You and I can barely speak with each other."

Corban clears his throat. "Uh…" He aims a thumb at the people passing our table. "Touching in public is risky business, if you get my drift."

I yank my hand away. "Sorry."

Marcela shrugs. "Kinkiness, you know."

I roll my eyes.

"My apologies for interrupting." Corban's blue eyes shine with sincerity. He's such a nice guy, not at all like egotistical Vance. "Please go on with your story, Marcela."

"Let's see…where was I?" She sips her coffee. "The moment Ruby Jade got wind Dad was balking and she couldn't change his mind…"

Marcela and Corban exchange another long look, and she says, "That's when she moved me and Robert out of my parents' house into another home and made Robert change jobs. But at least we were able to hug my family before we parted. Not everyone gets a chance to say goodbye."

"Have you seen your family since then?" I ask.

"I ran into my mom once at the grocery store. My brother and sister were with her. We hugged and cried. I wish my dad had been with them, but maybe I'll see him another time."

"What in the world convinced you two to stay?"

"Our car was on its last legs. Ruby Jade promised to give me and Robert each a nice car."

"What?" I'm incensed. "She *bought* your loyalty?"

"Even more important, Cassandra…" Marcela's eyes flash. "She said she'd forgive my inappropriate bonding with my parents and that Robert and I would be guaranteed a place in heaven. God won't send us to hell when we die."

"Are you kidding me? That's not—"

"You'll learn the FFOW way." Ever vigilant, Corban scans the crowd. "After you hear a few more Ruby Jade sermons. According to her, a person has to meet certain prerequisites to go to heaven, prerequisites only available and achieved at FFOW."

"That's the most ludicrous thing I've ever heard. Where does the Bible say that?"

"In Matthew."

I blink. "Really?"

Corban rests his forearms on the table. "As Jesus said in Matthew, lots of people say, 'Lord, Lord,' but only those who do the will of his Father can enter the kingdom of heaven."

"I don't get the connection with FFOW."

"Ruby Jade believes God tells her what his will is, so she can deliver it to the Faithful." He shrugs. "By her criteria, everyone else is outside his will." His monotone delivery and unsmiling eyes suggest he doesn't agree.

I turn to Marcela. "Which would include your parents and your brother and sister. Do you believe they're all going to hell?"

"I don't *want* to believe it, but—"

"Break's over." Corban yanks his earlobe. "Inez is coming."

By the time she's made her way to us, we've tossed our trash and are giving flyers to anyone who'll accept them.

Dressed in an expensive red pantsuit and matching heels, Inez marches straight for Corban. Her gold-plated necklace flashes in the sunlight. The first words out of her mouth are, "Where's Vance?"

"He said he was going to brunch with his mom," Corban says. "That was…" He checks his watch. "Maybe forty-five minutes ago."

"Oh. Ruby Jade asked me… Never mind." Pivoting, she smacks into a man, regains her balance and shoves through the throngs.

Corban chuckles. "Lost him again."

CHAPTER TWELVE

I give Corban a questioning look. "Vance? Lost?"

"His mother has a hard time keeping track of him."

"You mean he still lives at home?"

"When he's not at his dad's house in California."

"His parents are divorced?"

"Long ago."

"I wondered why I hadn't seen a Mr. Paradise."

"Vance has a different last name," Marcela says.

"The dude is almost thirty years old..." Corban peers at Marcela. "You with me on this?"

Once more, some sort of understanding or agreement passes between them.

She nods.

"He's figured out how to live the good life by playing his parents against each other," Corban says. "Flies to California every couple weeks, wears expensive clothes and has a fancy car. He also owns a car repair shop, but he spends his days at the gym or playing video games on his work computer."

He lowers his voice. "His employees, who are of course all FFOW members, say they do the work. The only thing he does is deposit the money in the bank." He snorts. "What more could a spoiled, lazy guy want?" Shaking his head, he moves to the other side of the narrow intersection.

"Cassandra..." Marcela comes alongside me. "Vance has his eye on you. Be careful."

"Well, I don't have my eye on him." I wrinkle my nose.

"Cold shoulders haven't stopped Vance in the past."

"Seems Ruby Jade would have hooked him up with someone by now, like she did you and Rodrigo." I hold out a flyer to a couple. The man says, "No, thanks," and they keep walking.

"You must call my husband by his approved name, Cassandra. Or I'll have to report you."

I sigh. "Okay."

"Vance has been married, twice." She turns to offer a flyer to a group of teenage girls. "Do you girls enjoy concerts?"

"What kind?" one of them asks.

"Choir. It's our church's spring concert."

"We go to church," says another. "Don't we, girls?"

The others snicker.

"Just kidding," the first girl says. "But I hope you Jesus people have a fun day in your polyester pants."

They move on, glancing back at us and laughing.

I brush a crumb off my slacks. "That's the first time I've had someone mock my choice of clothing." Well, not exactly my choice. If I had my way, I'd be wearing Levi's and a sweatshirt.

"Get used to it." She waves a flyer in a man's face, and he pushes it away.

I'm concerned her tactic is a bit too strong, and am thinking I should separate from her, when she starts talking again.

"Vance's first wife left him, and Ruby Jade kicked his second wife out after she had a miscarriage, according to the rumor."

Marcela slips a side glance my direction. "Some things can only be learned by leaks trickling through the congregation."

"What about Corban and his brother? They're old enough to be married."

"They almost were."

"Almost? Both of them?"

"Logan was engaged to Kalina for three or four years. They'd been good friends from elementary school on."

"And then?" I offer a flyer to a middle-age woman. She smiles but doesn't stop.

"And then Vance decided he wanted Kalina for himself, so Ruby Jade switched her engagement from Logan to Vance." She lowers her voice. "This is for your ears only. No one else."

"Got it." I give her an affirmative nod.

"Promise?"

"Cross my heart and hope to die."

She frowns.

"I'm joking. Of course, I promise."

"Logan was heartbroken. He asked Kalina to run away with him, but she was afraid to leave FFOW and Jesus. She didn't want to go to hell. She said she'd never stop loving Logan, yet I got the feeling she was excited to join Vance's family. Ruby Jade promised her all kinds of stuff."

"Not exactly a reason to marry someone." I smile and hand a flyer to a middle-aged couple.

"We're kind of old-fashioned at FFOW," Marcela says. "You know, dowries and such."

"Sounds like bribery to me."

"Well, anyway…" She shrugs. "Kalina and Vance were all smiles at the wedding, but their marriage didn't last long. Before the wedding, she was his queen. He bought her gifts none of the rest of us are allowed to have, like perfume and short skirts. I never heard why they divorced, but I suspect he reverted to his true self.

Would have been a shock for Kalina, who was used to sweet Logan."

"Did she and Logan try to get together again?"

"She disappeared. And, as I said, we're not allowed to have contact with people who leave." Marcela fans herself with the flyers in her hand. "Getting hot out here."

"That's really sad, and a little scary." My heart clenches. "I hope no harm has come—"

"I'm sure she's fine."

How can you accept someone's disappearance as though it's no big deal? When I was on the streets, if I didn't show up at the shelter for a day or two, someone would come looking for me to make sure I was okay. "What about Corban? Did Ruby Jade interfere with his love life, too?"

"Please don't use that term, Cassandra. It suggests, you know…"

"I didn't mean it that way."

"Try explaining that to Leadership. Anyway, Corban was engaged to Shelby and about to marry her, when she contracted a lethal pneumonia and died within a week. Because her parents took her to a hospital instead of having a FFOW healing ceremony for her, Ruby Jade kicked them out of the church and didn't allow them to have the funeral there or bury Shelby in the church cemetery."

I think of FFOW's beautiful cemetery filled with model citizens, by FFOW standards, who are now no different than every other deceased person. Before I can dwell on how long Eric has been dead and how his body has changed, I focus on Marcela and what she's saying.

"Ruby Jade said God told her no FFOW member could attend the funeral at the Baptist church because we'd be overcome by their false doctrines and fall into sin. And she insisted the word from God included Corban and his family. He didn't get to be with her in the hospital *or* go to her funeral service."

"How awful," I whisper. "He wasn't able to say goodbye."

"But…" Her eyes narrow. "Leadership must have gone to the funeral because they laughed about the Baptist service for weeks after. According to them, the pastor said Shelby went to heaven. But we all knew better than that."

I groan. Sitting through Eric's funeral was the worst thing that ever happened to me. But even worse would have been to miss it—and to listen to my pastor and others say he went to hell. How did Corban survive such a horrible, painful time? Apparently, he didn't turn to alcohol, the way I did.

"I'm sorry," she murmurs. "I shouldn't have told you."

I glance over at Corban, who's talking with an elderly couple, smiling and shaking their hands. "How can you stay in the church, Marcela, after watching your friends go through emotional abuse? How can they stay? I've been here less than three days, and I'm ready to run as far as I can from this place."

"I, we…" Her eyes click to the zombie stare. "If we leave, we'll go to hell." Her voice is lifeless, almost robotic. "Jesus said, 'In this life, you will have trouble.' He also said we each have burdens to bear. This is *our* trouble, the burdens we must bear in the same way you must bear the loss of your husband."

"But God and friends and family help us carry those burdens."

"Ruby Jade says our burdens won't be lifted until Jesus comes. That's when he'll end our bondage."

"Bondage?"

"Yes, bondage to this world's tribulation and sorrow." Her green eyes blank as marbles, she twists to give a couple in cowboy hats and western clothing a flyer. When they show interest, Marcela comes alive and tells them all about the upcoming concert. I'm impressed she can act so enthusiastic after relating such a sad story. Maybe later I'll suggest her bondage is to FFOW and her tribulation and sorrow come from the leaders.

If we weren't in a public place, I'd walk over to Corban, give him a hug and tell him I understand, that I'd like to ease his pain. But really, after all these years, what can I do for him? Nothing in this world can reverse or remove the suffering and cruelty he and Logan have endured.

Although I don't enjoy shoving posters in people's faces, I have interesting conversations and meet several nice people. I'm beginning to think this isn't such a bad way to spend a Saturday morning when a lady in dark sunglasses grabs my arm. Leaning close, she murmurs, "Ruby Jade Paradise is a charlatan and a crook."

I try to see her eyes. "Why do you—?"

She pulls her sun visor low and vanishes into the crowd. What is she afraid of? A feeling of foreboding settles in my soul. What should I be afraid of? I wish she'd stayed long enough for me to ask her questions.

Just when my legs are ready to buckle, Olivia comes to get us. "We need to hurry home to fix lunch and clean the house."

I wonder if Marcela can read the question in my eyes. *Do we ever get to rest?*

Olivia shifts from us to Corban. "Why don't you have a partner? You know you're not supposed to be alone with two females."

"My partner for this project was Vance Longpre." His eyes flicker. "Before his mother called him away."

"Oh." She swivels and marches back the way she came.

I give Corban a discreet thumbs-up.

He grins and winks.

The women tidy the house, and the men sweep the huge garage. They also remove fluid drips and tire tracks from the garage floor and wash the small windows at the tops of the doors. I see all this because I walk through several times to shake the dust mop outside.

Following a late lunch, we hurry to a widow's house in town. She's not a FFOW member. Our assignment is to entice her to join us and to scrape old paint from the siding. We'll paint the house later. The woman is sweet and grateful and serves us lemonade and cookies on her porch. I enjoy sitting almost as much as I appreciate visiting with someone who's not in the church, someone who doesn't measure her every word and movement or judge mine.

Saturday night is a big deal in our household. The men and boys appropriate the bathrooms to shower and shave—except the bathroom I share with Marcela. All FFOW men are cleanshaven, I've noticed. The women and girls will have primary use of the bathrooms in the morning. We must look our best at the Sunday services.

While the men are showering, we're to check our clothing for spots, tears and wrinkles, our shoes for dirt, and our nylons for runs. I haven't worn nylons in years and am not looking forward to pantyhose and restrictive clothing. The men will examine their clothes and shine their shoes in the morning. All this activity, I'm told, has something to do with the Israelites presenting spotless lambs to the priests as sacrifices for their sins.

We wash, mend and iron for the entire household. Our scheduled time to use the washers and dryers is Saturday night, but Marcela and I have to wait until the others are done with the laundry equipment. Finally, shortly before the hall clock strikes two a.m., we crawl between clean sheets.

Breakfast is served at the usual time Sunday morning. However, because we'll be "hearing the Word" this morning, the household guardians don't read from Lamentations. I'm tempted to read ahead in Marcela's Bible—mine hasn't arrived yet, but it would take the fun out of trying to guess what the strange verses might mean each day.

This morning, we go through two big pots of coffee. No one asks about plans for the day. Evidently, we're all doing the same thing, going to the same place. The children are adorable in their Sunday-best outfits. They're admonished to eat carefully, but towels are also hooked about their necks to cover their clothing.

Olivia's morning prayer includes a request for God's Word to fall in power upon Ruby Jade.

I eye our leader's picture on the opposite wall. *What about the rest of us?*

She finishes with, "And may your message to us through her fall on open, receptive, submissive hearts. May no rebellion taint this household."

Is that a hint to everyone around the table or just me? As far as I know, I'm the only one with a rap sheet. I hate to question every little comment, nuance and prayer, but acclimating to FFOW has been more challenging than figuring out the jail culture.

I didn't know anything about incarceration the first time I was arrested, so I had few expectations. On the other hand, because I grew up in church and around church people, I thought I knew what to expect at FFOW. What a joke. This place has very little resemblance to normal churches.

The people are nice enough, but there's something restrained about them, a sort of fearful uneasiness. On the other hand, I've never seen a group openly adore their pastor the way these people adore, maybe worship, Ruby Jade. How many Bible passages say our worship belongs to God alone?

Marcela and I walk into the church building together. But then she says she's going to the married women's Sunday school class and tells me where to find the single women's class.

I clomp down the wide hallway in my new flats, a pair I haven't broken in yet, thinking about my roommate's weird marriage. If Robert passes Marcela on his way to the married men's class, will he ignore her or wink at her the way Corban winks at me? Can she smile at her husband or is she supposed to act as though he doesn't exist?

I blow out a breath. Will the questions ever end?

Corban comes alongside, but he doesn't look at me. Staring straight ahead, he singsongs a barely discernable, "Me-ow," and hurries to join his brother who's several steps ahead.

I suppress a grin, touched he dared to tease me in public, and pleased he has a sense of humor, despite this rigid environment and the heartache he's suffered. Biting my lips to keep from laughing out loud, I remind myself that my public interactions, especially with the opposite sex, must be stealthy as a cat.

At least fifty women are already seated on metal folding chairs when I arrive at the single women's Sunday school class. Their ages range from young adult to a handful of ladies who must be in their eighties. Everyone's hair is beautiful, not a highlighted strand out of place, and their expensive clothes are immaculate. From what I can see, they wear lots of jewelry—rings, bracelets, necklaces and earrings. But only one earring per ear. Some of the older women have jeweled pins on their collars.

I find a seat in the back row and slide onto one of the hard metal chairs. From here, I can watch how the others interact. I'm interested to observe the teacher, the way he or she addresses such a diverse audience, and the women's responses. I'm also hoping to get a better idea of FFOW teachings. A curly-haired woman three seats over smiles and nods at me. The others talk quietly with each other.

At exactly eight o'clock, according to the big clock over the door, Inez breezes into the room and approaches the lectern at the front. Her short white-blond hair curves behind her ears, and she's wearing a navy-blue ankle-length skirt with a white top and a navy jacket. Accessories include pearl earrings, a pearl-and-silver bracelet and a three-strand pearl necklace.

I have a feeling they're real pearls, not fake. My mother could tell the difference. Like Noreen, Inez has a Bluetooth on one ear.

She lays a folder on the podium. "Good morning, ladies."

No wedding ring. Interesting...

The women respond in unison, reminding me of a first-grade class. "Good morning, Inez." Hands in their laps, they focus their complete attention on her. Some women fidget, a barely discernible mannerism Followers employ to suppress their inner discomfort. At least, I assume it's the reason why they twitch.

144 | Rebecca Carey Lyles

Inez surveys the room. "Joyce, you've gained weight and your roots are showing."

A forty-ish blond woman clasps her hands to her head. "I am so, so sorry, Inez. I let go of Jesus. I haven't been vigilant with my personal appearance." She presses her lips together, obviously suppressing tears. "I'll make an appointment first thing tomorrow morning."

"Tell the receptionist I insist they get you in immediately." Inez taps the podium. "I want you to begin dieting today. Come to my office after the service, and I'll teach you how to count calories."

"Yes, ma'am."

What? I bet Ruby Jade weighs twice what Joyce weighs.

"Stephanie…" Inez zeroes in on a dark-haired teenager. "I told you to wear more makeup to cover that horrid acne."

The girl cowers. "I've been using a little bit more, but my doctor said—"

"If Dr. Baker doesn't want you to wear makeup, then he needs to fix your face. You did go to Dr. Baker, as I told you to, right?"

Stephanie nods, blinking rapidly. Her lips quiver.

"I'll call him and set him straight. If he can't do any better, we'll send you to Salt Lake City or Denver for treatment."

By now, I'm cringing in my seat the same as all the others, praying I'm not Inez's next victim.

She eyes an older woman. "Mother, you wore the same outfit last Sunday. Do I need to lay out your clothes each week, along with everything else I do for you?"

"No, Inez." The woman lowers her head.

Heaving a heavy sigh, Inez grasps the sides of the lectern and turns to the audience. "Welcome to the single women's Sunday school class." She smiles, opens the folder and pauses before saying, "Ladies, did you know the Bible talks about eye makeup?"

I clamp my teeth to keep my jaw from dropping. *What just happened?*

As synchronized as their greeting, the women relax their shoulders and glance at each other, half smiles on their faces. I'm still clutching my chair seat. How can they so quickly change gears? Are they accustomed to these personality shifts that happen without warning?

A middle-aged woman says, "I had no idea."

"Yes, the Good Book discusses eye makeup—and it doesn't mince words." She focuses on each woman, one at a time, as if this topic is of utmost importance to our faith.

One young girl brushes the corner of her eye, then ever so discreetly checks her finger.

"The prophet Jeremiah wrote of women enlarging their eyes with paint, and in Second Kings, Jezebel painted her eyes before she was thrown to the dogs." Inez leans forward, hands on the podium. "What do you think of that?"

When no one responds, I raise my hand.

"Yes?" She gives me an encouraging nod.

"Jezebel wasn't thrown to the dogs because she painted her eyes. She had a history of evil actions."

"True, but don't you find it interesting she wanted to look her best for her death?"

I wish I had a Bible with me. I thought of borrowing one this morning, but Marcela told me members don't carry Bibles to church. The Scriptures are either printed on the screen, or Ruby Jade quotes them from memory.

"I grew up going to Sunday school and church. As I recall the story…" I sit a little taller. "Jezebel didn't expect to die. And even if she did, she was trampled by horses into an indistinguishable mass of blood and gore. Her eyelid color was no longer apparent."

The woman beside me groans, and a chorus of "Eww, gross" circles the room. One young woman jumps to her feet and runs out the door. The girl in front of me turns to whisper, "She has a weak stomach."

"Sorry." I lift my palms. "But the truth is, the biblical account is more graphic than what I described."

Inez studies me for a moment, lips pursed. "This is not where I planned to direct this lesson." Her voice is as hard as her eyes. She motions to me, her lacquered nails glittering beneath the fluorescent lights. "Please stand."

CHAPTER THIRTEEN

Uh-oh. I've offended the queen bee's lackey. Despite deep misgivings, I do as Inez asks.

"Class," she says, "welcome FFOW's newest member, Cassandra Turner. She comes to us from the confines of the Gallatin County Detention Center to be enrolled in our Transformation Way program."

Confines. Intriguing word choice, considering how confining this group is.

The others chorus, "Welcome, Cassandra," and clap polite little pat-pats with the fingertips of one hand on the palm of the other. They stare at me a bit too long, like they're searching for handcuffs or tattoos—or maybe a steely inmate glare. I'm tempted to cross my eyes and stick out my tongue or give them the finger, just to see their reactions. Instead, I nod my head and start to sit.

"While you're standing," Inez says, "I need you to help me with a demonstration. Please move to the first row."

I'm tempted to ask, "Why in the world are we talking about eye makeup in a Sunday school class?" But I do as she says and make my way to the front. No doubt bucking an Inez directive will get me nowhere except called into Ruby Jade's office.

Once I'm seated, she says, "Ruby Jade, Noreen and I spent three-and-a-half hours discussing this subject because we want to be faithful followers of the entire Word of God, not merely certain parts of it."

I smile. Good to know.

"We decided painting the eyes is the point of these verses. Also, painting with the purpose of enlarging the eyes is the sin God wants us to avoid."

What?

I'm now close enough to see Inez's neck wrinkles and the single blond hair coiled on the shoulder of her navy jacket. She's wearing eye makeup, as well as foundation, blush and lipstick. How is she going to justify her own appearance? And how is she going to use me to do so?

"As a result of our prayers and discussion," she continues, "Ruby Jade has heard from God. From this day forward, FFOW women are to utilize three types of eye makeup—eyebrow liner, eyeliner and mascara. If you have blond, red, auburn or light-brown hair, purchase those items in brown-black. If you have dark-brown or black hair, purchase black. Those with silver or white hair, use blue-black. Any questions?"

A woman to my left asks, "At what age should our daughters begin wearing eye makeup?"

Inez's answer is immediate. "When they enter the young women's class."

"Thank you."

"About painting the eyes," she continues, "God told Ruby Jade the phrase refers to eye shadow applied with a brush. From now on, only leadership and those onstage, whether here at FFOW or in the community, may wear eye shadow. The color must be approved beforehand, and the shadow must be applied with a cotton ball instead of a brush. It must not be used to enlarge the appearance of the eyes, but rather, to enhance."

Do I dare ask what the difference is between enhancing and enlarging our eyes?

Inez crooks her finger at me. "Cassandra, please come to the podium." Her "enhanced" eyebrow twitches.

Uh-oh. I rise to my feet and step to her side, smiling at the class. "Face me."

Once more, I do as I'm told.

She examines me with her cold gray eyes. "You're not wearing makeup. Is that correct?"

"Correct."

"You're no longer a washed-up vagrant in baggy orange clothes and stringy hair, hidden from the public behind bars." She snickers. "You can use makeup now."

"I choose not to."

Her eyes spark and her brow furrows. "Noreen sacrificed considerable time and money to provide the perfect shades of makeup for you." She aims a painted fingernail at my chest. "And you have the gall to refuse to use it?"

I clasp my hands. "While in jail, I discovered how liberating it is to shower, dry off, add a little face cream to counteract dry skin and be done for the day. I appreciate the makeup, a very generous gift—very generous, and I'm sure I'll use it for special occasions."

"Are you saying...?" Her nostrils flare. "Are you saying our church services are not special? And honoring Ruby Jade and God with your appearance is not important?"

"The Bible says man sees the outer person, but God sees our hearts." The jail chaplain mentioned that truth from First Samuel at least once a month.

Inez's eyes blaze.

I knew before I quoted the verse I should keep my mouth shut. But I couldn't help myself. After all, this is supposedly a church.

"I know all about men and their lust." She's so mad she's spitting. "How they can't keep their eyes off women."

I back away, but she stays in my space. "I'm talking about reverence for God and for Ruby Jade, who receives his words for us. You..." She shakes her finger in my face. "In the same manner as all FFOW women, especially unsightly women like yourself, you will dress and fix your face to honor both Ruby Jade and God." Hands on her waist, she glares at me for at least half an eternity. "Got it?"

I open my mouth to respond, but the conversation has so derailed I've lost track of what we're talking about. Unsightly?

"Say it."

"Say what?"

"Did you leave your brains in jail?" She swears under her breath. "Say you'll honor God and Ruby Jade."

"I…I will."

"In the way you dress, in the way you walk, in the way you talk, sing and pray—and in the way you apply makeup." Her upper lip curls. "But don't use lipstick until you get those awful teeth fixed. They're revolting. You're like those women at the holy-roller church in town, an embarrassment to the Faithful."

One thing I learned in jail was how to keep a poker face, how to control my reactions. But this is going too far. I'm about to give Inez a piece of my mind, when I hear, "Excuse me, Inez."

Ruby Jade is standing in the doorway, her dark eyebrows knit into caterpillar clumps. As always, she's wearing eye makeup, including brown shadow. Oh, right. One of the many privileges of leadership. "I need to speak with you, Inez," she says. "Send your class to the sanctuary to pray for the service."

Inez shoves past me.

I should be grateful for the interruption to my public humiliation. But Ruby Jade will get an earful from Inez about me, and then I'll get an earful from Ruby Jade. So be it. I can't wait for the Transformation Way program to begin. I need a break from this church's craziness. One year. Just one year. I can do this.

The class files out of the room. No one speaks. No one pats my arm in empathy. Are they afraid my jail germs or my bad teeth will rub off on them? Or that associating with me will put them in precarious standing with Inez?

I follow them into the women's restroom and join the line for the toilets. No one talks, which is unusual for a bunch of women. Somehow, they all manage to avoid eye contact with me, even those facing the long mirror above the sinks.

One person is washing her hands, but the others stare into the mirror and dab at their eye shadow with dampened paper towels. GCDC residents would have been seriously vocal about such an absurd edict. But here, no one complains or questions the rule change. These church women are more confined than I was because they're not allowed to have opinions of their own.

From the restroom, I follow a group of single women into the sanctuary, mostly because I don't know my way around the building. I stand inside the doors, adjusting to the rosewater scent and searching for Marcela. I'd like to sit with someone who doesn't make a big deal about how I look.

Corban and Logan walk in the open double doors, carrying instrument cases. They're both wearing ties.

"Hi, you two. I hardly know anyone here. Would you mind if I sat with your family?"

"Uh…" Logan stammers, "It's not, I mean, we'd…"

"What he's trying to say…" Corban clears his throat. "We don't sit with our parents. We're with the single men and you're with the single women."

"You mean my Sunday school class, the people I sat with Wednesday night?" People who act as though I don't exist.

Corban lowers his voice. "We'd better go…cameras."

"I forgot."

"Never," Logan murmurs. "Never ever forget."

Corban brushes hair from his forehead and sends me a furtive wink from beneath his palm.

I watch him follow his brother to the platform, where two men are playing scales on trumpets. Others are assembling instruments and placing sheet music on stands. I wish I could tell Corban I got skewered in Inez's class, for no good reason. I'm sure he'd sympathize.

From the first time I met Inez, I had a feeling she disliked me. If that's how she felt before, she hates me now. I'll have to tread lightly around her.

My class members are finding seats on the opposite side of the large sanctuary. I join them, settling beside a beautiful lady with short white hair. She pretends to pick lint off my sleeve. "Hold tight to Jesus, dear. Hold tight."

Before I can ask her how Followers "hold tight," another woman slips past me to sit on her other side.

The white-haired woman says, "Missed you in class this morning, Edna."

"Noreen drafted me to help in the nursery. It's full today. Thank God, they have enough people to cover the church service."

The comment is ordinary church talk similar to what I heard as a kid. But I'm struck by the fact three women run the huge church and the school. From what Mrs. Watkins told me, Ruby Jade is the superintendent of schools, Noreen is the elementary principal, and Inez acts as the middle and high school principal. God help those children.

And then there are the outside businesses Marcela mentioned. And Transformation Way. Do the Fearsome Threesome, which I've decided to call the Leadership team, run the rehab program, too? The thought of never escaping their authority sends a chill down my spine. What have I gotten myself into?

A middle-age woman drops into the seat on the other side of me. I offer a smile. She raises her chin, lowers her eyelids and looks the other way. Yep, another Inez protégé.

The Sunday FFOW service has many similarities to the Wednesday service. This time, women in ankle-length outfits lead the singing from the platform steps, accompanied by the ensemble behind them. Like the other group, they sing unfamiliar songs, melody only, at top volume. I've had enough voice training to know they'll harm their vocal cords, if they make scream-singing a habit. No wonder so many members are hoarse.

I hum along, trying to match the melodies with the words. The timing is difficult, and the rhymes are forced. I'm impressed at how well Corban and Logan and the others play the music and that the singers somehow manage to stay together. They must practice often.

The thought of leading one of the music groups was exciting at first. Now, I'm wondering how difficult it will be to interpret and lead Ruby Jade's songs. I'd be tempted to change them to make the words more lyrical and logical and the melodies easier to sing and play. Plus, I'd want to add harmonies.

After several lengthy repetitive songs, I'm tempted to sit, but the older women remain standing. I don't dare give in to my exhaustion. The only seated person in sight is an elderly man near the front in a wheelchair.

Vance leans on the doorframe of the nearest entrance, arms crossed. From what I can see, his fist is beneath his bicep. My guess is he thinks it creates a bigger bulge. What a moron. While the other men wear suits and ties, he has on a short-sleeved black t-shirt and chinos. One of the perks of being the pastor's son—or of being a guard? And exactly what is he guarding?

The music ends and Ruby Jade enters through a side door, this time without fanfare. She stops in the center of the stage. "Good morning, Faithful Followers."

"Good morning, Ruby Jade." The exuberant response fills the room.

"PGIH."

I mouth the expected echo along with the others, but I don't shout. It isn't in me this morning.

"Before I bring God's words for today to you," she says, "I need to deal with family business."

A tangible tension rustles through the congregation. Jaws clamp. Shoulders and necks stiffen, legs uncross, feet plop to the carpet. I swear I can hear it all, including the sound of pounding hearts. Or maybe it's the thrum of my own heart. On the platform, Corban and Logan and the other instrumentalists stare straight ahead.

I smell sweat and resist the urge to sniff my armpits. Could be the woman beside me is the source. She rubs her hands together, clasps them, unclasps and rubs some more. The older woman on my other side isn't quite as agitated.

"Arnold Spencer, Robert Perez and Marcela Perez, come to the platform."

I gasp and cover my mouth. Why Robert and Marcela? And why do I have a bad feeling about this? Those around me seem to melt with relief. At the same time, a sense of impending doom fills the room.

Several rows ahead in the married section, Marcela stands and slowly makes her way to the stage. When she turns toward us, her face is almost as white as the walls behind her. If I didn't know better, I'd think she was sleepwalking.

A door opens on the other side of the sanctuary, and Robert steps into the room. His gaze shifts from Vance's doorway to the double doors at the rear of the big room. Is he searching for an escape route or checking for guards?

I'm surprised when the third person is the guy in the wheelchair. One push at a time, he wheels his way to the base of the stage.

Ruby Jade tells Robert and Marcela to stand at each corner of the platform. How hard being so close yet barred from living out their marriage must be for them. I want to shout, "Run to each other. Hold one another like never before. Tell Robert how much you love him, Marcela. Robert, tell Marcela you'll never leave her again. Then give Ruby Jade the finger and walk out."

But, of course, I don't.

"Frank, bring three microphones," Ruby Jade orders. "Now."

A fortyish guy comes running with mics in his hands. He lays two on the edge of the stage, gives one to Arnold and trots away. I get the impression he's glad to be out of the spotlight—or, more likely, out of Ruby Jade's reach.

She motions to Robert and then Marcela. "Put on your happy faces."

They each manage a weak smile.

"You can do better than that." She rolls her eyes and sighs.

The tremulous grins they force onto their pale faces bring tears to my eyes.

Ruby Jade walks to the edge of the platform and peers down at the wheelchair-bound man. Even from nine rows away, I can tell he's shaking. Pointing her fingernail at him, she screams into the microphone attached to her ear, "Arnold Spencer!"

I jump, along with Arnold and everyone around me.

"You were healed last week," she declares. "What are you doing in a wheelchair?"

Looking up at her, he says something, but his words aren't amplified.

"Switch on the microphone, Arnold."

With trembling hands, he twists it this way and that. Finally, he finds the switch. Raising the mic to his lips, he whispers, "Sorry."

"I repeat," she says, sounding miffed. "You were healed last week. What are you doing in a wheelchair?"

"I, I…" His voice quavers. "When I tried to walk out of church…" He sucks in a shaky breath. "My legs gave out and I fell over. My doctor said—"

Her scream could rival that of any witch. "You listened to a doctor? You wicked, wicked man." She glares at him. "You trusted in man, not in the God who created those legs." She holds her hands over him, fingers splayed, diamonds glittering, and then flips them over. "In the name of Jesus, arise." Like a puppeteer pulling a puppet to its feet, she slowly raises her palms heavenward.

Arnold pushes upward, clutching the wheelchair arm with one hand, holding the microphone in the other.

I stretch forward, willing him to victory.

Half crouched, he releases his grip, holds the pose for three seconds, at most, and collapses on the seat. Shaking his head, he lifts the mic to his lips. "I can't, Ruby Jade." Everything about him pleads for understanding. "The doctor said I'll do permanent damage if—"

"Out!" She whips her arm around, aims a long fingernail toward the back of the sanctuary, and shouts, "Get–out–Arnold Spencer–and–never–return. If you do, I'll have you arrested."

He stares at her, mouth agape. "I'm a founding member of this church. I've been here since before you—"

"You're a pagan bound for hell. Guards, take the microphone away, escort him out, and lock the doors behind him."

Vance steps from the side doorway, grinning and rubbing his hands together like he's excited to throw an infirm senior citizen from the building. He yanks the mic from Arnold's hand and tosses it onto the stage. It clatters and shrieks. Onlookers cover their ears.

Grabbing the wheelchair handles, Vance whips Arnold's chair around and barrels up the aisle toward the exit. A brawny guy in a black t-shirt and chinos charges from the opposite side door. Racing along the wall, he reaches the sanctuary doors just before Vance and Arnold and yanks one open. The three of them disappear through the opening.

A stone-faced usher walks over to close the door.

I whisper a prayer for Arnold and turn my attention to Ruby Jade whose face is now red and contorted. Her shoulders rise, and she inhales through flared nostrils. The amplified sound rumbles like a gathering storm.

Please, God… I swallow. Don't let her hurt Marcela and Robert any more than they've already been hurt.

She blows out a long breath. "For those of you new to FFOW, Arnold Spencer is an RP—a reprehensible person. He is dead to us and will be shunned by Followers from this moment forward. No one is to ever speak to him or acknowledge his presence when you encounter him in a public place, such as a store, restaurant or gas station. Unless, of course, he returns to his senses and stands like a man.

"Cecelia, Arnold's sweet wife, was precious, so very precious. But Arnold…" She shakes her head. "He's a piece of work, isn't he?" Spreading her arms wide, she yells, "Right?"

As one, the congregation echoes, "Right, right, right."

Someone shouts, "Amen."

The woman at the flea market was not joking. Ruby Jade is a charlatan. Real pastors are loving, nurturing shepherds, not heartless witches. I met some tough cookies in jail, but she could out-tough any of them.

Ruby Jade walks to the center of the stage, folds her hands over her stomach and closes her eyes. Her thumbs twirl, fast at first. Finally, they reverse and slow. She opens her eyes and motions to Robert and Marcela. "Come close, my darling ones."

CHAPTER FOURTEEN

I raise my eyebrows. *Darling ones?*

Maybe she's going to let them live together now. I'd hate to lose my sweet roommate. We get along great. Still, I'd be over-the-top happy for both her and Robert...Rodrigo.

They move to stand on either side of Ruby Jade, who instructs Robert to pick up the microphones and give one to his wife.

He does as she says. I notice he doesn't look at Marcela, and she's focused on the floor. I can only imagine how painful this must be for the two of them.

Ruby Jade's voice dips to a whisper. "Do you miss Robert, Marcela?"

Marcela nods her head.

"Speak into the microphone."

Marcela lifts the mic to her lips. "Yes."

Ruby Jade then addresses Robert. "Do you miss Marcela?"

"Yes."

The auditorium is deathly quiet. Is everyone hoping for what I'm hoping for, or do they know something I don't know?

Vance saunters to his station at the doorway. He folds his arms and rests against the door jamb, smiling like he's expecting a good show.

My heart sinks.

Ruby Jade swivels to Marcela. "How long have you two been separated?"

"Just over three months."

Without comment, Ruby Jade asks Robert, "How much time is left in this discipline?"

"A little under three months."

"Come on, now." She chuckles. "How many days?"

"Eighty-seven." He ducks his head.

"I thought so." Her smile fades. "You both well know the duration of your discipline, yet you had the audacity to arrange a clandestine encounter at the flea market yesterday."

Marcela gasps. "No, we didn't." Her eyes are wide and terror-filled.

"That's not true." Robert appears mystified.

What is Ruby Jade talking about? I was with Marcela all day. The two of them never got together.

"Liars!" Ruby Jade shouts the word.

Marcela and Robert jerk.

We all jerk.

"First, you're filthy fornicators. Now, you're liars." She shoves them away from her. "Is there no end to your wickedness?"

What is she talking about? They're not fornicators. They're married. And they're not lying.

I'm about to jump to my feet to say I was with Marcela all day yesterday, and she was never with Robert. But a movement beyond the frozen congregation, beyond Ruby Jade, catches my eye. It's Corban. His eyebrows are tight, and he's pinching his earlobe. I get the feeling he's trying to tell me to cool it.

I sit back. Interfering would probably make the nightmare worse for them.

Marcela holds out her hands. "Robert and I have been true to the rules of the discipline all these weeks."

"I have it on good authority…" Ruby Jade glares at her. "That you both were at the flea market yesterday."

"I was there with my household." Marcela's voice falters. "Handing out flyers for the spring concert."

I give her a thumbs-up behind my folded arms.

"And you?" Ruby Jade faces Robert. "Where were you yesterday?"

"I was at the flea market, but—?"

Marcela looks over at Robert. "You were?"

"Enough." Hand high, Ruby Jade slices the air between them with the blade of her hand.

Marcela straightens, a soldier standing at attention before her commanding officer.

"What were you doing at the flea market, Robert?"

"I was assisting the Scout troop with its fundraiser, like you asked."

"And you purposely made a point to contact Marcela."

"I had no idea she was there. I happened to catch sight of her on my way from the restroom to the Scout booth. And, yes, I admit I stopped for a second, hoping she'd see me, and I could wave to her. But she didn't, and I moved on."

Marcela's eyes widen, and a tiny smile creases her cheeks. I'm sorry I didn't tell her. I thought knowing her husband was momentarily close would be painful for her.

"You lusted over her body."

"I did not."

"I have it on good authority you were overcome by the lust demon."

"It was…it was good to see my wife. That's all."

Vance. He's the one who ratted on Robert, who lied about him and Marcela. I'm sure of it. Only the side of the jerk's face is visible, yet I can tell he's enjoying their distress.

I check Corban's reaction. He's watching Vance, eyes narrowed on his otherwise impassive face. He glances at me, and I know he knows. Yanking his earlobe, he averts his gaze.

I focus forward.

"I am sickened," Ruby Jade is saying, "by your immoral, nauseating behavior. You two let go of Jesus."

Immoral? How can she accuse a married couple of immorality? Especially two people who rarely have a chance to make eye contact, let alone touch each other.

"Six more months." Ruby Jade holds six fingers high, emphasizing the words. "God and I are adding six *more* months to your original discipline. You are not to associate with each other for a total of twelve months. At that time, I will reconsider your case to determine if you have clung to Jesus and are worthy of a FFOW marriage."

She motions for them to come near again.

As if in a daze, they shuffle close.

She wraps her arms around their waists, pulling them to her, bringing them closer than they've been in months.

They gape at each other over her head, mouths open, eyes wide.

She addresses the audience. "I love these two cherished ones like a son and a daughter. This discipline is for their good, to make them more like Jesus."

Yeah, sure. Or to satisfy the cruel streak running from the top of your head to the bottom of your fat feet.

She releases her hold, puts her hands on their shoulders and pushes them apart. "Dismissed." Swiping her palms together as if brushing off their filth, she motions the couple she united in marriage aside.

Robert leaves the way he came in. Marcela stumbles to her seat, head and shoulders low. The congregation exhales a collective sigh, whether of sympathy or relief, I can't tell. Vance watches Marcela return to her seat. His grin is anything but sympathetic, more like *I gotcha, and I gotcha good.*

Ruby Jade smiles and extends her arms. "Now, God's message for us today."

I don't follow a word she says, and when the service is over, I stumble into the Pritchards' van to sit beside Marcela in the rear. When I'm certain no one can see us, I squeeze her hand.

She pulls away and stares out the side window.

I look out the opposite window, trying to arrange the FFOW puzzle pieces in a pattern that makes sense to my jumbled mind. If only I could talk with Marcela for more than a couple minutes while we brush our teeth. Why does she tolerate the humiliation and abuse? Does she really believe she'll go to hell if she leaves? Why does Rodrigo stay?

I don't believe I'll go to hell if I leave. Despite what Corban said, that's not indicated anywhere in the Bible. So, why do I stay?

Closing my eyes, I rest my forehead on the cool window glass. I stay because I have a court order to be with these people, at their recovery center *and* their church. A good attorney could get the judge to change his mind. But any attorney, good or bad, would cost money. My parents might be willing to help me. However, I've already cost them a fortune in legal fees and unfinished rehab programs.

I remember Noreen's expression after I reluctantly signed the FFOW documents, as though I was a fly she'd trapped in her spiderweb. I rub my tired, makeup-deficient eyelids. *Help me, God. And help Marcela and Rodrigo. Show me how to support them.*

At lunch, we're told our household will return to the house we worked on yesterday. We'll caulk, do more scraping, replace bad siding, clean the gutters and tape off the windows for painting. I come so close to swearing I have to cover my mouth.

Olivia gives me a funny look.

"Excuse me," I whisper, pretending I burped.

I was hoping for an afternoon nap followed by family phone calls. My mom, my dad and my brother have all left text and/or voice messages, which randomly surface in the lineup of Ruby Jade's endless texts admonishing us to keep hold of Jesus. Or, she chews everybody out for a splattered bathroom mirror or a solitary gum wrapper in the parking lot.

"Go change your clothes, girls," Olivia orders me and Marcela. "The young ones will stay home with their mothers to rest. Sunday evening church tends to run long."

Marcela takes her plate and leaves the table, head down.

Does anyone else notice? Is anyone as worried as I am about her? Not one word was mentioned about Ruby Jade's latest edict at lunch. Do the others sympathize or assume Marcela and Robert deserve the punishment? Do they care? Or are they glad they weren't the ones castigated this time? Already, I'm jaded, and the program hasn't even started.

Owen clears his throat. "Marcela."

She stops.

I wait. Maybe someone noticed after all.

The others push back their chairs. Silverware clangs on plates, but I focus on Owen.

He smiles at Marcela. "Don't forget to put on your happy face."

One side of her mouth twitches and she keeps walking.

Maybe Owen thinks he's helping Marcela, but I want to slap the man. I flip around and follow her into the kitchen. I had hoped to tell her tonight I want to help her. But we evidently have another late evening ahead of us. Do these people ever stop?

And then it hits me. For the next twelve months, I'll be one of "these people." In fact, I'm already one of them. Not a happy-face thought.

Marcela and I are scraping the final sections on the backside of the widow's house when Corban comes around the corner with a ladder. "Hey, ladies." He looks pleased to see us. "I didn't know you were assigned to this project."

"Hi, Corban." Seeing him brightens my day. I don't know him well, but he strikes me as an island of sanity in the midst of madness. "Our household is working on this one, except for those with napping children."

"Probably why they called me and my brother over. To fill in the gaps." He sets the ladder against the house and tests its stability.

"What's your job," I ask.

"Cleaning gutters. Logan's doing the same thing on the front."

A scoop and a whiskbroom in one hand, he's two steps up the ladder when he bends our direction. "Psst, Marcy..."

She squints up at him.

"I'm sorry about..." His eyes are soft. "This morning."

Her lips quiver. Blinking away tears, she whispers, "It's my fault. I let go of Jesus."

"Not true." I search our surroundings for listening ears. This may be my only chance to tell them what I want to do. "Corban, I want to help Marcela and Robert, but I'm so new here I have no idea where to begin. Can you—?"

"Don't," Marcela whispers. "She'll roast you alive, the way she did Robert and me." She swipes at the tears. "You two were with me at the flea market. You know I didn't—" She stops, mouth open, and stares from me to Corban. Her eyes go blank. "You told..."

"No, never." He shakes his head. "Vance the Nasty strikes again."

"Vance and I saw Robert at the same time," I add. "He said Robert was a glutton for punishment. I didn't get what that meant until this morning."

"You knew Robert was there?" She narrows her eyes. "And you didn't tell me?"

"I'm sorry." I give her a sad smile. "I only saw him for a second, and then he was gone. I didn't tell you because I thought knowing he was so close might be painful for you. The way he looked at you with such love and longing broke my heart."

The light returns to her eyes. "He misses me." As quickly as the light came, it's replaced by utter hopelessness. "But, six more months…"

"We'd better get busy, before someone comes around the corner." Corban starts climbing. "I want to help. And I know Logan will join in. The lunacy has gotten out of hand."

A robin flies at him, barely missing his head.

He shouts, "Hey," and brandishes the whiskbroom.

The bird settles on a nearby tree branch, squawking a loud protest.

"Oh, no." I throw my arms out wide. "We forgot."

"Forgot what?" the others chorus.

"Today is Palm Sunday."

Corban shrugs. "So?"

"You know, kids waving palm branches, sermons about Jesus' triumphal entry and all that."

"Palm Sunday…" Marcela frowns. "My family hasn't celebrated Palm Sunday for so long, I'd forgotten all about it."

"Palm Sunday is a happy day in other churches," I say. "Not a day to humiliate people and ruin their lives."

Corban peers into the gutter. "Every day's the same around here."

We get back to work none too soon because Owen comes to check our progress. Corban is by now cleaning the middle of the gutter and debating whether to move a nest—the reason for the robin's outcry—from the gutter to a nearby tree. He says it has three eggs in it.

In a display of compassion rare among Followers and unlike his earlier callous comment, Owen says, "If you move the nest, the parent birds might abandon it. Clean around it as best you can but leave it alone. And don't touch the eggs. We'll give the owner a bit of a discount. I'll stop by now and then, and when the young ones have departed, I'll remove the nest."

When Owen leaves, I whisper, "She's paying us? I thought this was a volunteer job to help a widow lady."

"We're volunteers. No doubt about that." Corban snorts. "The money bypasses us and goes directly to Ruby Jade's bank account."

CHAPTER FIFTEEN

The Sunday evening service mimics the two previous services I attended, opening with yet another vocal group in coordinated clothing. This one is a mix of men and women, which surprises me. The men stand on the top two levels and the women stand on the bottom step and the floor. I'm pleased because this means I can have both genders in my music group.

They're accompanied by a solitary piano player and are mostly on pitch, but the music lacks beauty and the songs lack rhythm and continuity. I realize that's my opinion. Everyone around me seems to be into the songs. I suppose sincerity matters more than rhythm in God's book.

I steal a peek through the middle section of congregants, searching for Corban in the men's section. I can barely see him, but when I spy him, he glances my way. He must have sensed my gaze. I'm rewarded with a half-closed eye.

Ah, a sneaky wink. I look away, hiding a smile. Having a friend makes navigating this unfamiliar terrain a bit less daunting. I'll ask him to help me put together the instrumentalists for my music group, unless the powers-that-be micromanage the music as well as everything else around here. I have a funny feeling they do.

After the usual PGIH business, Ruby Jade goes directly into her sermon without singling out any victims to chastise. The relief in the room is tangible. I'm struggling to stay awake when she says something about "devil car radios."

I snap to attention. *Devil car radios?*

"You pretend you don't listen to the devil's music or carnal talk shows in your cars. But Security has found your radios tuned to the supposed *Christian* station, a station that in actuality is pagan and plays idolatrous songs with a fleshly beat." Hands folded on her stomach, she twirls her thumbs and scans the sanctuary. "You know who you are. I won't ask you to come forward. Instead…"

She bends toward us, hands on her hips. "I've heard from God. He and I are going to remove temptation from your feeble fingers. For a mere ninety-five dollars per car, my son's repair shop, Vance's Vehicle Repair, will disconnect your radios and CD players." She straightens, beaming. "What do you think about that?"

After a second, scattered applause splinters the awkward silence.

"WHAT…?" Fire blazes from her eyes. "Do–you–think–about–THAT?" Each word is punctuated with jabs of her taut hands, her fingers claw-like.

The ever-faithful, or maybe the ever-scared-out-of-their-wits, Followers jump to their feet, cheering and clapping and shouting, "Hallelujah!" I stand with them, clutching the seatback in front of me. I can't clap. I can't cheer. This is beyond weird.

I'm putting breakfast dishes in the dishwasher the next morning, when Olivia tells me Noreen will pick me up at eight to drive me to the dentist. Inez certainly got on that fast. I should be grateful for free dental care, but after her insult Sunday morning…

I stop what I'm doing. "Does Mrs. Watkins know?"

"Of course."

"Why am I the last to know? I'm the school employee *and* the dental patient. Why didn't Noreen tell me? Or at least send me a text? I have a phone now."

Olivia folds her arms and gives me the same scowl she gives her teenagers. "If I were you, Cassandra Turner, I'd watch my attitude. You're not in a place to question your superiors."

That word *superiors* raises my hackles. "I'm trying to figure out how things work around here."

"Now you know."

From the kitchen window, I watch Olivia's van drive away. The kids are going to school without me, which makes me sad. I enjoy working with the third graders. They're so sweet and cute.

But that's not why I'm here, I remind myself. I'm here for Transformation Way, and I intend to find out today when the rehab program will begin for me and how many people are already enrolled. I have yet to run into anyone who's in it. I'd love to hear what participants have to say about their progress.

Before someone in the household saddles me with another chore, I tiptoe up the stairs to my bedroom. I have twenty minutes before Noreen bustles into the house. I don't mind work. In fact, I like to stay busy. But when I can't find a free moment to communicate with my family, something is way off base.

From the privacy of our bathroom—with the door closed and the window open to the spring morning, I send each of my family members texts. I know better than to use my phone in camera view. God only knows what kind of rule-breaking the Sentinel perverts might fabricate. I also leave a short, quiet voicemail for my mom, promising more later.

Hearing a car, I peek out the half-open bathroom window. It's Noreen's Lexus. I shut and lock the window, inspect my mandated eye makeup in the mirror and hurry down the stairs.

The night I moved in, I learned windows must be closed *and* locked at all times to prevent break-ins. I could tell them locked windows never stopped a thief. And I doubt a person so inclined would carry a ladder to reach the second floor. The rule probably came from Leadership. From what I've observed so far, arguing with them is a lost cause.

By the time I reach the bottom stair, Noreen is already in the house. Olivia must have left one of the big garage doors open for her and the kitchen door unlocked. Or, could be Noreen knows the code to enter our home anytime she wants, an unnerving thought.

I smile. "Good morning, Noreen."

She nods in an absentminded way and wanders about the kitchen, running her finger over the counters, the stove and the stove hood, peering into the oven and cupboards. Is she inspecting the house? She passes through the dining room to the living room. I follow.

Seated on a couch, Candice is nursing her baby. She slides a receiving blanket over Tristen, but he pulls it off.

Noreen stops. "I can't believe what I'm seeing."

Candice's face is blank.

I look from her to Noreen. *What's going on?*

Noreen puts her hands on her hips. "Ruby Jade told you breastfeeding is sensual and unclean. Your son will have degenerate thoughts."

"The Bible talks about breastfeeding."

Noreen rolls her eyes, like that was the stupidest comment ever. "They didn't have bottles then."

"My son has digestive issues. Dr. Bennett instructed me to breastfeed him."

"With prompting from you, no doubt. Maybe your child needs to be raised in a home where—"

"Noreen, please don't do that." Candice hugs the baby closer to her body. "Talk to Dr. Bennett. He's a FFOW member. He knows Ruby Jade's policy. He'll explain."

The baby starts to cry. Candice slips her shirt down and lifts him to her shoulder. Tears cover her cheeks. "Talk to him, please, Noreen. And please don't take Tristen. You already took Mylea."

"Nobody *took* your daughter. She was delivered to another home for a better upbringing than you and Scott can provide for her." Noreen sneers and flips around. "I need to check the bedrooms before we go." High heels clicking, she marches across the wood floors and up the stairs.

A door squeaks open, probably ours. It's at the top of the stairs. I pray everything is in its proper place. Tiptoeing over to Candice, I kneel before her. "I'm so sorry," I whisper. "Let me know what I can do to help."

"Nobody can help us." She chokes back a sob. "When Ruby Jade decides to do something, no one can stop her. I mean, when she hears from God."

"Why do you stay?"

"I don't want to go to—"

"What's the real reason?"

"The real—" She looks away. "If we leave, we'll never see our daughter again."

"Nonsense." I touch her arm. "The courts would give her to you in an instant."

"Ha." Her laugh is bitter. "You're new here." She shakes her head. "You have no idea how many parents have gone to court and lost."

"How terrible." My voice grows louder. "The judge shouldn't—"

Pointing at the ceiling, she whispers, "Quick. Get a drink in the kitchen."

I get the hint. I need to distance myself from her and the baby as well as do something to cool my anger.

I'm finishing my glass of water when Noreen's heels hit the landing. Evidently, *her* anger hasn't cooled. She grabs my arm. I barely have time to deposit the glass on the counter before she pulls me toward the front door. "Spineless, sniveling women make me sick." She glares at Candice one last time before yanking the door open.

Once I'm through, she slams it so hard I'm surprised the glass oval doesn't break. My heart hurts for Candice. The fear of losing a second child has pierced her soul and will soon pierce Scott's soul, too. *God help them.*

I ease into Noreen's car, my head reeling. I can't believe she threatened to steal a nursing baby from his mother. I once thought she was a somewhat caring member of the Fearsome Threesome. I was wrong, so wrong. They're all evil. Why do they separate kids from their parents, anyway?

She opens the door and drops onto the driver's seat. Her perfume replaces the new-car smell, and a smile replaces her scowl. "This is a big day for you, Cassandra. You'll look wonderful when Dr. Collins is done with you."

How could I forget? It's all about appearances around here.

When I don't respond, she lowers her sunglasses and eyes me over the top. "You do want to have your teeth fixed, don't you?"

"Do I have a choice?"

"No, but so you know, Ruby Jade does not tolerate ingratitude."

I want to ask, *What DOES she tolerate, other than kowtowing fake but perfect-looking people who enhance her church's image? People who let her steal their children.* But I keep my mouth shut over my "disgusting" teeth. I learned on Sunday questioning a supposed superior can have disastrous results.

"After your teeth are fixed…" She lifts her sunglasses to check her lipstick in the mirror, something I don't need to do, per Inez's decree. Not that I normally wear lipstick. "Which will require two, maybe three visits," she says. "But whenever the dentist is finished with you, I believe you'll be ready for a FFOW member to befriend you. Wouldn't that be nice?"

What a strange way to talk about friendship. "I already have people I'm getting to know in my household and in the Sunday school class." I don't mention only one person from the class has spoken to me so far. "And I'm excited to meet the other Transformation Way participants."

"You silly girl." Her laughter has a snooty tartness to it. "*Befriend* is the precursor to *betrothed.* Before members of the opposite sex enmesh themselves in a long-term commitment, we encourage them to become friends, in a wholesome manner, as befits a Follower."

She starts the car and rolls across the long driveway and onto the street. "Our church has several young men in good standing in your age range, plus or minus ten years or so. I can ask Ruby Jade—"

For sure, I'd be stuck with either a pimpled teenager or a paunchy bald guy. Good thing I I don't plan to be in her twisted church forever. "No, thank you." I shake my head. "I'm not interested."

She frowns. "I didn't ask if you were interested."

"I was married to a wonderful man, and we had an amazing marriage. I'm grateful for the year-and-a-half we had together. I don't need another husband and, frankly, I don't want another one in my life. Eric was enough for me."

"Don't you want someone to go home to after work?" She acts as though I've lost my mind. "Someone to snuggle with at night?"

"The way Marcela snuggles with *her* husband?" I don't mention the fact my roommate is one of those spineless, sniveling women who silently cries herself to sleep because she's not *allowed* to snuggle with the man she loves. As for me, I was done crying at night, until I came to FFOW. Now, I miss my husband more than ever.

Noreen grips the steering wheel like a racecar driver navigating a curve. "Don't ever, *ever* backtalk me again, Cassandra Turner. Leadership decisions are not yours to question."

"I'm not questioning. I'm saying separating couples doesn't make marriage desirable for others in the congregation."

"Ha." She snorts. "We've got dozens of couples waiting in line for approval to befriend and betroth." She removes her sunglasses and shoots me such a fiery glare I'm amazed my hair doesn't burst into flames. "I was going to lobby to push your name to the head of the list. But not now. I'll make sure you *never* remarry and you remain a spinster the rest of your life."

I grit my teeth. Should I tell her I'm a widow, not a spinster, that I'll never be a spinster because I was once married? Um, maybe later. But I do find it fascinating she believes she has power over the remainder of my life. As my grandma would say, *I think not.*

On the way home, after what felt like an eternity holding my mouth open, I rub my jaws and ask about Transformation Way. I'd rather not speak to Noreen, but I have to ask. "This is my second week here," I say. "When do I start the rehab program?"

She raises an eyebrow. "When Ruby Jade decides you're ready."

"That's not what the judge's order says."

"Doesn't matter what it says." She lifts her chin.

I study her profile with her expensive glasses perched above her perfect nose and flawless cheeks. Since when does a judge's order not matter?

"As I told you earlier, we have friends in high places." She adjusts her glasses. "Ruby Jade and Judge Snow went to school together. They're *very* close. He'll do whatever she asks him to do."

"I didn't realize he attended FFOW."

"He doesn't." Eyebrows arched, she adds, "He can do us more good on the outside than on the inside."

Yeah, for a price.

Noreen drops me off at the school with orders to mind my p's and q's. "That is," she says, "*if* you want to get into the program."

I close the car door and walk the steps to the school. Being handed a jail sentence wasn't as mind-blowing as learning my future is in the hands of three heartless tyrannical women fed lies by Ruby Jade's nasty son. If they can destroy a marriage or take a child away from his parents, ruining my life will be a piece of cake for their demented psyches.

Mrs. Watkins is at the front of the classroom, teaching a math lesson. "Cassandra, I'm so glad you're here. With Taylor absent today, I don't seem to have enough hands. Can you walk children to the music room? We have five who are taking trombone lessons from a teacher named Corban Dahlstrom."

"I'd be glad to."

"Do you know where the music room is in the church building?"

"The one with the baby grand piano?"

She nods.

"Noreen showed it to me."

Corban welcomes his students with a wide smile and sneaks me a wink when they bend over their cases to pull out their instruments. I show him a notebook I brought with me. "I was a music major in college. I thought I'd jot notes for the kids." I clear my throat. "Um, children, to remind them of what you want them to practice."

"Great idea. The school can't afford music books, so every little bit helps. I photocopy the music for the lessons."

"Photocopying music is illegal, you know." I stop. "Did you say the school can't afford music books? This place is swimming—"

Brow lowered, he grasps his ear and his gaze flicks toward the kids and then the video camera in the corner.

I get the message. "Do you want me to make them each a practice page with your instructions and a melody line to work on?"

"Sure, if you have the time."

"Like this?" I balance the notebook on my forearm and write in small print, *When and where can we talk?* I want to know if he has any ideas about how to help Marcela.

He acts like he's contemplating my suggestion. "Maybe bigger notes. This group is making great progress, but they're early learners. Let me show you what I mean."

I erase my words.

He takes my pencil and writes in small, light print. *Greenhouse beside cemetery.*

I frown. I'm a little apprehensive about cemeteries since Eric's death.

He writes. *Gardener a friend.*

Okay. At least it would be private. I nod.

He erases his words and then draws large notes across them, filling in the circles.

I murmur, "When?"

He looks at his students. Several of them have their instruments at their mouths and are moving the slides in and out. "Ready?"

"Almost," says one.

He scratches his nose, hand covering his mouth. "Friday lunch."

"I'll try." I don't know how I'll get past Hank and Pete, but I'll try.

CHAPTER SIXTEEN

The rest of the afternoon passes in a blur, as do the supper preparations. Neither Marcela nor I contribute to the dinner conversation. As usual, the others engage in surface talk, except when disciplining the children. That's when they get down to business. All the adults correct *all* the children, no matter the child. From their table manners to their posture to their speech and behavior, anything less than perfection is reprimanded.

The kids' parents don't even flinch at the harsh rebukes. I'm grateful Eric and I never had a child. Poor Zachary gets it from all sides. Is it because, as Olivia says, he's not one of them?

I'm also hearing more snippets of bickering around the house. "You were supposed to get my dry cleaning for me." "You should have given me money to pay for it." "You used all the laundry soap." "I did not. Deanna was the last person to use the washer."

And on it goes. No yelling, only little jabs when Olivia and Owen aren't around. Earlier, I was so enamored with the group I didn't notice. Either that, or they put their shiny side out for me. The teens are sullen, the younger ones cry a lot, and Olivia is crabby.

Before the children's bedtime, we all go to the living room for a mandatory Ruby Jade webinar. Her topic, I'm told, will be the FFOW spring celebration. Marcela went upstairs after supper, so

Olivia sends me to get her. Knowing they're waiting for us, I run the stairs two at a time and burst into the bedroom.

"Marcela?" I check the bathroom, but she's not there. Where else could she be? Hearing a noise, I return to the bedroom. "Are you—?" My words catch in my throat. "Oh…"

She's huddled on the closet floor.

I rush to her side. "What's the matter?"

Though she hides her face from me, I'm hit by a pungent whiff of chocolate. "What are you—?"

Hand over her mouth, chocolate leaking between her fingers, she shoves me aside and crawls on her knees and one hand to the bathroom.

I follow her in and close and lock the door. This needs to be private.

Still on her knees, she lifts the toilet lid and begins to retch. The bowl fills with dark-brown vomit, and a chocolate odor fills the room.

I put my hand on her shoulder.

Finally, she sits back, whispering, "I OD'd."

"On chocolate?"

"I know. It's dumb. I was only going to eat one, but I couldn't stop. I kept shoving it in."

"It's not dumb. It's a normal reaction to trauma. I've been there, done that." After what she's been through, I totally understand. In the same way the big bottle of vanilla extract in the kitchen calls my name, chocolate calls hers.

"We're supposed to go downstairs for a Ruby Jade webinar," I tell her. "And we need to hurry, before they come looking for us. Open the window and switch on the fan. I'll get you some juice to rinse away the chocolate."

"Thanks, Cassandra. I was at the end…"

"Yeah, I know."

I rush to the living room. The others stare at me, brows creased. Does anyone trust anyone around here?

"Marcela tossed her cookies," I tell them. "But she should be fine now that her stomach has emptied. I'll take her some orange juice to rinse out her mouth."

"Hurry," Olivia says. "The webinar starts in two minutes. We report attendance and tardiness to Leadership, so don't be late."

Nice way to show your love and concern, household guardian lady.

I pour a glass of orange juice and grab a mint from the bowl on Olivia's desk. She's never offered me a mint, but she's never said I couldn't have one. I bound up the steps.

Inside the bedroom, I close the door and dash into the bathroom. "Here you go." I set the juice and the mint on the counter. "This should help." I say the words more for the perverts observing our every move than for Marcela.

She's washing her face, which I'm glad to see, and has changed her top. I wipe a chocolate smear from her hair with a damp cloth and whisper, "Swish the juice around your mouth to remove the brown from your teeth."

Satisfied she looks and smells okay, I hurry to join the others. Marcela stops in the kitchen to rinse the juice glass and place it in the dishwasher before she takes her seat. The others glance at her, but no one mentions a chocolate odor or asks how she's feeling. I'm relieved and peeved, at the same time.

The camera is on Ruby Jade. She's seated behind the marble-topped desk in her office, dressed in black. Her makeup is subdued. She doesn't smile.

I'm prepared for her to tell us how important and solemn this season of the year is, how our faith revolves around Christ's death, burial and resurrection. How he died a terrible death to save us from our sins. All we have to do is repent of those sins and accept his free salvation.

I expect her to say we shouldn't miss a single Passion Week service—and for her to explain why we failed to commemorate Palm Sunday. Doesn't make sense to me, but maybe she has a good reason. I also assume she'll tell us to spend Saturday preparing for the big day.

As a result, I'm caught off-guard by her Easter rant. I'm not surprised the children won't be allowed to hunt Easter eggs or receive bunnies or chicks, real or stuffed. I figured she'd eliminate the fun from the holiday. But I'm shocked when we're told anyone using phrases such as *Ash Wednesday, Maundy Thursday, Good Friday* or *Easter* will be publicly shamed. No wonder I didn't hear any mention of Palm Sunday.

"We do not live as the pagans live," she says. "Ishtar…" She practically hisses the word. "Is the pagans' goddess of…pros-ti-tu-tion." She glares into the camera, her purple eyes fierce. "Easter, rabbits and eggs are all about fertility and s-s-sex."

Somehow, the way she says "sex" makes it sound really nasty. I notice the teens, as well as the young kids who shouldn't be hearing this, are way too tuned into her words. "Rabbits breed and multiply," she says, "like, well, uh…like rabbits."

For a moment, she appears flustered. But then she regains her moxie. "They're *not* what the death and resurrection of our Lord was about."

I peek at Marcela to make sure she's okay. Her face is pale, and she has the zombie stare, but she seems calmer. How she can watch and listen to Ruby Jade is beyond me. Maybe she's ignoring her. If my roommate ever needed her husband and her parents, it's now. Yet, she's not allowed to contact either.

I blink, twice. *That's it.* Excitement rises in my chest, and I sit a little higher. Corban, Logan and I will become a communication channel for Marcela and her loved ones.

Beside me, Candice shifts and gives me a what's-your-problem frown.

I don't have a problem. I have an answer.

She places the baby on her shoulder and pats his back. His burp is so loud heads turn. Candice whispers, "Sorry."

I squint at her. *Apologizing for your baby doing what babies need to do?*

She elbows me, and I focus on Ruby Jade, who's scratching her red arms and explaining all the things we can and can't do in the next week. Surely, she's seeing a doctor about her rash. If not, lack of money couldn't be what's holding her back.

Her most important directive is to forbid us to commemorate Christ's death the way the "worldly" churches do. We will have no Ash Wednesday ashes, which I find puzzling. Ash Wednesday was six weeks ago, and the ashes are long gone. No Maundy Thursday feet-washing is permitted, and definitely no Good Friday sadness. "Followers celebrate Christ's life," she informs us, "not his death. You will put on your happy faces."

We *are* allowed to accept the free turkeys our employers give us and purchase hams on sale, but we cannot cook them until after Easter. The same goes for buying related on-sale items like potatoes, eggs, mayonnaise, green beans, cream of mushroom soup and French-fried onions.

In fact, we're supposed to stockpile eggs while they're cheap. We can make stuffed eggs, but we must call them *divine eggs* not *deviled eggs*. She also informs us devil's food cake is chocolate cake and angel food cake is heavenly cake. Really? Surely, she can come up with more creative names.

From food rules, she transitions into clothing instructions. We must dress our best, as is expected every Sunday. But she's quick to warn that anyone who enters the church wearing an Easter hat or dress gloves will be asked to give them to a guard to dispose of properly.

I'd roll my eyes, if I thought it was safe to do so. This is Montana, not Florida. I remember Easter Sundays when the wind blew sixty miles an hour and the ground was covered in three feet of snow. Women wore down coats, sweaters, pants, insulated gloves and snow boots to church—if the roads were plowed and open. Since I moved to Bozeman, more than one woman has told me she never bothers to buy Easter dresses, let alone white gloves and fancy hats.

On the other hand, according to the weather update we saw while waiting for Ruby Jade's broadcast, this Easter Sunday is expected to be gorgeous. The favorable forecast is due to the early spring plus the fact the holiday occurs near the end of April, making it the latest Easter in recent history. Maybe she was wise to warn us against wearing those offensive hats and gloves. You never know. Montana weather can change as fast as her moods.

The male members are not left out of the spring attire instructions. Men and boys must wear solid-color ties and black, navy or gray jackets with white or light-blue shirts. *Isn't that their normal Sunday attire?*

They should clean and polish their black leather shoes—no showy, carnal, patent leather allowed. No silly ties, patterned ties, untucked shirts or tennis shoes allowed. Black socks only.

Our pastor, prophetess and psalmist then proceeds to tell us what we have to do to prepare for the spring concert. The church building *must be* cleaned from one end to the other, with special attention given to the parking lot, front doors and sanctuary. Members' cars must be washed *and* waxed.

Appearances. More confirmation this place is all about looks.

She goes on, but I can't listen any longer. It's all too much, too much. I need to think of ways to help Marcela get in touch with her loved ones. A clandestine meeting or phone call now and then won't do. It's time for her to get a life.

Silence, like a void, invades the room. I turn my attention to the wide screen in time to see our fearless leader close her eyes. Her breathing slows and becomes ponderous, giving the impression she's about to snore.

My housemates send furtive glances to each other.

Ruby Jade blinks and jerks. Staring into the camera, she seems to reorient and come to her senses again. Strange. Who falls asleep while delivering a speech?

Without an explanation or an apology, she picks up where she left off, like nothing unusual happened.

I return to my roommate's plight. My first thought is to get Marcela a prepaid burner phone. However, if it was discovered, I can only imagine what Ruby Jade would do to her. I've heard of anonymous phone numbers, but I'm not sure how those work or how one would help her. We could devise a method to deliver handwritten letters between her and her family members. Yet, a paper trail is riskier than a burner phone.

I chew at my lip. I'll discuss possible options with Corban when we meet in the cemetery. My stomach jitters, and I pray we don't get caught. Talking to him might be as dangerous as Marcela talking with Rodrigo.

God... I close my eyes. *I just started brainstorming, and I'm already out of ideas. Where do I go from here?*

Ask Marcela about her schedule.

Who said that? I glance around. All eyes are on the big screen.

Shortly after midnight, I return to our bathroom. The first thing I do is open the door, close the window and switch off the fan. The combination did the trick. No more chocolate scent. Too bad. It was more pleasant than the room deodorizer we're expected to use. However, explaining it to Olivia might have been difficult.

Marcela walks in.

I stop the water and whisper in her ear. "Are you ever alone at your job?" I picture her surrounded by people all day at the factory. But it's worth a try.

Her expression says, *Are you kidding me?*

"Ever?"

"Bathroom breaks." She shrugs. "Sometimes I'm the only one in there."

I wet my toothbrush, stop the water, squeeze on the toothpaste and decide to try a different approach. When I finish brushing, I rinse the toothbrush and put it away. "Maybe we could meet for lunch sometime. Where do you usually go to eat?"

She spits toothpaste into the sink. "I always eat at my desk."

"That's too bad. I was hoping—"

"I only have a half-hour lunch, and the factory isn't near any restaurants. Besides…" She laughs. "You don't have a car. How could we meet for lunch?"

"Good point." I lean close. "Your daily schedule… Are you *ever* alone? Think about it and tell me tomorrow."

Her eyes brighten for the first time since I met her. "Oh, you're—"

I put my finger to my lips. "Let me know."

We don't have a chance to talk before breakfast, but afterward, we share the mirror while we fix our hair and apply makeup. Marcela says, "Your teeth are nice."

"Thank you." I check my teeth for the first time since the dental visit. I was so traumatized by Noreen's comments I didn't bother to examine them earlier, but I must admit my appearance is vastly improved. Thanks to his state-of-the-art equipment, the dentist was able to cap my chipped teeth and whiten all of them in one long visit.

I should be excited to have a more attractive smile, but after Inez's insult, I really don't care. Mostly, I'm delighted Noreen won't be driving me to the dentist again. With any luck, I'll never again have to be alone with her. Evil woman.

Marcela whispers, "I heard what happened in your Sunday school class. Inez can be…"

"Mean and nasty."

She frowns. "You shouldn't—"

"Now you know why I started wearing makeup."

She switches her hair blower on and sets it on the counter. The two of us move behind the door.

"How do you stay so strong?" she asks. "What happened to me and Robert makes me want to crawl under my bed and never come out. Or jump off the roof. Life is so…so impossible."

As soon as she says those words, her eyes go blank and she lowers her chin to her chest. "I shouldn't have said anything. I let go of Jesus."

"You told the truth," I murmur into her hair. "Truth is good. Remember, Jesus is holding you. The Bible says *no one* can snatch us out of his hand."

She switches off the hair dryer. "Really?"

"Really." I turn the water on full force. "Do you have an answer to my question?"

"Yes." She comes to life. The spark in her eyes, small as it is, gives me more hope than I've felt in days.

A knock on the bedroom door makes us both jump. "Marcela," Olivia calls, "your ride is here."

Marcela checks her watch. "She's early."

"Well, she's here and waiting. If she parks too long in the driveway, she'll drip oil on it."

I whisper, "I thought you had a car."

"We alternate driving to work," Marcela murmurs. "One of us confesses our sins out loud while the other one drives. Gotta leave. Sorry." She smooths her hair and rushes from the room.

I follow at a slower pace to make a lunch in the kitchen. How can I devise a plan without some solid facts to work with?

Olivia is at her desk in the corner of the kitchen, making a list. I assume she's getting ready to grocery shop.

"Olivia…" I open the fridge door. "What do you suggest I put in my lunch today?"

Without raising her head, she says, "PB and J. Apple."

"Okay." I take the peanut butter and jelly from the shelf in the door and close it. "Thanks." Sliding the silverware drawer open, I grab a table knife. "Do you have time for a question?"

She looks over at me. "What is it?"

"I've been wondering about Zachary." I bump the drawer closed with my hip.

By her frown, I gather she didn't appreciate the hip-bump.

I ignore the frown and keep talking. "Did you adopt him, or is he a foster child?"

"Why do you ask?" She puts her pen down.

"I was wondering if he's an orphan or if his parents are still living."

"He's not an orphan."

"So, he's a foster child."

"In a sense, yes. But not technically, not in the legal sense. He had…well, let's say, inadequate parenting. Ruby Jade asked us to assume his upbringing. Owen and I have been glad to do that for Zachary."

Zachary doesn't seem too happy about it. And I'll bet his parents aren't either. "Are his parents FFOW members?"

"Of course."

"Great. I assume they get to visit with him now and then."

"Never." Her voice is flat. "It would only serve to confuse Zachary and ruin everything we've done to help him unearth the gift of God within him."

I turn away, sickened not only by her self-righteous arrogance, but by her disregard for Zachary's feelings.

I'm talking with Mrs. Watkins at her desk when Inez comes into our classroom, hands the teacher an envelope and swivels to go.

Mrs. Watkins says, "Do you have a paycheck for Cassandra?"

Inez rifles through the envelopes. "No, I guess not. Remember, they're delayed by two weeks."

"I haven't filled out any employment forms." I try to talk without showing my teeth because I don't want to give Inez the satisfaction of knowing I capitulated to her ridicule. She probably knows, but still…

"In fact," I say, "I haven't filled out an application for this job."

"Well, no wonder." She spins on her heels and strides out of the room, high heels hammering the floor.

Mrs. Watkins starts to say something, but then her eyes dim. "Ruby Jade's secretary should be able to help you with the paperwork. I'll cover recess duty. You can go over to the office then."

CHAPTER SEVENTEEN

On the way to the school office, which Mrs. Watkins told me is the same as the church office, I walk the long hallway that leads to the music room. Hearing trombone music, I peek through the window. It's Corban.

I smile and tap the window. He doesn't hear me. I consider opening the door but decide I should stay in the hallway, for his sake as well as mine. He must sense my presence because he stops playing, does the slow half-wink thing, and gives me a wide grin. I clap silently and wave goodbye. I know better than to loiter.

In the office, Evelyn glances up from her work, registering my presence. But that's all, as far as I can tell. Her smile barely creases her cheeks, and her eyes remain shuttered.

My request for employment forms triggers a wide-eyed stare. I can't decide if she didn't know I was working at the school or if for some strange reason teachers' aides don't normally fill out the forms. For a moment, she gawks at me, her mascara-coated eyelashes blinking over dull eyes. Finally, she turns to her computer screen.

The office reeks of rosewater yet feels sterile. Could be due to the washed-out flower picture on the white wall behind the reception desk and the big vase of beige flowers in the far corner. What's with all the anemic flowers around this place?

The printer beside Evelyn whirrs to life, spitting out printouts in rapid succession. She hands them to me.

I rifle through the pages. "When I'm finished, I'd appreciate a copy of the forms."

That request flusters her even further. "No… I can't. I mean, this office doesn't provide copies of anything."

Now, I'm the one to stare. "Really?"

"Uh-huh." Her cheek twitches. "Really."

"Well, lucky for me…" I brandish the pages. "You printed two of each form."

"Oh, no." She covers her mouth. "Please, I mean…" Her voice drops to a whisper. "I let go of Jesus and forgot to change the number of copies after the last print job."

Birdlike, her focus flits from Ruby Jade's closed door to the ceiling camera in the corner to the doors on the other side of her desk. One gold nameplate has Inez's name etched on it and the other has Noreen's.

My heart goes out to the woman. Surrounded by the Fearsome Threesome day in and day out must give her nightmares all night, every night. I can only imagine how high her blood pressure must be.

"Thank you so much, Evelyn." I lean over the counter. "You've been a wonderful help. Remember, if you've asked Jesus to be your Savior, you're God's child. He *never* lets go of you. The Bible says *no one* can snatch us out of his hand."

A glimmer of light slips into her lifeless eyes.

I stop in the restroom to give myself a few minutes of solitude before I return to the third-grade classroom. But I can't relax. If I linger, someone will come looking for me. I'm sure of it. They'll tell me I let go of Jesus and gave in to the devious devil.

When I return, Mrs. Watkins is at her desk with a stack of standardized tests. I remember the days of filling in those little round circles with number-two pencils.

She sighs. "This is going to take forever."

"Can I help?" I ask. "All I need is a list of correct answers… True or false?" I chuckle, amused by my little joke.

Being a typical Follower, she doesn't get the humor. "False. This is a bit more complicated than that."

"Okay. What do you want me to do instead?"

She scans the quiet room. Heads bent over their books, the kids are either reading or writing. "The children are doing their social studies worksheets," she says. "Maybe this would be a good time for you to assist me."

She hands me an answer sheet with a child's name at the top. "He answered five questions wrong, and we're only allowed three per student. Using this guide…" She hands me another sheet. "Pick two wrong answers and correct them. You'll need a number-two pencil with a good eraser." She digs through the tray in her desk drawer and hands me a sharpened yellow pencil.

"I'm confused." I tilt my head. "Isn't the purpose of testing to determine weaknesses, so you can help a student improve?"

"This school has ranked at the top of *all* Montana private schools every year since its inception. Ruby Jade is determined not to lose that status."

I hold out both sheets. "I'm fairly certain changing a student's answers is illegal. It doesn't give a true—"

She cuts me off with a frown. "Ruby Jade is our spiritual leader as well as the superintendent of our schools. She knows best. I do what she tells me."

Shaking my head, I lay the papers on her desk. Beside the fact I don't want to add another crime to my record, I never once thought of cheating in school or helping anyone else cheat. Changing a student's answers is not only an illegal, spurious way to make the school look good, it doesn't help the child. Once again, I'm reminded appearances are more important than people in this place.

The teacher's gaze hardens. "Go help Emily. Her hand is raised."

That afternoon, the kids are getting their colored pencils from their cubbyholes for an art project, when one of the boys shouts, "You're having devil thoughts. You let go of Jesus."

I spin around in time to see him shove Zachary, who shoves back. "I am not."

Before I can stop the altercation, Mrs. Watkins says, "Ryan, Zachary, sit down. Save it for recess."

Save it for recess? My insides churn the peanut butter sandwich I ate for lunch.

She avoids my questioning gaze and hands me a stack of construction paper plus a basket of glitter glue. "Please give every child one sheet of paper and a bottle of glue."

By the time recess comes around, I assume Ryan has forgotten his accusation. But the class is hardly out the door when he lays into Zachary. The other kids circle the two boys, even the girls.

"Punch him," someone shouts. "Zachary has a devil in him."

Another child yells, "He let go of Jesus."

"Stop it!" I rush to them. "Stop it now."

Two teachers, a man and a woman, come running. I'm about to thank them for their help, when the woman yells, "Stay out of it," and pulls me away.

The man raises his palms. "This is not ours to referee."

"What does that mean?" I scowl at him.

"Ryan must have heard from God."

"And that allows him to pound on another child?" Livid, I jerk from the woman's grasp and charge into the group. By now, all the third-grade boys are slapping, slugging, shoving, kicking Zachary. Tears squeeze from his closed eyes.

The girls cheer, "Hit him again, hit him again. Knock the devil out, knock the devil out."

I push the boys aside and pull Zachary to me, bending over him and taking his punches until the girls quiet and the frenzied boys realize what they're doing. One by one, they wander away. I rock the sobbing child, patting his back and whispering, "It's over, it's over."

The woman teacher looms above us. "Do you realize what you've done?"

I squint at her. "Isn't it obvious?"

"You interfered with the work of God in this boy's life. His spirituality may be forever stunted because you stopped a cleansing opportunity."

"Cleansing opportunity?" *What are you talking about?*

"His devil thoughts need to be pounded out of him. Now, they're trapped inside his body with nowhere to go." She spins around and marches to the other side of the playground, arms stiff.

"Zachary, that's not how God works." We're alone now, but I'm whispering in Zachary's ear. "He knows all our thoughts and forgives the bad ones when we ask him to. They're not trapped in our bodies." *These crazy people are trapped by their sick beliefs.*

I walk him to the kitchen that adjoins the gym and wet some paper towels. Placing them on his bruised cheek, I tell him, "You're going to have quite the shiner, but this should help the swelling. If it gets to hurting a lot, tell me, and I'll go find the school nurse." I peer into his eyes. "The school has a nurse, right?"

He shakes his head. "When someone gets sick, Mrs. Watkins calls their mom to come get them."

"I see."

"I don't want…" He looks away. "I don't want Mrs. Pritchard. I want my mama." He falls against me, sobbing from the depths of his broken heart and broken body. My own tears wet his soft hair.

Mrs. Watkins comes into the kitchen. "Cassandra…"

I twist away from her, pulling Zachary with me. Teachers are supposed to care for their students, not encourage them to beat on each other.

Why, God? I stare at the ceiling. *Why does such a sweet little boy have to suffer so much in this God-forsaken place?*

Because... The answer comes to me. Because this truly is a God-forsaken place. Like the idolatrous Israelites in the Old Testament, the Followers don't realize God wants nothing to do with their atrocious practices.

I wipe Zachary's face and then my face and place a spare set of wet paper towels in a plastic bag. We make our way to the classroom as a trail of sweaty but subdued children file inside the building. They don't acknowledge Zachary or me. Mrs. Watkins shakes her head, obviously disgusted with my actions.

Why do I get the feeling a trip to the superintendent's office figures in my near future? So be it. I did what I needed to do, what I believe God wanted me to do, and what Zachary's parents would have wanted me to do.

Lord, please reunite Zachary with his parents, no matter how "inadequate" Ruby Jade thinks they are. He needs his real mommy and daddy.

When the kids are in their seats, Mrs. Watkins says, "Children, put on your happy faces."

Though their eyes belie them, fake FFOW grins pop onto their somber little faces. Zachary manages a small smile.

"Miss Turner is new to Faithful Followers of the Way. She's never been cleansed, nor has she observed an adult cleanse session. She didn't understand what you were doing."

Never been cleansed? Are you kidding me? For some silly reason, I thought Mrs. Watkins was an oasis of sanity in this sea of craziness. But, no, all the members are tainted by madness, except Corban...maybe.

"I don't know about your version of cleansing," I say, "but Jesus' blood washed my sins away. He cleansed me, once and for all. Our God is a God of love and compassion. He doesn't hurt us. He heals and helps us. And he wants us to do the same for others."

The wide-eyed children stare at me like I stepped out of a horror movie—not that they've ever seen a movie, and Mrs. Watkins is eyeing her cell phone on her desk. I can guess the debate that wars within her.

Do I call Ruby Jade, or not? If I do, I could be blamed for this mess. And suffer the consequences. If I don't, I could be blamed for this mess. And suffer the consequences.

I'd hate for her to lose her job or have her pay docked, or whatever the queen bee might dream up. For her sake, and for the kids' sake, I shut my mouth. The last thing any of them need is for Ruby Jade to send in the guards to usher me out. Their intrusion would only add to the afternoon's chaos.

Later, when I climb into the overly air-conditioned van for the trip to the house, Olivia's glower could scorch my eyeballs. I smile, determined to take the high road. How long I can hang onto an unflappable demeanor and retain my sanity, I'm not sure. To Zachary, whose eyelid is now a greenish-blue and swollen shut, she says, "Put on your happy face."

I worm my way to the rear of the van and slump in a corner to get as far away from her radar as I can. Staring out the window, I balance my future on two mountains in the distance. On one snow-topped peak, I picture Judge Snow seated behind his bench. On the other crest, I visualize my guitar and the music career I hope to reestablish. Between the two tall pinnacles is a deep valley with a wide raging river running through it.

The river is FFOW, an endless series of tortuous class-six whitewater rapids, whirlpools, boulders and snags. I've barely navigated one hazard when I'm upon another, with no time to rest or regroup. Is that the intent of this place?

I could climb Judge Snow's mountain to petition him for a transfer. But I'd have to make the climb on my own because I can't afford a lawyer to act as my "trail guide." The judge's decision and an opening at another rehab facility could be months in coming. In the meantime, where would I live? Would he send me to jail or to a halfway house? Or make me stay with the Pritchards? Wherever I landed, my career would remain on hold.

If I jump into the river, ignoring all my fears and reservations, I might eventually make it through the recovery program to the opposite shore and start the climb to reestablish my career. But is it possible? Even if I knew all the FFOW rules, I'm fairly certain I couldn't keep them all. Somehow, I'd mess up, which I assume is the Fearsome Threesome's goal.

And if I somehow managed to please them, I couldn't stand by and watch people being abused. The Followers work day and night on very little sleep, marriages are arranged and splintered, children are illegally separated from their parents, and the "cleansing" beatings are evidently common, for children as well as adults. On and on it goes. I have a feeling I'll discover much worse, if I stay with the group.

To be honest with myself, I'm not sure I'm ready to leave. Marcela, Zachary and Candice are all desperate to be reunited with their loved ones. As a newcomer, maybe I can help them foil the system. Truth is, I'm merely an ignorant, powerless, fresh-out-of-jail alcoholic, dreaming about the vanilla in the cupboard and wishing Eric was around to help me navigate life. Is it possible for me to be of use here?

Lord, please show me how to help my friends—and whether I should leave the program before it starts.

I expect Olivia to lay into me once we get home, but she says nothing. Instead, she marches into the house ahead of me and the kids.

I pat Zachary's head. "Hang on a minute." I run up the stairs, grab a washcloth from my bathroom and hustle down to the kitchen. Taking a handful of ice cubes from the freezer, I fold them into the cloth. "Lie on the floor in the living room with this on your cheek." Olivia would have a fit if water dripped on the furniture. "It'll help keep the swelling down. You feeling okay?"

"Uh-huh. I hope I don't ever get..." He lowers his voice. "You know...anymore."

"I know."

"Children," Olivia calls from the living room. "Come in here, please." A moment later, she appears in the opening that separates the dining room from the kitchen. "That includes you, Zachary."

She huffs. "Leave him alone, Cassandra. You've done enough damage for one day."

I squeeze his shoulder and climb the stairs to my bedroom. Poor little guy. If I had a car, I'd drive him straight to his parents, wherever they are.

Our bedroom is the first one at the top of the stairs. Beyond it is a long hallway. I've never ventured past the room I share with Marcela. One of these days, I'll have to do some exploring. I wish I could also explore the residents' minds. Has everyone in the household bought into FFOW ideology, hook, line and sinker? Do they agree with all the weird rules? Do they approve of the cleanses?

I take my cell phone from the pink purse and sit on the end of my bed. I'm about to call my mom, when Marcela charges in. Her face is alive with excitement. Before I can question the dramatic change in her demeanor, she crooks her finger. "Come with me. Hurry."

I lay the phone on the nightstand and follow her. She bounces down the steps, looks both ways, and darts through the kitchen door into the huge empty garage. As soon as I close the door, she pivots. I smile, expecting her to answer my question about a time when she's alone each day.

Instead, she whispers, "When my ride dropped me off, I saw two big boxes on the front porch. I checked, and they have your name on them...your other name, that is. Isn't that exciting?"

"Great. The things my mom sent must have arrived."

"There's only one problem."

"Problem?"

"Getting them up here without anyone seeing us."

"Why is it a——?"

"If certain people notice you have packages, they'll want to know what's in them."

"It's nobody's business."

"Our household guardians would disagree."

I fold my arms. "What do you suggest?"

"The only person in the living room is Aunt Marjorie. I asked her where everyone was, and she said Olivia took the children to the basement to teach them how to fold laundry properly. You probably saw Ruby Jade's text with the new instructions."

Whoops, missed that one. "What's the deal with laundry?"

"Read the text."

I sigh.

"Aunt Marjorie is sitting on a couch, knitting an afghan. Her back is to the window." Marcela opens the garage's side entry, which leads to the backyard. "If we go around the backside of the house and sneak onto the porch, she'll be less likely to notice us. She probably wouldn't tattle, but you never know around here."

"Amen to that." I'm surprised she used the word *sneak*, but I don't mention it.

We circle the huge house the opposite direction of the laundry room, which is beneath the garage. Ducking below the windows, we come to the front and tiptoe onto the porch. Aunt Marjorie is still in the living room, bent over her work. She seems intent on her afghan, but one squeaky board could ruin everything.

We grab the boxes and, moving as fast as we can with our cumbersome loads, return the way we came. Marcela giggles with every step, a rare reaction from her.

I whisper, "You're enjoying this."

"Maybe too much..." She grows serious. "I must be letting—"

"Remember, Jesus hasn't let go of you. I can show you verses that say so."

At the garage's side entrance, Marcela sets the big box on the stoop, cracks the door and peeks inside before opening it farther. We carry the packages into the garage, and I silently shut the door. We're about to enter the kitchen, when I stop Marcela. "What about the camera? Will the Sentinel perverts tell Ruby Jade?"

"Don't call them that," she whispers. "Yes, they might see us, but I can stand behind you and block their view, like I'm watching over your shoulder. Don't hold stuff high or make a big deal about anything."

"It's not a big deal. My mom sent stuff from home. Nothing exciting."

"Ruby Jade doesn't want us to talk about homes and families outside of FFOW. Our family is *here*, she says. The family of God."

I sigh. "I don't get it."

"I'm going to open the kitchen door now." Her voice is barely a murmur. "If someone is in there, or coming from the basement, we'll act as if bringing in packages is normal. If they ask why we didn't carry them through the living room, we'll say we thought it'd be easier to come around closer to the stairs. Or maybe say we didn't want to get in the way of whoever's fixing dinner. Okay?"

For someone worried about letting go of Jesus, she seems rather cunning. Maybe she doesn't totally buy into the FFOW party line, after all.

She twists the doorknob and opens the door.

CHAPTER EIGHTEEN

I can't believe our luck. No one is in sight. The house is usually crawling with people, especially after school lets out. And no one is working on dinner. They must all be in the laundry room, learning proper folding techniques.

We slide the boxes up the stairs and into the bedroom, quickly shutting the door behind us. Marcela stays close to block the camera view as much as is possible while I scoot the boxes between our beds.

I drop to my knees, the parcels in front of me, Marcela behind me, and bedspread-covered mattresses at my shoulders. "I should have grabbed a knife from the kitchen to open these."

"I keep hair scissors in the bathroom to trim my bangs," Marcela says. "I'll get them for you." She brings me the scissors and stations herself behind me. "I can't wait to see what your mom sent." I can tell by her tone she's tempering her enthusiasm.

Closer to my ear, she whispers, "This is almost as good as getting a package from my own mom."

Pleased I can share a happy moment with my roommate, I murmur, "Sweet." I wish I could hug her. However, slugs and slaps have replaced hugs in the FFOW world.

Seeing my mom's handwriting makes me feel less lonely and isolated. I slip a scissor blade into the tape, slide it across the top and cut the tape at each end. I lift the flaps and smell home.

Eyes closed, I breathe in the memories. Mom. Dad. Kip. Love. Laughter.

When I open my eyes, the first item I see is my Oregon Ducks sweatshirt. It's the most comfortable thing I own. I love it. I'm about to take it out when Marcela says, "What a nice sweater." But then she whispers in my ear, "Hide it, Cassandra. Faithful Followers don't wear sports attire."

"But, it's my fav—"

"What else do you have in there?" Her voice comes from above me again.

I paw through the contents. "She sent both winter and summer clothes." *Mom apparently expects me to stay a while.* How can I tell my mother I don't know how much longer I can hold out? Or that I can't wear most of the clothing. Jeans and shorts are not allowed. Neither are sleeveless tops and dresses, of which I have an abundance.

I lift a rectangular-shaped object covered with bubble wrap. "Good, she sent a family picture." I remove the bubble wrap and show the photo to Marcela. "Eric is on my right."

"Your family looks really nice. But our love and allegiance belong to God. We don't display family pictures at FFOW."

"Oh, right. I forgot." I twist toward her. "But he gave us our families."

"Ruby Jade does our interior decorating for us. She says family pictures ruin the effect."

"Whatever..." I drop the picture on my bed and dig once more into the box. "Hey, here's my Bible. My parents gave it to me for my sixteenth birthday." I hug it to my chest. Crazy, but I feel as though I've found a sanctuary inside a dangerous foreign land.

"May I see it?"

"Sure." I hold it above my shoulder.

She takes it, and I hear her flipping pages while I dig deeper into the box. After a pause, she says, "This isn't a King James Version."

"No, it's not." I twist to look at her. "Is that a problem?"

"Followers only use the KJV."

Of course. I should have known I'd have the wrong Bible version. "There's nothing wrong with the KJV," I tell Marcela, "but it was translated in 1611. Maybe I'm dense, but I understand contemporary translations better than older ones."

"Shh. Don't talk so loud."

I pull out the Oswald Chambers devotional book my parents' church gave me when I graduated from high school. "I s'pose this doesn't meet FFOW code, either."

She returns the Bible to me and takes the Chambers book. "Looks like it was written by a human, not by God."

"I see..." Truth is, I don't see, but by now I know better than to buck the system.

I picture my mother lovingly going through my things, praying for me, trying to decide what I can use. What a waste of her time and energy—and money. Must have cost her a fortune to send two huge packages.

My shoes are at the bottom. Stuffed in one of them is a plastic bag that contains my driver's license and a note from my mom, which makes me smile. She says she prays for me every day and hopes they can visit me soon because she misses me. I sigh. I miss her and Dad, too. But from what I know about this place, the chances of seeing them are not good.

I read the date on my driver's license. It won't expire for another year. Maybe I'll have a car by then.

The shoe collection includes a pair of black dress flats, one pair of tennis shoes, and three pairs of sandals. I love my sandals and used to wear them every day it didn't snow. But like my clothes, I'll have to wait to wear them. I have a new normal. Or maybe I should say normal is not a norm in this place.

I turn my head. "Marcela, will this box fit in the closet?"

She whispers, "I think we can squeeze it in the side."

I rummage through the clothes one more time, searching for my framed picture of Eric and our wedding album. Mom didn't send either one. A hint to move on, perhaps?

In the middle of everything is a bag of cookies. Don't know how I missed it earlier. No wonder the box evoked images of home.

Marcela murmurs, "I'm excited to know what's in the other box."

I slide the first box into the closet, pull out the underwear and stuff it in a dresser drawer. Then I motion for Marcela to join me in the closet. Hidden by the bifold door, I dangle the cookie bag before her eyes. "Care for a baked-by-my-mom treat?"

She grins.

"Mom's chocolate oatmeal nut cookies are the best. Plus, they're good for you." I open the bag and hand her a cookie.

"Tell your mother 'thank you' for me." She bites into the cookie. "Mmm, this is delicious, but it makes me miss my mom so much."

I give her a sympathetic nod. "Yeah, I get that."

I'd love to take the time to savor my cookie. Even better would be to enjoy it with a cup of coffee or a glass of milk. Instead, Marcela and I chew fast, so someone doesn't come running to check for closet kinkiness. We wipe our mouths and back out of the closet. She resumes her post at the end of the beds, and I slide the second box close.

But before I have a chance to open it, someone knocks on the door. Are we in trouble already for eating cookies on the sly?

Marcela opens the door, but not all the way. One of the teen boys is standing in the hallway. "Mom said you and Cassandra need to peel potatoes for dinner."

I blow out a breath and shove the box under my bed.

Marcela and I peel the potatoes over a garbage can in the garage. I love raw potatoes. If I had a saltshaker, I'd cut a slice, salt it, and eat it fast. I hate to be devious, like the devil, but I don't suppose Olivia would approve of me helping myself to a snack.

The six-car garage is full, which means everyone is home from work and in the house. We should be alone for a while. I whisper to Marcela, "I made a lot of people mad today."

"Oh, no... What happened?"

"I stopped the third graders from thrashing Zachary."

"You what?"

"The teacher called it a cleanse."

"Oh, Cassandra..." Her face constricts. "Interfering in a cleanse is interfering with God's work in a person's life. Ruby Jade will be furious."

"No doubt she's already furious. The word got out hours ago. But the fact is, I stopped a *beating*. I hate to think how bruised Zachary's little body is." My own body is plenty sore from where the boys hit me.

"Cleanses can be rough on children."

"And they're not hard on adults? Have you been through one?" The thought of a bunch of church people beating on each other makes me sick.

"I've been through several, both as the recipient and as a deliverer of truth."

"Deliverer of truth?" Potato in one hand and peeler in the other, I gape at her.

"We hear from God when someone has sin in their heart and let go of Jesus."

"Marcela, Jesus promised he won't leave us or abandon us. He'll be with us till the end of time and into eternity. Why do Followers believe they can let go of him?"

The kitchen door opens. "You girls about done?" Olivia's fists are on her hips.

"Last two potatoes," Marcela says.

As always, superficial chitchat permeates the dinner conversation. *How was your day? Fine, thank you. How was your work today? Pass the potatoes, please.* No one asks about Zachary's bruised cheek, which is gaining color, although the swelling isn't too bad. And no one speaks to me or mentions my blunder…or even looks at me, for that matter.

After supper, Olivia invites all the women and girls to ride with her to Walmart to shop for groceries and personal items. I'm anxious to open the other box, but I don't know if I have the freedom to refuse her invitation. Plus, Marcela is going. She says she needs shampoo and a couple other items. Because I want her to be with me when I pull my guitar from the box, I decide to delay the grand opening and tag along to Walmart.

Before we leave the bedroom, I put my cell phone in my shiny pink purse and slip the strap over my shoulder. I don't have a solitary penny in the purse, but I can pretend. Isn't that what FFOW is all about? Faking it?

The silly purse makes me and Marcela laugh. We both need a laugh, and I love the rare instances when she lets down her guard. She has a beautiful smile.

Seated in the back of the van, I review my text messages, grumbling beneath my breath. Ruby Jade's been busy. Does the woman have nothing better to do than to harass members? I skim the texts to make sure I didn't miss something important, like an announcement she kicked me out of the church *and* the rehab program.

But nothing is related to today's events. Text after text tells everyone where they should be when, along with her latest rules. She calls them "FFOW-Wow Insights from God." I bet God would prefer she not give him credit for her craziness. I skim the laundry-folding decree but stop on one titled "Stray Dogs." *Stray dogs?*

Stray dogs, Ruby Jade informs us, have many terrible diseases, including rabies, distemper and fleas. *Hmm, I've never thought of fleas as a disease.* They attack other dogs, cats, squirrels and people. They also knock over trash cans and spread the contents across driveways and into the street. This is unsanitary and reflects poorly on FFOW. All trash cans must now be secured with bungee cords.

As if people don't know how to deal with their garbage?

I sigh and continue scrolling. My brother, father and mother have all left text and voice messages. I love hearing their voices. I'll call them after we return from the store, provided Olivia doesn't find another video to watch or a chore to tackle.

In her phone message, Mom says she overnighted two large boxes yesterday afternoon. "I tried to pick your favorite clothes, several items for each season. And I threw your U of O sweatshirt in at the last moment. It's a bit worn around the cuffs, but I know how you love it. It'll be nice for evenings or if you happen to go to the mountains."

I huff. *Like that'll ever happen.*

"I wrapped yards of bubble wrap around the instrument case," she adds. "But be sure to let me know if your guitar is damaged during transit. I insured both packages."

I won't call her until I open the box. With all the bubble wrap, I'm sure it's fine, but I'm anxious to check.

We reach Walmart, and I stow the phone in my purse. After the greeter, we separate, two women head for the children's department, others to the grocery section and others to women's clothing.

Marcela tells Olivia we need to go to the personal-care department to find shampoo and deodorant. Olivia gives us her okay but tells us to keep our cell phones on, so she can let us know when she's ready to leave. I can't believe I'm twenty-eight years old and asking permission to walk to another part of a store, like a child would ask his or her parent. This is way too similar to jail.

When half a store length separates us from the others, I grab Marcela's arm. "Tell me, you've got to tell me about…"

She jerks her arm away.

"Sorry." I twist my neck to make sure Olivia didn't see us. She and her daughters are already rummaging through clothing racks.

I lower my voice. "Tell me about your, uh, work before I lose my mind."

We pass the greeting card section. If Followers don't celebrate Christmas, Easter or birthdays, I have a sneaking suspicion greeting cards are "of the devious devil."

Marcela stops at a chocolate egg display. "Don't these look yummy." Almost as soon as she picks up a package, she puts it down. "What am I doing? They're Easter eggs."

Yeah, and they taste the same as any other chocolate. I elbow her. "Tell me, Marcela."

She slips into the shampoo aisle but checks both ways before she speaks. "I don't know how this can help…" Her voice is barely above a whisper. "But my boss leaves the factory every day at approximately ten-thirty to make the bank deposit. He tries to get it in before noon, so Ruby Jade doesn't call and ask him about it."

I frown. "Why would she do that?"

"As far as I know, she has access to the bank accounts for all the church-owned businesses."

"She's a pastor and a school superintendent—and she has time to monitor bank accounts?"

"Shh." She holds her finger to her lips. "Inez and Noreen help her with everything—the church, the school, the businesses."

I pull her into the corner where the shampoo and conditioner shelves meet the hair-coloring and styling shelves, so we can watch both directions. Soap scents waft around us. "Such all-encompassing control is wrong, so wrong." I shake my head, trying to clear the exasperation each new FFOW revelation sparks in me. "But we can't do anything about it, at least not now."

Her expression says, *Why would I want to?*

"What we *can* do," I say, "is find a way for you to talk with your husband and your parents during the time your boss is gone. How long is he out of the office?"

"Forty-five minutes to an hour. He eats lunch while he's out."

"You can't leave the building to get lunch, but he can?"

She arches an eyebrow.

"I know, I know." I raise my palms. "I make a big deal about every little thing." *But every little thing is warped in the FFOW world.* I adjust the purse strap on my shoulder. "So, he's gone from about ten-thirty to a quarter after eleven, maybe eleven-thirty? Is that correct?"

"Once in a while, he has an emergency or a lunch meeting and has to change his schedule."

I reach for a can of hairspray, stuff I never use, in case a household member comes our way. Staring at the label, I ask, "Why does the factory need to make deposits every day? Do they get a lot of cash or checks?"

"We have a small store in the front where we sell trinkets and toys. Although the store doesn't bring in much money, Ruby Jade doesn't want the cash to accumulate. She wants it deposited every day because you never know when someone might burglarize the place."

"She wants it deposited even if it's only a few dollars?"

"Even if."

I snort and place my hand over my mouth. "Sorry. It's just so…" I set the hairspray on the shelf and try not to obsess over our leader's greed. "Is your boss the only one who makes the deposits?"

"I've never known anyone else to do it."

"Do other employees enter your work area while he's gone?"

"Not usually."

"What about when they leave for lunch? Do they walk through your office?"

"Most people pack their lunches and eat in the lunchroom."

"Do you?"

"Like I told you, I eat at my desk."

"Hmm…" I tap my jaw. "This has potential, Marcela. Let's consider how we can use it to your advantage."

"Oh, no." She blinks to a wide-eyed stare. "I wouldn't want to do that."

"Do what?"

"Take advantage of the company."

"You aren't taking advantage of the company. You're reclaiming the time your employer stole from you. By law, you should be able to make personal phone calls, go out for lunch, relax, have fun."

She doesn't look convinced.

I pound my fist into my palm. "It's *your* time, Marcela. Hours and hours have been stolen from you. Now, you're going to use and enjoy those hours."

Her brow furrows.

"I have a sneaking suspicion your pay is low. Am I right?"

"It's not a lot." She shrugs. "I mean, they can't afford—"

"Hogwash." I suspect Ruby Jade profits nicely from the plastics company and God only knows how many other companies, while workers like Marcela struggle to make ends meet.

"Okay, but if anyone finds out—"

"Is your family worth the risk?"

Without hesitation, she says, "Yes."

I blow out a long breath. Maybe she's going to be okay after all.

"They're all worth it," she says. "My husband, my parents, my sister, and even my ornery brother." She bounces on her toes, grinning the way Kip does when he talks about climbing mountains. "I can't wait to talk to Robert."

"Rodrigo. Call him by his real name, Marcela."

"Yes. Rodrigo." Her eyes sparkle beneath the fluorescent lights. "My sweet husband."

For once, we don't have chores waiting for us. Shopping seems to have sucked the last of Olivia's work-assigning energy. Marcela and I run the stairs to our bedroom, ready to open the last box. I know what's in it, but I want to see the surprise on her face when I pull my beautiful guitar from the case. I can't wait to hold it and play it.

Marcela hands me the scissors I left on her bed and takes her position behind me.

I slide the long, narrow package from beneath my bed and slit the tape. Ever so slowly, I bend back the flaps, glancing over my shoulder to be sure she's watching. On top of the well-wrapped guitar case are two three-ring binders with all the songs I've written. "Mom sent my notebooks. This is so exciting."

"Talk softly," she murmurs. "What's in the notebooks?"

"Songs. This one has my secular songs and this one has worship songs."

"What's beneath all the bubble wrap?"

I cut through the plastic to reveal the black guitar case.

"A musical instrument?"

"Yes."

She's not as excited as I expected.

"What kind?"

"Guitar. Want to see it?"

"No!"

The sharpness in her voice startles me. I turn my head. "I thought you'd—"

"Put the box back, and let's go brush our teeth."

Uh-oh. What'd I do wrong this time? I fold the flaps inward and push the box under the bed.

In the bathroom, we take our toothbrushes from our separate drawers, a result of another Ruby Jade edict. No toothbrushes are to be left on the counter because bugs or germs from toilets might crawl on them or flies might land on them. And then we'd breathe those germs at each other, maybe even on her.

Marcela starts the water. Raising her voice, she says, "I need to warm the water before I wash my face."

We slip behind the door, toothbrushes in hand.

"Ruby Jade," she murmurs, "hates rock 'n' roll music, hard rock music, folk music, jazz, blues and anything else that uses a guitar, including Christian music on the radio. She says it's the devil's instrument because it's shaped like a woman's body."

I stare at her, mouth agape. "That's insane, the craziest thing I ever heard." I emphasize my words with my toothbrush. "I heard classical guitar music playing in her office when I met with her. To say no one else can listen to it or play it is—"

She puts her finger to her lips, and I cover my mouth with my hand.

"Don't show the guitar to *anyone*," she says. "Don't play it in front of anyone. And don't show your songs to anyone. Ruby Jade is the *only* person who composes music here."

Tears spring to my eyes. "I've waited months to play my guitar, to hear the songs in my head come alive."

"I'm so sorry…" She backs out of our cramped little corner. "I'd better get the water."

I toss the toothbrush on the counter, grab my washcloth and wet it. Covering my face, I do my best to stifle my sobs. Finally, I gain control and dry my face.

"I'm sorry about your husband," Marcela whispers to the mirror.

Seeing the sympathy in her eyes, I burst into tears again and bury my face in the towel. She pats my shoulder. Two lonely women, missing their men. But at least her guy is still alive. I've got to do everything in my power to help her have a normal, happy, together-in-the-same-house marriage.

And I've got to find a safe place for my guitar. Maybe I should mail it to Kip.

CHAPTER NINETEEN

Peering over the towel, I whisper to the mirror, "Why do you stay?"

Marcela lifts her chin. "Because I don't want to go—"

"The truth." Between sniffs, I give her my sternest look.

"If, if Rodrigo and I..." Fisting her left hand, she aims her rings at me. "Ruby Jade selected *and* financed our wedding rings. She also planned and paid for our wedding. We still owe her almost ten-thousand dollars."

"What about the cars she promised you? Do you owe her for those?" I refrain from mentioning the absurdity of letting someone else pick their wedding rings and plan their wedding.

"She gave those to us, like she said she would, but her name is on the titles, along with ours." Lowering her hand, Marcela adds, "The main reason we stay is because she has Rodrigo's passport and his birth certificate. He's working to gain citizenship, but she told him if he causes any trouble for FFOW or leaves, she'll report him as an illegal alien. She'll have him deported and will make me file for divorce."

Now, we're both crying.

After a bit, I gain control, dab my cheeks with a hand towel and open the bathroom window. "It's a beautiful night out there. Let's go for a walk before bed. Fresh air will help us feel better."

Marcela's sob is a half-snort. "First, we'd have to ask Olivia for permission, and you know how she is. And then, she'd have to approve two more household members to walk with us. If it actually happened, we could only walk for twenty minutes, at the most."

I blow out a breath, astounded by the detailed layers in FFOW rules. "Can Owen give us permission?"

"Well, yes." Her forehead furrows. "But he'd have to clear it with Olivia, so it's easiest to go direct."

"In other words, she's the real boss around here."

"I guess you could say that."

"Forget the walk. I'll go sit on the porch and call my parents."

Her features darken.

"Don't say it." I start for the door. "I need to talk with my family, and this is a good night to do it."

The front porch has two wooden rocking chairs on it, which gives the house a cozy, welcoming appearance, when in truth, it's cold and inhospitable. The potted cactus by the door more accurately conveys reality, in my mind, anyway.

I slide one of the chairs to the corner and settle into it, pleased I can watch a sunset while we talk plus breathe fresh air. I wipe my eyes with my sleeve and call my brother first because I know the call will be short. We love each other and enjoy talking, but he's usually headed off to volunteer somewhere or to do something fun with his friends.

He doesn't answer. No surprise. I leave a message and speed-dial my parents' home phone. My dad answers.

"Hi, Dad, this is Cas—" I almost say Cassandra. "This is Cassie. How are you doing?"

"Great, now that I'm hearing your voice. Your mom and I were becoming concerned."

"I'm so sorry to worry you. This place keeps us busy day and night. By the time I have a break, it's way past your bedtime."

"Busy doing what?"

Yep, that's my dad. Get to the facts.

"Well…" My mind switches to high gear, racing through all the things I've done at FFOW. What can I say that won't cause my parents to look at each other and whisper, *What has Cassie gotten herself into this time?*

My mom gets on the bedroom phone. "Cassie, how are you?"

"Great, Mom. I'm sorry I didn't call earlier. I've been super busy. But I wanted to be sure to thank you for the packages."

"I hope I sent clothes you can use," she says. "I considered including dressier things, but you're still in Montana, so I mailed casual items."

"I appreciate all the thought and time you put into those boxes. I felt the love the moment I opened them. Or, maybe it had something to do with the smell of your famous chocolate oatmeal nut cookies, which, by the way, my roommate and I are both enjoying."

"Hey…" Dad exclaims. "I didn't get any of those cookies."

"Edward," Mom says. "I baked the cookies last week and sent three of them with you for your coffee break."

"You need to bake another batch to refresh my memory."

Their banter makes me long for home. Maybe I should tell them what's going on. With a lawyer's help, we could get the judge to let me live with them until he found another rehab program.

The door at the other end of the porch opens and Olivia glowers into the dusk. "Who's out here?"

I cover the phone's mouthpiece. "It's me, Cassandra. I'm talking with my parents."

"You shouldn't be out after dark."

"It's not quite—"

"Quit sassing me and get inside." She slams the door but then opens it again. "Or I'll take your phone away."

What?

Again, the door bangs closed.

"Cassie, are you there?" Mom asks.

"I, I have to go. I'll call soon."

"Are you sure? This is like when you were in jail. We rarely get to speak with you, and the calls are always so short."

"I know, Mom. I'm sorry. I love you both. Goodnight." I can almost taste the vanilla-flavored alcohol in the cupboard.

I slowly get to my feet and slide the chair to its original location. Not only was the call way too short, I forgot to ask how Grandma is doing. I'm tempted to do a quick callback, but a text is safer. Olivia wouldn't hear it.

As tired as I am, I'm still wide awake long after Marcela has fallen asleep. For the first time since I became her roommate, she didn't cry herself to sleep tonight. I pray I haven't given her false hope.

Assuming the perverts are on duty, I sit up with my back to the camera and slip on my robe. Tiptoeing across the room, I open the door, peer into the silent, empty hallway, and make my way down the stairs. I tread carefully, one bare foot at a time, trying hard not to squeak the wooden steps. This is the first I've felt their smooth coolness.

We're supposed to always wear shoes in the house, so we don't spread athlete's foot or other fungi, I've been told. Socks and slippers cannot be substituted for shoes. We might slip and sustain an injury. Which, of course, would keep us from doing God's work.

I make my way through the dim kitchen. The only light comes from the water dispenser on the fridge door. I open it as noiselessly as I can and remove the milk jug. My plan is to heat some milk and then add vanilla, a lot of it, and honey. If anyone questions me, I'll tell them it's an old family recipe. I hate to lie, but I've got to file the edge off the lost, hopeless feeling that plagues me, especially after the aborted call to my parents.

I shut the door and stare at the solitary fridge magnet. I've read the words before—God loves a cheerful giver *and* worker. But until now, I hadn't noticed the person in the small picture at the top is

Ruby Jade. She's wearing a blinged-out western vest and cowboy hat.

Huh? Maybe I'm bitter, but her get-up strikes me as an insult to real cowgirls. My grandpa would say she's a she-bear in satin—or in this case, western clothes.

Glancing from the stovetop to the microwave, I debate which one will be the least noisy. Probably the stovetop. I yawn. But how will I lift a pan from the drawer below the oven without making a ruckus?

"Cas-sandra! What are you doing in here?"

I pivot. Olivia is standing in the doorway between the kitchen and dining room. "Hi, Olivia. You scared me." Does an alarm ring in her first-floor bedroom when someone opens the fridge, or does she have a sixth sense?

"I asked you, what are you doing?"

"My stomach's upset," I lie. "I thought warm milk might settle it."

"Ridiculous. You haven't eaten anything bothersome. Put the milk away and go to bed. If you continue to imagine discomfort in the morning, you may approach Leadership for a cleanse." She turns and disappears into the gloom as silently as she came.

A cleanse for an upset stomach? I shake my head and walk the stairs to my bedroom.

The next morning, Marcela is brushing her hair, and I'm blow-drying mine. The smell of warmed coconut conditioner fills the small room. She nudges me with her shoulder. "Why do *you* stay?"

"That's easy. Court order."

"The truth…" She gives me the same frown I gave her yesterday.

"The truth?" I focus on the ceiling. "The truth is, I want to help you and Zachary—and Candice and Scott." I lean in. "Noreen threatened to take their baby. I was there."

Tears form in her eyes. "Not another one."

"You know who has their daughter?"

She nods.

"Good. We'll start there."

I say "good morning" to my housemates, but Candice and Zachary are the only ones who respond with more than a grunt. Everyone else is strangely silent. No one asks anyone about their plans for the day.

Coffee and bacon aromas, pleasant as they are, do nothing to dispel the tension in the room. I consider asking if something is wrong, but I fear the answer will be, "You, Cassandra, you're what's wrong."

Olivia concludes the quiet meal by reading three more mystifying verses from Lamentations. When she finishes, she lifts her chin. "Cassandra."

I push my plate forward, clasp my hands and rest them on the table edge. "Yes?" Here's where she tells me I'm the problem.

She stares down her nose at me, observing me from beneath lowered eyelids. "I heard from Ruby Jade regarding your future."

Ah, now the supreme master's gavel strikes. I wasn't expecting to receive her verdict at breakfast, but I shouldn't be shocked. She seems to enjoy catching her victims unaware and making public spectacles of them. I give Olivia my best GCDC poker face.

"You will not be allowed to sing in the special service."

That's it? "I didn't know I was supposed to sing in the special service. I haven't been to any practices—"

"And…"

Of course. There's always more.

"I will no longer transport you to work."

I maintain my impassive expression. *What am I supposed to do, hitchhike?*

When I don't respond, she lowers her chin. "Ruby Jade has transferred you to another position."

My first thought is, *why am I not surprised?* My second is, *poor Zachary. Now he has no one to protect him.*

Out of the corner of my eye, I see his lip quiver, and I know he already put two and two together.

She waits.

And, so do I. No doubt, she's dying to tell me how I disappointed Leadership.

Instead, she says, "You've been given the *privilege* of doing yardwork at Ruby Jade's home."

I could swear she's gloating.

Eyebrows raise across the table—and then quickly lower.

Privilege? I try to think of something positive to say. "Sounds interesting."

"Yes, indeed." Her tone reminds me of a melodrama villain rubbing his hands together, anticipating the train about to run over the heroine tied to the tracks.

I keep my gaze on Olivia, determined not to flinch from her indignant stare. Is she peeved I thwarted Zachary's cleanse, or is she jealous I'll be working at Ruby Jade's place? The other household members eye their plates. Evidently, they don't see the *privilege* in this assignment.

Why, I wonder, *does Olivia dislike me? I've always been polite to her.*

"You must be there by eight a.m. sharp."

"Okay." I reach for my coffee.

"Would you like to know where she lives?"

"Yes, of course."

"She's up the street to the north, about a mile and a half." She smirks. "You'll have to walk."

"It's a three-story white house," Owen offers, "with tall columns and purple trim—and lots of trees, bushes and flowers. You can't miss it."

Olivia glares at him. Apparently, she hadn't planned to give me a description of the house.

"Thank you, Owen." I fight to hide my elation. I won't have to ride to and from the school with Olivia, and I'll have time to myself. Olivia acts as though walking three miles a day will be a hardship. For me, it'll be a pleasure.

I'll have time to gather my thoughts, call my family, enjoy the outdoors, relax, breathe fresh air and do something for my health. I'll miss the third graders, especially Zachary, but I'll encourage him however I can when I'm home.

I stand and gather my plate and silverware. "I'd better go get ready."

"Wear tennis shoes." Again, the smirk. "You'll be working outside, in the heat and bugs and s-snakes."

Once more, I struggle to hide my delight. I'd much rather work outside the demented leader's house than inside. With any luck, our paths will never cross.

Walking the stairs to our bedroom, two negatives come to mind. I may work outside the house, but I'll be dangerously close to Ruby Jade, the last person on earth I want to be around. In fact, I'll probably have to go inside her house to use a bathroom. Not a good thought.

And I won't be able to meet Corban on Friday. Will he know what happened to me? How will I contact him now?

I'm rummaging through the closet, trying to decide what to wear with my polyester pants, when Marcela comes into the room. She reaches for a blouse on her side of the closet and whispers, "Beware of Vance. Never let him catch you alone."

Three strikes against my new job already. Maybe the positives will outweigh the negatives. I pray for a safe, positive, fun environment. Asking for fun in a FFOW job may be wishful thinking, but it can't hurt to ask.

Although I can easily walk a mile in fifteen minutes, I leave the house at seven-twenty. I won't have to walk super-fast, yet I should arrive early. Before Owen left for work, he told me to knock on

Ruby Jade's front door and talk with her butler, a man named Sebastian.

I thought only the super-wealthy had butlers. But maybe she fits that category. I'll soon find out.

If I didn't fear being seen by a Follower, I'd sing and dance in the early morning sunlight, and twirl my pink purse through air sweet with the scent of new blossoms. Instead, I lift my face to the heavens, focus on the clouds and thank God for this amazing change of circumstances. Green grass, sunshine, bright-yellow forsythia bushes, and birds singing in the treetops. What more could a girl want?

The freedom to not only be alone with my thoughts but to be outdoors feels too exquisite not to share. How I wish Marcela were either with me or allowed to go to college to get a teaching degree, like she wants.

I stop myself. I will not dwell on all the downers in life. Instead, I will thank God for this wonderful moment surrounded by his creation, where tree buds are bursting into tiny soft-green leaves, sparrows flutter and chatter in the bushes, and tulips and daffodils sway with the breeze. In the distance, cotton-ball clouds float over blue mountains as if they haven't a care in the world.

If only I were hiking those mountains, kayaking the rivers, canoeing the lakes—with Eric. I suck in a long breath and blow it out. I can't live in the past. I must move forward, God at my side.

I break into a run because I can, but I slow to a walk when a van similar to the Pritchards' vehicle exits a driveway two houses ahead of me. With a name like Fellowship Neighborhood, numerous other FFOW members must reside in this isolated neighborhood. I don't want a Follower to report me for acting unseemly.

Sure enough, I recognize the driver as one who drives children to and from school every day. I also recognize the kids inside. The woman ignores my wave, but several of the children wave and smile. May God preserve their innocence.

I reach a three-story colonial house with two tall columns. Fronted by a treelined driveway and a sizeable lawn, the house sits some distance from the road. Its bright-white paint is accented with purple—purple double doors, purple shutters, and purple trim around the windows and eaves.

A curved red-brick walkway leads from the porch to a purple mailbox with the word "Paradise" stenciled across the side in gold calligraphy. Below it is a tube with a rolled newspaper inside.

I look from the mailbox to the house. One of the purple doors opens and a man in a cowboy hat steps out. He ambles along the brick path toward me.

With all the purple opulence, this looks like Ruby Jade's house. But the guy has a mustache and is wearing a plaid western shirt with the sleeves rolled above his elbows, worn blue jeans and cowboy boots. He doesn't fit the Follower mold.

I've never seen a FFOW male, other than Ruby Jade's son, wear anything but dress pants. Cowboy hats are a common sight around Bozeman. However, this is the first one I've seen since I arrived at FFOW. Same goes for mustaches.

And a newspaper? If no media is allowed in Follower homes, she wouldn't have newspaper delivery. Or would she?

As the man comes near, I notice his mustache has as much gray in it as brown. He smiles, revealing nice teeth, but not sparkling perfect Follower teeth.

"Mornin', ma'am," he says. "Mighty fine day, ain't it?" He doffs his hat, like in the movies, revealing more gray hair.

"Yes, it is. I'm looking for Ruby Jade Paradise's home."

"This is where she hangs her hat."

I give him a quizzical look, finding it hard to imagine her with something other than a tiara on her head. But then I remember the picture on the Pritchards' refrigerator.

He adds, "So to speak..."

"I'm supposed to talk with someone named Sebastian."

"You're gawkin' at him."

"Oh…" I don't hide my shock. "I was told you're a butler."

He chuckles. "You pictured me in a black suit and a high-collared white shirt, right?"

"Well, yes. I mean, everyone at the church dresses in suits, so I…"

"One thing's for certain, I'm not an English butler. In fact, a better title would be 'property manager.'" He props an elbow on the mailbox. "Between you and me, I have a notion R.J. gets a kick out of telling people she has a butler."

"But jeans? I heard jeans—"

"Are outlawed for the FFOW folks?"

I nod.

"I don't go to my boss's church."

"Oh…" I close my wide-open mouth. "I'm surprised—shocked, actually—to think she'd let anyone outside the church manage her affairs. Or call her R.J."

"I'm the only wrangler who gets by with calling her by her initials. Maybe it's because we go back a long way. But so you know, I stay out of her personal affairs, and she stays out of mine."

"Sounds like a good arrangement." I change the subject, though I'd love to ask how the arrangement works. Ruby Jade has her nose in everyone's business. "I assume you're my new boss."

"Righto, bucko, if you're the new hire." He holds out his hand. "Sebastian Longpre."

I take his hand. His grip is firm. "Nice to meet you, Sebastian." *Longpre…* I pull away. Is he related to Vance? Is that why he works here? "I'm, uh… Ruby Jade changed my name to Cassandra Turner, but you can call me Cassie or Cat, if you want."

"Cat. I like it. A good feisty name." He steps around to the other side of the mailbox. "I'll grab the mail and then show you the spread. If I remember right, your last name is True."

"Correct."

"Good to know you, Cat True." He removes the newspaper from the tube and the mail from the mailbox and closes the door.

Following the brick path to the house, we walk alongside each other, Sebastian with the mail and newspaper tucked under his arm and me with my pink purse dangling from my shoulder. "I don't get it," I say. "You're Ruby Jade's employee, but you're not afraid of her the way everyone else."

He stops. "And neither are you."

"How do you know?"

"When I heard R.J. was sending you over here, I checked into your history, something I do with everyone who works the property. With your background and all you've seen, I figure you're not as gullible as the average church girl. You've been out of commission for a bit, but now you're back in the saddle with wide-open eyeballs. And knowing you made my boss mad enough to reassign you to what she considers menial work is a big plus in my book."

He reaches out his hand again. "I wanna shake your hand for the way you went to bat for the kid whose classmates were beating the tar outta him." He pumps my arm with painful enthusiasm. "That was the clincher for me. I knew you and I would get along like liver and onions."

I massage my hand. "Liver and onions?"

"Yep. Nothin' better."

"Debatable." I make a face, daring to disagree with Ruby Jade's property manager. "About being feisty, all I want is to lay low and get through the Transformation Way program on time."

"Ah, Transformation Way." He arches an eyebrow. "Did anyone tell you the program director left?"

"I heard he did, but he'll be replaced soon, won't he?"

"Maybe, maybe not. He and his wife, the program's mental health therapist, both left, which isn't always the case at FFOW. Oftentimes, the couples split. One stays, and one goes."

"They must have other staff to keep the program going."

"Nope. They were the only employees. The program folded."

"You mean the judge sent me here for a year when—?"

"A year, huh?"

"Yes, and if there's no program, then…" All this craziness and wasted time for nothing. I put my hands on my hips. "Would you please give me a ride to the courthouse?"

"Whoa, Nelly, not so fast." He raises his palm. "R.J. is syrup on pancakes with most everyone over at the courthouse. Includes the secretaries and the janitors, the spider in the corner and the flies on the walls. Hang tight and let me do some snooping."

"I…" I study his faded blue eyes. Can I trust him? Or have I already said too much? "I appreciate you checking for me." I'm not sure what he's *snooping* for, but he has a better idea where to begin than I do.

CHAPTER TWENTY

I follow Sebastian onto Ruby Jade's wide white verandah. "Is she…?"

"No one's home but me and the dogs."

I silently blow out a relieved sigh.

He grips the handle on one of the tall doors. "We're gonna slip inside slick as a whistle and shut the door real fast-like. R.J.'s dogs are wily little escape artists. The ornery boogers mutate into greased lightning when they see the slightest opening."

"Okay…"

"If you ever see 'em runnin' around loose outside, grab 'em. R.J. doesn't want 'em to dirty their dainty paws. And, being dogs, they enjoy nothing better than diggin' in the dirt."

We manage to worm our way into the house without losing either of Ruby Jade's Shih Tzus, Francis and Fenwick. Despite his disparaging comments, the dogs adore Sebastian and warm to me fast. Their coats are clean and fluffy. Their blue collars are studded with diamonds. Surely those are fake, but they shoot off brilliant flashes when they catch the light.

Sebastian gives me a tour of the main floor, dogs at our heels. Funny thing—the house has a strong rosewater aroma throughout. When I leave the program, will I ever be able to forget the smell?

Ruby Jade lacks for nothing. Once more, the words "cradled in opulence" come to mind. The huge kitchen has the latest of every tool and appliance. I consider asking if she does her own cooking, but the fact she has a butler suggests she probably has a cook and a maid or two, maybe a gardener. Oh, wait—I just became her gardener.

Grandiose furniture carved from ebony and upholstered in pale brocades fills the living room, dining room, office and TV room. *TV room? For the weather channel?*

The matching drapes are thick, the carpets plush. Flowers, both fake and fresh, and paintings of flowers adorn every room. Her house reminds me of the church sanctuary—or a funeral home.

At the foot of a spiral staircase, Sebastian points up the stairs. "R.J.'s master suite and four guest bedrooms plus baths are on the second floor." A large beige vase filled with pastel flowers sits on the landing halfway up.

"The third floor has four more bedrooms and baths," he says. "And downstairs…" He turns to the other side of the foyer, where a gated elevator sits beside a stairway entrance. "Vance's domain is in the garden-level basement, along with the laundry room, the family room, a movie room and a game room big enough to hold a billiard table and a pool table plus a snooker table."

Movie room? Game room? If Followers don't go to lounges, I bet they don't hang out in poolhalls. Unless their name is Vance Longpre.

He gives me a side glance. "Vance, as you may know, is R.J.'s son."

I nod.

"But you may not know he's also my nephew."

"So, you're Ruby Jade's—"

"I'm Vance's uncle on his dad's side. Quentin is my youngest brother, by several years, and R.J. is my *ex*-sister-in-law." He emphasizes "ex."

Why would anyone voluntarily work for the woman, especially a former in-law who must know full well what she's like?

"I can tell your wheels are spinnin'." He scratches at his mustache. "Long story. I have my reasons for working here, one being to keep an eye on Vance for Quentin. The kid is a pilotless ship headed for an iceberg."

Sebastian shakes his head. "Actually, Vance is way too old to be called a kid. Problem is, he's about as mature as a tadpole."

I get the impression he doesn't have much hope for his nephew.

"Best I can do," he says, "is play a game of pool with the knucklehead now and then and offer a little so-called fatherly advice."

He leads me through the kitchen, out a backdoor and across a wide patio to a good-sized shed with lots of windows. Inside, it's light and airy and holds whiffs of dirt and metal tools and something else, maybe compost. "I call this my hideout," he says. "R.J. doesn't come back here. Neither does Vance. They're both afraid of bugs and snakes."

I eye the shed's wood floor. *Snakes? Maybe Olivia was right.*

"I've never had a snake inside the shed," he adds. "But we occasionally run across bull snakes and garter snakes on the property. When I first came, I left a dead bull snake—big ol' bruiser—outside the door for almost three weeks, in case R.J. and Vance came snooping. I also mention sightings fairly regularly, to keep the pair out of my territory."

He chuckles. "Truth be told, the snakes are harmless." He taps a shelf. "You can drop that neon purse anywhere you can find a spot. Better yet, hide it under something. It ruins my hideout's masculine ambience."

"Masculine ambience? I didn't know such a thing existed." I laugh and place the purse on a low shelf beside a bag of grass seed. "Why do you tell me all this stuff? I mean, we just met. Everyone at FFOW is so secretive, but you're telling me, a stranger, that Vance is a problem and your ex-sister-in-law is a…"

I'm not sure what to say. Maybe he's trying to get me to say something negative he can report to Ruby Jade.

"Burr under the saddle?"

I shrug.

"I don't shoot straight with everyone, but as I said, your eyes are as open as the Montana sky."

"My eyes are open because I'm trying to gather enough information to make sense of the church. What I've seen so far confuses me."

"Keep those peepers open. Keep 'em wide open."

He lifts a straw hat from a hook and plops it on my head. "No sense getting heat stroke."

I tap my polyester pant leg. "Any chance I can wear jeans when I work here?"

"You have some? Last I knew, only Followers who work construction jobs—or who work for me—wear jeans."

"My mom sent me a box of clothes with several pairs of my old jeans in it. I'd wear the ones without holes."

"Fine with me, holes or no holes. And you'll probably want to ditch those long sleeves, unless you're trying to avoid a sunburn." He lifts a bottle of sunscreen from a bin that also contains bug repellant and medical supplies. "Feel free to use any of this anytime you need."

Jeans and a t-shirt. This job is getting better all the time. I look out the shed window. The backyard is beautiful—and big. I can't wait to get started on the flowerbeds. Maybe I'll think differently when I'm hot and tired, but right now, I'm excited.

Something's been niggling at the back of my brain since I arrived, and it finally hits me what it is. "I have a question."

My new boss nods. "Shoot."

"At church, I can only be around women, but here…"

"Yeah, won't be the first inconsistency you run across. And I won't be the only male you'll encounter on this property. I have orders to keep the genders separated, but it's not my priority. My priority is gettin' the work done."

He grabs an electric trimmer off a hook and separates it from the charger cord. "One more thing. See that door?" He points to a door in the corner. "It's the bathroom for the yard help, as R.J. calls us, when she forgets I'm her butler. She doesn't want us traipsing in her house with dirty shoes, although I go in and out all the time."

"Great." Knowing I won't have to step inside her house every time I need the restroom eases the tension in my shoulders.

He leads me to a hedgerow running from the side of the big house almost to the rear of the extensive property. "Know how to use one of these things?"

"My mom has a green thumb, which means I've trimmed grass, bushes, vines and trees. It also means I've planted gardens, deadheaded flowers, dug dandelion roots and pulled more weeds than I care to remember. When it comes to yardwork, there isn't much I haven't done."

"Good to know. Sounds as though you're well-experienced." He gives me a thumbs-up. "Trim the twigs you see sticking out from the hedge and keep to the basic shape. None of that blasted fancy stuff, no poodles and swans."

"You don't have to worry about shrub art with me. My husband was the artist in the family." I'm pleased I can mention Eric without crying.

"I read you lost your young man." His eyes are soft and sorrowful. "I'm sorry."

"Thank you."

He hands me the trimmer. "You'll run out of juice in about an hour and a half. When you do, carry this to the hideout, plug in the charger, and then go sit at the picnic table under those big trees over there." He indicates a cluster of tall maples at the back of the property. "Can't see the table due to all those trees and bushes, but it's there. I'll bring out lemonade and water, unless you prefer another drink."

"Sounds wonderful." I don't tell him I'd love a beer, or maybe a whiskey sour. "Lemonade is great, thanks. I should have brought water and a lunch, but I forgot. I was too worried about being late on the first day."

"I'll get you a water bottle. And don't worry about bringing a lunch when you work here. I always serve our workers lunch on the picnic table, weather permitting. During downpours, we eat on the patio, and when it's blustery, we eat in here."

"Very kind of you."

"Least I can do. Lunch is at high noon." He grins. "I promise it'll be better than the peanut butter and jelly sandwiches the Followers choke down every day."

"You have them pegged." I almost said, "you have *us* pegged," but I'm not ready to consider myself a Follower.

He looks at his watch. "The mowers will be here soon. Our riding mowers are loud, so don't be surprised when they pass by the hedge or one of the guys runs a weed whacker at the base."

"Thanks for the warning."

"Let me know if you have any trouble with Vance."

What is it about Vance that has everyone warning me about him? I get it he's a creep, but how much of a creep is he?

Sebastian takes off. I lay the trimmer on the grass, roll my sleeves and adjust the hat. The bushes are tall, about two-feet taller than I am, but the leaves are small, not yet fully developed. The trimming shouldn't be too difficult. I set to work.

My new boss returns with a water bottle and goggles. "Wear these to protect your eyes."

Already, I like the guy, the first down-to-earth person I've met since I came to FFOW. He reminds me of my grandpa. I ask if he has a ladder I can use to reach the top of the hedge.

"Don't worry about it," he says. "I'll catch the top later. And don't get too picky after five or ten feet in on the fence side. You're small enough to squeeze between the shrubs and the fence, but R.J. will never see beyond a few feet, if you catch my drift."

Amazed at his audacity, I laugh and shake my head. Even so, I keep waiting for a big fist to come out of the sky and clobber him over the head.

He grins and walks away.

I get right to work, humming a tune in my head, one I was composing in jail. This is the first chance I've had to focus on my songs since I left GCDC. A butterfly flutters above the hedge, and once again, I thank God for the wonderful change of circumstances. I like this job. If I stay off Ruby Jade's radar, maybe she won't transfer me. I should ask Sebastian about paperwork. Will the forms I filled out yesterday suffice for this position?

Hearing lawn mowers, I find a hole in the hedge and eye the intruders who ruined my peaceful morning. On the far side of the property, two mowers are starting across the vast expanse of lawn broken only by trees, bushes and flowerbeds. The mini-tractors, which are manned by men, as far as I can tell, separate and go opposite directions.

Like Sebastian, they wear cowboy hats. A riding mower might be fun, but I'm enjoying solitude and the fresh scent of morning air. I'm also having a good time finding words for the melody playing in my head. But will I be able to hear it with the noisy machines coming closer and closer?

Soon, the hay-like aroma of cut grass filters through the hedge. When one of the mowers comes near, I peek through branches. Corban Dahlstrom is not more than fifteen feet away. I yell, "Corban, Corban."

He's wearing ear protectors and can't hear me over the sound of the mower.

I shove my arm through the greenery and wave my hand.

His eyes grow wide, and the mower veers.

Uh-oh. I stop waving. I don't want to make him have an accident.

He kills the engine and gets off the machine, calling, "You need help?"

"Corban, it's me." I wiggle my fingers. "Cassie."

"It is?" He pushes the brim of his hat upward, his expression confused. "Are you stuck?"

"No, I'm trimming the hedge." I pull my hand out of the bush.

"I thought you worked at the school." He steps closer and peers through the branches.

I slide the goggles to the top of my head. "I interfered with a cleanse of a third-grader. I thought the little boys' classmates were beating on him, which is actually what they were doing. Anyway, that was yesterday, and today, voilà, I have a new job. Didn't have a chance to get bored at the last one."

"Sorry." He sighs. "That's how things go around here."

"What about you? Don't you work at Macy's?"

"I'm there afternoons and evenings. Logan and I usually mow in the mornings as part of our volunteer hours. Actually, we were conscripted, but it's still considered volunteer work."

"You're not paid to mow all this grass?"

He shrugs. "We've done it for years and have yet to receive a paycheck."

"If you don't get paid, does it mean I won't get paid?"

"Strong possibility."

I have a *strong* urge to swear, but I'll stew over working for free later. "I still need your help, Corban. But I can't meet you at the cemetery, the way we planned. Can we talk here?"

"Yes, during the break. The picnic table in the trees is private." He looks across at his brother, who's circling a tree with his mower. "I'd better get busy or we won't finish in time."

He slides onto the mower seat and winks a full *real* wink. "You scared the daylights out of me, Cassie True, but I'm glad to see you."

"I'm glad to see you, too, Corban Dahlstrom."

He drives slowly onward, and I return to clipping the hedge. What a morning. I awakened expecting to work at the school, but then I got the news of an overnight job change in a rather rude manner. And now? Now, I have sunshine, solitude and a non-FFOW boss. Plus, wonders of wonders, when I thought I might never have another chance to talk with Corban, I discover he and his brother are yard help, like me. Amazing. *Thank you, Jesus.*

If the three of us put our heads together, I'm convinced we can figure out a way to reunite Marcela with her husband and family. And Candice and Scott with their daughter. And Zachary with his parents. Maybe we can help a whole bunch of people escape Ruby Jade's tentacles.

But we have to hurry. When the judge learns Transformation Way is no longer operating, he'll send me elsewhere, no matter how close he is to Ruby Jade. He's a judge, after all. And the sooner I complete a rehab program, the sooner I can get on with my life.

Last night, I was furious with Olivia for denying me my vanilla concoction. But today, I'm grateful I didn't have the first sip, which could have led me into active addiction again. Just because I haven't had a drink since my last arrest doesn't mean I'm no longer an addict.

I plug in the trimmer and walk across the grass to the picnic table hidden by bushes and surrounded by big shade trees. Corban and Logan are already seated, wiping their foreheads with red bandanas. They greet me and stuff the bandanas into the back pockets of their worn blue jeans.

I set my hat and goggles on the table. "Jeans?"

Logan shrugs. "Work."

"But only," Corban adds, "because years ago our mom told Ruby Jade she was tired of us ruining good pants. If she wanted us to keep doing volunteer work, she had to let us wear jeans. It was the only time I remember her standing up to Ruby Jade, but it worked."

230 | REBECCA CAREY LYLES

'Good for your mom." I ease onto the bench seat across from them. They smell sweaty, but so do I. "I'm definitely wearing jeans tomorrow, maybe cutoffs."

Corban and Logan eye each other.

"I wouldn't go *that* far," Corban says. "Ruby Jade or Vance might look out a window."

I cringe. Spending a summer outside in long pants, wondering if those two obnoxious people are spying on me, is not my idea of fun. But I can't let my mind go there. More important issues are at stake. "I have a question for you guys before Sebastian gets here."

"Shoot," Logan says. "If I can't answer it, Corb here can."

Corban elbows his brother. "Maybe, maybe not."

"Why do you stay at FFOW?"

They respond in unison. "To keep from going to hell."

"Okay…" I lift my chin. "Now, the real reason."

The brothers share a glance. Logan nods, and Corban says, "Because our mother suffered a spinal cord injury in an accident and lost the use of her legs."

"How awful. I'm so sorry." I lean forward on the table. "Must have been a huge life-changer for her—for all of you."

"Yes." Corban picks at a loose sliver on the tabletop. "It's been tough for Mom, although you'd never know it because she doesn't complain. Insurance paid for a wheelchair and other necessities, but it didn't pay to renovate our house, so she could get around in it. Thank God, Dad has had construction experience. We helped him build ramps and modify thresholds. We also lowered the bathroom and kitchen cabinets and counters and made the office and laundry room accessible."

"And built raised garden beds," Logan says. "Mom has always had big vegetable and flower gardens. We poured cement paths from the patio ramp to the garden boxes and all around, so her wheelchair can't get stuck in the dirt."

"Was Ruby Jade mean to your mom, like she was to the elderly man on Sunday?" I shudder. "She was so cruel to him. Oh, sorry…" I jerk back. I shouldn't be sharing my opinion with these guys I barely know. "I spoke out of turn. Maybe you thought he deserved—"

They shake their heads, and a fierce expression flashes across Corban's face. "Ruby Jade came to the house and did a similar healing routine over Mom..." "When our severely injured mother didn't jump out of bed and run around the room, Ruby Jade yelled at her and told her she wasn't submitting to the will of God. Called her a weakling and said she was going to hell."

"I thought Ruby Jade would never quit screaming." Logan makes a face. "Afterward, we all had headaches."

"No surprise." Her amplified screams from the pulpit are bad enough. I can only imagine how overwhelming the sound would be in a small room.

"She assumes anyone who depends on a walker or a wheelchair is useless," Corban says. "Which is okay with Mom. Now that she's not expected to do volunteer work twenty-four seven, she can concentrate on helping those who are truly in need."

"Did Ruby Jade kick your mother out of the church?" A breeze rustles through the trees. I lift my hair to let the draft cool my neck.

"No, she didn't." He grunts. "Maybe she hopes to save her soul someday."

Logan snorts. "Might have something to do with the fact she'd lose the tithes of four people. Mom has the same job she had before the accident, but she works part-time from home now—and gives enough to the church to make Ruby Jade believe she's still tithing."

"Pastors with integrity have no idea who contributes how much. She is so, so wrong." I pound the table. "And poor Arnold. I s'pose he's on Social Security and couldn't donate enough money to please her. I felt awful for him on Sunday. He was a sad and broken man."

"Don't worry about Arnold, Cassie." Corban winks. "We're taking good care of him. Since the night Ruby Jade was so cruel to Mom..." He pauses, glances at his brother and then says, "Let's just say our family focus changed course."

"You guys are the best." I hope they can't see the blush I feel creeping onto my cheeks. Something about a Corban wink across a narrow table makes my stomach flipflop.

"But, why do you stay at the church? Why do your parents stay? According to Ruby Jade, whether you stay or leave, your mom is headed for hell." I raise my hands. "Which, by the way, I don't believe for a minute. Her salvation has nothing to do with membership in any church."

Corban looks beyond me. "Here comes Sebastian with the lemonade." He lifts his hat and runs his hand through his hair. "Part of the reason we stay is because Ruby Jade funded the renovation."

"What?" I can't believe my ears. "She raked your mom over the coals for not walking on paralyzed legs and then paid to make your house wheelchair accessible?"

"That's Ruby Jade for you." Logan scowls. "Nasty one minute and fake nice the next."

"Yeah," Corban nods. "Believe me, she didn't offer the money out of the goodness of her heart. She *loaned* our parents the money and now has a lien against their home. If they leave the church, she can call in the loan, in which case, they'd probably lose the house.

"Dad has kicked himself a thousand times for not getting a second mortgage. But Ruby Jade made it so quick and simple at a time when he was desperate to do all he could to make Mom's life easier."

I smile, grateful to be reminded some people at FFOW actually care for each other. "He must love her a lot."

"He does." Corban smiles.

"What if they got a second mortgage now?"

"The lien could be a problem," Logan says. "Plus, the wording of the agreement suggests they have to stay in the church and pay Ruby Jade a certain amount each month. Early loan payoff would result in a *substantial* penalty, a ridiculous amount. But Dad recently hired a lawyer to review the contract. He wants to know if it's legal. If it is, does it have a loophole he can use?"

Sebastian is getting closer, and I want to ask the brothers if he's a safe person. But I also want to know the whole story. Why do such nice guys stay in the group when they could easily walk away?

"The other factor is due to the fact our parents were with the original church," Corban continues, "when it was normal. Before Ruby Jade took the reins. They were not only founding members, but very active. Served in several capacities. If they leave, they'll lose lifelong friends, as well as their home."

"Corb and I would lose all our friends, too," Logan says. "We grew up at FFOW and have no friends outside the church because Leadership forbids it. As you've seen, it's exclusive. But we could handle the loss better than our parents, I think. Mom and Dad's only outside contacts all these years, have been coworkers and others they interact with for business purposes.

"However, situations like those with Mom and Arnold—and others—have convinced them we need to go. They're biding their time, hoping to take lots of friends with them when that day comes."

"About the house..." Corban leans his elbows on the table. "For most people, being forced to leave a home is hard, but ours is now specifically customized for Mom, which makes moving even more difficult. We're checking options—new-builds or prebuilt handicap-accessible homes, but it's not easy. Ruby Jade owns half of Bozeman, you know."

CHAPTER TWENTY-ONE

I tilt my head. "No, I didn't know."

"Didn't know what?" Sebastian is holding a tray with a tall pitcher of lemonade on it plus four glasses and a plate of pastries. He sets the tray on the table. Ice cubes clink in the pitcher.

"Your sister-in-law owns half the town," Logan says.

"*Ex* sister-in-law." Sebastian sits beside me. "R.J. may think she owns Bozeman, but I have it on good authority she owns less than a fifth of it." He turns to me. "Care for a glass of lemonade?"

"I'd love some." Deep down, I'm disappointed it won't be the huckleberry vodka lemonade of long ago. It would taste really, really good right now. On the other hand, I'm grateful Sebastian's concoction won't spin my life out of control.

He pours my drink and sets it in front of me. "I hope you're not allergic to nuts, Cat True."

Corban grins. "No matter what Ruby Jade says, Cat fits you better than Cassandra."

I smile, feeling more like myself than I have in days. I love seeing this anti-FFOW side of him.

"As I was saying..." Sebastian scowls at Corban, his eyes twinkling. "These here energy bars are sugar-free, gluten-free, protein-rich and nut-full, not nut-free."

"No." I shake my head. "I don't have a nut allergy." I sip the lemonade and then raise the glass high. "This is heavenly, Sebastian. Is it fresh-squeezed?"

"Sure thing."

"Your energy bars are the best." Logan takes two. "And so is your lemonade. But you don't have to do this for us every time we come."

"Can't have my help collapsing on me." Sebastian pours lemonade for the others. "Might have to do the work myself."

The only sounds are the birds singing above us, a dog barking in the distance, and a small airplane headed for the Bozeman airport. I haven't been this at ease since before I left jail. Hard to believe I was more relaxed there than I am in a church setting. "This place is so peaceful, Sebastian, and your food is so good. I could sit here in the shade all day."

He gives me a side glance. "I don't s'pose Olivia allows you a moment's rest."

"She'd probably lose her household-guardian status if she did."

"Glad I can provide a short break." He checks his watch. "We'll have a longer sit-down for lunch."

"Just being away from the Pritchards' house is a treat. And then you feed us a wonderful snack, like we're royalty."

"Isn't that what the Bible says?" He plunks his glass down with a decisive clunk. Ice cubes crash against the sides. "We're children of the King of kings."

I sigh. "I tend to forget."

"Forgetting who we are is easy to do at FFOW." Corban reaches for another energy bar. "Ruby Jade, Inez and Noreen are the only royals there."

Logan says, "I bet our tithes pay for your good cooking, Seb, as well as their fancy clothes."

SHATTERED DREAM | 237

"Don't know and don't care to know." Sebastian's jaw muscles twitch. "I make it a point to stay a couple mountains and three or four gullies away from my boss's money dealings."

I've reached the end of the long hedge and started around the front when Sebastian comes across the yard carrying a tray loaded with chips and sandwiches. By then, I'm happy to take another break—and anxious to talk with the brothers about Marcela and Rodrigo. But I'm not sure I should I mention them with Ruby Jade's manager present.

Logan and Corban drive to the picnic table, cut the motors and climb off the lawnmowers. Gas fumes mingle with the smell of newly mown grass.

Corban rubs his lower back. "I'm gonna be dreaming about grass in my sleep."

"You can say that again." Logan places a foot on a bench seat and stretches his legs.

Sebastian sets the tray on the table. "I'll go get the drinks."

"Can we help?" Corban asks.

"Nope. Take a seat and relax." He heads for the house.

Already, the shade feels wonderful. I hang my goggles and hat on a low tree branch and run my hands through my hair. "You two seem comfortable with Sebastian. Can he be trusted with, uh, sensitive subjects?"

"Yes and no." Logan grabs a sandwich.

I fold my arms and lean against the tree trunk, waiting for more.

"Sebastian keeps his distance from anything that might suggest he has power or influence in FFOW." Logan swings a leg over the bench seat to sit at the table. "Dad thinks Seb is biding his time and won't be around any longer than he has to be here."

"But why does he *have* to be here?"

"From what our parents tell us," Corban says, "Sebastian was a rabble-rouser back in the day. Even after Ruby Jade split with his brother, Vance's dad, she kept bailing Sebastian out of jail.

Eventually, he landed in prison, which is where he found God—in prison, not at FFOW. And God radically changed him. When he got out, she hired him to be her manager, or butler, as she calls him."

"Funniest-looking butler I ever saw," Logan says.

"How many have you seen?" Corban sits beside him.

Logan raises his chin. "Enough."

"If you're like me," I say, "the only butlers you've seen were on TV or in movies."

"Not that we've ever watched television or movies." Logan grins.

"Of course not." I turn to Corban. "So, why does Sebastian stay?"

"Could be his past keeps him from getting another job. Or, could be he owes Ruby Jade for all the bail money she put out for him."

"With interest, I bet." Logan talks around the food in his mouth. "You forgot the other possibility. He has something on Ruby Jade she wants to keep under wraps, and they made some kind of deal."

"Interesting." Brushing a leaf off my shoulder, I leave the tree trunk and sit across from them.

"What's the sensitive subject?" Corban takes a sandwich half from the stack.

"Marcela. I already told you I want to help her reunite with Rodrigo and her family. What Ruby Jade did to her on Sunday—to all of them—was wrong, unspeakably wrong."

"I agree. She was mean and nasty, treated innocent, vulnerable people like trash." He brandishes the sandwich. "Logan and I have been bouncing around ideas, but so far we've drawn a blank. Have you thought of anything?"

"You two have a better understanding of the church and the town than I do. All I know is Rodrigo works at a French restaurant where lots of the employees are FFOW members, and Marcela works at a church-owned factory, where everyone belongs to the church. Private times or personal phone calls, I assume, are impossible."

"The way Leadership likes it." Corban bites into the sandwich.

"But I did learn one positive piece of information from Marcela. I believe it has possibilities."

In tandem, they raise their eyebrows and lower their sandwiches.

"As I understand the setup, because she's the receptionist at the plastic factory, her office is separate from the manufacturing plant and the other employees. Her boss's office is evidently near hers, but he leaves every day around ten-thirty to make a bank deposit and go to lunch."

"Of course." Logan snaps his fingers. "I should have remembered."

"You guys amaze me." I reach for a sandwich. "You know everything."

"The only reason I have any inkling about the plastic factory is because I used to work there, until Ruby Jade decided I needed a change, for whatever weird logic."

"What do you do now?"

"I'm a delivery driver."

"Like me, he delivers the goods." Sebastian plops a jar of iced tea and a pitcher of water on the redwood table.

"Speaking of 'good,' these sandwiches are wonderful, Sebastian." I give him a thumbs-up. "Delicious."

"Careful with your sign language," Logan says.

"What?"

"Followers only use their pointer fingers to indicate heaven. Anything else is considered *profane*." He grins. "Don't worry about us but be careful around the others."

"I had no idea."

"You've only just begun, Cat True." Sebastian says. "You've only just begun. Iced tea or water?"

"Tea, thank you."

He pours me a tall glass.

"Thank you. I have a question for you, if you don't mind."

"Shoot." Sebastian waggles his mustache.

"This is serious," I say, but I giggle anyway. "When Olivia told me this morning I was no longer employed at the school and would be working here instead, I was thrilled. But I didn't get paid at the school, at least not yet, and I'm wondering if I'll get paid here."

"Hard to say." He slides onto the bench seat. "I may be your boss, but I have nothing to do with paychecks. From previous workers, I got the impression pay depends on whether R.J. considers this a volunteer opportunity, a punishment or a job."

"Olivia also said I can't sing in the spring concert, so I probably fall into the punishment category."

By the smirks playing at the corners of the brothers' mouths, I get the idea the spring concert is no big deal.

"I didn't know I was supposed to sing," I tell them, "and I hadn't been informed of any music practices."

"Inez should have contacted you about singing with the single women's class," Corban says. "Each class performs a song."

"Like the winter concert?"

"Yes."

"I saw the video." I look from Corban to Logan. "What's so special about the concerts?"

"Nothing." Logan chuckles. "Except Ruby Jade has a chance to be centerstage in front of townspeople as well as church members. Apparently, she hasn't noticed fewer and fewer outsiders come each time. The locals have figured out if you've seen one boring FFOW production, you've seen them all."

"Will you two be playing in the band?"

"Band?" Corban's eyes are huge and his mouth twists.

"Did I say something wrong?"

Logan laughs. "*Never* say *band* at church. It suggests rock bands and all the other 'devil music' Ruby Jade abhors."

"What do you call your music group? An orchestra?"

"Yes, or an ensemble. And to answer your question, we play for several of the classes, but not all of them. Some sing acapella, and some only use piano accompaniment."

"Ruby Jade told me I might be able to lead a music group. I was a music major before I dropped out of the university."

"I heard you playing the piano in the music room," Corban say. "You know your way around a keyboard."

"Thanks." I trace a pattern through the condensation on my iced tea glass. "I was hoping to ask you two to help me pull together a band—an ensemble—to accompany the group. But I'm not sure what she's thinking now, after I interfered with a cleanse."

"Hang loose," Sebastian says. "Whatever she thought this morning could have already changed. She's fickler than the Montana weather."

"I was also hoping to play my guitar, but Marcela says—"

Corban, who was about to take a drink, thumps his glass on the table. "You have a guitar?"

"Yes, but—"

"Where is it?"

"Under my bed. Marcela said—"

He elbows his brother. "We gotta get it out of there."

"Why?" I ask, confused by the urgency in his voice.

"If the Fearsome Threesome find it—"

"Hey," I exclaim, "that's what I call them, too."

Both Corban and Logan high-five me, and then Corban says, "If they find your guitar, they'll take it away."

"But it's mine." I pound the table with my fist.

"Ruby Jade hates guitars," Logan says, "almost as much as she hates Nike shoes."

"Because..." Sebastian interjects, "My brother plays the guitar *and* wears Nikes." He snorts. "To get her goat, Quentin wore brand-new Nikes to both of Vance's weddings."

"Did it work?"

"Oh, yeah. You could almost see the steam rising from R.J.'s tiara." He laughs. "At least those weddings weren't as dull as most Follower weddings."

"Back to my guitar. No matter what she thinks, it's mine, whether she approves or not."

"We'll get it out of there and put it in a safe place." Corban eyes his brother. "Right, Logan?"

Logan straightens, excitement and determination written all over his face. "I like search-and-rescue missions the best."

"Thank you." I smile. "I appreciate your help. You guys know the ins and outs of this place better than I do." Whether or not they can sneak past the powers-that-be, I appreciate their willingness to help me.

"On another subject..." I point to a small house nestled between evergreens near the rear of the property. "The yellow house behind those trees. Does someone live there?"

"Yep." Sebastian nods. "R.J.'s mom."

"Oh..." Funny how I'd thought of Ruby Jade as an atypical being without parents or siblings. For all I know, she could be an alien who dropped out of the sky complete with tiara and satin finery.

"She's a great lady," Corban says, "a good friend to our whole family."

I turn to Sebastian. "I'm amazed Ruby Jade doesn't have her mom with her in the main house. It's big enough."

His lips twitch. "I get the impression they live separate by mutual agreement."

"I see." Already, I like Ruby Jade's mother.

Corban and Logan leave after lunch, promising to brainstorm ways to rescue Marcela and relocate my guitar, and I'm left to myself for the afternoon. I wouldn't want to trim bushes every day, but repetitive work lets my mind sift through the songs I wrote in jail and some of those I wrote earlier.

I wish with all my heart I could play my guitar, but the important thing right now is to keep it safe. Somehow, we've got to move it from the Pritchards' house to…I have no idea where. Maybe I'll ask Kip to store it for me, although I don't know how I'd get it to him. Too bad Mom went to all the effort and expense to mail it to me.

Corban said he and Logan mow two to three times a week because Ruby Jade prefers a manicured look. I have an internal debate as to what day this is and finally decide it's Wednesday. How is it I've only been here one week? Seems like forever.

I don't know when the guys will mow again—maybe Friday, but when I see them next, I hope they'll have ideas for Marcela. Should I tell her they're working on a plan to help her and her family? Or surprise her when the plan comes together?

I snip a clump of leaves. She's had so many disappointments. I should probably wait.

I'm halfway along the front of the hedge when Ruby Jade's dogs come running. I switch off the trimmer, lay it on the grass and kneel. The bouncing white furballs lick my hands, but as quickly as they came, they race for the rear of the property. I run after them, chasing them all the way to the yellow house I noticed earlier.

I hear yipping and dash around a carport with an older-model blue Chrysler parked beneath it. The dogs are seated on the back stoop, tails wagging.

The screen door opens, and a woman's voice calls from the shadowed interior, "Come in, boys."

The dogs charge into the house.

The door closes.

Taken aback, I stand there for a moment, trying to decide what to do. Finally, I knock on the door.

"Yes?"

The way the sun is shining, I can't see through the screen. "Hi, my name is Cassie. I've been trimming the hedges, and Sebastian told me—"

"I told Cat…" Sebastian is coming around the carport. "If the dogs got loose, she should catch them. But I didn't tell her they'd head straight for their favorite lady who spoils them rotten."

He has blue leashes in one hand and daffodils in the other. "I'll give you two a proper introduction inside."

"Come in," the woman says, "come in."

She opens the door and I step into a small kitchen, followed by Sebastian. The dogs hop around us as if we're their long-lost friends.

"Myrtle Mae Fleming," Sebastian says, "Please meet our newest Follower volunteer, Cat True."

Myrtle May extends her hand, and I take it. Ruby Jade gets her height and violet eyes from her mother but not her width. The petite woman is wearing a blue blouse and a knee-length navy skirt, the shortest skirt I've seen at FFOW. Funny it's on an older woman, not a teenager.

Similar to Ruby Jade, her long, straight hair is streaked, but it's silver-gray with white highlights rather than black with silver-gray highlights. Tiny wrinkles radiate like sunbursts at her temples and emphasize her beautiful eyes. Her smooth alabaster skin is flawless.

"You can call me Cassie," I tell her, "or Cat—or Cassandra, the name Ruby Jade gave me."

"Don't let her confuse you, sweetie." She wraps both hands around mine. "You are who you are, not who she tries to make you to be. Changing names is one of the many ways my daughter attempts to separate people from their true selves and make them feel inferior."

"Thank you. I appreciate your advice." I'm stunned. While hundreds of Followers practically worship Ruby Jade, her mother criticizes the way she belittles others.

She squeezes my hands before releasing them. "Eleanor Roosevelt once said, 'No one can make you feel inferior without your consent.' Those are words worth pondering."

"I'll keep them in mind, for sure."

"Sorry I didn't warn you about the dogs," Sebastian says. "Every morning and afternoon, we make a trek over here to say hello to Myrtle Mae and grab some treats. Huh, guys?"

Both sets of ears perk.

I laugh at their response. "Smart dogs."

She opens the refrigerator and pulls out a plastic container. "Don't tell Ruby Jade, but Fenwick and Francis love cooked kidney beans. I feed them each three beans every time they visit." She smiles at the dogs. "Don't I, boys?"

Their tales wag in unison.

"Sit."

The dogs stop wiggling and sit.

"Up Fenwick, up Francis."

Once they're balanced on their hind legs, she drops three beans into each of their mouths.

Sebastian shakes his head. "S'pose they'd do that for me? Ha." He takes a vase from the cupboard above the refrigerator, fills it with water and adds the flowers.

The dogs swallow the beans and go straight to the door.

"Not so fast." Sebastian sets the flowers on the table and kneels on one knee to attach the leashes to the dogs' collars. "Now that they've had their treats, they'll run wild, sticking their noses into God only knows what. Then I'll have to bathe them again because R.J. wants them spic-and-span at all times. But they're dogs, blasted dogs. Thank God she gets them trimmed, or they'd be a hairy nightmare."

I laugh. "Sounds as though they keep you busy."

"Yeah, and I'd better go make busy."

"Me, too." I start to follow him out the door, but he says, "Stay and get acquainted with Myrtle Mae. She makes a mean cup of tea."

"Oh, but…" *But I'm volunteering my time. I should be able to visit with a sweet little lady for a few minutes.* I turn to her. "If you're busy…"

"Not at all." She goes to the door with Sebastian. "Thank you for the flowers."

He winks. "R.J. will never miss 'em." The dogs pull the leashes taut, and off they go.

Myrtle Mae lifts a teakettle from the stove. "Dear Sebastian knows how lonely I get. I'm delighted to have someone to visit with for a few minutes."

"Does your daughter come back here to see you?"

"Not often, which is okay by me."

"Why do you stay? You have a car." I backtrack. "I mean, I saw one in the carport..."

"Here in my little house where I know my way around, you may not notice I have a visual impairment. However, the macular degeneration has reached the point where I can no longer drive."

"I'm sorry."

"Ruby Jade was supposed to move me to an assisted living facility, but I guess she didn't want the cost to come out of her inheritance." She holds the kettle under the faucet and turns on the water. "I had hot water simmering in this, but I'll add a bit more to be sure we have enough. If I'd known my daughter was going to bring me here, I'd have kept my cat, instead of giving her to the nice family next door.

"Bramble was a sweet kitty..." She looks wistful. "He would have kept me company. I don't have a telephone. Or a television. My daughter says TVs are the devil's tools, but I happen to know she has one in her bedroom. My brother says he sees the blue light flashing when he sneaks over at night."

Her brother has to sneak to visit her? "What's your brother's name?"

"Norman." She stops the water and carries the teakettle to the stove. "Ruby Jade hates him, even though he's her uncle. Norman tells it like it is and won't join her church."

CHAPTER TWENTY-TWO

"Can't Sebastian and Norman move you where you want to live?" I ask. "I'd help."

"Very sweet of you to offer, dear." Myrtle Mae motions to a small table beside a window on the other side of the room. "Please have a seat. So rude of me to keep you on your feet after you've been working."

"No problem. I sat while we ate lunch." I pull out a chair. Like the table, it's made of wood and painted white. A gentle wind ruffles the turquoise-and-white gingham curtains, bringing whiffs of grass and spring flowers. I'm reminded of my grandma and her cozy country kitchen.

"You can pick a teabag from the basket on the table." Myrtle Mae smiles. "Or you can sample my special concoction. It has lots of cinnamon in it."

"Sounds really good. I love cinnamon."

"I believe you'll like it." She places a trivet on the table. "Now, where was I?"

"We were talking about how Ruby Jade moved you here instead of the assisted living facility."

248 | REBECCA CAREY LYLES

"The facility is lovely, but I wasn't excited to join the old folks and eat institutional food when I can cook and care for myself. Truth be told, I enjoy it here. Beautiful surroundings with birds singing in the treetops. A rooster crows in some neighbors' yard every morning, and an owl hoots from the big ponderosa every night." She indicates a tall pine outside the window above the sink.

A soft cross-breeze wafts between the kitchen windows. "It's a charming little cottage." I peer into the living room. "You've decorated it so cute." Unlike the Pritchards' sterile house and Ruby Jade's showy mansion, Myrtle Mae's home is intimate yet welcoming, with beautiful landscapes on the walls and cute knickknacks on the doily-covered end tables.

"Thank you." She pours water from the teakettle into a flower-covered china teapot and sets it on the trivet. "I would have had more people to talk with in the retirement center. My friends who still drive are leery of my daughter, so they don't come around any more. Even friends from the church hesitate to visit. But like I said, my brother keeps an eye on me and so does Sebastian."

"Does Vance visit you?"

"My grandson, my *only* grandchild, look in on me? Ha." A wry smile creases one cheek. "He's as obnoxious and self-centered as his mother, maybe worse. Greed has done in the both of them."

Her bemused expression suggests she doesn't understand either her daughter or her grandson. "From the day she was born, Ruby Jade had her father, Kenneth, wrapped around her little finger. Whatever she asked for, he gave it to her. I tried to talk sense into his head, but she was his 'precious princess,' as he liked to call her, and could be denied nothing. Now, it appears she's raised her son to follow in her self-indulgent footsteps."

Interesting how no one, not even his grandmother, has anything good to say about Vance.

She places matching teacups on dainty saucers and brings them to the table. From the basket, she selects two cheesecloth balls tied with string. "This is my special pick-me-up tea for the middle of the day. You can add honey and cream, if you want."

After filling our cups, she steps over to the counter. "I always keep a few goodies on hand, in case someone stops by." She lifts the lid from a ceramic cookie jar. "Care for a peanut butter cookie?"

"Sounds good, but I hate for you to go to any more trouble for—"

"This is no trouble, no trouble at all."

"You and Sebastian are going to make me fat. Ruby Jade will get suspicious and figure out I spend more time eating than working in her backyard."

"I know how hard you Followers work. You deserve to sit down and enjoy life once in a while." She arranges several cookies on a small plate and sets it in front of me. Then she fills a cream pitcher and brings it to the table, along with a honey jar shaped like a beehive.

"When you say 'you Followers,' I get the impression you don't attend the church." A wonderful spicy aroma rises from the tea. I inhale deeply. "Mmm, wonderful."

"Actually, I do attend, when my daughter remembers to send someone to drive me to services." She sits across from me. "I don't agree with the nonsense that goes on, but I do enjoy visiting with the folks there."

"Are you in the single women's Sunday school class?"

"Yes." She peers at me, her head at an angle. "I do believe you're the young woman Inez tried to humiliate last Sunday."

"She didn't just try. She skewered me good."

"Pay no mind to the bully." Myrtle Mae flips her hand, as if swatting away a fly. "Inez is a heartless twit who tears others down to make herself look better, or so she thinks." She pushes the cookies closer to me. "Please, help yourself."

I take a cookie.

"Remember," Myrtle Mae says, "God sees hearts, not eye shadow and lipstick. She's jealous because you're young and beautiful, and she's far from either."

"Thank you." I fan my cheeks. "You make me blush."

"It's true, dear, all true."

"You had your hair up on Sunday." I study her. "And you were sitting near the window with several other, uh, older women."

"Ruby Jade doesn't approve of my long straight hair." Myrtle Mae slips a gray lock behind her ear. "She says I'm trying to look like a teenager, but I've always worn it this way. I only put it in a French roll on Sundays, so Inez doesn't waste class time ranting about how childish I am."

She touches my arm. "I'm sorry you were the subject of her wrath last week. She's always hunting for someone to castigate."

"I've been lectured by judges, but they never spewed venom the way Inez and Noreen do."

Myrtle Mae raises a well-defined eyebrow, which is darker than her hair. "Judges?"

"I just got out of jail. Noreen drove me here."

"I see. You'll have to tell me all about it one of these days." She seems interested in a good rather than gossipy way. "But for now, I want to say I regret my daughter is a role model and mentor for Inez and Noreen. They were both decent young women when they first came to the church."

Inez and Noreen decent young women? I find her words hard to believe, but I don't argue.

Myrtle Mae looks so sad, I change the subject. "I should have realized the similarity between you and your daughter last Sunday. You're both very beautiful."

"Thank you, dear." Her lavender eyes are bright and clear. "Kenneth was a handsome man, and she was our only child. Like I said, he spoiled her rotten. He didn't just buy her a car when she got her driver's license, he bought her a *new* car. Not only that, it was a sportscar. Attracted boys like flies to honey."

I'm not surprised by the revelation. However, being spoiled by her father can't be the whole reason for Ruby Jade's craziness. Her sex hang-up suggests to me she might have a background similar to several women I met in jail who'd been molested. But who knows? The catalyst could have been something totally unrelated.

I ask the question I've had since the night I joined FFOW. What better person to give me the facts than Ruby Jade's mother? "I've been told Ruby Jade Paradise is not her real name. Is it an assumed name?"

"Good grief. The silly name she uses now sticks in my craw every time I say it." Myrtle Mae wrinkles her nose. "Kenneth and I named her after her grandmothers, Marilyn and June. She was and is Marilyn June Fleming—or Longpre, which is Vance's last name, in case you haven't heard. Kenneth started calling her Marilee when she was in junior high, and the nickname stuck. But she said she didn't like any of those names. Said they were for weak girls, not her."

She raises her gaze to the ceiling, a slight smile on her flawless face. "When Marilyn was three, the neighbor girl gave her a hand-me-down Superwoman outfit. She loved it and looked so adorable in it—wore it constantly, sure she was the real thing. We thought her delusion was cute."

With a sigh, she adds, "Until she didn't grow out of it—the delusion, that is. Except now, she not only thinks she's Superwoman, she thinks she's God's mouthpiece." She shakes her head. "About her name, she went by Marilee until she got the jewel bug. Came from her love for jewelry, I suppose. Actually had her name legally changed.

"My daughter..." Myrtle Mae stands again and walks to the cupboard. "Is impossible. Always has been. I love her, but..." She opens a drawer and pulls out two spoons. "Got to yacking and forgot to remove the teas." She hands me a spoon.

I use it to lift my handcrafted, cheesecloth-wrapped tea blend from the cup and slip it onto the saucer. "This smells wonderful."

"Thank you."

"If you can't drive, how do you shop and go to doctor appointments?"

"Norman lives not far from here. If he's unavailable, Sebastian graciously drives me wherever I need to go."

"That's good."

252 | Rebecca Carey Lyles

"I appreciate the opportunity to buy groceries, so I don't have to eat those tasteless low-calorie microwave dinners my daughter crams in my freezer. She's convinced I'm too blind to cook real food. I've shown her otherwise, but once she gets an idea in her head..."

I sip my tea. "Delicious blend, Myrtle Mae. Doesn't even need sweetener."

"I'm glad you like it."

"I'd be happy to drive you wherever you need to go." I put the cup down. "I don't have a car, but I do have a driver's license."

Her eyes darken to purple. "Very kind of you, dear, but..." She reaches across the table to clutch my forearm. "You need to get away from this place—far, far away."

I am nearing where I started on the hedge, when I see Sebastian coming my direction. I straighten and turn off the trimmer.

He pulls a blue bandana from his back pocket. Wiping his neck, he says, "Quittin' time, Cat True."

"I only have a few feet to go. I hate to quit now."

"Okay, you can finish up. But you'll be feeling it tomorrow. Don't forget to plug in the trimmer when you're done and, for sure, don't forget that pink purse of yours. It severely diminishes the manliness of my shop."

I roll my eyes. "Traumatic for you, no doubt."

A grin tugs at the side of his mouth. He scans the long hedge row. "Nice job. I'm heading out now. Catch you in the morning."

He's gone before I remember I wanted to ask him about getting a phone for Myrtle Mae, one that accommodates her limited vision and isn't tied into the FFOW network. And maybe one of us could drive her to the animal shelter. A cat would keep her company when no one else is around.

I check my watch. Five o'clock. I'm now working longer hours than I did at the school, which I don't mind. But I hope they shorten my hours when the program gets going.

Finished with the hedge, I return to the shed, take off the hat and plug in the trimmer. I chuckle when I grab my purse, remembering Sebastian's comment about diminishing the manliness of his shed. Funny guy. So far, he seems like a great boss.

I walk around the garage. With any luck, I won't run into Ruby Jade or Vance. At the front corner, I lean out and look around. Neither person is in sight.

Hurrying along the brick walkway toward the street, I pull out my phone. Twenty-three text messages, twenty-two of them from Ruby Jade. I skim through her directives. Most of them are instructions for those participating in the spring program. I'm grateful I'm not included.

A solitary FFOW-Wow informs us God's favorite flower is a rose because the rose of Sharon is revered in the Bible. That's news to me. My mother, who knows her flowers, would question the "insight" for another reason. She once told me biblical experts say the rose of Sharon could be a lily, a jonquil, a crocus or a tulip. Maybe even a hibiscus. Apparently, the queen bee isn't required to substantiate her supposed words from God.

The other message is from my mom, asking about the rehab program. I push the icon to return her call. She answers, and I smile, happy to hear her voice. "Hi, Mom. It's me."

"Cassie, sweetheart. Are you free to talk longer this time?"

"I have twenty or thirty minutes before I arrive at the house, where I'll probably need to help with supper." Or whatever chore Olivia has in mind. I didn't bother to read the refrigerator list this morning because she's always quick to inform me of my duties.

"Are you driving?"

"No, I'm walking. My work is close enough to the house I can walk." And if I take my time, I can stretch our conversation to a half hour.

"That's wonderful, especially when you're without a vehicle."

A tall black van with dark windows drives slowly past and parks in front of a house across the road. I can't see the driver clearly, which gives me the willies. I continue walking. A mere handful of

254 | Rebecca Carey Lyles

days at FFOW, and I don't trust anyone. No one is above suspicion, especially in Fellowship Neighborhood. But the van seems harmless.

I ask Mom, "What mischief have you and Dad been into lately?"

"You won't believe it. We're redoing the living room."

"Didn't you redo it a couple years ago?"

"Well, yes, but I found this gorgeous couch I adore and—"

"And your present décor doesn't quite work with it."

"You know me too well." Mom laughs. "You should see this couch."

She's describing it to me—and the matching chair, when Vance rolls by in a silver sportscar. I pretend not to notice him, but then the car brakes to a squealing stop and reverses. He lowers the passenger window, bends my direction and looks me up and down. "Well, hel-lo, Cas-*san*-dra."

I put my hand over my ear like I'm in the middle of an important conversation, which I am. I haven't had a good talk with my mom in forever. I'd love to tell him to get lost, but that probably wouldn't be my smartest move.

He calls my name.

I ignore him and keep walking. Finally, he hits the gas and his car shoots up the street.

"How do you like Transformation Way so far, Cassie?" Mom asks.

"It's, well…it's different." Lying was not one of my vices before I came to FFOW, other than deluding myself about my dependency and trying to convince cops I was sober. Each time I was caught stealing, however, I always came clean.

But now, I'm even lying to my mother. "I got to be outside a lot today. Perfect spring day. Very relaxing and therapeutic. Gave me time to consider where I've been and where I want to go." I purse my lips. *Mostly true.*

A calico cat runs from the bushes to the sidewalk. I stoop to pet it, and it rubs my legs. I start walking. It stays with me, weaving around my feet. I have to step carefully, so I don't trip on it.

I tell Mom about the cat, and she tells me the neighbors had to put down their old dog, Rocket.

"Too bad," I say. "He was a good dog. Kip and I used to play tug-a-war and fetch with him. He loved to chase balls."

She laughs. "After you two were gone, he'd bring his ball to your dad when he got home from work and they'd play for a few minutes. I think it helped your father unwind from his day."

The cat sits on the sidewalk. When I look back, it's still watching me.

All too soon, I near the Pritchards' place. "I'm almost there, Mom, so I'd better let you go." With any luck, Olivia's project will involve sitting. I'd love to get off my feet.

I stuff the phone in my purse and enter the house through the front door, feeling as bad as I did each time I had to tell my parents I was incarcerated. This time, I failed to tell the whole truth. I didn't tell Mom about my job change or about the nonexistent rehab program.

Olivia calls from the dining room, "Cassandra, you're home. Wash your hands and help Marcela husk the corn."

I head for the stairs. "I'll be down in a minute." Where she found corn on the cob so early in the season is a mystery to me. Could be it came from Mexico or Guatemala. Wherever it originated, it must have cost a pretty penny.

Once more, we head to the garage. And once more, we stand with a garbage can between us. Marcela says, "Olivia *loves* corn on the cob. But she gets upset if any silk is left on it, so be sure to pick it all off."

I rip away a husk. "Okay." The fresh sweet scent of ripe corn fills my senses.

"Did you enjoy working at Ruby Jade's house?"

"Loved it. I got to be outside all day." I lower my voice. "I thought of you stuck in that factory and wished you were with me."

"Oh, well." She shrugs. "I can tell you got a little sun. Do you like Sebastian?"

"He seems to be an okay guy. Do you know anything about him?"

"I've never met him. Some say he's a criminal Ruby Jade is helping go straight, and others say he has something on her, so she keeps him around to protect her secrets."

"Did you know he's her ex-brother-in-law?"

"I'd heard he was somehow related."

"He told me he's Vance's uncle on his dad's side. Have you ever met his father?"

"He came for Vance's weddings. Both times, he wore bright-white Nikes, of all things. So inappropriate." She scowls and shakes her head. "He doesn't smile, and he doesn't stay around to socialize."

"Understandable." I pick at a particularly stubborn silk strand. "How about your, uh, solitary time? Any changes?"

"No. It's as predictable as ever. I timed it today. Fifty-nine minutes, exactly."

"Great. We can work with that."

"Who is *we*?"

Whoops, I wasn't going to tell her about the Dahlstrom brothers. "You know—you and me and anyone else we can find to help us."

"Good luck with that. Oh, no." She covers her mouth. "I let go of Jesus. Followers don't believe in luck."

I shake my head.

Marcela gives me a look. She knows what I'm thinking.

"Have you thought about applying for my teacher's aide position?"

"They already gave the job to an older man who worked in shipping-and-receiving at the factory."

"You're kidding. You applied to work at the school months ago."

"He started this morning." She sighs and tosses an ear onto the tray. "Did you notice we're not eating at the church tonight?"

No, but I noticed you changed the subject. "I hadn't thought about what day it is. How come we're not eating there?"

"Tonight, we eat the same food as all the other Followers and we receive an offering, as usual. Then we pray for the spring program."

"Separately or together?"

She laughs. "Followers rarely do anything by themselves. This is a household prayer meeting. Be prepared for a long night." Scooting closer, she whispers, "I always feel sorry for the children. They'll let the little ones fall asleep, but not the older ones."

At dinner, the residents ask each other about their day and about their jobs—everyone, that is, except me. Aren't they the least bit curious to know what it's like to be one of the worker bees at the queen's ritzy hive? Or maybe they've all been there, done that.

Remembering Marcela's comment, I watch Olivia chomp row after row of corn off cob after cob. The rest of us get one ear each. No one seems to notice but me.

The conversation turns to the spring program, which is Saturday night, three days away. I'm left out of the chit-chat, which I don't mind. They're all excited about the concert. The women are especially concerned their shoes and jewelry complement their outfits. Not for the first time, I wonder how they afford all the fancy clothes and if shopping and getting their hair and nails done is how they get their jollies.

That's when it hits me. These people are similar to many of the women in jail—walking dead. They only come alive when they talk about new clothes, new cars, new babies or the next big thing at FFOW. GCDC residents came to life when their favorite addiction was the topic of discussion, whether it was alcohol, drugs, food, sweets, men, sex or movies. One woman talked incessantly about the actors in her favorite television series.

As Marcela promised, the household prayer meeting begins with passing a basket Olivia brought from the kitchen. "Like any other fellowship meal," she says, "we'll collect five dollars per person to donate to the outreach fund."

When I hand off the basket without dropping in a five, Olivia says, "Cassandra. I realize you didn't pay the fee last week, but this week, you're required to contribute to the fund."

"I wish I could," I say. "But I haven't received a paycheck, although I've worked every day since I arrived. Maybe next week I'll have money." I can hope.

She huffs. "Next week, and no more excuses."

Owen offers a sympathetic smile. The others stare at their hands.

Before the prayer time, we watch another Ruby Jade video. This one instructs us on how to pray. Dummies that we are, none of us has a clue how to talk to God without her direction. I fold my arms and remind myself to keep my mouth shut and my negative thoughts to myself.

Marcela, who's seated beside me on one of the couches, nudges me and taps her thighs, ever so slightly. I get the message. Folded arms will earn me a trip to the superintendent's office. So many rules, so many rules.

The video is surprisingly short, only about fifteen minutes. We're to pray the FFOW guards are alert to any potential troublemakers, which strikes me as odd. I'm pretty sure this won't be on par with a rock concert.

We're also to pray for protection of the property and for the grass not to be trampled. I'm confused, but maybe they've had vandalism in the past. We're to pray no one stumbles or sings out during a pause, for the children to get ahold of Jesus and show him to the people, and for visitors to perceive the perfection of the saints and to be drawn to join us.

Perfection of the saints?

We pray in order around the room. No way can I get out of participating. Some pace the room, calling out to God in loud, plaintive voices with groans, eerie wails and fervent hand waving. Others yell, "Amen. Hallelujah."

They punch the air, demanding God bring vanloads of visitors to the spring program. From beneath half-closed lids, I watch Zachary plug his ears. I don't blame him.

When my opportunity to pray comes around, I go off-script and remain seated on the couch. Hands on my knees, I pray, "Dear God, what an opportunity this is to show your love to the community, to show them how much we love each other and you. I pray the music will not be jarring or discordant but will be so beautiful the words reach deep into listeners' hearts and draw them to you—and you alone. I pray for the singers to have good pitch and sing beautiful harmonies as well as melodies."

Remembering Corban and Logan, I add, "Please give the instrumentalists sensitive hearts, good timing, correct notes and nimble fingers. In the name of the Creator of music and the One who, as Zephaniah wrote, sings over each of us, amen."

Unlike the previous prayers, mine is short and elicits no "hallelujahs" or "amens" from the others. I've blown it, but I don't care. I prayed from my heart, and God heard.

Shortly after midnight, Marcela and I are in the bathroom, brushing our teeth. How the prayer meeting went so late, I don't know. But I'm sure Ruby Jade will be impressed when Olivia reports to her. Somehow, every day at FFOW is the same, yet different. Weird.

Marcela rinses her toothbrush. "I loved your prayer. I wish I could pray the way you do."

"Always remember you're talking to Jesus. He loves you more than you can imagine." I drop my toothpaste tube into the drawer. "And say what you're feeling and thinking."

"Hard to do around here."

"Yeah, I know. I also know my rebellion against the status quo will backfire sooner or later. Probably sooner."

CHAPTER TWENTY-THREE

Once Marcela leaves for work, I slip into my favorite blue jeans and a short-sleeved t-shirt. The worn cotton clothing feels so good I almost cry. Funny how normal has become a rare pleasure.

Knowing Fellowship Neighborhood is thick with Followers, I button a blouse over the t-shirt and pull yesterday's polyester pants over my jeans. I hate the stuffed feeling, but I'll be able to shed the top layer in Sebastian's hideout.

I hook the purse strap over my shoulder and bounce down the stairs. But then I remember I don't want to act too enthused about my job and slow my steps. If Leadership learned I enjoy working outside, they'd move me indoors to some awful place, like one of their factories.

Candice is in the living room with Tristan. He's asleep on her shoulder, and she's rocking back and forth on the couch. I kneel beside her and whisper, "I'm praying about what Noreen said the other day."

"Thank you." Tears spring to her eyes. "I don't know what I'd do if—"

I touch her arm. "I'm also praying for your daughter."

"Thank you, Cassandra. I pray for her every day, all day, but…" Her voice trails off.

"But it's not the same as having Mylea with you."

"I wasn't a good enough—"

"Stop." I raise my palm.

She blinks and stares at me, wide-eyed.

"Stop believing the lies and start believing you'll be reunited with your daughter."

"I'll try." She sniffs. "I miss her so much."

I pat her shoulder and get up to go. "Remember, you're praying to the God who created the universe. He loves you and has more than enough power to answer your prayers." I'm reminding myself of those eternal truths, as well as Candice. "Mylea was a wonderful gift from him to you. Trust him to return her to you and Scott."

Closing the front door behind me, I step off the front porch and check my phone. Ruby Jade's been busy, as usual, and Kip called last night during the prayer meeting. He didn't leave a message, which is totally my brother. I dial his number, but he doesn't answer. No surprise. He works during the day. I leave a message, so he knows I'm not ignoring him.

I stuff the phone into my purse and hurry along the sidewalk, trying not to swing my arms or reveal the fact I'm loving this beautiful morning. Fresh sweet air, green grass and the feel of something intangible all tease at my senses. What is it?

I smile. Freedom, that's what it is, though it doesn't make sense. I'm headed straight into the lair of the one who stole my freedom.

Sebastian is as welcoming as yesterday. He seems happy to see me, a much more pleasant response than I get from my robotic housemates. "Today," he says, "we'll tackle the flowerbeds."

He leads me to one with clusters of daffodils, tulips and a mix of yellow and purple pansies. "The pansies and tulips are fine, but these daffodils can be deadheaded. And those weeds should be pulled while they're small and easy to pluck."

Another bed has jonquils, hyacinths and crocuses surrounded by alyssum. "Same thing here," he says, "except...see those grass blades?"

"Uh-huh."

"We need to dig 'em out. When grass takes root, it's a doozy to eradicate."

"I understand," I tell him. "My mom goes nuts fighting grass. It constantly encroaches on her flower garden."

He walks me to his hideout. "You're welcome to borrow the sunhat any time you need and use gloves from the basket over there. I forgot to offer 'em yesterday."

"Thanks." I glance at my fingernails. The pearl polish is still intact. "I wore jeans and a t-shirt beneath my Follower clothes. Do you mind if I leave them on a shelf with my purse?"

"No problem, but I'll make myself scarce before you step out of your duds. You never know when Vance might be snooping around."

"He comes out here?"

"Only when he's cruisin' for trouble."

I blow out a long breath. Just when I have a moment to relax and enjoy life...

"Don't you worry, Cat." He pats my shoulder. "I'll be on the lookout and run interference. He knows I play hardball."

"Thanks, Sebastian."

"Just 'cause trouble comes a visitin' doesn't mean you have to offer it a chair."

I nod, but I know I'll be deciphering that thought for weeks to come.

Working in the sunshine in comfortable clothing, I feel as though I'm on vacation. The only distraction is an occasional bee and the feeling someone is watching me. I'm probably being paranoid. So many people have warned me about Vance. I can't let down my guard. From the first time I met him, he's been too friendly, too brash. Lecherous might be a better word, but it doesn't mean he's watching me right now.

I'm on my knees, digging a dandelion root out of a pansy patch, when Francis and Fenwick attack me with licks and nuzzles. They smell like shampoo. I drop my tool and hug the energetic pair. They don't stay long. Instead, they make a beeline for the yellow house.

Sebastian moseys over. "Care to join us at Myrtle Mae's for a break?"

"Sure."

"Good job with the dandelions." He helps me to my feet. "You're getting the entire root."

"Thanks to what you've done with the soil. It's loose and easy to dig into." I remove the gloves, letting them fall beside the dandelion digger, and stretch my back. "Feels good to stand."

"I hear you," he says. "I've been tilling out front. R.J. decided she wants a big rose garden in the middle of the grass."

"Sounds like hard work."

"It's a paycheck."

I place my hat on top of the gloves, and we walk across the wide expanse of grass together. The dogs are nowhere in sight, but by the sound of their barking, I picture them poised on Myrtle Mae's doorstep, tails wagging. I ask Sebastian, "Do you have a family, other than Vance and his dad?"

"I have a brother in Idaho and a half-sister who lives back east, plus three nieces and two nephews, in addition to Vance. If you're wondering about marriage, I've had some close calls, but I never walked the aisle."

"Close calls. You're too funny."

"Learned something helpful from all those close calls."

"What's that?"

"I came up with two theories 'bout arguin' with a woman."

"Oh, yeah?"

"Yeah. Neither one works."

I laugh and slap his shoulder. "I should have seen it coming. But you never know, Sebastian. Marriage could still happen for you. Never say *never.*"

"At this age, I don't expect to tie the knot, as they say, which is okay by me. I'm a bit of a loner."

"I highly recommend marriage, at any age, because I loved being married to Eric. But I don't plan to marry again."

He raises a questioning eyebrow.

"I can't imagine how marriage to anyone else could be as good as it was with him. We were soulmates."

He chuckles. "Never say *never.*"

Myrtle Mae greets us at the door and hugs us both. "I'm so glad you're still here, Cassie. Seems I just get to know the volunteers who care for the property, when my daughter decides to move them elsewhere."

"Oh…" I stare at Sebastian. "I hope, I mean… I don't—" Switching me from the school, where I worked less than a week, to this job happened overnight. It could happen again.

He grins. "I'll go to bat for you."

"Thanks."

He draws a deep breath. "Somethin' smells mighty good, Myrtle Mae."

"Zucchini muffins," she says. "Fresh out of the oven."

After she gives "the boys" their three kidney beans each, Sebastian tells them to lie down. The dogs obey, plopping side-by-side on the small rug before the door. He and I sit at the kitchen table. Myrtle Mae bustles about, preparing her special tea and arranging muffins on a flowered dish.

"They're warm enough to melt the butter." She sets the muffins and a crock of butter on the table and then goes for the tea.

She's placing cups and saucers in front of us, when Sebastian says, "Sit, Myrtle Mae, before you wear a rut as deep as a trail to the outhouse. I replaced the linoleum in here once. Don't want to do it again."

"Quit your grousing, Seb." She carries a third cup to the table and sits at the end between me and Sebastian. But then she hops to her feet again. "Silly me. I forgot plates for the muffins. And napkins."

Satisfied we have everything we need, she sits down and immediately picks up the muffin plate. Holding it in front of first me and then Sebastian, she insists we take two or three muffins apiece. I may not be able to eat more than one, but I put two on my plate just to see her nod of approval, something I don't ever expect from her daughter.

"Cassie…" She stirs honey into her tea. "Last time we met, I monopolized the conversation, talking about myself and my family. Today, it's your turn. I'd like to get to know you."

"Okay." I scoop butter out of the crock and smear it on a muffin. "Where do you want me to start? Birth?" I bite into the muffin.

Sebastian chuckles. "Better yet, you could tell us when your ancestors came to America."

"You're always so helpful, Seb." Myrtle Mae shakes her spoon at him. "Cassie, how about you tell me where you're from, if you're not from here, and what brought you to the Followers."

"I'm from Oregon." I set the muffin on the plate. "These are yummy, Myrtle Mae. Quite a treat for someone who's been eating institutional food for months on end."

Sebastian chuckles. "The same ole, same ole FFOW meal routine getting to you?"

"I had noticed a lack of creativity. The food, at least at our house, isn't much different from what they dished out at GCDC."

Sebastian smirks, like he knows what I'm talking about.

"The jail?" Myrtle Mae asks.

I nod.

"You mentioned incarceration the other day."

"That's not what brought me here. I came to Bozeman to attend MSU on a music scholarship."

"Wonderful." She claps her hands. "You're a musician. Are you still in college, or have you graduated?"

"Neither. I dropped out of school when my husband began his cancer treatments."

"Husband?" Myrtle Mae stares at me, a startled expression on her face. "You're so young. I never once thought..."

"His name was Eric." I rest my folded hands on the table edge. "Eric Blaine True."

"You dear, sweet girl." A tear slips from the corner of her eye. She dabs it with her napkin. "I am so sorry." She covers my hands with one of hers. "I can only imagine how terrible losing him was for you. And how you must miss him." She pauses, searching my face. "If you don't mind, I'd like to know the circumstances of his death."

I somehow manage to recount Eric's cancer saga without shedding a single tear. Maybe I'm finally getting over his absence from my life. Or maybe it's Sebastian across from me, reaching for a third muffin.

"And that's how I landed in jail," I say. "I should have returned to school after he died, but I couldn't face it then. Maybe I'll finish later. I wish I had a picture of Eric, but even if I did, I couldn't display it at the Pritchards' house."

Sebastian's forehead furrows. "You were incarcerated because your husband died?"

"In a roundabout way." The jail chaplain's voice echoes in my head. *Transparency is the key to transformation. Transparency is the key to transformation.*

"Not long after Eric's death..." I take a breath and begin again. "My next-door neighbor, who was probably tired of listening to me cry, brought over brownies and huckleberry vodka lemonade. She burrowed into my couch and spent the afternoon—I make air quotes—*consoling* me. I'd never drunk so much as a beer before she came over. Needless to say, my path to addiction was a downhill ride from there."

Sebastian nods as if he's remembering his own journey.

"How did you get from jail to FFOW?" Myrtle Mae asks.

"I'd served a year of a two-year sentence when Judge Snow decided I could finish my time at Transformation Way."

"But…" Her beautiful brow creases.

"I know." I make a face. "The program isn't happening right now."

Shaking his head, Sebastian carries his cup to the counter.

I stand. "I have a feeling our tea break is over."

Tired but happy, I leave work with a smile on my face and daffodils and yellow and orange tulips in my hand. Sebastian said I could take a bouquet to Olivia. My mother would be thrilled with the beautiful colors, but you never know about Olivia. Flowers are a big deal at FFOW. The question is, will they alleviate the perpetual frown on her face?

The tulips' sweet aroma fills my senses. If she doesn't want the flowers, I'll keep them in my bedroom.

I dig my cell phone out of my purse with my free hand and speed-dial my brother. Kip answers after the first ring. "Hey, sis, how you doin'?"

"I'm great. How was the mountain climbing?"

"The bomb. New Zealand is an awesome country, and their mountains are amazing. Three-thousand glaciers—can you believe it? The more I'm immersed in God's creation, the more I'm awed by who he is. You've got to go with me sometime."

"I'd love to." My brother's enthusiasm for God and for life is contagious. And one of these days, I'll be free to do whatever I please. "How many peaks did you climb?"

"Ten. That's about half of those over ten-thousand feet."

"If I'd been with you, you'd have lost me before the second mountain. Why did you stop at ten?"

"We wanted to leave a little time to do the tourist thing."

"I'm impressed. Skipping the other summits must have been difficult for you mountaineering maniacs."

"We're *mountaineering enthusiasts*, Cassie…*enthusiasts.*" He belches and snickers. He knows it bugs me.

"S'cuse you, Kip."

"S'cuse me, Cassie."

I ignore the sarcasm in his voice. "Was it hard to go back to work?"

"You'd better believe it, but it's the only way to pay for the next trip."

"Where are you planning to go?"

"We want to take a couple weeks to tackle Colorado's Fourteeners."

"Didn't you tell me Colorado has over fifty of those? You can't climb them all in two weeks, can you?"

"No, but we'll give it the ole college try." He heaves a sigh. "Oh, to have the whole summer off. But, hey, enough about me. How's it going in the new program?"

The calico cat intercepts me on the sidewalk. I'd pet it, but I don't have a free hand. Instead, I stop so it can rub my legs. But then I remember the hair I had to pick off my pants last night and walk faster.

How much should I tell him? If I ask him not to tell Mom and Dad, he'll honor my wishes. And he'll pray for me, like he always has. "It's an odd, situation, Kip, one I'd rather you keep to yourself."

"My lips are sealed, Super Glue sealed."

"Ugh, not a pretty picture."

He laughs. "Live with it."

I tell him about the strange church, the nonexistent treatment center, my name change, my friends' problems. I'm beginning to tell him about my new job when Olivia's car rolls my way. "I'd better go. I'll explain later."

"Cat…" His voice has lost all hint of playfulness. "That place sounds psycho. Want me to come get you?"

"You can't. I have a court order to be here."

"Got it, but I don't like it." He growls his frustration. "Love you, Sis. Keep me informed."

"Love you, too. Bye."

Olivia pulls alongside the curb, rolls down the window and crooks her finger at me. I step close. Cool air swishes through the window, though the outside temperature is perfect. She doesn't need air-conditioning. But who am I to tell Olivia Pritchard what's what?

"You're needed in the kitchen, Cassandra." She taps the steering wheel. "I have to make a quick run to the grocery store in town."

"Okay."

She eyes the flowers. "Did you steal those from Ruby Jade's yard?" The frown lines between her eyebrows crease.

I tell a little fib, hating that I'm afraid she'll reject the flowers if she believes they're from me. "Sebastian sent these for you. He thought you'd enjoy fresh-cut spring flowers."

She quirks an eyebrow, but before she can question me further, I ask, "Where can I find a vase?"

After a moment's hesitation, she says, "The cupboard over the refrigerator." She closes the window and drives off.

I wonder if Owen has ever given her flowers. He seems like a flower-giving kind of guy. And, surely, she hasn't always been so coldhearted. For the first time, I feel sorry for Olivia. She's as much a victim of Ruby Jade's lunacy as Candice and Marcela are.

I also feel triumph. She didn't say "no." She's letting me contribute flowers to the household décor, without Ruby Jade's approval.

At the opening from the dining room to the kitchen, I say hello to Deanna and her children, who are all working on dinner preparations. Sliding a chair in from the dining room, I set it in front of the fridge. Flowers in one hand and my pink purse flapping from my shoulder, I slip out of my shoes and climb onto the chair.

Whatever's on the stove smells like pork roast, but I know better. The only pork the Followers are allowed to eat is bacon, and only for breakfast.

"Cassandra..."

I look down.

Deanna, who must have taken the kitchen reins when Olivia left, has a horrified expression on her face. "What on earth are you doing?"

Her daughters, Hannah and Heidi, glance at each other, their foreheads puckered. Bradford, their brother, has an interested, almost envious expression on his face. My guess is he's never been allowed to climb a chair, let alone a tree.

"Olivia told me this is where the vases are kept."

"Did she say you could stand on a dining room chair? It's not—"

"She didn't tell me *how* to get a vase, only where to find it." I sort through the vases until I find an appropriate size. "Would you hold this, please?" I hand the vase to Deanna.

"Those are beautiful flowers." She offers her hand to help me down. "Where did you get them?"

"Sebastian sent them home with me. All kinds of spring flowers are blooming in Ruby Jade's yard."

She frowns. "I hope it's okay with Ruby Jade."

"It's not as though I can glue the flowers back onto the stems."

"But..."

"Sebastian knows what he's doing." I put the flowers in the vase, fill it with water and set it on the table.

Deanna tells Hannah to carry the chair to the dining room.

I thank Hannah, fiddle with the arrangement and then step away to admire it. If Olivia doesn't like the flowers on the table, she can move them.

I tell the others I need to use the restroom and dart upstairs to remove my underlayer. Tossing the jeans and t-shirt into the laundry basket in the closet, I hurry down to the kitchen. Deanna puts me to work making rice to go with the stir-fry chicken and vegetables she's preparing.

I peek over her shoulder. "I thought I caught a whiff of pork." Small squares of bacon are mixed with the chicken and veggies she's stirring.

She scowls. "I'm only doing this because Olivia wanted to use the last few slices from a package she bought last week. Ruby Jade wouldn't approve, but Olivia's the one who'll have to answer to her, not me."

I'm tempted to say, "Don't count on it." But I bite my tongue and lower the flame beneath the rice, which is about to boil over.

CHAPTER TWENTY-FOUR

I'm pleased the flowers remain in the center of the table during dinner, probably because Olivia rushed in after we prayed. But no one mentions the flowers or asks about my day. I feel invisible, and maybe that's their intent. Could be they've been told to give me the cold shoulder because I stopped a cleanse. I need to ask Marcela how long shunnings last around this place.

No one speaks to Zachary, either. His eye seems better, but he's such a sad, lonely little boy. I wish I could put my arm around him and tell him how special he is. Maybe Marcela will help me contact his parents.

After supper, we're sent to our rooms for individual times of soul searching, an annual FFOW routine. I'm told this involves confession and crying out to God for forgiveness as well as prayer for the spring concert. Clothing preparation is also permitted, but no sleeping or excessive Bible reading.

Excessive Bible reading? Why would a church be against Bible reading? Is Ruby Jade concerned we'll come across something contrary to her teaching? Or does she fear God might dare to bypass her supposed authority and speak directly to us through his Word?

We may pace as we pray, and we may kneel beside our beds, but we may not lie on them. Neither snacking nor conversation is allowed. Since when did prayer get so complicated?

Because we weren't told how to dress, an oversight on Ruby Jade's part, I'm sure, I gather my nightgown and robe and go into the bathroom to change. Might as well be comfortable during the ritual.

I would never publicly suggest Ruby Jade might have missed a beat. Corban told me she considers herself above reproach. In fact, according to her, she once was a sinner, a long time ago. But now, she's supposedly reached perfection and can do no wrong.

The woman has a problem, a serious mental problem. God help us.

When I walk out of the bathroom, Marcela is coming into the room. Her back to the camera, she eyes my attire and offers a discreet thumbs-up. I'm pleased she's reverting to her "pagan" ways. Good thing Ruby Jade doesn't know what a terrible influence I am.

Dropping my clothing into the laundry basket, I decide this would be a good time to pick out jeans and a t-shirt for tomorrow. I turn on the closet light, grateful the door blocks the camera view. First, I'll find slacks and a blouse, and then—

I stop, mouth open. The box of clothes Mom sent is gone. I push Marcela's clothing aside to check her corner of the closet. Nothing. "Marcela." I whisper. "Come here."

She appears at my side, murmuring, "What's wrong?"

"My box, it's gone. With all my things and the cookies Mom made." I check my shoes. Sure, enough, the hiking boots are also missing. "And my hiking boots. Eric gave me those boots."

She sucks in a breath and does the same thing I did—searches from one corner of the closet to the other. "They must have taken…" She groans. "Those cookies were so, so good." Her eyes widen. "Your guitar. Do you think…?"

I swivel. *The jerks. If they—*

"Don't." She grabs my arm. "Don't be obvious." Lowering her voice, she murmurs, "You can look while you're praying. Get on your knees by your bed, and I'll pretend to drop something. Then I'll stand behind you."

"Ohh..." I'm near tears. "If they took my guitar..."

"We'll find it," she whispers. "We'll find it."

I close my eyes to her empty promise. She may be gaining a sense of self, but she's as powerless as I am in this place. I stumble to my bed and fall on my knees. Hands clasped on the bedspread, I bow my head, trying not to cry.

Marcela taps me on the shoulder.

I lift my head.

She gestures as if she's looking for something, motioning toward the bathroom and then the floor. What an actress. Did I teach her to be deceptive, or was she already practiced at playing the system?

I give her a questioning stare.

She points beneath her bed.

I lift her bedspread and bend down. Nothing. Sitting on my heels, I shake my head.

She moves behind me.

Switching to my bed, I raise the bedspread and peer underneath. Nothing. I feel around, to be sure. Finally, I sit back, shaking my head. "Gone," I whisper. "It's gone."

"Uh-oh." She moans. "I'm so sorry."

I bury my face in the bed, crying, "Oh God—oh God—oh God..." I don't care what the perverts report to Leadership. My heart is broken. I love my guitar. It's part of me, the conduit for the music in my head to flow through my fingers and reach the world.

"No, no." I rise onto my knees but then fall onto the bed again.

Marcela whispers, "What's wrong?"

I blubber into the bedding. "Later..." Musical instruments need to be kept at moderate temperatures. If my guitar is in a hot place, it'll warp and be ruined forever.

I fight the urge to run down the stairs and pound on Olivia and Owen's door, demanding to know where my guitar is—and my clothes. And the cookies. Mom made them for me. Those are *my* possessions. They *stole* them from me.

I clutch the tear-dampened bedspread, wadding it into clumps. I've got to find my things and leave this nuthouse before I lose my mind.

Marcela paces the narrow area between the beds and the door. "Lord…forgive me, for I have sinned." She moans again. "I drove twenty-seven miles per hour in a twenty-five zone today. I let go of Jesus and didn't check the speedometer until I'd driven three blocks. I'm grateful to you no law-enforcement officer stopped me. But still, I sinned."

Is she for real? I twist my head.

She spreads her fingers and winks through the gap. If I wasn't so heartbroken, I'd laugh. Instead, I resume crying out to God. Marcela may be putting on an act, but I mean every word I sob into the bedspread.

Groggy from a lack of sleep, I stir dusty-smelling oatmeal in a slow circle. The oatmeal makes me think of Mom's cookies. Not that I've forgotten my missing boxes for a single minute.

Across the kitchen, Marcela slices pungent oranges in half. Ruby Jade believes *fresh* orange juice prevents Followers from succumbing to colds and flu—and from missing work, which could affect her income. My suspicion, anyway.

Olivia comes up from the basement with a loaf of sliced cinnamon bread in her hands.

I turn from the oatmeal to look her directly in the eyes. "Olivia, I need to report a theft. Several of my items were stolen from our bedroom yesterday. I don't know if someone in this house took them or someone broke in, but the sheriff should be notified."

"No!" She jerks to a stop, squeezing the bread. "Followers *never* involve the authorities in our private business."

"I see." I'm not surprised by her response. "What do you do?"

"We deal with such things ourselves."

"You and Owen?"

She shakes her head.

"Should I talk with Leadership?"

"Your contraband items were not stolen." She inhales and seems to expand before my eyes. "They were *removed*, so you won't be tempted to use them."

"My *mother* sent me those things."

"Your *mother* should have asked Leadership first."

The thought of Mom asking Ruby Jade's permission to send me a package is so ridiculous I could scream. I draw in a long breath and tell myself to stay calm. "I'm mostly concerned about my guitar. Extreme heat and extreme cold can ruin instruments. They need to remain at moderate temperatures. Do you know where it is?"

"I'm not at liberty to discuss the matter." She motions to the oatmeal pot. "Watch what you're doing. It's about to burn."

I lower the flame and stir several more times. "Are you the one who snooped through my stuff?" I realize I'm pushing her buttons, but I need to know how things work in this household.

"For your information, young lady, I do not *snoop*." Her eyes flash and her face reddens. "My job as household guardian is to *inspect* every room of this home to ensure they meet FFOW's high standards. Not only is your guitar an instrument of the devil, I did not want those ungodly songs of yours tainting our household and causing members to give in to the unclean. Or your worldly clothing to seduce Follower men and boys."

Behind her, Marcela is still as a statue, holding the knife in midair. Her gaze darts from Olivia to me and back to Olivia.

Poker face in place, I ignore Olivia's diatribe and push another button. "You opened my boxes without my permission."

"I am the authority in this household. I don't need your permission for anything I do." She brandishes the bread in my face. "Your rubbish is in a place where it cannot corrupt the Faithful. That's all you need to know, Cassandra Turner. Case closed. You will never speak of this again."

I lift an eyebrow. *Bet me...*

Judson walks in.

Olivia shoves the squished bread into his hands. "Get the butter from the fridge and hurry with the toast. Breakfast is served in ten minutes." She marches out of the kitchen and into the dining room.

Stirring furiously, I try not to splatter myself with hot cereal. *Not at liberty, my foot.* Olivia knows exactly where my stuff is. I'll have to ask Corban and Logan what to do.

Is this a mowing day for the brothers? I stare at the ceiling in a futile attempt to clear my thoughts. Since the night I came to this fruitcake place, I've been confused as to what day it is.

As quickly as she left the room, Olivia returns with the flowers I brought her last night. She drops them into the garbage, dumps the water in the sink and plunks the vase on the counter. With a "so there" glance my direction, she swings around and stomps away.

I bite my lip to keep from saying what I'm thinking—toddler tantrums don't look good on middle-aged women. Turning to the oatmeal, I send her a mental message. *Believe me, Olivia Pritchard, when I say this case is NOT closed. I will speak of it again and again until my so-called rubbish is returned.*

As soon as Olivia leaves the house with the kids, I retrieve the t-shirt and jeans I wore yesterday from the laundry basket. They can't steal clothes from me if they're on my body. Or maybe they can. Who knows how far the Fearsome Threesome will go to enforce the FFOW lifestyle. Over my work clothes, I button a long-sleeved blouse and step into the polyester pants I designated as work pants after the first day of snags and cat hair.

Downstairs, I hurry through the kitchen and dining room and peek into the living room. Her back to me, Candice is seated on one of the couches with her baby. Too bad. If no one was here, I'd treat myself to a nip or two of vanilla extract. After all I've been through lately, I deserve it.

Whoa, Cassie. I stop and give myself a mental slap. "You deserve it, Cassie," is what got me into trouble in the first place. Self-pity is a slippery slope I don't want to slide down again. Was it two days ago I was praising God because Olivia interrupted my vanilla-with-milk-and-honey plot? I am such a wishy-washy wuss.

Forcing a smile onto my face, I walk into the room and sit beside Candice.

She's bottle-feeding Tristen, who squirms and flails his arms. He's a good baby. I rarely hear him cry. Maybe he senses crying isn't in his best interest.

"Tristen doesn't understand..." Her voice is low. "We're putting on a show for the...you know." She glances at the muted television, where a still shot of the local forecast predicts a nice day in the Bozeman area.

The way she looks at the TV screen makes me think it may have a video camera. Really? In addition to the two ceiling cameras?

"When he gets this way," she murmurs, "I let him fuss for a few minutes, and then I go into the bathroom to nurse him."

"Any more threats from—?"

"No, but..."

"Yeah, I'm seeing how things work around here."

"Please don't say 'yeah' again, or I'll have to report you."

All I can do is shake my head, wave goodbye and head for the door.

My walk to work this morning is far from lighthearted. The sun shines and the birds sing, but I'm heartsick. My guitar is my most precious possession.

When I realized I was losing my battle with alcohol, I knew I had to send the instrument to my parents before I hocked it for one more drink. Despite my drunken haze, I was aware I had to protect my guitar—from myself.

An older friend at the shelter where I slept on sober nights loaned me the money for shipping, saying if she didn't give it to me, she'd spend it on uppers. The money came out of her Social Security check. I need to find her and repay her—after I get a job with benefits, like a paycheck.

When I near Ruby Jade's house, one of her three double-car garage doors opens and a black Lincoln Town Car backs out. It's not Vance's car, so it must be Ruby Jade's. She's the last person I care to encounter today. In fact, I'd love to never see her or her cronies ever again.

I hope she'll ignore me, but I know better. Why would she overlook an opportunity to abuse an underling? I reach the brick path almost the same moment her front wheels touch the street. She rolls down the window and beckons to me. Country music drifts from inside the car.

A radio? Worldly music? Guitars? What a hypocrite. Apparently, her son hasn't gotten around to disconnecting the Lincoln's stereo.

I steel myself for a tirade regarding *my* guitar and *my* ungodly songs—like the one she's listening to on her outlawed radio—and walk over to her. How will I react when she attacks me? Will I burst into tears or tell her where to go? I'd hate to give her the satisfaction of either reaction. *Help me, God.*

I smile a fake FFOW smile. "Hi, Ruby Jade."

She looks at me over the top of her gold-rimmed sunglasses, and her coral-coated lips part. "Hello, Cassandra."

Her dogs are in the car with her. They hop from the passenger seat and onto her lap, their paws on the doorframe and their tails wagging.

Ruby Jade smiles and hugs them. Her loose sleeves slip down her arms, revealing the rash I noticed earlier. "Cassandra," she says, "meet Francis and Fenwick."

They lick her chin. She doesn't seem to mind.

I tentatively reach out to pet them and they jump all over her in their eagerness to sniff my hand and lick it.

"Fenwick, Francis, settle down." She pushes them over to the passenger seat and tells them to sit, which they do, although their little bodies quiver. "They're excited because we're going for a drive. They don't get out of the house often."

Really? Does she not know Sebastian takes them to visit Myrtle Mae twice a day?

"They're cute dogs," I tell her. "Very friendly. I like their names."

At the sound of my voice, they edge onto her lap. She says, "Sit," and they stop, yet their tails still wag. She squints at me. "Cassandra, you-not wear-ing lipstick." As has happened before, some of her words slur and blend together. Strange.

I blink, caught off-guard. "I, I'm here to work, not... I mean, no one sees me, except Sebastian and—"

"I'm seeing you."

"I..." I'm so close to apologizing, I have to clamp my mouth shut to stop myself. "Yes, you are."

"Surely, you have some in that silly pink purse." Her voice is back to its normal haughtiness.

"No, I don't." I quickly add, "Noreen chose this purse for me."

She rolls her eyes. "How many times have I told her...?" Leaning out the window, she stares at me like I've got spinach between my teeth. "Your Jamaican heritage has corrupted your skin tones. I'll have Noreen purchase bleaching cream for you. To be a true Follower, we need to rid you of the Mark of Cain and its curse."

All I can do is mouth, "What?"

She twists her wrist to glance at her huge diamond-studded watch. The jewels sparkle in the sunshine. "Work hard today, Cassandra Turner. God will reward you in heaven, if you make it." She raises an eyebrow. "Will I see you there?"

I watch her drive away, my mouth opening and closing like a fish out of water. which is what I am, a fish out of water. I don't fit with these crazy people.

One thing I've figured out—God will have to do the rewarding, 'cause it's not going to happen around this place. She won't even reward my labor with a paycheck. And what kind of person tells someone their skin color is wrong and then suggests they might not make it to heaven, but she will. I've heard worse insults on the streets. Somehow, the jibes hurt more coming from a supposed pastor.

Too mad to cry, I stomp along the driveway and around the garage to Sebastian's hideout. I'm going to tell him I'm done with his ex-sister-in-law, that I'm sorry, but I have to leave. I must go *now*.

Maybe he'll loan me money for a ticket home and give me a ride to the bus station—after I pack my few possessions that survived Olivia's supposed inspection. If Sebastian won't help, I'll ask Kip to come get me. He'd do it in an instant.

I don't see Sebastian anywhere on the property, but that doesn't mean much. He could be working behind a clump of trees or visiting Myrtle Mae. I hope he's in his shed. The mere sight of his hideout makes me feel better, as though I've found a shelter in the midst of a hurricane. I hurry inside, anxious for its earthy odor and Sebastian's steady presence.

But he's not there. Instead, a piece of notebook paper hangs from a nail with CAT printed in big letters at the top and smaller writing below. I drop my purse on a shelf. Unbuttoning my blouse, I slip off one sleeve then the other as I read the note. His handwriting is neat and easy to read.

Got to run to the hardware store. Won't be long. I left annuals on the grass by the rose garden out front. You can start transplanting them. Tools are in the bin at your knees. Space the flowers along the brick edges and around the fountain. I bought a variety, so arrange them how you want. You have a good eye. I trust your judgement.

The last line destroys my shaky composure. I burst into tears, sink to the floor and bury my face in my blouse. No one has trusted me in a long, long time, not even my parents, who are afraid I'll fall off the wagon again.

Bars, nightclubs and concert halls don't trust me, for good reason. My ex-landlady doesn't trust me. No one at FFOW trusts me to do anything but housework and yardwork. They don't trust my music, they don't trust me with the school kids. Yet, Sebastian has confidence I can plant flowers in a manner that will satisfy his persnickety boss.

My sobs slowly subside. I feel silly for letting such a small thing bring me to tears. Ruby Jade's nasty comments must have pushed me over the edge. Grabbing onto a shelf, I pull myself to my feet and wipe my face with the blouse. Good thing I'm not wearing eye makeup, or the fabric would be a ruined black mess. *Take that, R.J.!*

I kick off my shoes, slip out of the polyesters and swipe at my nose. I'm still sniffling, but I have to admit I feel better after the cry. I was so ready to unload on Sebastian, as if he has the answers for my problems. Fact is, he chooses to work for Ruby Jade. Why would he understand my desperate need to escape her clutches? I remember Myrtle Mae's words and repeat them again to myself. "No one can make you feel inferior without your consent."

I hang the blouse on a nail to dry, stash my purse and pants on a low shelf and put on the sunhat. Trowel in one hand and the cultivator in the other, I step outside the shed. Rather than walk around the garage, I skirt the other end of the house. I haven't seen the property on that side.

With the wide expanse of lawn and beautiful mature trees, Ruby Jade's yard could pass for a park. No wonder she needs volunteers to help Sebastian maintain it, but someone could have told me not to expect a paycheck. I sigh and remind myself I didn't have a choice about this work, paid or otherwise.

Which brings me to my debate whether to stay at FFOW or leave as soon as Sebastian drives me to the bus station. Should I stick it out until they restart the Transformation Way program, which may or may not happen? Or should I hang on long enough to help my friends reunite with their families, no matter how much time it takes?

I round the front corner of the house. Why do I keep forgetting I can't leave town? I have to go to the courthouse to talk with Judge Snow, not to the bus station. He might send me back to jail, but so be it, as much as I dread the idea. But whether I go or stay, and whether Olivia approves or not, I need to report the theft to the sheriff.

A tall flowing fountain already occupies the center of the rose garden. Short brick paths spiral out from it, with park benches at the sides. A half-dozen rose bushes lie in a neat row on the grass and a nearby pallet is stacked with more. From the pictures on the packaging, they'll produce a wide variety of types and colors.

Flats of bedding plants are everywhere. This project will keep both of us busy most of the day. That is, if I stay.

CHAPTER TWENTY-FIVE

I tear four-packs of flowers from the flats and then alternate white and purple alyssum with multi-colored petunias to get an idea of how to space the flowers. As I space them along the bricks, I think about how much I enjoy working with plants and with Sebastian. But I'm not getting paid, and I'm not progressing in a rehab program.

Something has to change. I'll ask Sebastian to drive me to the sheriff's office and to the courthouse. Surely, the judge will see the need to reassign me to a different program. I sit back on my heels. What if he grants my request? What if he sends me to the other side of Montana or to another state? I hate to get too far from my guitar, wherever it is.

I hear a garage door open and look up from my work. Neither Ruby Jade's Lincoln nor Sebastian's faded green pickup is approaching the house, which means someone is exiting the garage. The tail end of Vance's sportscar appears, and I slip to the opposite side of the water fountain. I'm not well-hidden, but with any luck, he won't glance my direction.

The garage door closes, the car stops, and Vance gets out. When he starts my direction, I sigh and focus on the flower packs I'm breaking apart. As much as I'd hoped to avoid him, a one-on-one encounter with the jerk had to happen sometime.

He stops not far from where I'm kneeling on the grass. "So, Cas-*san*-dra, you're one of my mom's flower girls."

I raise my head. "If that's what you want to call it." His aftershave is as strong as the day we met in the church office. Blended with marijuana, it's disgusting.

"Better than being called a hooker."

I squint at him. "What are you getting at?"

"You know, a streetwalker."

A bird swoops low, like it's about to land on the fountain, but then it changes course.

"I know what a hooker is." I stand to be on equal footing.

"You oughta." He sneers. "You lived on the streets—"

"Doesn't mean I sold myself." I almost add, *to scum like you,* but think better of it.

"You got money somehow."

"I had my ways. However, prostitution wasn't one of them."

"Someone as hot as you? I find it hard—"

"Excuse me." I drop to my knees. "I have work to do."

"I saw you walk past my window, Cas-*san*-dra. Love that sexy swing. You look *real* good in jeans."

I grab a multipack of pansies and start snapping apart the individual flower containers to steady my trembling hands. *This isn't fair, God.* First Ruby Jade, then Vance. I rip a single pansy cell from the pack, trying not to squish it.

"I'd like…" He steps closer. "I'd *love* to show you around my suite. You'd be impressed. Most of the lower level is my—"

"Don't you have a job to go to?"

"I have a business, my own *business.*" He sounds like a petulant child.

Yeah, a business other people's tithes bought for you.

"The peons can run the place till I get there."

I stare at him. "Peons?"

"Yeah, you know, people like you, who're nothing at FFOW, unless…" A sly grin accentuates his haughty features. "You hook up with someone who's an insider, someone with money." He holds out his hands. "Come on, baby, you know what you want. And you can have it *all* with me."

I grab a trowel and stand, tired of him, tired of the threats, tired of the power plays.

Vance smiles a knowing smile and reaches for me.

I raise the trowel.

He hesitates.

"If you're talking about living off other people's hard-earned money, I don't want a penny of it." I point the tool at him. "If you're talking about treating people like they're trash to make yourself feel superior, I don't want that either. In my book, yours is a pathetic, poverty-stricken, godforsaken life. In no way does it appeal to me. In fact, I can't imagine a worse way to live."

"You stupid tramp." He jabs his finger at me, emphasizing his words. "You sleep in gutters and eat out of garbage cans. How dare you suggest this…" He waves his arm at the house and the acres of lawn and trees and bushes. "That this is poverty."

"Poverty of soul, Vance. Poverty of soul."

"My mother's church is the most religious church in the state, in the West. I'm going to tell her you said—" The sly expression returns. He crooks a forefinger. "Come with me, Cas-*san*-dra, and I won't say a word to my mother."

"For the last time, Vance…" I stare him in the eye. "N-o. No. Now, please leave and let me do my work." *Where are you, Sebastian, when I need you? You promised—*

"No one tells me 'no.'" His nostrils flare. "Come with me or—" His gaze darkens and shifts beyond my shoulder. "Damn doofus brothers." He sneers. "I stole one of their girlfriends. They can't seem to get over it."

"Apparently she didn't stick around."

"Shut your mouth, tramp." He pivots and tromps over the grass to his car. Slamming the door, he squeals a wide U-turn in the driveway and jets into the street, tires screeching.

Corban and Logan, who are standing beside their car, watch him leave before they start my direction.

Without warning, my legs give out and I sink to my knees.

"Cassie," Corban calls. "You okay?" He comes running and kneels beside me. "Did he hurt you?"

"No, but I'm glad you guys came along when you did." His clean, soapy smell is like a fresh breeze compared to Vance's oppressive stink.

"One of these days…" Logan says.

Corban shoots him a warning glance.

"Don't worry about me." I smile at Logan. "I totally understand."

"Still…" Corban helps me to my feet, his grip warm and firm. I don't want him to let go. "The less you know," he says, "the safer you are around here." He gives my arm a gentle squeeze before releasing it.

In an attempt to get my mind off Vance, I aim the trowel at the rose garden. "Hasn't Sebastian done a nice job with this new rose garden?"

"Yeah." Corban grins. "Less grass for us to mow."

Logan shakes his head. "Mowing the curves and trimming along the bricks means it'll take us longer."

"Look at the bright side," Corban says. "The more time we put in, the more we get paid."

"Yeah." Logan snorts. "Zero plus zero is zero. And zero times zero is zero. No matter how you figure it, we're—"

"Don't say it." Corban shakes his head. "It is what it is."

The reminder that, like me, they don't get paid for their work makes me wonder how many other Followers go without paychecks. "I'm curious to know," I tell them, "how you two fit this volunteer job into your real work schedules."

"I work afternoons and evenings at Macy's," Corban says.

"I alternate mornings and afternoons at a produce delivery service," Logan says. "Work is a big deal for the Followers. After all, Proverbs ten-four says, 'Lazy hands make a man poor, but diligent hands bring wealth.' One of Ruby Jade's favorite verses."

"Don't forget," Corban says, "idle hands are the devil's tools."

I laugh. "You mean *devious* devil, don't you?"

"Yeah." He gives me a wry grin.

"It's true. Diligent hands bring wealth...to three people." Logan clasps his hands behind his head and stretches. "The more we make, the more we put in the offering plate—and the more the leaders pocket."

"But it's never enough," Corban interjects. "We're expected to do volunteer work on our time off, for Leadership as well as for some of the wealthier members and people in the community. Hours and hours each week."

I remember the house I helped prep for painting. Was it just last week? "You mean members volunteer at Noreen and Inez's houses, too?"

"Yep."

"I wonder why I was assigned here, not at one of their places, not that I care to work for either of them."

"Probably because this is within walking distance for you."

"Makes sense."

"Or maybe Ruby Jade wants to keep an eye on you." Corban glances at his watch. "We'd better get to mowing, or I'll be late for work. But we wanted to tell you we have a plan."

"A plan?"

He grins.

I love his smile. It makes me want to smile too—and helps me push the Vance encounter to the recesses of my mind.

"We figured out a way Marcela can communicate with Rodrigo and her parents. Or, actually, how they can communicate with her."

"How exciting, Corban." I toss the trowel aside and clap my hands. "Tell me. What is it?"

"Your tip about her boss leaving for forty-five minutes or so every day was the clincher. Her parents can call the factory while he's gone. If someone is around and it's not safe for her to talk, all she has to do is say, 'Sorry, you must have a wrong number,' and hang up."

"Mom and Dad are in on the plan," Logan says. "They got pretty excited about it. In fact, Mom wanted to invite Marcela's mom over for lunch to tell her, but getting with a so-called reprehensible person is too chancy in this small town. Instead, Dad will stop by her dad's lumberyard to talk with him this afternoon. He's his insurance agent, so a private conversation in the office with the door closed won't be suspect."

"Your mom could call Marcela's mom."

"Yes, but…" Logan says.

"But, what?"

"Have you noticed a big black van with dark windows driving slowly through your neighborhood?" Corban asks.

"Now that you mention it, I have. What does it—?"

"The van is outfitted with audio equipment. Ruby Jade's stooges listen in on members' phone calls and report suspect conversations to her."

My heart jolts. The black van was here, in this very neighborhood, listening to me talk with my mom and my brother. Thinking of all I told Kip, I'm about to panic, when I remember the van wasn't around that day…if I remember right.

"A suspect conversation could be anything," Logan says. "Almost every word we say has the potential to be labeled unclean, perverted or wicked. Those are the primary evils around here."

"Are you kidding? How ludicrous." Doesn't fail—when I think I've heard the worst of what goes on in this place, I learn something new.

"Yeah, well, it's true." Corban rights a pack of flowers Vance knocked over.

"How do you guys communicate? Do you avoid using telephones?"

"At the moment, they only have one surveillance van," Corban says. "Before we make a call of any kind, business or personal, we check for the van and keep the calls short."

"Noreen gave me a phone, so I assume they can access my phone records. Do you and your parents have FFOW phones, too?"

"No," Logan says. "We have our own family plan, thank God. Yet, we still need to be careful with calls, especially on the landline."

"Why, if they can't access your phone records?"

"Same reason—someone could be snooping in on our calls. We always listen for clicks."

"What about Rodrigo? He could call Marcela from the restaurant where he works. They don't listen in on businesses, do they?"

As far as we know, they don't," Corban says. "But most of the employees are Followers. A private conversation, even a short one, would be nearly impossible. Have you been to Restaurant des Delices?"

"Noreen took me there." If I'd realized how I was being manipulated that day, I might not have capitulated. Instead, I ignored my gut instinct because I wanted to get out of jail free, like in Monopoly. Only, this isn't a game.

"I deliver to the restaurant's back door off a private alley," Logan says, "three times a week."

"Oh…" Before my mind can go wild formulating possible scenarios, I ask, "What's your plan?"

"Burner phones. We've got several at the house. I'll arrange produce boxes in the back of my truck to give Rodrigo a private corner to talk to his wife for a few minutes. If anyone happens to notice him missing, I'll cover for him."

"I get the impression this isn't the first Dahlstrom family caper."

They smirk and shrug their shoulders.

"Quick question," I say. "I, uh, heard something about darker-skinned Followers like me bleaching their skin to make it lighter and, supposedly, to rid themselves of Cain's curse. But Rodrigo and others in the congregation have dark skin, some darker than mine. I don't understand."

"As with most policies around here…" Corban swats at a wasp buzzing between us. "It doesn't have to make sense. I've heard female Followers should aspire to have ghost-white skin like Ruby Jade's. But for men, skin color doesn't seem to matter. Go figure."

"Here comes Sebastian." Logan waves at the pickup coming up the street. "We'd better get at it."

Corban tracks the vehicle's progress with his eyes. "Tell Marcela to expect short phone calls from ten-thirty to eleven-fifteen. If someone is with her, she should say it's a wrong number and end the call. Her parents will take turns calling and will work with Rodrigo through Logan to figure out what days work best with his restaurant schedule."

"Got it." I hold up a finger. "One more question." I glance at Sebastian's truck that's turning into the driveway. "I know I've asked before, but I need to be sure. Can I trust him?"

"Seb's a good guy," Corban says. "He helps out when he can. But he told us he's learned the only good reason to ride a bull is to meet a nurse."

I tilt my head. "Meaning?"

"Meaning he has no intention of butting heads with his boss. If Ruby Jade got wind he'd betrayed her, we all know she'd do everything in her power to destroy him."

"Sometimes I get the feeling," Logan counters, "he's biding his time, waiting for an opportunity to put her in her place."

"Could be," Corban says, "could be."

They walk toward the back of the property, reminding me of the clean-cut guys who used to come to our door in pairs, peddling their organization's skewed beliefs and literature. As the brothers go, I realize I haven't asked them to help me find my guitar. I'll have to tell them about its disappearance during our break, if we have one. Things change so fast around here, I can't plan on anything.

Corban and Logan don't stop for a break. Sebastian understands their time limitations and gives them each a water bottle and more homemade energy bars to eat while they work. Feeling like I've piddled away too much time, I follow suit and continue to work, which is silly when I'm not getting paid. But I've always been a hard worker, and I don't want to give Ruby Jade anything else to throw in my face.

While Logan is cleaning the lawnmowers, Corban comes to the rose garden to say goodbye, which makes me feel special. My housemates can't be bothered to say good morning.

"I need your help," I tell him.

"Vance?" His eyelids narrow. "He looked ready to pounce on you this morning."

"He was, but I'm safe as long as Sebastian is around." Unless, of course, Vance informs his mother he saw me wearing jeans.

"Be sure to tell Seb about it."

"Okay, but I have another more pressing problem."

He lifts an eyebrow.

"I know you need to get to your job, so I'll give you the short version. Someone, probably Olivia, took my guitar and two binders filled with songs I wrote, plus all my civilian clothes, including hiking boots my husband gave me. But she won't tell me where she put them."

"I'm sorry." He groans. "We should have gotten on that, but we were so focused on figuring out a solution to Marcela's—"

"It's not your fault, Corban. The boxes disappeared almost as soon as I got them. Before I left this morning, I told Olivia I wanted to report the theft to the sheriff, and she had a fit."

"Of course, she did."

"Should I file a report, anyway?"

"Hold off." He knocks a clump of grass from his pantleg. "I'll call another family meeting tonight, and we'll do some brainstorming, if you don't mind."

"I appreciate any help I can get. My parents gave me my guitar years ago. I'm afraid it'll be ruined."

"We'll outline a plan and get your input."

"Thanks. I'll be praying for you."

"Thank you. We need it." He ducks his head. "I've been praying for you, 'cause I know you've had a tough time since you came here."

"Hey, Corb…" Logan comes around the corner of the house. "I'm ready when you are."

Corban reaches out and clasps my shoulders.

I blink, surprised he's touching me. No one at FFOW touches anyone, except for a side hug now and then between women. From what I hear, Ruby Jade believes "bosom contact," as she calls it, will lead to the kinkiness she obsesses over.

Along with his soapy essence, I get a hint of grassy sweat, but it's not unpleasant.

"Hang on, Cat True." He gazes at me with eyes even bluer than I remember. "I have a feeling the ride is gonna be rough, but never forget, we're in this boat together." He grins. "Know what the best part is?"

I shrug, enjoying the weight of his strong hands. I have no idea where he's leading with this.

"When Jesus calmed the wind and waves, he was in the boat with his disciples—and he's in this battered, rocking boat, right alongside us. He'll get us through the storm."

"I appreciate the reminder, Corban." I place my hands on his arms. "I needed it."

He releases my shoulders and takes my hands. With a squeeze and a wink, he turns to join his brother. They wave goodbye and trot to their car.

Like a tsunami, a barrage of emotions crashes through my spirit. Happiness because Corban seems to truly care about me and my concerns. Sadness for all the pain and abuse my friends have suffered and continue to suffer. Fear I might never find my guitar and my songs—or my Bible and hiking boots. Anger at Ruby Jade and her minions for their callous exploitation and greed.

And finally, despair because I don't know how to escape their talons.

Yet, Corban reminded me the story doesn't end here. I cross my arms and rest my hands on my shoulders, shoulders his warm hands held so firmly. Lifting my face to the sun, I close my eyes and thank God for his faithful presence. The deluge of emotions dissipates like a receding wave, trickling and foaming at the edges of my soul. Yes, Jesus has stilled the waters.

Sebastian and I eat a quiet lunch at the picnic table. He tells me Myrtle Mae's brother, Norman, took her to town for a dental visit, but she hopes to be home in time for afternoon tea with me. "She loves visiting with you."

I smile, touched she enjoys our time together. I certainly enjoy her. She's like a mountain spring, always refreshing.

Earlier today, I wanted to beg Sebastian to drive me to the sheriff's office to file a complaint about my missing guitar. Afterward, I hoped to go to Judge Snow's chambers to find a way to leave. But now that I've talked with Corban, I'll wait until his family discusses the guitar theft before I do anything rash.

And then there's the Vance problem. Should I tell Sebastian his nephew came close to attacking me this morning? I can't be sure, but assault appeared to be his intent.

"You still drinking upstream from the herd?" Sebastian asks.

I give him a confused look.

"You're not letting the church's manure foul your waters, are you?"

And then I get what he means. I unscrew the cap on my water bottle. "I wish I knew a way to avoid the manure, as you call it. The only time I have any freedom from the church is when I'm here.

Except this morning, when I ran into Ruby Jade. She chewed me out for not wearing lipstick." I tip the bottle for a drink.

He grunts. "She used to be smart, but she got over it."

I spew water across the table. "Sorry." Hand over my mouth, I sputter and cough. "Struck me funny."

"One of my grandad's favorites." He chuckles. "Truth be told, R.J. is a smart woman, shrewd as a coyote. You gotta be wilier than she is."

"I don't want to be wily. I had to watch my back on the streets and fight to outsmart those who tried to take advantage of me in jail. Relaxing now and then would be nice, which a person ought to be able to do in a church group."

"Yeah, I know what you mean. Been there, done that. Hard to slack off the reins when varmints are breathing down your neck."

CHAPTER TWENTY-SIX

On the way to the Pritchards' house after work, I pull out my phone to call my dad. Maybe I can catch him on his drive home from his office. I've just dialed him, when I see the black van at the other end of the street, and I remember what Corban told me.

I end the call, hoping it didn't ring on Dad's end. I don't plan to say anything negative about FFOW, but I know my father wouldn't appreciate someone listening in on our conversation. I certainly don't appreciate it.

For the millionth time, I ask myself, *What's wrong with these people?* A church staff that spies on parishioners—even the most intimate acts. Parishioners who do their every bidding. Children taken from their parents. Parents allowing it.

Shutting off my mental list before I lose the calm I had earlier, I watch the van pass by. Two indistinct forms are visible through the darkened windows. I'm fairly certain they're men.

The vehicle stops in the same place it parked the first time I saw it. I wonder if it's the best spot to monitor the neighborhood. If the residents weren't all Followers, they'd assume someone was stalking them and call the sheriff. Truth is, someone *is* stalking them, stalking me.

I wonder how Kip would respond, if he knew. Actually, I know what his response would be. My big brother would get serious, for a change. *Sis*, he'd say, *I'll drive all night and be there first thing in the morning. Have your things packed and ready. We'll go straight to the judge, and then I'll deliver you wherever he feels you'll be safe from those crazies.*

Taking a long breath, I blow it out. *Calm the waves, Jesus. I need your peace in the midst of the storm.* Step number eleven in the Alcoholics Anonymous Big Book says we should pray only for the knowledge of God's will and the power to carry it out. How simple that seemed in the protected confines of the Gallatin County Jail.

Show me your will, God, and help me understand it. This place is so confusing. I need the power to do what you want me to do. Seems the only people around here with any power are the Fearsome Threesome—and Vance.

Olivia meets me at the kitchen door. "Wash your hands, Cassandra, and help Marjorie with the salad. We must eat on time because Ruby Jade has another message for us this evening."

No "welcome home" or questions about my day. Just get busy. *Now.* Like Logan said, work truly is a big deal for the Followers. I wonder if they believe scrubbing floors and scraping houses will get them to heaven. I miss Eric. He always asked about my day.

At supper, something feels off. The others ignore me, but that's nothing new. Marcela peers at me from time to time, her eyes wide with expectation. I hope we don't disappoint her. The Dahlstroms' plan seems failsafe, but that would be under normal circumstances. The Followers aren't normal.

I survey the table. The food smells okay—nothing rotten or sour, despite its boring appearance. Skinless chicken, mashed potatoes, white country gravy, steamed cauliflower, and a barely browned dinner roll.

Wait a minute. Where's Zachary? He's not in his usual seat. I lean in and glance from Olivia's end of the table to Owen's, but I don't see him. Dread seeps into my soul, and I chide myself for being pessimistic. Maybe they returned him to his parents. I hope so. To be with them again would make him so happy.

I look at those seated near me. "Where's Zachary?" The others freeze, as though they've been zapped by a wizard. Marcela flashes me warning signs with her eyes. I ignore her. "Did he go home to his family?"

Olivia places her hands on each side of her plate and clears her throat. Her husband stabs a piece of cauliflower and shoves it around his plate. Their children stare at the ceiling.

"Zachary," Olivia informs me, "is in timeout."

I wait for more, but that's all she says.

I shift my gaze from person to person. Other than Marcela, who has wide, frightened eyes, they avoid my gaze. I ask, anyway. "Can someone tell me what timeout means?"

Olivia blows out an impatient huff. "It means exactly what I said, Cassandra. Time. Out. You need no further explanation."

"But Zachary—"

"Dinner is done." She claps her hands. "Time to do the dishes and prepare for worship." She glares at me, her face scarlet and pinched, her eyes pinpricks of hatred.

Pushing away their chairs, the others eye the food still on their plates and give me side-glances, which suggest I'm the cause of them going hungry. I've lost my appetite and can't believe they haven't done the same. Something bad has happened to a precious child. I can tell by the way everyone is acting.

Less than fifteen minutes later, we're all seated around the living room like a group of friends about to watch the Super Bowl together. However, no easy banter or loud laughter enliven the occasion. The atmosphere is deathly quiet, thick with tension. The room is stuffy, and Olivia's mother, Alice, who's seated beside me, doesn't bathe often. Her body odor could best be described as stale perfume with urine undertones.

Every few minutes, Olivia shoots another eye dagger my way. I feel like I should apologize. But inquiring about a child's disappearance isn't a crime or an insult—in the *real* world.

She jumps to her feet and strides across the room to the thermostat. "Who turned off the air-conditioning?"

"I did," Owen says. "When I walked in from work, this place was as cold as—"

"Don't exaggerate, Owen." She adjusts the thermostat. "You know it's a sin. You should consider others' needs above your own."

I feel the air whoosh on. In a few short minutes, I'll be wishing I'd brought a sweater downstairs. But maybe the circulating air will diffuse Alice's stench.

"Olivia," Owen says, "you're the only one who wants the air-conditioning on all the time." He lifts his hand. "Who feels this house is too cold?"

Three people tentatively raise their hands.

Olivia whips around, eyes blazing. "This is *not* a democracy, Owen Pritchard."

The three rebels quickly lower their hands.

"If I say this house is hot…" Her shrill voice grows louder. "It's hot."

He sighs. "There you have it."

"And just what do you mean by such an asinine comment?"

He doesn't respond.

She stomps to the recliner in the corner opposite him. The other residents are either seated elbow-to-elbow on the three couches or are perched on dining room chairs. But Olivia and Owen always get the recliners. After all, they're the household guardians.

We wait for ten long, cold, silent minutes before Ruby Jade appears on the screen. I feel awful about the aborted meal. We had plenty of time to finish eating, but I pushed Olivia for an answer. The only way she could handle her irritation was to make everyone suffer.

Like before, Ruby Jade is seated at her desk. I glance at my housemates. The kids look bored already. But the adults, especially the women, focus on their leader, slight smiles on their faces.

As if her constant texts aren't reminder enough, Ruby Jade takes twenty minutes to inform us only the devious devil and his minions would call Christ's death *good*. "In fact…" She scowls at the camera, eyebrows lowered. "To think the words *Good Friday* or say them out loud is worldly and must be confessed immediately to remain in God's favor."

After the do-or-die pronouncement, she giggles, which catches me off-guard. I'm never prepared for her temperament changes.

"Those carnal, pretend Christians are so silly," she says. "So silly. No one knows the dates of Christ's death and resurrection. We have to endure this bloody pagan pageant year after year because the pope wants another excuse to ride around in his popemobile and act holier than thou."

I swallow my own giggle. Since when does the pope make worldwide holiday decisions?

Hands beside her mouth, she whispers, "But *we* know better. Remember the children's story *The Emperor's New Clothes* and what happened to the emperor? Well..." She sits back, eyebrows lifted. "I have it on good authority the pope will get his due, same as the emperor."

The others in the room smile at each other. Do they dislike the pope? Or do they enjoy knowing their leader has an inside connection with God? I wonder if any of the children in the room have been allowed to read *The Emperor's New Clothes*. I also wonder if Ruby Jade ever read the book to Vance.

Her eyelids flutter over her constricted pupils and her head twitches. Something has unsettled her. But as quickly as her composure faltered, her self-importance reappears. "Don't you assume for one minute I'm recommending you read a pagan book. My comment was for the sake of..." Her words run together. "Illustra-shun-on-ly."

Across the room, Owen's eyebrows twitch. No one else seems to notice.

Ruby Jade blinks, hesitates, and then finishes her thought. "My point is, the pope is a poophead."

I snort and then cough, hand over my mouth, to cover my laughter. *The pope is a poophead?* I'll have to tell Kip. He'll die laughing. I can see him now.

302 | Rebecca Carey Lyles

"It's true," Ruby Jade is saying. "Do not follow his misguided footsteps."

With that final vague proclamation, she orders the households to sing a *hallelujah* song she wrote to help us celebrate, not mourn, like the world mourns. The words flash onto the screen.

Similar to the church services, the singing is loud, jarring and in unison. When I throw in harmony, which is a challenge to find in the cacophony of harsh, discordant noise, Marcela elbows me.

I frown. *What now?*

She whispers, "Melody."

I refrain from rolling my eyes, struck by the realization this moment is a perfect example of what life is like at FFOW. Individuality is suppressed and uniformity expected. The end result is chaos.

The song's meter is off, but we muddle through. Guitar accompaniment would provide rhythm and keep everyone on pitch, as much as is possible with this crowd. Which brings me to my missing instrument…and a missing little boy. Finding Zachary is far more crucial than finding my stuff.

I want to jump to my feet and scream, "What's wrong with you people?" They all seem to know what happened to Zachary, and they act ashamed, or maybe secretive. Whatever the case, I'd gladly sacrifice my guitar *and* my hiking boots to ensure the child's wellbeing. I wish I could call Corban to ask him what to do.

Later, in the bathroom, Marcela informs me harmony is only used when "under authority," which means authorized by one of the leaders. Her explanation blows my mind. The Fearsome Threesome actually have the audacity to control the members' singing. I could go on a long rant about how they're stealing the gifts of creativity and beautiful music—*God's gifts* to us. Instead, I ask, "What is 'timeout'? What does it mean?"

Her gaze slides away. "I'd rather not tell you."

"That bad?"

She averts her gaze.

"Tell me, Marcy."

She murmurs something I can't hear.

I bend closer, my head almost touching hers. "What?" Chocolate tinges her breath.

"Seclusion."

My heart plummets. I can barely breathe. "An eight-year-old boy is in seclusion?" I stare at her. "By himself?"

"I don't know."

"Why?"

"I'm not sure, but I heard a rumor Leadership feels he wasn't properly cleansed because you interfered. Ruby Jade doesn't want him to become bigheaded and get the idea he's above discipline."

Hands clenched, I close my eyes and start to scream my rage, but she quickly covers my mouth. "You okay, Cassandra?" Her voice is loud. "Did you choke on your mouthwash?"

I push her hand off my face and suck in short gasping breaths. She whispers, "Cough."

I cough, three times. Ruby Jade's obnoxious son is the one who belongs in timeout, not an innocent child. "Where is he?"

She turns on the water. "The leaders have a special wing in the men's dorm where they send men and teenage boys to timeout for days, sometimes weeks or months. But I've never heard of younger boys being sent there."

"What?" I gape at her in the mirror.

Marcela whispers in my ear, "I'm sure you're aware males have a greater problem with lust than women, visually and physically."

I clasp my chest and hack once more, this time out of shocked horror. Timeout is one more way for Ruby Jade to destroy families. Eric loved to caress me every chance he got. And I loved his tender touch. "Is that where Rodrigo is, in the men's dorm?"

Her sad eyes and pressed lips tell me all I need to know.

"Marcela…" I hug her. "I'm so sorry."

She stops the water.

I pull her behind the door. "A child has disappeared. Does no one care? Do his parents know?"

She shrugs.

I open my mouth.

She covers it. "Stuff it, Cassandra."

Bile rises in my throat. I step to the toilet, lift the lid and lose my supper, what little I ate.

Exhausted, I fall into bed, but I can't sleep. If I could, I'd pace the room or the hallway. However, prying eyes are everywhere. I'd go to my Bible for comfort and direction, but Olivia took it away with the rest of my things.

Are women ever banished to solitary confinement the way men and boys are? How about young girls? I'll have to ask Marcela.

I'm about to roll over, when the thought comes that this is the perfect time to search the basement for my belongings. What if my guitar is right under my nose, maybe in the storage room behind the laundry room?

The room also has an unused woodburning stove with a cooktop and big blue barrels scattered about. I assume the Followers are preppers, stockpiling for Armageddon or whatever. Could be the cupboards are filled with canned and dehydrated foods, but I won't know until I check.

If I find my guitar, I won't remove it. But I'll know it's close, not in a hot attic or a damp shed. I grab my robe and sit up. "Marcela," I whisper. "You awake?"

Her response is a garbled, "Huh..."

For the perverts who may be watching, I say, "My stomach is still bothering me. I'm going to the kitchen to find something to calm it."

She moves a bit but says nothing, which is okay by me. For her sake, the less she knows about my nocturnal activities, the better. I'm about to leave the room but stop, hand over my mouth. I was so upset about Zachary I forgot to tell her the Dahlstroms' plan.

I slip out the door, closing it as quietly as I can, and peer both ways into the dark hallway. Empty. So far, so good. Barely breathing, I hug the stair railing and place one bare foot at a time along the edge of each stair. As I hoped, the wood is silent. The only sounds are my heartbeat and the kitchen clock, which governs all meal preparations with great precision.

At the landing, I turn toward the basement door, grateful I don't need to walk through the kitchen. I'm convinced the Pritchards have a motion alarm in their bedroom. Slowly, ever so slowly, I twist the handle. The latch's release is loud as a hammer strike in my ears.

Holding my breath, I wait. No one stirs. I feel my way down the stairs and along the shelf where the Pritchards keep candles, matches, flashlights, batteries and such for power outages.

I find a small flashlight, point it at the floor and push the switch. The circle of light on the tile floor is small, which is good. If someone has a bedroom down here, I don't want to attract their attention with a bright light. The basement is dark and cool and suffused with an earthy mushroom smell.

I tiptoe into the laundry room, where four washing machines face four dryers. The basement odor is replaced by that of detergents and dryer sheets. Foldout ironing boards on the far wall hang near a garment steamer and a shoeshine pedestal. A clothesline spans a corner.

The door to the storage room is at the rear of the laundry room. I slip inside. Shining the flashlight on the cabinets, I notice for the first time they have built-in locks. Should have known. I move from one side of the room to the other, tugging handles, but no dice.

Quietly closing the door behind me, I return to the laundry room. From there, I walk out into a long hallway lit by a solitary nightlight. The cement floor's chill seeps into my feet. I direct the flashlight beam into the hall. The doors on each side are closed, as far as I can tell.

Should I try them?

Yes, I decide, *I should.* This is a unique opportunity to search as much of the basement as I can access.

But what if someone hears a doorknob rattle, comes unglued and screams—and wakes the entire household? I have no idea where everyone sleeps. We're forbidden to visit each other's bedrooms—one more queen-bee effort to prevent "kinkiness" amongst the worker bees, I assume.

Farther along the hallway, I aim the light ahead and listen for snores. Hearing none, I crisscross from one door to the next, my destination being the red exit sign glowing at the end of the hall. Carefully, quietly, I test each doorknob. They're all locked.

When I first moved into the house, the exit signs over the doors seemed strange to me. But then I saw the sprinkler heads hanging from the ceilings and figured such a big house with so many residents required extra safety features, like the jail had. This exit sign surprises me because it indicates an outside entrance I didn't know existed. I ran past it when Marcela and I retrieved my boxes from the front porch, but I was riveted on our mission and didn't notice.

Close enough to catch sight of an empty space beyond the wide exit, I shine the light into the void. It reflects off what looks like a vault door. Really? Maybe it's where they store their gold and silver for end times. I'm tiptoeing toward it, when a strange sound stops me. I switch off the flashlight and pivot to scan the hallway behind me, but I don't see any shadows or movement in the dim light.

Holding my breath, I fight to focus my hearing beyond my loud heartbeat. The noise comes again. It sounds like muffled yelling or crying but not like a baby. A cat, maybe?

Rank-and-file Followers who don't have leadership privileges can't have pets inside their homes. They're unsanitary, according to one of Ruby Jade's FFOW-Wows, and spread hair, dander and germs. Even so, a feral cat or some other animal might have somehow become trapped in the basement. Fellowship Neighborhood is far enough out of town that I've seen deer, rabbits and raccoons and an occasional frog.

The barely audible cries continue. I know I should go back to bed before Ruby Jade's camera goons get suspicious. Yet, I also know I won't sleep if I haven't found the source and released whatever it is. I creep along the wall toward the noise. It seems to be coming from the last door on the left.

Dropping to my knees, I place my ear against the narrow gap between the door and the doorframe. Though the sound is muted, as if the room has been soundproofed, I'm certain I hear someone calling "Mama" amidst heartbreaking sobs.

Zachary. It has to be him. I don't know the boy well, but I'm positive it's his voice. To catch his attention, I switch on the flashlight and flicker the beam below the door. His wails continue. I lean close and whisper, "Zachary, it's me, Cassandra."

No response.

I wait for him to take a breath and whisper as loud as I dare, "Zachary, it's your friend Cassandra."

First a stifled sob and then his childish voice rasps through the narrow crack. "Mama?"

"This is Cassandra. I want to help you."

"It is?"

"Yes. I just found where they put you."

"They s-said I was b-bad." He stutters through sobs. "I-I should have l-let the others hit m-me."

"I was the one who stopped those boys, not you. Who put you in the room?"

"Miss Olivia and Miss Inez."

Fury churns my chest. How can they be so heartless? "They're the bad people for locking you in this room."

"I'm s-so scared." He whimpers. "It's very l-loudly quiet in here."

A light at the far end of the hallway flashes on.

I switch off the flashlight and whisper, "Someone's coming. I need to leave, but I promise to help you."

He sniffles and hiccups. "Will you f-find my m-mama?"

"I'll try. Lie down and pretend you're asleep."

"Okay."

"Remember, Jesus loves you and so do I."

CHAPTER TWENTY-SEVEN

S till crouched, I scoot around the wall, which divides the long hallway from the alcove where the vault sits. A short set of stairs on my left leads to a landing, where another red exit light reveals the shadowy outline of an exterior door. I'm about to sneak up the stairs, when the hall lights come on, and Olivia's voice proclaims, "I'm positive she came straight down here."

She's at the other end of the basement, but her words are loud and clear. Apparently, she's not concerned about waking anyone. The irritation in her voice is more pronounced than usual.

"But she doesn't know where the boy is." Owen's voice. "Her confusion was obvious at supper."

"She's street-smart and dangerous. I knew it the minute Ruby Jade assigned her to this household."

"Seems like a nice girl to me."

"She's a slut, Owen, and don't you ever forget that."

"Just because she was in jail doesn't mean—"

"She was in jail for a reason. Only someone as naïve and dense as you would be dumb enough to think she's anything more than a street tramp."

"Olivia, that's not—"

"Keep running your mouth, Owen, and I'll report you for lusting after the whore. Ruby Jade will banish you to the men's dorm for a year, maybe two. Now, open the door and hand me the keys. We need to check inside every room."

The jangle of keys is my cue to dash up the stairs to the exit, not that I wouldn't love to hear all the other kind words Olivia has to say about me. How did a nice man like Owen marry a witch like her? And her poor kids. I bet they leave home the first chance they get.

I turn the lever to unlock the deadbolt. It slides silent as silk, and I breathe a grateful prayer. Pressing the door handle downward millimeter by millimeter, I plead for the hinges to not squeak and opening the door doesn't trigger an alarm.

It opens without effort or fireworks. No ear-splitting sirens, no flashing lights. I tiptoe onto a cement stoop and carefully pull the door closed behind me. For a moment, I linger beneath the three-quarter moon, getting my bearings and breathing in the cool night air. But I know I have to keep moving.

As I understand the house's layout, I'm by the Pritchards' bedroom windows. Thank God they're not there. Even so, I hunker low as I hurry past. Moonlight provides enough illumination I don't need to use the flashlight.

At the front corner, I stop and peer both ways. This is when I have to make a decision. I could sneak inside the house, creep up the stairs and climb into bed. And pretend I never left, that I don't know the Pritchards are searching for me. From what I can tell, no upstairs lights are on, which suggests they haven't involved the entire household in the search. But the bedroom camera is a problem. I can't return without the perverts seeing me. They must have alerted the Pritchards.

I could say I felt nauseated and stepped outside for a breath of fresh air—and then act shocked they're concerned about me—which would truly be a shock. But then, how could I help Zachary who needs to be rescued before any more harm is done to his poor little psyche?

What's done is done. However, the terror needs to end. Now. This is my opportunity to show him at least one person in the world cares. Besides, I promised I'd find his mama.

I make my decision. I'll run to town, find someone on the street with a phone, maybe one of my former friends, and call the sheriff. Then I'll call the Dahlstroms, provided their home phone is listed. If I had my cell phone, I'd call the authorities right now, so they could rescue Zachary immediately. But the phone is in the bedroom. Someone would see me for sure.

Maybe the Dahlstroms can help the department locate Zachary's parents. If they can't or won't rescue their son from Olivia's clutches, Child and Family Services will. I'll also tell the sheriff about the Johnsons' little girl and beg them to reunite her with her family.

I break into a run across the damp grass and onto the sidewalk that meanders through the rural neighborhood. I've heard the distance to town is slightly over ten miles. My bare feet may be trashed by then, but the highway is paved. I won't have to endure gravel roads.

And it's nighttime. Shouldn't be much traffic. If someone asks why I'm outside in my nightgown in the middle of the night, I'll say I fled a domestic situation, which is entirely true.

I feel as though I'm flying. My feet barely touch the cement. Freedom never felt so good. I can make my own decisions and plan how to help my friends. But I must be quite a sight with my hair and my robe floating behind me as I race beneath streetlights.

If some little Follower kid happens to peek out a window—not that such independence or curiosity is encouraged—they might believe they're seeing a fairy or an angel. Or a character from a Peter Pan book.

Oh, right. FFOW kids probably haven't heard of fairies and Peter Pan. I slow to catch my breath. Why am I thinking about angels and fairies? My mind is all over the place tonight. I rest my hands on my thighs and drop my head to catch my breath. Probably has something to do with experiencing real freedom for the first time in a long time.

At the corner where the main road through the neighborhood intersects with the highway, a pair of spotlights highlight the engraved Fellowship Neighborhood entrance rock. "Farewell, Fellowship Neighborhood," I whisper, "and all you misguided Followers."

As I expected, the highway is deserted. I walk until I regain my wind, and then I run until I'm out of breath. Unlike the sidewalks in the neighborhood, the road is littered with gravel, which bruises the soles of my tender feet. Followers only remove their shoes when they sleep because feet are considered sensual body parts. How sensuality fits with the athlete's-foot concern, I'm not sure.

King Solomon, I was told, provided the juicy nugget about feet in the "Song of Solomon." I was also informed reading his sensuous song is off-limits for anyone under sixty years of age. The mental picture of Olivia's mother reading Solomon's ode to sex makes me laugh out loud. Why is the book in the Bible, if God doesn't want us to read it?

Crickets chirp, and a gentle breeze rustles the grass that edges the road. A rabbit hops across the pavement. I'm not alone, which is okay with me. Lately, I've come to believe insects and animals are far safer than people. A faraway dog barks, and an owl hoots from somewhere nearby. The air smells of prairie grass.

Montana summer nights are the best.

My feet slap rhythmically against the asphalt. Smacking an occasional pebble takes my breath away, but I ignore the pain. I'll deal with my feet later.

In the distance, moonglow reflects off snow-covered peaks. Cloud wisps float over the moon, yet I have sufficient visibility without the flashlight. I'm grateful for small blessings. An early rising farmer might notice a circle of light bobbing along the road and send his dogs after me.

The night has cooled, and the breeze has strengthened, but I'm hot. Running in a flannel robe over a flannel gown, which all female Followers wear, no matter the season, is a recipe for a heat stroke. I slow to a walk, remove the robe and throw it over my arm. Relishing the fresh air, I continue at the slower pace. What a beautiful night, one I couldn't have enjoyed if I'd stayed in my bedroom.

My heart dances. I have escaped the FFOW trap. Free at last. Thank you, Jesus. Now, to free my friends. The old me would be planning where to grab a celebratory nip when I get to town. Instead, I have the unfinished song fragment running through my brain, with additional phrases.

> *Cradled in opulence, swaddled in decadence,*
> *delusions of grandeur, great poverty of soul.*
> *Playing a prophetess, stealing their innocence,*
> *charlatan psalmist, wicked master of control.*

Pleased, I decide these four lines—or some version thereof—will be the chorus. I'm working on stanzas describing the Fearsome Threesome and their tactics, when car lights appear on the horizon. I quickly slip on the robe and button all the buttons as fast as I can.

Should I flag the oncoming driver in the hope he or she will be willing to turn around and give me a ride to town? Or should I drop into the barrow pit beside the road? Hitchhiking has its dangers, and I have nowhere else to hide. No trees or bushes line the highway, only prairie grass and fences.

The barrow pit isn't steep. I could easily climb down the bank, if my feet weren't so sore. I'd have to lie on the bottom, which could be muddy, and where weeds and stickers would cling to my flannel nightclothes like iron shavings to a magnet.

And I might come nose to nose with a skunk or a rat—or a snake. I shudder. I may have a growing fondness for wild animals, but I have to admit I can't fathom a cozy relationship with certain critters.

Coming upon a long drive to a farmhouse a quarter mile off the highway, I stop and wait. A cattle guard straddles the dirt road that leads to the house, and a barbed-wire fence abuts the wide metal grate on each end. I ready my domestic-abuse excuse for wandering a Montana highway, in my nightgown, in the dark.

I'm surprised the car is still far away. Seems it would be nearing me by now. It's not only traveling slowly, a searchlight flashes from it, probing one side of the road, then the other. They're looking for something…or someone. I hope and pray it's not me.

I use the wait to catch my breath. I don't know how much time has passed since I left the Pritchards' house. From the rise I'm standing on, I can see the lights of town blinking in the distance. My guess is it's less than five miles away. I think my feet could make it, but a ride would be wonderful.

The car approaches, driving twenty or thirty miles an hour. Moonlight bounces off the white SUV, and I see "Sheriff" printed in big letters on the side. "Gallatin County" is in a smaller font. Perfect. The deputy can initiate Zachary's rescue, and I won't have to run all the way to Bozeman. My feet are beginning to hurt, a lot.

I'm tempted to wave the flashlight, but the spotlight will catch me soon enough. Dropping the flashlight behind me, I kick it into the barrow pit. I can retrieve it later. Right now, I'd rather not have something that belongs to the Pritchards in my possession.

When the spotlight lands on me, I twist my head from the powerful beam.

The SUV screeches to a halt and pulls onto the shoulder. Dirt roils around me.

I cough and can't see a thing in the dusty haze, but I hear a door open, followed by footsteps. I'm glad I'm wearing the robe. The light is so strong, it would have shone right through my nightgown.

"Well, well, well… If it isn't Miz Cassandra Turner."

I nod. "Yes, I'm Cas—" *Wait. I'm not Cassandra Turner. I'm Cassie True.* My heart begins to thump. *How does he know my FFOW name, and why is he so sure it's me?*

"Out for a little midnight stroll?"

I'm tempted to respond to his sarcasm with my own brand, which Eric said could blister paint. But Zachary's sobs ring in my head, and I bite my tongue. All that matters is rescuing a little boy, no matter how much the officer's aggressive tone unsettles me.

Hearing noises behind me, I pivot. Three cows are on the other side of the cattleguard, every hair on their heads illuminated. Their big curious eyes reflect the spotlight, and I catch a whiff of manure.

"Face me, with your hands up."

Hands up? I rotate. *Like I've done something wrong?* I do as I'm told, even as a sense of foreboding invades my soul.

"Get in the car." His voice is harsh, as if I'm being difficult. "Keep your hands above your head, or I'll cuff 'em."

I follow orders, hobbling through the light and squinting until I'm able to see again.

He opens the door.

I climb in.

"Fasten your seatbelt."

I comply. The rubber mat feels smooth and cool beneath my battered feet. I'm relieved to be able to sit, though the vinyl seat is hard and smells like more than one drunk has laid on it.

The officer stands by the door, gazing at me. He rubs his jaw. Is he trying to decide what to do with me? Enough light bleeds over from the spotlight that I can read his nametag. Deputy Lawrence Manning. I don't remember seeing the stocky man at the jail.

Behind him, the bovine trio has been joined by other curious cows. And behind them, the farmhouse lights are ablaze. I didn't mean to cause a commotion, but one thing seems to be leading to another. I wish I knew how to stop the dominoes.

"What do you have to say for yourself, Cassandra Turner?"

"Why do you assume that's my name?"

Manning snorts. "Add a missing-person report to a woman wandering around in a nightgown, and—" He snaps his fingers. "The answer is you."

"It's not my real name." I find it hard to believe Olivia filed a missing-person report after telling me Followers don't involve authorities in their private matters. Seems she would have come looking for me herself.

"You think I don't know your other names?"

"More important than my name is rescuing the little boy who's being held prisoner in the Pritchards' basement."

He rears his head back. "What?"

316 | REBECCA CAREY LYLES

"Do you need a search order to look for him? I can take you directly to where they're keeping him."

"Olivia and Owen Pritchard are upstanding FFOW members." He juts his chin. "They wouldn't do anything without Ruby Jade's approval."

"Are you a FFOW member?"

"Sure thing." Manning's barrel chest expands. "And proud of it."

Yeah, and your search for me was authorized by the queen bee herself, not the sheriff. "Whether Ruby Jade approved or not, imprisoning children is illegal—and cruel."

"Sometimes..." His voice is softer now, less macho. "Sometimes Leadership puts teen boys in timeout for discipline purposes. How old is this kid?"

"Eight."

"Eight?" He eyes me for a moment. "And he's locked in a basement, not in the men's dorm? You sure about that?"

"Positive."

"What's his name?"

"Zachary Russell."

The deputy's head jerks, like I slapped him.

"You know his parents?"

Fists clenched on his duty belt, he stares at the ground.

CHAPTER TWENTY-EIGHT

I've struck a nerve, but I don't know which one. "Do Zachary's parents know how poorly their child is treated? Olivia Pritchard is nasty to him, and his classmates beat him up. I saw them do it. The teacher called it a cleanse."

When he doesn't respond, I ask, "Are you familiar with cleanses?"

"Yeah." He grunts. "But I didn't know kids get them too."

"Any idea who his parents are? You could call them—"

"I, uh…" Manning rubs his jaw. "Huh…"

His hesitation disturbs me. "Please, officer, you've got to help him. When I left, he was crying for his mother. I promised to find her for him." It's all I can do not to fall at his knees and plead for mercy for the little boy.

"His mother's name is Trina." Manning finally looks at me. "I probably shouldn't tell you this because Leadership hasn't announced it to the church yet, but Trina Russell just became my fiancée."

Now, I'm the shocked one. "Oh, wow, that's—"

"From what she's told me," he adds, "she knows very little about her son's day-to-day happenings. But she misses him. He's everything to her."

"Then, why did she—?"

"Like you, she spent time at GCDC. Meth addiction. Before she was released, she was accepted into the Transformation Way program and assigned a room in the women's dorm. But she was told her son needed to be with a family, not in a dorm with women. Ruby Jade was afraid he'd get—he finger quotes—*kinky* ideas."

Tempted to swear, I press my lips together. Ruby Jade's obsession manifests in so many ways. "You know the rehab program is on hold?"

"I knew the director and his wife left, but only because Ruby Jade ranted from the pulpit for over an hour. Said they'd abandoned God's vision and were headed to the hottest dungeon in hell. Called them Judases. She even said they ought to hang themselves, so vultures could rip apart their bodies. A bit of an overreaction, I'd say."

Yeah…

He shakes his head. "I figured someone else had taken their positions."

"Trina didn't tell you?"

"We rarely get to spend time together. And then, we have to be careful what we say."

"From what I've observed, your communication may not change after you marry."

He gazes off into the distance.

"Where did Zachary live while his mom was incarcerated?" I ask. "With his father?"

"His dad was killed in Afghanistan shortly after he was born." He glances at the cows and then back at me. "Trina's brother and wife kept him while she was at GCDC. They offered to house them both while she was in the program, but Ruby Jade wanted her on campus, and Trina wanted her son with her."

My first instinct is anger at Trina, but I'm sure she had no idea Ruby Jade would flip her life upside down by taking her son away. Like I had no idea what I was getting into. "Does she ever visit him?"

He shakes his head. "Not allowed."

"Then, she must talk with him at church."

"No. She sits in the overflow room. Ruby Jade doesn't want Zachary to see her and get upset."

If my feet weren't so sore, I'd kick the seatback in front of me. Such disregard for people's feelings is beyond me. "He's a little boy who desperately needs his mother. I left to get help for him."

At the sound of shrill barking, the deputy whips around. Dark coats shining in the moonlight, two big dogs are headed our way at a full sprint. The cows bellow and disappear. Manning shoves my door closed, dives into the driver's seat and slams the door so hard the car rocks.

The dogs leap over the cattle guard and jump on the SUV, growling and clawing the doors, their fangs mere inches from my face. I shrink as far away as the seatbelt allows.

Manning lowers his window a half inch. "Go on, git outa here."

The dogs continue their frenzied attack.

He guns the motor and the dogs back off. Switching off the spotlight, he speeds onto the highway, heading toward the neighborhood I fled a few short hours ago.

I bang the metal grid that separates the seats.

The deputy slows the vehicle and turns on the red dome light. It paints the SUV's interior a hazy red-pink. He eyes me in the mirror.

"Please..." I shake my head. "I don't want to go to the Pritchards' house."

He screeches to a stop in the middle of the deserted road.

I grab the partition for support.

"My only other option is to take you to the detention center," he says. "Judge Snow's orders are for you to remain in the rehab program until completion. If you leave—"

"How can I leave what doesn't exist?"

"The judge doesn't know that."

"I bet he does." I return his stare without blinking. My pulse pounds my temples.

"You're probably right." He blows out a breath. "But I can't change his ruling, and I gotta get back to work. As an officer of the law, I can drive you to the jail and book you, or I can drop you off at your Follower household." With a shrug, he adds, "Your choice."

I close my eyes. How did a sleepless night come to this? How did my earlier debate as to which mountain to scale reach a climax so quickly?

Two mountains, two options. If I return to GCDC, I'll escape FFOW and Ruby Jade's craziness, or at least I hope so. She seems to hold a lot of sway in this town. But I'll disappoint my family, and my parents will have to hire a lawyer to wrangle with the judge over a different rehab program. And I won't be able to help my friends.

Opening my eyes, I ask, "What about Zachary? Are you going to remove him from the basement and from the Pritchards custody?"

"I'll contact the Child Protective Services hotline when I get off duty in a couple hours. I'd call sooner, but I doubt you want it to appear like you had anything to do with the report. By the time CPS takes action, you'll have been at the Pritchards' house or the detention center for several hours."

"Will you reunite him with his mother?" My feet are beginning to throb.

"I don't have that authority, but I'll do what I can."

"Realistically, what *can* you do?" I cock my chin. "You're a FFOW member."

"Not for long. Ruby Jade's unhinged tirade about the T.W. director and his wife didn't sit well with me. And I'm tired of her using me to do her dirty work, like tracking you down. When I thought no one was listening, I hinted to Trina the possibility of moving on when she finishes the program. She seemed open to the idea." He pauses. "I have a feeling this situation with her son will trigger an earlier departure."

"I'd like to meet Trina and tell her how much her son loves her."

"I'm sure she'd appreciate it. Now, where to?" He puts the car into gear again.

Moon-silvered grasses wave in the breeze drifting over the prairie, and a hint of sunrise rims the eastern mountains. I wish I could enjoy the peaceful scene. Unfortunately, that's not possible. Officer Manning needs to get to work.

And I need to make a decision.

I release my seatbelt and slide forward. The movement sends sharp pangs up my legs. Grasping the metal grille, I lean close. "Do you promise?" My red fingers on the grid look like something out of a sci-fi flick. Beyond the dashboard, broken yellow highway lines glow in the headlights.

He meets my gaze in the dimly lit mirror. "Promise what?"

"Promise to get Zachary out of the Pritchards' basement and into his mother's arms?"

Manning twists my direction. His face is a pale red, and he smells like Irish Spring soap. "I promise," he says. "Scout's honor. I will do *everything* in my power to reunite Trina and Zachary. And I'll search out other children who've been taken from their parents or are in so-called timeout. Trina's son may not be the only one."

"They took my housemates' daughter."

"Tell them to call me." He reaches into his shirt pocket. "Here's my card." Bending it, he shoves the card through the grid.

I squint to read it in the dim light. "One more thing."

He looks at his watch. "What?"

"No one inside or outside Faithful Followers of the Way needs to know you and I met tonight. I'm not asking you to lie, but—"

322 | REBECCA CAREY LYLES

"Haven't you noticed?" He chuckles. "We Followers are first-rate liars."

"Now that you mention it, yes, I have noticed."

"Of course, no FFOW member would ever publicly condone lying. Ruby Jade preaches against it on a regular basis, but..." He pauses. "It's a self-protection tactic."

"From what?" I ask, although I know the answer.

"Leadership."

"I get it." I push the card into the grate. "And for the same reason, I can't keep this card. But I memorized your number. You'll be hearing from me."

"Where to?" he asks. "Your household or jail?"

I groan. "This is killing me."

He clears his throat.

I get the message. *Make a decision—and make it fast.*

"Okay. Take me to the Pritchards' place." I fumble for the seatbelt. "It's not my home, but it's where I live."

For now.

DISCUSSION QUESTIONS

1. As *Shattered Dream* unfolds, it becomes increasingly obvious FFOW is more than a religious community. It is, in fact, a cult. Cults have been documented in the United States since the 1800s. Have you ever been part of a cult or have you known anyone who's been embedded in or deceived by one? What did it take for you/the person to break free? What were the consequences of leaving?

2. Cassie ignores the red flags that nag at her as she signs the Transformation Way forms. She left her jail life behind, only to be imprisoned by a religious cult. Compare and contrast an inmate's life with a cult member's life. What does each environment allow the individual to retain? What is stripped away?

3. Having renewed her faith while in jail, Cassie encourages fellow cult members to remember Jesus holds onto them. Their salvation doesn't depend on them holding onto Him moment by moment. How might a "prison" experience or difficult circumstances be part of God's plan to use you to encourage others? Are you willing, like Cassie, to step up and risk the consequences?

4. From taking passports to installing cameras in private bedrooms, the Fearsome Threesome see themselves as above the law. List other illegal actions or activities they commit or condone. Who or what, both inside and outside the cult, enables them to get away with breaking the law?

5. Ruby Jade presents herself as God's appointed pastor, prophetess and psalmist for FFOW. Brainstorm as a group the differences between Jesus' leadership example and Ruby Jade's leadership model. What do you think causes the differences?

6. FFOW members have very little control over their personal lives. How are power, authority and control exercised at FFOW? Who are the primary power brokers? Have you ever experienced abuse of power in a religious community? What was the result?

7. Ruby Jade gives every member an "approved" name. What is her purpose for doing this? What affect does it have on the recipient? Would you feel comfortable being given a mandatory new name?

8. Little Zachary's "cleansing" is an overtly brutal form of manipulation. What other, but perhaps more subtle, forms of manipulation are used to insure FFOW members' unquestioning compliance? Which do you think would be hardest for you to see through or resist? Does manipulation ever have a positive aspect?

9. What benefits do FFOW members receive in exchange for giving up their rights to personal opinions and personal decision-making? Would you be willing to relinquish the same rights to receive the same benefits? What personality types might be attracted to this arrangement, whether in a leader or follower role?

10. Where does Cassie find solace and strength to endure life in the FFOW cult? Who does God put in her life to encourage her? What "way of escape" has God provided for you in a tough situation? Who has He sent to stand alongside you and encourage you in your faith journey? Whom might you encourage?

Questions crafted by Pat Watkins

RELIGIOUS CULTS

"If I were asked for a yardstick to discern good from bad spirituality, I would suggest three criteria to be detached from: material gain, self-importance, and the urge to dominate others. Unfortunately, much of what is labeled spirituality in America today moves in the opposite direction. It means using the names of God and Christ to promote one's own importance, material gain, and right to oppress others."

(Rosemary Radford Ruether, Professor of Theology; quoted in "Toxic Faith: Experiencing Healing from Painful Spiritual Abuse" by Stephen Arterburn and Jack Felton)

"My experience has taught me that a cult can potentially recruit anyone regardless of his or her education or special background. No one is invulnerable or somehow immune. ...The issue of destructive cults isn't limited based on geography, a demographic, a nationality, or one's political ideology; rather it is an issue of human welfare, which transcends such boundaries."

("Cults Inside Out: How People Get In and Can Get Out" by Rick Alan Ross)

"Whether male or female, most [cult leaders] are equal-opportunity victimizers, drawing men, women, and children of all ages into their webs of influence."

("Take Back Your Life: Recovering from Cults and Abusive Relationships" by Janja Lalich and Madeleine Tobias)

"[ISIS] is a political cult that uses religion to lure and indoctrinate people. It exhibits many of the classic signs—recruiting people through deception, whisking them away to isolated locations, giving them new names, clothes, controlling their access to food and information, implanting phobias, and making false promises."

("Combating Cult Mind Control: Guide to Protection, Rescue and Recovery from Destructive Cults" by Steven Hassan)

Cult Awareness

Advocates for Awareness of Watchtower Abuses: http://aawa.co/

Cult Education Network: https://culteducation.com/

Cult Research: http://cultresearch.org/

Cults in America Article: https://bit.ly/32Yro6q

Ex Mormon Christians United for Jesus: http://www.unveilingmormonism.com/

Ex Mormon Files: https://www.exmormonfiles.com/

Facts about JWs: https://www.jwfacts.com/

Families Against Cult Teachings: https://familiesagainstcultteachings.org/

Freedom of Mind: https://freedomofmind.com/

Holding Out Help: https://holdingouthelp.org/

International Cultic Studies Association (ICSA): https://www.icsahome.com/

MeadowHaven: http://www.meadowhaven.org/

Open Minds Foundation: https://www.openmindsfoundation.org/

Religious Cults Info: Resources, Answers and Hope: http://religiouscultsinfo.com/

Safe Passage Foundation: https://safepassagefoundation.org/

Spiritual Abuse Characteristics: http://thewartburgwatch.com/2013/07/18/spiritual-abuse-and-common-characteristics/

Watchman Fellowship: https://www.watchman.org/

Wellspring Retreat: https://wellspringretreat.org/

SHATTERED DREAM
ACKNOWLEDGEMENTS

So many, many people have helped *Shattered Dream* become a reality. My dear hubby, Steve Lyles, and sweet daughter, Alissa Ketterling, graciously trudged through the first draft for me, not an easy challenge. Pat Watkins patiently read two or three drafts and then provided wonderful feedback plus wrote excellent discussion questions.

Along with the cult survivors I spoke with, Rev. Robert Thompson and therapists Jean Thompson and Beatrice Carroll provided valuable insights into high-demand organizations and their members.

My critique group's brilliant insights and suggestions always keep me on track. Amber Bennett, Laurie Bower, Val Gray, Lisa Hess, Marguerite Martell, Michelle Netten and Kathy Schuknecht, you're the best! Laurie Bower went the extra mile to line edit *Shattered Dream*, twice!

In addition, several gracious friends gave of their time and brainpower to serve as beta readers and proofreaders. What a gift! My eternal gratitude goes to Sharol Aranda, Lori Charlier, Pat Cory, Gail Harmon, Norma Hubka, Mary McGuire, Linda Newport and Joyce Stoddard. They not only found typos and grammar errors, they discovered factual errors I had included in the story out of ignorance or oversight. Whatever errors remain, blame me, not them!

Want to know what happens next to Cassie and Corban and gang? Turn the page for a peek inside "Tangled Truth," the second book in the PRISONERS OF HOPE SERIES.

PRISONERS OF HOPE SERIES
BOOK TWO

TANGLED TRUTH

REBECCA CAREY LYLES

I buckle the seatbelt and cover my face with my hands. What have I done? Did I just make the worst decision of my life? I've made so many bad choices, but this...

Deputy Manning hits the gas, and the SUV shoots up the highway, slamming me against the backseat.

He gave me two options—the detention center or Olivia and Owen Pritchards' place. I'd rather go back to jail than return to their hostile household and horrid so-called church, Faithful Followers of the Way. Yet, I've chosen the warped world I escaped not that long ago.

For a brief moment, I was my real self again, Cassie Anita True. But for the next year, I'll be called Cassandra Turner, my church-approved name. The thought is so depressing, I lift my head, so I don't start crying.

The SUV zips along the deserted two-lane highway. Fence posts with their rumpled moon shadows whip past my backseat view. I have a feeling the deputy is exceeding the speed limit by at least twenty miles per hour.

I clamp my teeth to keep from screaming, Stop! I changed my mind! I've come up with some dumb ideas while under the influence. But right now, I'm stone-cold sober—and craving cheap whiskey to rescue me from the reality that lies ahead.

In some ways, Followers' lives are worse than those of inmates. Rather than steel bars, mental and emotional bars block their freedom. I'm jumping right back into the "frying pan" I fled last night, solely for the purpose of helping FFOW members escape the hellhole. I'm not sure how I'll do it, but I trust I'll have more opportunities to do so outside jail than inside.

Way too soon, the deputy brakes to a halt in the middle of the road, directly across from the floodlit "Fellowship Neighborhood" sign.

I unbuckle my seatbelt and reach for the door handle.

"I'll get your door," he says.

How could I have forgotten? Backdoors in patrol cars don't have handles on the inside.

He steps from the front and opens my door.

I start to get out, but my feet stick to the rubber mat. I suck in a breath.

"What's wrong?" He sounds impatient.

Biting my lip to keep from crying out, I pull one foot at a time off the floormat. The pain is incredible and even worse when I maneuver from the vehicle and shift my full weight onto my feet. I moan and grab the door.

Manning frowns. I'm sure he's thinking, What's your problem?

I slide the mat out of the car and hold it so it catches the light.

He stares at my bloody footprints and then at my feet. "You can't walk like that. I'll drive you to the door."

"No!" My voice in the quiet night is louder than I intended. "We can't be seen together." I'm already worried someone coming home from an all-night work project or leaving early for a Saturday-morning project will see us. I hand him the mat and close the door. "You'll want to rinse it first chance you get. Thank you for the ride."

I start to hobble across the road but stop and look at him over my shoulder. "Don't forget your promise."

"I'll be on it the instant my shift ends." He glances at the mountains, which are now edged with light, and opens the hatchback. "Sorry about your feet." Laying the mat inside, he pushes the door down and is about to leave, when he says, "The least I can do is help you to the sidewalk." Taking my arm, he slowly walks me to the curb.

I flinch with every footstep, but with his assistance, I'm able to step up onto the smooth, cool cement.

"Good luck." He releases my arm. "You'll need it." With that, he trots to his vehicle and takes off.

I watch the taillights fade into the distance and am turning to go when a reflection on the floodlit sidewalk catches my eye. Bloody footprints—mine. Kneeling, I use the bottom of the robe to wipe them from the concrete as best I can. I don't dare leave behind clues of my nocturnal wanderings.

I sidestep from the sidewalk onto the night-chilled grass. It feels wonderful under my feet. With any luck, it'll also hide my messy trail. Of course, Followers don't believe in luck, despite what Deputy Manning said.

Actually, I have to agree, which may be a first for me since I joined the church. I breathe a quick prayer. Better to trust God rather than vague, elusive luck.

I break into an awkward, painful run across immaculate lawns, not because I'm anxious to return, but because the sun is rising. I can't be seen in my nightgown. The residents would be scandalized. Dread replaces the freedom I relished mere hours earlier. The grass, which felt good at first, now stabs at my raw feet.

Finally, as the first rays of sunlight touch the treetops, I reach the Pritchards' property and stagger behind the garage. Olivia didn't bother to tell me the keypad code when I moved in, but Owen did. I've never used it and hope and pray I remember it correctly.

I punch in the number. The deadbolt releases. Thank you, Jesus. Slowly, ever so slowly, I twist the knob and slip inside. The garage smells of rubber and engines, but not of garbage, which is never to be left inside the garage. I shut the door as soundlessly as possible, lock it, and aim for the kitchen door. Each silent stumbling step across the cold cement is soothing yet excruciating. I'm grateful my bedroom is the first one at the top of the stairs. I'll have to make the climb on my knees.

Trusting the code is the same for all outer doors, I tap it into the keypad by the kitchen door. The lock clicks, thank God, and I turn the knob, millimeter by millimeter, all the while questioning the wisdom of returning to this house and to these people. If I were smart, I would…

What exactly would I do? Now that daylight is breaking, what could I do in my nightclothes with trashed feet? I blow out a long breath. I've made my bed with the Followers. I've got to lie in it, for better or worse—probably worse.

I push the door, barely opening it. Chicken and cauliflower aromas from last night's meal sift through the crack. Soon, those odors will be replaced by coffee and bacon and other breakfast smells. The thought triggers mixed emotions.

First come happy memories of Saturday morning breakfasts at my grandparents' Oregon farm and Sunday morning breakfasts with my family in town. But those sweet recollections are soured by a vision of Olivia marching through the kitchen, telling each person how to do his or her task better. None of us can do anything right, in her lofty opinion.

I open the door and peek inside. I can see the kitchen, the stairs to the second floor, and by craning my neck, the doorway to the basement stairs. The Pritchards must have left the door open.

No lights are on, and no one is in the kitchen. Maybe Olivia and Owen gave up on me and went back to bed. The mere thought of Olivia turns my stomach. Owen isn't so bad, but Olivia…

The gloom below triggers another vision, this one of little Zachary imprisoned at the far end of the house, huddled alone and afraid in the cold dark basement. My foot pain is nothing compared to his suffering. I burst into tears, biting my knuckle to keep from sobbing out loud. Oh, how I'd love to whisper to him, "Hang on, little guy. Help is on the way." But Olivia has probably posted a guard—or a camera.

"God," I whisper under my breath, "help Deputy Manning keep his promise."

I wipe my eyes with a sleeve and step inside. Quietly closing the door behind me, I'm about to crawl up the stairs when a desperate thirst assaults my parched throat. I was thirsty when the deputy found me and should have asked if he carried bottled water. But I was too distracted to pay attention to my bodily needs until now.

Cringing with each step, I cross to the cupboard, swipe at my nose, and reach for a glass. I fill it, down the water fast and am filling it again, when I hear, "Cas-sandra Turner!"

Tangled Truth coming soon. Watch for it on my website http://beckylyles.com/ and my Amazon Author Page: https://amzn.to/31UUcNb

ABOUT THE AUTHOR

Rebecca Carey Lyles grew up in Wyoming, the setting for her award-winning *Kate Neilson Novels*. She and her husband, Steve, currently live in Idaho, the beautiful state that borders Wyoming and Montana, the setting for this story. Together, they host a podcast called *Let Me Tell You a Story* (beckylyles.com/podcast). In addition to writing fiction and nonfiction, she serves as an editor and a mentor for aspiring authors. *Shattered Dream* is the first book in the *Prisoners of Hope Series*.

Email: beckylyles@beckylyles.com
Facebook author page: Rebecca Carey Lyles
Website: http://beckylyles.com/
Twitter: @beckylyles

NOTE FROM THE AUTHOR

Thank you for reading this story and caring about those ensnared by religious cults. I hope you enjoyed *Shattered Dream* and will consider leaving a review or rating online wherever you share your thoughts about books.

If you'd like to learn about my other books as well as future releases, I invite you to go to my website – beckylyles.com – to register for my rare-and-random newsletter. You'll receive a free eStory as a "thank you."

http://beckylyles.com/newsletter---freebies.html

Made in the USA
Middletown, DE
15 June 2024

55856644R00205